0045475

WITHDRAWN

DUE

SKIHARR99
13.95

THE HARROWING

AINSLIE SKINNER

The HARROWING

RAWSON, WADE PUBLISHERS, INC.
NEW YORK

Library of Congress Cataloging in Publication Data

Skinner, Ainslie.
The harrowing.

I. Title.
PR6069.K48H3   1980   823'.914   80–5980
ISBN 0–89256–153–X

This work was originally published in Great Britain by
Martin Secker & Warburg Limited
Copyright © 1980 by Ainslie Skinner
Composition by American–Stratford Graphic Services, Inc.,
Brattleboro, Vermont
Manufactured in the United States of America by
Fairfield Graphics, Fairfield, Pennsylvania
Designed by Francesca Belanger

First U.S.A. printing

This one is for my parents and my children . . .
and because of A.H.—Terynged i'th nerth, ddewin

ACKNOWLEDGEMENTS

I wish to express my thanks to Mr. Patrick Smith, FRCS; to Dr. Cheyne McCallum of the Burden Neurological Institute, and to those other physicians, surgeons, and psychologists I've talked to in friendship—for their kindness, patience, expert advice, and information.

None of them is to blame for what I've done with it.

Less than 100 years ago, an American newspaper printed the following editorial:

A man was arrested yesterday, charged with attempting to obtain money under false pretenses. He claimed he was promoting a device whereby one person could talk to another several miles away, by means of a small aparatus [sic] and some wire. Without doubt this man is a fraud and an unscrupulous trickster and must be taught that the American public is too smart to be the victim of this and similar schemes. Even if this insane idea worked it would be no practical value other than for circus sideshows.

The man arrested was Alexander Graham Bell. . . .

Charles Panati, *Supersenses*

THE HARROWING

PROLOGUE I

The man behind the desk looked up in annoyance as his secretary came in through the side door. The Bill on his blotter was only half-read, and the stack of Proposed Amendments loomed thickly next to it. Already the sun was dropping behind autumn trees that seemed to have set Ottawa in orderly flames.

"There is a man, sir—with a letter. His clearance is very high, and the message is personal, for your eyes only. I said I'd ask."

"From?" He put his pencil down with a click of annoyance.

"He's British, sir."

There was a brief, shadowed flicker in the level grey eyes, and then it was gone. "Very well, I'll see him. If I ring, come back immediately."

The secretary nodded his head and went out, to return with a pale, elegantly neat man at his heels. The stranger advanced towards the desk and drew a long ordinary white envelope from an inside pocket. When the man behind the desk had accepted it, the messenger drew back and stood waiting quietly. The secretary went out and closed the door.

"Do I know who sent this?" the man holding the letter asked, reaching for his ivory knife and slitting the sealed flap.

"You met him once at Chequers, sir," the messenger said softly. "His hands were very dirty at the time, I understand. Some blood had been drawn."

"Ah." Slowly he drew out the closely written sheaf of thin airmail paper, unfolding it as he spoke. "And is he well?"

"He was when I left, sir. But that was . . . two days ago."

The grey eyes glanced up from the letter, taking in the expression evident only upon close inspection. There was pain there, and not much hope, although the stranger held himself under tight control.

"You'll be going back with my reply?"

"Your reply will be for me alone, sir. And I am to remain here . . . in your country."

"I see." But he did not. His eyes returned to the message, and he leaned back in his chair, holding the pages up slightly. The red of the setting sun made them glow with a bloody sheen, and at first he found the words hard to make out. Gradually they came into focus:

> If we make it, none of this will matter.
> But if we don't, I want you to know what happened and why.
> Somebody should know the truth.
> Somebody should make them pay for what they did to us.
> And are probably going to do to you . . .

I

The white and gold twin-engined Cessna had circled the island once, and now swept low over the grey-green hills on its approach. Elliot squinted as the afternoon sun angled in and caught him across the face. Below, a scurry of black-faced sheep ran ahead of the descending plane, wheeling and scattering, like a twist of lace blown across the grass.

"You're scaring the livestock."

"Them or you?" Longjohn Hawkins lifted both hands from the controls to pull the peak of his baseball cap further down his nose, momentarily dislodging his wraparound sunglasses. Elliot glared at the empty wheel until the long-fingered hands returned to steady it.

"You *always* scare me," he growled.

"You are pitiful, you know that?"

"I know it, I know it. Watch out! You're going into the *water!*"

"That's not the water, that's the runway," Hawkins said calmly, as the Cessna touched down, sluicing along the shining beach and skewing slightly to the left. The "airport" had only recently surfaced. All landings on the island of Mhourra in the Outer Hebrides were made onto the hard-packed sand of the beach, and that was only accessible when the tide was out. The creamy scallops of retreating water were still visible, and strands of seaweed lay glistening where they had been caught by the fenceposts that divided beach from moorland.

Elliot leaned back to unbuckle his seatbelt. "Now, you're sure you've got everything you need for this conference at Edinburgh? Papers, diagrams, charts, schematics . . ."

"Phil." Hawkins regarded the smaller man benignly.

"What?" The buckle was stuck.

"Shut up."

Elliot glanced over at him, ready to snap out a reply, then surrendered with a sigh. "You're right."

"Speaking clinically, I never saw anyone who needed a holiday more, you know that? You've never flown white-knuckled *all* the way before."

"Just because I own the goddamn plane doesn't mean I have to like riding in it." Elliot finally got the buckle undone and dropped the belt on either side irritably. "Throw my bag out to me, will you?"

Longjohn paused to clear his take-off with the voice from the control hut, then stood up to follow his colleague down the narrow aisle. He was so tall he had to crouch and bend double to retrieve the calfskin suitcase from between the empty seats. Holding it in his fingertips as if it did not weigh all of its forty-odd pounds, he gazed down at the stocky figure waiting on the sand below him. "Sure you don't want me to pick you up tomorrow?"

He received a glare for his concern. "Two weeks. It's just what I wanted and I'm glad to be here."

"Oh, I can *see* that, Phil," Longjohn chuckled, and tossed the case out abruptly. Fielding it without falling backwards (just), Elliot regarded the gangling pilot balefully, ill-concealed stubbornness squaring his jaw.

"Just get your Canadian backside over to that conference and behave yourself. I don't want to hear you spent all your time screwing the delegate's secretaries like last year."

Hawkins dropped a raincoat and briefcase onto the sand. "If I do you won't hear about it." He swung the hatch shut, then pushed it open to lean out again. "Unless you ask nicely, that is."

Elliot was brushing damp sand from his coat, and looked up. The hatch swung shut on the beginnings of his grin, and the lock clunked firmly into place. Taking the bulging briefcase in one hand and the suitcase in the other, he began to trudge across the sand, leaping lightly over the first of the larger puddles, then shrugging and walking straight through the rest. He had nearly made it to the fence when the Cessna revved suddenly and started its take-off. As he turned to wave he got a blast of loose sanddune in the face. The wings waggled twice and the plane faded to seagull size in minutes.

Turning back inland, he took a minute to assess what he let himself in for. From above, the small island of Mhourra had looked unfriendly. Now he could see that first impression had been misleading: Mhourra was downright inimical. The barren beach stretched long and white on either side, empty of everything except seagulls and rocks, until it curved out of sight around the island itself. Beyond the wire of the fence a few of the black-faced sheep munched phlegmatically on the first of the spring grass, and one of them gave him a mournful stare as a long strand of weed slowly disappeared between its grinding jaws. The band of moorland stretched beyond the beach and eventually gave way to low rounded hills that broke the horizon gently. Where the thin soil had been worn away, the base rock of the island showed sharp and razored edges. The two visible trees were bent over as if stricken with spinal arthritis, their backs turned against the constant shore winds. Periodically, racing clouds dragged their shadows across the hills, removing what little colour there was from the landscape.

"What, no badminton courts?" Taking a firmer grip on his bags, Elliot made for the lonely hut on the other side of the fence. Because he'd heard a voice on the radio he knew there was someone in there, but *only* because he'd heard a voice. In fact, there were two men inside—the radio operator and a big solid man with a weathered face and a pair of hands designed for someone twice his size. He extended one of them, and Elliot put down his suitcase to grasp it.

"Dr. Elliot? Macadam, I am. Come to take you across to the house. Welcome to Mhourra."

"Thanks. Glad to be here." Macadam you may be, Elliot thought, bloody liar I am. "That your car out back?"

The other two exchanged an amused glance. "Och, no." Macadam smiled. "That's young Bill's here. Our place is only a little way along—you'll be wanting to stretch your legs after being stuck in that toy plane all the way from London, surely?"

Elliot smiled gamely, but after the first mile he felt every bit of his thirty-eight years of sedentary life dragging at him. After the second mile, he decided that somewhere between Glasgow and eternity they must have ditched in the sea, and this was his reward for having spent a life of dissolution and despair. Hell was *not* hot, it was freezing and it was on this island. By the time they finally reached the two-storey stone cottage, he felt as if he had been lightly curetted from hairline to shirt collar by the icy wind, and would probably be forced to amputate his own nose before morning.

However, after putting on two extra sweaters from his suitcase and partaking of the considerable delights of Mrs. Macadam's tea-table, he began to relax at last, joining Macadam in front of the glowing peat fire and leaning his head wearily against the high wing of the chintz-covered chair. The light from the pink-shaded ceiling lamp gave the small framed photographs on the mantelpiece an antic life of their own as they peered out from between the bric-à-brac. He found the small room slightly claustrophobic. The furniture was too plentiful and too large, as were the abstract designs that exploded all over the carpet. But it was blissfully quiet, with only the faint murmur of the chimney's draw. He closed his eyes.

Macadam looked at the tired face across from his as the moving firelight threw the shadows under the eyes into deep relief. When he spoke, Elliot jerked slightly, as if someone had pinched one of his nerve endings.

"You'll be needing a rest, then, Doctor? George wrote you had been overworking at that place of yours . . . Talbot Hall, is it?"

"Yes. He sent his regards, by the way."

"Ah, thank you. You'll return ours, too."

Elliot nodded and watched his host filling his black, gnarled pipe. It made the cigarette between his own fingers look like a child's sweet. Overworking was an understatement. A week ago he'd taken more than a furtive look at himself while shaving and realized that if he didn't stop at once, something was going to stop him. Pneumonia, perhaps, or a nervous breakdown. He never considered himself beautiful, but the gaunt bruised-looking face in the mirror appeared downright pathetic. Hastily grabbed sandwiches and burned beans cooked too fast late at night—it was no way to run a human body. With his bone structure, he should have been solid and stocky. The outline was still there, but the substance was not. He felt as hollow as a rotten tooth.

"When he was here with us, George talked about you quite a lot."

"Oh?"

Macadam nodded, thrusting another match into the bowl of his pipe and drawing deeply. "Didna talk of much else, in fact. You're his hero, it seems."

"And now you see me face to face, you wonder if George sent the wrong man?" He gave a small embarrassed laugh.

The old crofter smiled around his pipestem. "You're very young, George said, to be head of a research establishment like Talbot Hall."

"I don't *feel* young, Mr. Macadam, I assure you. And despite George's enthusiasm, Talbot Hall is just a small Government investment in the future that a lot of people think should be cashed in on something real, like car parks. Maybe they're right."

"Brains, George said. You're a brain doctor."

"I'm a neurologist, that's all. Nothing very special in it."

"And this place you work in—you and George . . ."

"And quite a few others."

"Mmmmm. You work on brains there, do you?"

Elliot shifted uneasily in his chair. "There are a lot of projects under way at Talbot, most of them classified, I'm afraid."

"Ah. Mind your own business, you nosey old man, is that it?"

Dismay widened Elliot's eyes. "Not at all. I'm sorry if I sounded . . ."

It was Macadam's turn to chuckle. The temptation to bait this over-serious young scientist faded quickly in the face of Elliot's very real concern at the possibility of having offended his host.

"Of course not, man. I know well you canna discuss the work you do. I shouldn't have gone on at you."

Elliot lit a cigarette, dropping the match into the ashtray, and noticed the unfinished stub he had propped there a moment before still smouldering. "Oh, it's not that. Most of it is pretty run-of-the-mill, if you want the truth. I suppose we get into the habit of—you practically have to sign the Official Secrets Act every time you want a fresh roll of toilet paper put into the loo down there." He hurriedly extinguished the shorter of the two cigarettes. "I do a lot of work on the various aspects of extrasensory perception, relating them to the areas of the brain for which we've found no apparent function as yet."

"Mind-reading, you mean?"

"That's what the press like to call it, yes." He was apparently resigned to the description.

"That's a little . . . far-fetched, isn't it?"

"Not really. You see, there are two opposing views on

this. One group of scientists maintain that what we collectively refer to as 'instincts' are really just the remnants of mental abilities we once had when we existed on a simple animal level and gradually lost through becoming socialized. You've only to watch a wolf-pack hunt to see there's some kind of communication going on that has nothing to do with noises or gestures."

Macadam laughed. "Man, ye've only to watch a good dog work a flock to know that—they *anticipate* what the sheep are going to do. I've seen it time and again—quite magical, it is."

Elliot nodded. "Wonderful, I agree, but not magic. In my opinion it's just an example of low-level extrasensory perception. I belong to the *other* group, you see. The scientists who believe that all the things we're studying at Talbot Hall are just the first manifestations of the ultimate development of the brain. Not something we're losing, but something we're only beginning to explore. Up to now mankind has been so busy simply *surviving* that we've had no energy to spare. Now that we've got machines to do so much for us in physical terms, we're finding time to look in rather than out. Hence the upsurge in ESP research over the past sixty years or so."

"And what is it you're *doing*, exactly?" Macadam asked, leaning forward slightly in his curiosity.

"I'm looking for the human mind," Elliot said. "As a neurologist I've operated on or dissected hundreds of brains, but never found a mind. Now, if I had you in my lab at Talbot Hall, I could show you hard physical proof that such a thing exists, over and beyond the structure of the brain itself. I could show you a photographic trace of it. I could let you listen to it humming as it worked. Perhaps, with training, I could even teach you to read someone else's."

"Hah!" Macadam said, leaning back with satisfaction. "I knew ye'd say that. I tell ye it's impossible. I'm no mind-reader. Nobody is."

Elliot looked at him and then began to laugh. "You've

just proved my point," he said after a minute.

"How so?"

"You said, 'I knew you'd say that.' *How* did you know?"

"Ye're a man with a mission. Ye obviously believe . . ."

But Elliot was shaking his head. "My point is, you've used that phrase hundreds of times. We all have. And it *isn't* always a matter of logic. Any more than it's logical for a person to step back just seconds before a cliff gives way under him, or to suddenly feel uneasy and phone home to find a loved one has fallen ill, or to suspect the motives of a stranger and eventually be proved right. Some say instinct—*I* say it's more often a demonstration of the ESP abilities we're developing as the inevitable evolutionary refining of the brain."

"Mebbe," Macadam said, reluctantly.

"You want specifics?"

"Aye, I do."

"All right. We divide extrasensory abilities into five basic categories." Elliot put down his cigarette to count off on his fingers. "One, telepathy—the ability to receive or transmit thoughts and images directly from one mind to another. Two, telekinesis—the ability to move or affect inanimate objects with the mind alone. That includes 'spoon-bending' and controlling the fall of the dice, among other things. Three, clairvoyance—the ability to 'read' inanimate objects for their connections with the people who've owned or touched them. There's a psychic named Peter Hurkos who's had amazing success helping the police find murderers and lost children using just such an ability. Four, precognition—the ability to 'see' into the future. There's a tremendous amount of testimony for this, from the Prophet Isaiah right up to a woman named Jeanne Dixon who predicted President Kennedy's assassination, and all those people who dreamt of the Aberfan disaster before it happened. And five, psychic healing. We're accumulating a lot of hard physical evidence on that, now, but we've had to wade through an awful lot of nonsense on the way. There's a famous American researcher in this field who, in addition to being a fine scientist, is also a nun. When she was criticized for investigating such matters, she simply pointed out that one of the earliest recorded psychic healers was a carpenter named Jesus. Now *she's* working on the enzymatic changes that . . .”

Elliot noted a slight stiffening in Macadam, and tardily recalled the strict religious attitudes of these isolated islands. “I'm not being blasphemous, Mr. Macadam,” he said, gently. “The Bible refers again and again to Jesus 'knowing what was in the mind' of this supplicant or that. And he predicted he would be betrayed. He knew where, when, and by whom. He made the lame to walk and the blind to see. By any criterion, that makes him a psychic healer of great power, a telepath, and a precognitive. Understanding the processes by which these things are achieved doesn't make them any less a miracle —or any less a gift from God.”

“Are ye a religious man, then, Doctor?”

“In the broadest sense, I suppose I am. Despite the wars and cruelties of history, all man's progress has been a matter of what I call 'reaching for the Good.' Even biologically speaking, evolution is clearly directed towards the refining and improving of every organism, including man. When we talk of a 'civilized' man, we usually mean someone who uses his mind rather than his fists to settle his problems. You see? Always back to the mind, as if we *knew* that's where our destiny lay.”

“Instinctively?” Macadam asked, with a twinkle.

Elliot had the grace to smile. “Yes.”

“Ye're no telling me Talbot Hall is a religious institution,” Macadam said pointedly.

“No, I'm not. Certainly very few scientists there share my idealistic attitude. We're after facts, as I said. Hard facts on which to build an understanding of what the brain is capable of achieving. Our instrumentation is improvised, our methods hit-and-miss, our successes few. It's going to take a long time, because what we're studying is the most complicated and powerful machine in the world. We design computers in its image, but they're pathetic imitations. They can't make a creative 'leap'—they have to work 'in line,' taking one step after another in rote sequence. Although they do it quickly, that's *all* they do. The brain perceives, computes, deduces, analyzes, organizes, and projects simultaneously a literally infinite number of concepts, using less electrical power than is required to light a fifteen-watt bulb. And it does all that while keeping your heart beating, your stomach digesting, and preventing you from falling on your face every time you take a step. We only use five percent of our brain's capacity, even so. Think what we could do if we only increased our abilities by another five per cent."

"That's what ye're after?"

"In a sense, yes."

"And will ye do it?"

"We already have," Elliot said, slowly. "We're much further along in ESP research than most laymen realize. If they did realize it, they'd be scared half to death. It often frightens me."

"What, the power of the mind?"

"No—that's inspiring. What's terrifying are the uses to which it could be put. The kind of applications I'm *supposed* to be developing at Talbot."

"Secret, I suppose," Macadam murmured, resignedly.

Elliot's eyes went blank for a moment, then he shook his head. "Not all of them. There's a lot of information available on recent ESP research if you know where to look. Just as there's enough information in a good public library to enable an averagely gifted physics student to build an H-bomb in his basement, given the materials. The Americans are very interested in cybernetic research, for example, which involves use of the brain in direct connection with a machine, either electronic or mechanical. The Pentagon already has a system that permits a man to fire a rocket by simply thinking the word 'Fire' into a computer terminal. Wired to his plane through a similar system, a pilot can fly it without touching a single

control. He just thinks 'right,' 'left,' 'up,' 'down,' and so on—
the computer does the rest. Then there's what's popularly referred to as 'mind-bending.' Theoretically a powerful telepath
could convince a politician that a certain course of action was
in his country's best interest when it patently was not. Or even
a platoon of soldiers on a battlefield that they were surrounded
and defeated, when they were not. The Russians pretend
they're developing telepathy as a means of improving com-
munications in the cosmonaut programme. It would save quite
a lot of roubles in copper wire, alone."

"But that's not the real reason?"

"Obviously not. How much simpler for a telepathic spy
to abstract secrets directly from the opposition's mind than
go to all the trouble and expense of buying or stealing them.
Cost efficiency has a very high priority in such circles." Elliot's
voice was bitter. "It's a truism that science leaps ahead during
a war, and it doesn't matter whether that war is a hot or cold
one. It's only because the Western governments are growing
paranoic about the Russians that *I* got a research budget at all.
The Russians have been at it longer than anyone else—they
spend over eleven million pounds a year on psychic and bio-
psychical research. That's the government's reason for funding
me. I have my *own* reasons for taking the money and using
their facilities to do what I want to do."

"Ye don't sound proud of it."

Elliot grimaced. "I'm not. But that's my problem, not
theirs. Or yours." He seemed to come to himself, and forced a
smile. "I appear to have been making a speech. I came away to
stop myself doing that—sorry."

"Nonsense, man. It's a fascinating subject. I can understand how it would take hold of ye so strong." The old man
put his pipe down. "Will ye take a dram with me, Doctor?" He
paused, halfway out of his chair. "Or don't ye?"

"I do and I would. Thank you."

The old man busied himself with the glasses, pouring out
generous inches of pale amber whisky from an unlabelled

bottle. He hesitated. "Something with it?"

"No, as it comes, please." Elliot accepted the thick glass and raised it slightly as Macadam turned back for his own. "You know—I did have another reason for coming to Mhourra, aside from the peace and quiet. Related to my work, in a sense."

"And what might that have been?"

"Your local ghost." Elliot's eyes narrowed as the old man's shoulders stiffened. "George came back with some stories about a deserted cottage that no one would go near, day or night? He knew I'd be interested—ghosts are a hobby of mine." Lying is another, he added, silently.

"Damn foolishness," Macadam muttered.

"George seemed pretty convinced, and he's not exactly the imaginative type."

Macadam returned to his chair without looking at the younger man, shook his head, and swallowed a large amount of his whisky in one gulp. "Mebbe not, but the rest of them are. Some people *like* to scare themselves of a winter evening. Silly children's games, that's all."

Elliot took an experimental sip of his drink, blinked, and took another. "Then you haven't seen, or rather felt, this ghost yourself?"

"Never."

"Or Mrs. Macadam?" He turned slightly to address the small woman who was still clearing tea-things from the table. She raised her eyes to meet his, and he was surprised to see a trace of dislike in them. Or was it fear?

"Never," the crofter repeated, saving his wife the trouble of answering. She looked down and continued to gather up the last plates and cups, her lips tightening over what she might have said.

"I see." Elliot settled back into his chair and took another, larger, swallow of his whisky. "But you know the place I mean?"

"Oh, aye. The old Craigie cottage. Long empty, not much

of a place and never was. It's true enough old Mrs. Craigie died there and wasn't found for several days, but what of it? She was just a simple old soul who never harmed anyone. If it's *her* ghost that's haunting, there wouldna be much in it." He picked up the pipe again and felt in his pockets for the matches. "No thrills at all."

Elliot's mouth quirked. "I'm not looking for 'thrills,' Mr. Macadam. Just curious, that's all. It's not ghosts that are interesting to me, it's the minds of the people who see them. Or think they see them." And what the results can be, he refrained from pointing out.

He wondered how Macadam would react if he told him the full story of George and his ghost. That before his experience in the Craigie cottage, George had been totally without psychic ability—so negative, in fact, as to be a positive gift as a control during psychic experiments. But after returning from meeting the Craigie "ghost," George had suddenly displayed the beginnings of psychic abilities. Not great, not marked, but *there* in his head, where they had no right to be on previous evidence. A lot of things could have done that to George—but not a "ghost." Elliot rested his drink on his knee and loosened his collar slightly. It would not have taken a mind-reader to see that his questions had upset Macadam and his wife. And that was odd, too, because most people loved to discuss lurid local superstitions and things that go bump in the night. Especially with outsiders. But instead of expanding on the subject, the Macadams had closed up, tight. Curiouser and curiouser, mused Elliot, watching the firelight through the remaining half-inch of whisky in his glass.

He also wondered what Macadam's reaction would be if he told him his *own* story. But of course, he could not. So, he politely enquired about the difficulties of running an efficient croft on an island like Mhourra. With obvious relief the old man launched into a list of the problems, leaving ghosts and the rest of the unsettling aspects of ESP researches out in the cold, and welcome to it. Two hours later, Elliot left the couple to the dubious delights of an old James Bond movie, relayed rather tweedily from the mainland in living colour (predominantly puce) and retired to the slant-ceilinged front bedroom over their heads. The bed was wide and soft, and Mrs. Macadam had tucked a hot-water bottle in at the foot, wrapped in a furry knitted envelope. She can't have disliked me all that much, he decided, picking up a bottle of sedatives from the table beside his bed. The wind rattled the window in its frame and he glanced towards it momentarily. Just the wind. Beyond the window, miles and miles of emptiness, open sea, and hardly a soul between him and Greenland. He tipped two capsules out into the palm of his hand and swallowed them with the water he carried back from the bathroom in his shaving mug. Then he settled himself under the two feather quilts and blanket, lighting a last cigarette to fill the minutes before the drugs began to shut him in for the night. In a little while he knew he would be free. Away from everything, isolated, safe, wrapped protectively in heavy sedation, with only his own dreams to disturb his rest.

Nobody else's.

2

It certainly didn't *look* haunted.

As a matter of fact it looked charming, nestled in the hollow of the hills. Just a small abandoned cottage, hardly remarkable in an area dotted with small abandoned cottages. The wind had eaten away at the roof, exposing a few weathered rafters, and the once-white paint had been washed away leaving a random pattern of grey stone and mossy patches. Some grass had begun to grow between the roof slates, creating a surprised set of eyebrows over the glassless stare of the windows and the gaping mouth of the door.

Elliot's heavy walking boots slid on the grass as he went down the slope. He noticed the wooden cover of a well beside the cottage and headed towards it. The salt of the air during his three-mile walk, plus the salt in the porridge and bacon Mrs. Macadam had cooked for his late breakfast, had left him parched. With any luck—yes, the bucket was still there, hanging down into the blackness. He hauled up some of the water and sipped handfuls of it until he was satisfied. Pulling his cigarettes out of the pocket of his old Navy anorak, he lit one and regarded the cottage through the smoke. According to George, it was *not* charming, no matter how it might appear.

It was, he had said, a very nasty place to visit indeed.

George had not "seen" anything. The horror of the cottage was in what he felt, he had told Elliot. And apparently sensation was more than enough, because even when George had talked about it afterwards the fear had shown in his eyes. And George was not a fearful man. Stubbing out his cigarette on the rough stone surrounding the low well, Elliot stood up. If there was nothing to see, sitting and looking wasn't going to answer any questions, was it?

The place was obviously very old. He had to duck his head under the doorframe, and the packed earth floor was a good six inches below the level of the doorstep. It was dark inside, but bars of light slanted in through the windows and gave him enough illumination to avoid tripping over the few broken bits of furniture that still lay scattered around the large main room. The breeze came in behind him, stirring white ashes in the soot-blackened hole of the fireplace. Some peat blocks were still stacked tidily alongside the grate, their edges dry and crumbling. There was only the main room, about twenty by thirty, and a smaller second room to one side. He walked carefully around both of them, looking, listening, waiting.

Finally he leaned back against the timber that was set into the wall as a rough mantel, resting his elbows on either side. "Well, George," he muttered, "I'm not impressed with your little place. Although it has possibilities as a sheep-shed, I suppose."

Apparently that was funny, because somebody laughed.

Straightening abruptly, he went to the door of the second room. Nothing. No one. Turning again to face the larger room, he called out: "Who's there?"

More laughter. Children. It had to be children, playing about. He crossed to the door and went out to circle the cottage, but again nothing, no one. He shook his head and re-entered the cottage, finding it as before. Then paused. No, it was not quite the same. He felt . . . different. No longer welcome. As if the cottage itself were emanating a sensation of dislike, as if it were alive and willing him to leave, get out, go. He stood in the middle of the room, refusing to move, and it got . . . cross. Go away. Go *away*. A cloud covered the sun. The bars of light disappeared from the windows, one by one, and the shadows seemed to gather around him. The sensations got stronger, and Elliot, despite his interest in what was happening, began to feel distinctly uneasy and uncomfortable.

He crossed his arms. "No," he said, deliberately, into the stillness.

Something pinched his leg. He started, kicked out instinctively, looked down. But there was nothing there, just a scuff mark he made in the dirt floor, and a few gnawed animal bones—rabbit, by the look of them. Then something pinched his arm. And suddenly he was being pinched and tweaked all over, hard. It hurt, it was irritating, it was damned annoying. He twitched and dodged, but could not escape the attack. After a particularly vicious stab of pain, he dragged back the sleeve of his anorak and stared at his forearm. Several blotches of bright red marked his flesh, and in one broken capillaries had begun to suffuse blood under the skin. Tomorrow there would be a bruise there.

"Bloody hell," he breathed.

And again, someone laughed. Not maniacally, not even wildly, but with the gleeful maliciousness of a child that knows it is doing wrong but doesn't care, because it is having fun. The pinching had stopped as quickly as it had begun, but the sensations of dislike were intensifying, until they became hate, and then loathing. He was repellent, he was disgusting, he should go, *go*, before something stepped on him. It was incredible, he simply could not accept that it was happening to him, and yet could not believe that it was *not* happening, that it was not perfectly real, and very frightening.

It was turning his guts to water, churning him up and dragging him down.

And now he could not move. A gull screeched overhead,

suddenly, its raucous noise almost like the laughter that was continuing to rise in the room. He very much wanted to obey, to get out, but something had hold of his legs, tight. Struggling against it, he nearly fell. Sweat began to inch down his back and chest, and beads of it began to break out on his face. He stared into the corners of the room, searching for a focus, someone or something to blame for the torment that was wracking him. Then suddenly there was a smell, a nauseating miasma of raw, rotting meat. He tried to hold his breath as he struggled against whatever was imprisoning his legs, but a long thin needle of pain slid under his ribs and he gasped involuntarily. Instantly the thick invisible sludge flooded his nostrils and started a slow crawl down his throat, causing him to gag and choke. At the same moment, something seemed to push at the small of his back and he went down, throwing his hands out in front of him in an effort to keep his head out of the filth he could not see but was convinced was there.

And still the laughter went on.

More needles pierced him in a hundred places at once, sending waves of pain rising through his body to bounce back and forth between his temples like a ricochet of razors. His brain felt like a lacerated mass of throbbing tissue, swelling and pressing against the bones of his skull, threatening to ooze out of his eyes and ears in a spongy grey bulge.

Straining, sinews cording his neck and jaw, he began to crawl towards the door and the fresh wind that blew past it. The ghost—or whatever it was—continued to express its vast amusement as he scrabbled along, nails clawing at the dirt floor, dragging his body behind him like a ton of flaccid, unset cement. Finally he reached the doorway and pulled himself up by the frame, lurching out into the air in one great endless fall as he moved forward to stay on his feet. Then he began to run. When he reached the top of the shallow depression in which the cottage sat, he slowed, stumbled, stopped. And looked back.

It was just an empty cottage.

He straightened up from the defensive hunch he had unconsciously assumed on turning and wiped his face with his sleeve, taking deep breaths of the fresh cold air, feeling it cleanse him, release him from the still clinging strands of imaginary filth. After a few minutes he began to get angry. It was simply his nerves, wasn't it? He'd been working too hard, he was over-sensitive, he had created for himself an atmosphere in keeping with what he had been told to expect. Damn George Lomax, anyway.

"You *are* pathetic," he informed himself. "You are operating on the level of a six-year-old. Go back in there and spit in its eye." He was already granting the cottage a persona. Still breathing raggedly, he looked around at the empty reaches of the meadows, the running shadows of the clouds, the metallic glint of the sea in the distance. There was no disputing the fact that he was utterly alone, except for the gulls and the crows. He was a grown man of reasonable size and sanity, and whatever it was—if it was anything—had defeated him without much apparent effort. Which was simply not good enough. In his work he had heard all kinds of accounts of manifestations, psychic experiences, hallucinations, and the rest of it. He knew better. He knew *better,* damn it.

Reluctantly, he started back to the cottage. This time he would be prepared, he would resist the thing, he would observe it with the detachment of which he knew he was capable even under duress. Gritting his teeth, he re-entered the cottage and strode to the centre of the room.

It was just an empty room.

The dust he had raised in his frenzy still drifted lazily through the bars of sunlight that again were slanting through the windows. The air merely smelt damp and slightly sour. He smiled wryly. He was a jackass.

Thirty seconds later he was a screaming jackass.

Pain poured into his head like liquid oxygen, simultaneously burning and freezing the flesh of his brain. Uselessly he clawed at his temples, trying to drag it out, let it out, but it would not stop. He staggered back and felt his breakfast trying to fight its way back up his throat. Remorselessly, strands of barbed wire began to tighten around his chest. The laughter came again, louder than ever, and although he could see that he was alone in the room, he *knew* that he was not. Something very evil was there with him, very close now, coming closer, reaching out. Yes. Its cold touch grazed the skin of his face, slid like slime across his mouth, encircled his neck, began to close over his throat, tighter, tighter, squeezing, choking . . .

This time he did not stop running until he had reached the sea and stood ankle-deep in the waves, letting them soak his boots and denims, glad of their icy reality, their wetness, their noise. After a while the convulsive sobs that shuddered through him began to abate, and he staggered back to a rock to sit, to shake, to stare. Across the moat of the sea the rising humps of the other islands at this tail-end of the archipelago broke the line of the horizon with their grey backs, misted by distance and occasionally darkened by the skating shadows of the clouds.

"Okay, George," Elliot whispered. "I believe you."

The gulls circled over him curiously, gazing down with black and beady eyes at the hunched figure that was now staring dully at the sand. Was it something new the sea had thrown up? Was it good to eat? Shrilly, they debated the possibilities, while Elliot tried to light a cigarette. It took him quite a while.

He was debating the possibilities, too. Did the water from the well contain some kind of hallucinogenic substance? Was the cottage filled with gas from an old volcanic pocket? Or something more sinister? There was a Government tracking station in the Hebrides. What other kind of facilities or installations might be here, nice and isolated and off-limits to over-curious tourists? He tried to consider everything, including the possibility that the ghost of old Mrs. Craigie *was* around. And the last, less acceptable explanation—that he was losing his mind.

For anyone else it might have been far too abrupt a conclusion. But it was a spectre that had stalked him for over twelve years, because Philip Elliot's mind was not like everyone else's. Not since that sunny afternoon in June when a drunken driver had come out of nowhere to send him sprawling against the kerbstone with a sickening crack followed by eight days of blackness. When Philip Elliot had hit the kerb he had just been appointed neurological registrar of the university hospital, a doctor like his father and his grandfather before him. Happy to be, and good at his work.

But when he had awakened from his coma, he found he had become something more.

He could read minds.

The first one he read belonged to the surgeon who happened to be standing beside his bed at the time. His thoughts were not cheerful, for Elliot's prognosis was poor, and his opinion was that this man was not going to make it. He was staring at the chart and so did not realize his patient was awake at last.

"I'll make it, you dumb bastard." The surgeon had jumped about a foot into the air, affording Elliot a great deal of unsuitable satisfaction. Then he got the full force of the surgeon's mind, and passed out again.

Basically, it hurt.

The startled human mind at bay is, at best, a cacophony of multiple and contradictory impulses. The human mind does not think in nice orderly sentences, nor does it think one thought at a time. It blasts. For Elliot it was like waking up in a room in which the walls, floor, and ceiling were covered with loudspeakers, every one of which was playing something different at full volume—some sending out music, some sending out words, some emotions, some sensory impressions, both surface and visceral, and some just the static and roar of mind machinery at work. He woke into a maelstrom of message and counter-message and was unable to put his hands over his ears. Unconsciousness was the only retreat, and he took it. When he came round again, a few days later, it was night and he was alone. He lay there for about ten minutes, then a nurse walked into the room, and down he went once more into darkness, gratefully.

He lost a year in hospital, and was soon transferred to a psychiatric ward because they simply did not know where else to put him. They drugged him heavily to insulate him against a pain they could see he was suffering, but for which they could detect no cause. He didn't tell them what was really happening because he couldn't, at first. Then, when he had gradually worked it out and could have told them, he didn't want to. They would not have believed him, and to them the next logical step would have been commitment. He was not crazy, not in the least, and he knew it.

Just totally telepathic.

Animals don't *like* being hurt, they try everything to avoid it. Using his medical training, he tried everything too. Something he tried finally worked, although he didn't know what. And still didn't know. But, little by little, the ability (or curse) began to fade. Instead of being full-blast and totally incapacitating, it became more or less like listening to a radio in the next room. One that somebody kept turning off every now and then for no apparent reason. If he concentrated he could get things pretty clearly, but it was hard work. Conversely, if he was very distracted or half-asleep, sometimes things could get *him* before he could defend himself.

Eventually he was able to convince the doctors that he was back to "normal" and they released him. He finished his medical training in the Navy and embarked on the course that had directed the subsequent years of his life. His intentions were simple, but his obsession was not. If he had simply announced his telepathic ability, his life would have been wasted trying to make everyone believe him. He would have been shunted into the "freak circuit," and he was not a freak. He was a scientist and he wanted to study and understand what had happened to him within a totally scientific framework.

He had to be able to provide the scientific community with irrefutable proof in their own narrow terms, because those were the *only* terms they would accept. Indeed, the only terms he himself would accept.

Knowing that something exists is one thing, proving it another. He needed a lot of money to cover the costs of equipment and assistance, and his income, and his attempts to supplement it, proved insufficient. In the end, there was only one alternative.

And that was why, using his peculiar advantages to thread the convoluted corridors of medical and political power, he had become Director of Research at Talbot Hall, paid and paid for by H.M. Government. Assigned to find a way to "get" the psychic Russians before the psychic Russians got them. Or the Americans. Or the Chinese. Or anybody else, for that matter, including little green men from outer space. It was a useful arrangement. The Government did not expect miracles—only Elliot expected miracles, especially of Elliot.

But they had not materialized.

And now, this.

He lit another cigarette with hands that were appreciably steadier. The wind blew his hair over his forehead and tugged at the collar of his anorak. Facing something squarely made it comprehensible, if not any more pleasant. His waning telepathic abilities might *not* have been the end, he realized, just one step on a long ladder of change. Twelve years after the accident, his scarred brain might still be echoing to that terrible impact. Perhaps, instead of merely picking up other people's thoughts, his brain was now manufacturing things for him, independent of his will. Perhaps that long ladder simply led back to a straitjacket and a padded cell.

To go insane is bad enough. To *know* you are going insane and not be able to stop it seemed a hundred times worse to him. No sea breeze was going to blow *that* away.

But George had not been brain-injured, and George had felt something, too. And all of it centered on that empty cottage back there in the hills. Whether he liked it or not, he would have to go back. Instantly his body reacted against his decision, and the resulting tremors sent the cigarette flying out of his fingers onto the sand, where it smouldered and went out. Eventually he got up and returned to face the cottage, but when he saw it again he knew he was totally incapable of entering it. So he sat on the edge of the well until his cigarettes ran out and the chill air of sunset began to penetrate his clothes. He had contemplated the place until his eyes crossed, but was no closer to understanding it than he had been in the beginning. An empty cottage, and an empty head.

Maybe he'd try again tomorrow. Maybe.

He started back towards the sea, but hadn't quite caught sight of it when the sensations from the cottage started to come over him again. Horrified, he stopped, and they immediately got stronger. Dear God, it *was* him! He resumed walking, and the sensations faded slightly. Closing down everything in his head he could reach, he concentrated on the grass, and stood still. Up they came, stronger and more unpleasant than ever— hatred and fear. Nothing he could do in his head would make them stop. After a few minutes he could no longer control himself, and began to walk, then trot, then run wildly towards the shore. But moving didn't do any good. It, whatever it was, was tracking him. The conviction that he was being chased by something terrifying, grotesque, and murderous kept building and building. It was going to get him . . . it was going to get him . . . there was nothing he could do . . . he would be torn apart . . . gutted . . . eaten . . . slavered over . . . tortured and . . .

"Stop it!" he screamed.

And it stopped.

So did he. The world seemed to hold its breath, and then he turned abruptly, instinctively.

Something *was* following him.

Three hundred yards back against the greenish twilight sky stood a ragged, shapeless black silhouette. Covered from

head to foot—if there were a head and feet—by fur or something like it. It stood on the top of the last hill, so inhuman
and strange that Elliot felt pure atavistic horror filling him as
he stared wildly at it. Slowly, it raised part of itself in an
eerie, ritualistic gesture of threat or accusation. He felt the
storm of terror rising in him—terror coupled with a kind of
astonishment. For an instant he faced it, helplessly frozen.
He opened his mouth to cry out, and was viciously thrown to
the ground by a blow so savage he lost consciousness before
his face touched the grass.

When he came to, it was dark. He raised his head slightly and
immediately regretted it. His arm was beneath his chin, and
he could see the faint glow of his watchdial. Past nine o'clock.
He had been unconscious for over five hours. The night wind
rustled the long grass around him, and the soft slush of the
sea came from the darkness ahead. Nothing else.

He rolled over onto his back and lay looking up at the
stars. Clear and bright they hung in the distance like crystals
of ice, and they glared back at him unwinking until his eyes
began to water and he shut them out. His head throbbed with
a dull pain that seemed centered on the right side. He lay still
for a while longer, wondering why he had been left alive and
untouched. There was a metallic taste in his mouth—he had
either bitten his tongue or smashed his mouth against his teeth
in falling. He got to his feet slowly, dizzy, sick, unsure of his
balance, and made for the sound of the sea. When he fell on
his face for the twentieth time and tasted sand, he knew he had
reached it. Keeping the waves on his right, he made his way
drunkenly along the shore until he saw a light coming towards
him, and stopped. It glowed sharply, swept left then right,
wavered, advanced. What now?

But it was only Macadam, come to find him. When Elliot
staggered into the beam of his torch, the old man gasped.

"My God, man, what's happened to you?"

Elliot took a deep breath and mumbled. "I . . . fell over

. . . some rocks. Must have knocked myself out . . ." But Macadam's eyes said otherwise. Taking the smaller man's arm, he steadied him and started back down the beach, retracing his own footsteps in the sand.

"We'll get you back and then I'll bring Baines over to take a look at you."

"Baines?"

"Our local doctor. Bit long in the tooth, but he's good. You could use some stitches in that lip by the look of it."

It seemed to take forever, but eventually Elliot was back in his room at the Macadam place, staring at his reflection in the mirror. His lower lip was badly split, his chin caked with blood and sand. But that was not what riveted his eyes in the glass.

Across his forehead and cheeks someone had scrawled strange markings with his own blood. In another land or another time, he might have called them hex marks. Leaning forward, he looked more closely at what at first seemed alien, but on second examination was very familiar. It was not until he realised exactly what the markings *were* that he could make sense of the thoughts he had been picking up from Macadam's head all the way along the beach. They had been erratic and intermittent, but perfectly clear when they came. Over and over:

Annie did this. Annie. Annie.

3

"Annie Craigie, old Mrs. Craigie's grand-daughter." Dr. Baines sighed as he cast a bleak eye over Elliot, who was now propped against his pillows, pale and weary. "Mind you, she never actually attacked anyone before. That isn't like her, not a bit."

"She didn't attack me, I fell. She was yards away," Elliot mumbled through a mouth stiff with the local anaesthetic Baines had injected before putting six careful stitches into his lower lip. He watched Baines repacking his battered medical case. One of those people it's hard to put an age to—over sixty, certainly. The old man's eyes were a deep infant blue, and lent a spurious innocence to his long narrow face that no doctor so long in practice could truly possess. Elliot had liked the elderly GP immediately, the quiet way he examined and assessed, the deft steadiness of his hand as he worked on the wound. He noticed Baines gazing curiously at the array of bottles on the bedside table.

"You take some pretty strong sedatives, I see. Have that much trouble sleeping, do you?"

More than you know, Elliot thought. "I've been over-worked—still have difficulty turning off at night. I'm hoping to get away from them by the time I have to go back."

Baines nodded and closed his case with a snap. "Aye, work can be the very devil, I know. Especially if you're a worrier. Are you a worrier, Doctor?"

"Tell me about Annie." It was not himself he wanted to discuss.

Baines hesitated and Elliot realized his natural reticence was struggling with an urge to share the problem and perhaps halve it. Especially since Baines knew he was a neurologist and this case was apparently in that area. After a moment Baines shrugged and settled himself on the foot of the bed, leaning an elbow on the top of the footboard and rubbing his forehead with a long arthritic finger.

"She's what you might call a recluse now. I delivered her myself not long after coming to Mhourra, twenty-four or -five years ago it must be. Seemed a perfectly normal wee babby at first, but she wasn't. After a few weeks she turned into a wild little thing, cried day and night, nearly drove her mother to distraction. Well, the mother was just a child herself really, no more than seventeen, and not married. She couldn't even remember the father's name."

"Was the baby injured during those weeks? Did the mother maltreat her? Or was she ill, high fever? Violent allergic—"

Baines shook his head.

"No battering, the grandmother would have put a stop to that. And no illness. We gave the baby all the tests there were then, but couldn't find a thing wrong with her, physically. She stayed wild, grew up wild. Screamed one minute, sat staring at nothing the next. Wouldn't be held, wouldn't be comforted. Couldn't or wouldn't speak, went into rages for no apparent reason, never looked directly at anyone. I understand there's a name for it now, if not a cure."

"Autism."

"Aye, that's it."

"Why wasn't she institutionalized?"

"The grandmother, mainly. She wasn't bright, but she was a proud woman. Born in Edinburgh, came here as a bride, but always set herself apart from the islanders. Particularly after her man died." He smiled briefly in recollection. "Anyway, one day Annie's mother just up and left on the ferry and has never been heard of since. It was all right, though, because the grandmother doted on the child and was really the only one who could handle her—Annie was reasonably quiet with her. So we just let her get on. I realize *now* that was a mistake, but hindsight is useless. Couldn't force the issue, after all. There's many a family that will put up with far worse rather than condemn a child to the purgatory of some crowded institution. I certainly wasn't keen on that idea myself. But the inevitable happened. Mrs. Craigie died, and there was Annie. Grown up in body, yes, but totally unequipped to deal with the world around her."

Elliot's head was pounding. "Surely that would have been the time to institutionalize her?"

The old doctor gazed at him pityingly. "Indeed, yes. But, man, we couldn't get *near* her. What would you have had me do—shoot her down?"

"But how does she *live?*"

"Your hostess, Mrs. Macadam. She was a Craigie before she married. Annie is her niece. She takes food and clothing to the cottage. Whatever the girl needs, she gets for her."

Elliot sat up angrily. "That's disgraceful. The girl could injure herself out there, fall ill . . . anything. How can you possibly countenance such a ludicrous situation?"

"How can I not? Mrs. Macadam is Annie's closest relative, she'll do nothing to help us. Oh, man, you've no idea how it can be up here, have you? Fear and superstition still govern a great deal of what goes on in these islands."

"I see." Elliot gazed at the old man thoughtfully for a moment, then leaned back against the pillows once more, folding his arms. "Obviously there's more to it than you've said."

Baines looked away. "Aye, more. Much more. There's some who say Annie can heal the sick, some who say she can cast spells, some who call her the devil's own and will have nothing done to tempt her anger. Others go into the hills for what they believe she can provide."

"Which is?"

"Magic, man." The voice was an empty husk. "Magic."

"Rubbish."

"Is it? I wonder. I've been doctoring a long time."

"So have I."

"Not long enough, mebbe. Don't you know yet that where the body leaves off the head sometimes begins?"

Elliot stared at him—he knew it better than anyone. "What are you saying?"

Baines turned and fixed Elliot with the blue eyes. "I don't know. I don't *know,* can't you see that? But I've had patients I could not cure who went to Annie Craigie and lived. *Lived.* I've seen things—things I couldn't explain but were there before my eyes. A hideous facial melanoma—gone. A confirmed diagnosis of advanced leukemia made ten years ago— the patient still alive today, and *whole.*" He looked directly at Elliot, weariness evident in his eyes. An uncertain old man, suddenly, ridden with guilt and confusion, unable to see his way clearly and too tired to follow it if he could.

"She harms no one," he muttered.

But she has harmed me, Elliot thought, staring at him. And more.

The next morning he faced a desperately worried and ashamed Mrs. Macadam across the breakfast table.

"She's a good girl, Dr. Elliot. A gentle girl, not a bad girl."

"Not a girl at all, Mrs. Macadam. A woman, living wild and alone God knows how out there, with no one to protect or care for her."

"I care for her. She canna bear anyone near her, that's

all. Let her be and no harm will come."

He pushed the egg and bacon around his plate, unable to do more with it. "How close do you actually get to her, Mrs. Macadam? Does she speak to you, does she talk at all?"

"Oh, yes. She's perfectly bright, she has some Gaelic and English both. She lets me near now and again, but there's not much need for words somehow. If she were ill I know she would come to me, she knows I love her, but she's never been ill at all."

"I'm going back to see her."

Mrs. Macadam stiffened, despair in her face. "But *why?*"

"I think I know what's wrong with her. I think I can help her. You'd want her to be helped, wouldn't you?"

"Leave her alone . . . please. Leave her as she is."

"I won't hurt her."

"No, you'll not *want* to hurt her. But you'll make them take her away, put her with a lot of crazy people, won't you? She's not crazy."

"I can't legally take her anywhere without your permission, Mrs. Macadam, or hers if she can give it. I certainly have no intention of 'putting her with crazy people,' either. That would be pointless. That's why I'd like you to go with me —so she'll see I mean her no harm."

"No."

"But don't you understand—"

"No." She kept her eyes down, refusing to meet his. "I won't do that. If you want to see her, you'll have to do it on your own." Reaching across the table she took his plate away and disappeared into the kitchen, leaving him with the pot of tea and a rack of cold toast.

Elliot knew that if he delayed, Mrs. Macadam would somehow manage to warn the girl and he would never be able to find her. He had no alternative but to ignore his exhaustion and go back to the cottage immediately. At any rate, his exhaustion was partially attenuated by his excitement. The local people thought Annie Craigie was "odd." He was reasonably sure, now, that she was much, much more. It was true she had exhibited all the classic symptoms of infantile autism. From his viewpoint, however, there was another possibility. Every one of those symptoms could also have been a reaction to a telepathic flood similar to what he had experienced after his accident. The room full of loudspeakers. He had been hit with it as an educated adult with medical training. But could she have had it in the cradle?

His conviction grew not from Baines's case history, nor Mrs. Macadam's descriptions of Annie, but from the marks that had been scrawled on his face the night before. There had been three of them. On his forehead, the Greek letter Psi. On the right cheek, the Greek letter Tau. And on the left cheek a rough caduceus, the snake and staff of medicine. He did not think that Annie Craigie wrote and understood Greek. But those three letters were something special to him, his own private shorthand for experimental notes. Psi—someone with psi or paranormal powers. Tau—a telepath. The caduceus—a psychic healer.

The only place she could have got those symbols was from his own head.

She had followed him and left her mark on him—or rather, his own mark on him.

Why?

Had she wanted him to know? Had she finally understood who and *what* he was?

As he strode along the sand, he decided it was his own powers that were causing the problem. It had happened before in the lab, not often, but often enough. A latent telepath would be on a test rig, and his own hidden abilities would cross over and set up an interface. Like shouting at himself and hearing his own echoes at the same time, on ever-mounting levels. The telepath would pick up Elliot's thoughts, Elliot would read the telepath as he picked them up, and back they would come, doubled and re-doubled, bouncing between them with increasing intensity as the subject, confused by what he was getting, added astonishment and eventually fear to the process. It was not easy to deal with, and Elliot always excused himself from the experiments with a "headache" or something of the kind. No one ever questioned it, because no one knew it was happening. Never once had he told his colleagues the extent of his abilities. It would have created too many side issues, too much confusion, too much time-wasting. Of course they knew he had *some* psychic ability; it would have been impossible to deny it to such trained observers. But they thought it was no more than many of the subjects they tested. They accepted it as a reasonable explanation of his continuing interest in ESP research and let it go at that. Not even Longjohn had guessed the truth.

The day was even wilder and windier than yesterday had been. The beach vibrated with the heavy thud of the waves, and the spray literally rained on his face. Despite the sun he was shivering, and kept his hands jammed into his anorak pockets. He did not look forward to his encounter with Annie Craigie, but he could not in all conscience avoid it.

She was not at the cottage, and it took a lot of purposely aimless walking before he got a faint glimmer of anything. Not much. A sensation of unease, no more. It increased as he approached a scrubby stand of bushes on the lee flank of a hill. As he came closer, the sensations strengthened. It was a bad hiding place, she could not break out in any direction without him seeing her, and it occurred to him again that perhaps she *wanted* to be found.

"Annie." She did not answer his call, but the sensations immediately sharpened. He stopped and waited. "Annie, I'm not going to hurt you. I only want to talk to you." Still no response. It was evidently going to be a test between his nerve endings and her stubbornness. He dropped down onto the grass, pulled out his cigarettes and started to light up. The next minute she was in his head.

It was like having ice water poured in through a hole at

the top of his skull. He could feel it trickling down and around and through his brain. At the same time, his own deepest and most private fears were picked up, amplified, and hurled back at him with violent intensity. Memories of closed spaces became more closed than ever, spiders and black dogs loomed and menaced gigantically, stagnant water lapped at him more chokingly than it had on that day he nearly drowned. Like a whirlpool of nightmares, all the monstrous senseless remnants of childhood fears and adult traumas engulfed him and began to drag him down, down into a dark and endless terror. He went into mild involuntary convulsions, triggered by the feedback of overload. His cigarettes and lighter flew in one direction, his body into another as he sprawled face forward into the grass and tried very hard not to wet himself.

"Stop it, stop it!" he bellowed. "Can't you see what you're doing? I'm not like the others . . . you *know* that . . . Stop it!" He was doing even more shouting in his head than he was into the grass, and after a few more seconds the bombardment ceased. He lay there, as close to being totally shattered as anyone could be, inside and out. There was a long, long silence. And then . . .

?

No words, just a question.

He lay utterly still, unable to quite believe it. It hadn't been a problem of interface at all. She *was* full power, as he had once been. More than he had been, in fact.

Because at distance, and at will . . .

She could *send.*

He put his first question up front in his brain, using a projection technique developed over the years in the lab.

Can you control it?

Negative, positive, negative, positive. She still wasn't using words, just sensations. He presumed the answer meant "Sort of."

Can you talk it?

?

Words. Can you put it into words, as I am?
Negative, negative, negative. Go away. Or sensations to
that effect. No pain or ice water this time, she was minding her
manners for the moment.
But you understand my English words?
Positive.
"Then why don't we talk?" he called out. "Face to face?"
Negative, negative, negative, go away.
"I can help you. I know what you've been through."
NEGATIVE.

Apparently he *didn't* know what she'd been through. He
took out a handkerchief and scrubbed ineffectually at his face
and clothes, brushing away the bits of grass and dirt, using
the activity to cover his own confusion. He was at a loss.
So accustomed was he to holding back in the lab and everywhere else that to encounter somebody who had all his powers
and more was a little unnerving. At least, he acknowledged,
she wasn't hating him all over the place. And she was correct
—he probably didn't have a real idea of what she'd gone
through in her lifetime. Bad enough to be forced to accept
the thoughts of others. But when she had eventually realized
she could get *back* at them, extrapolate from that to a normal
child's development, rages, tantrums, frustrations—why hadn't
she simply blown everyone off the island?

She picked that up, apparently, because he suddenly got
a picture of an old lady—the grandmother. The impression
helped to clarify things. Old Mrs. Craigie had been able to
handle her grand-daughter because she had been simple-
minded. Her brain-patterns had been so lacking in complexity
and depth that the child could just about tolerate them, and
they gave her a fairly easy pattern to follow and cling to. But
they certainly were not the only patterns she had encountered
over the years—Baines, her aunt, everyone else on the island.
It all must have poured in at one time or another. Why wasn't
she insane?

Sensation of laughter. Soft. Gentle. Maybe she *was* insane, the laughter said. How did he propose to tell the difference?

"You tell me."

Negative, negative, negative.

"You'd say that anyway."

?

"This is ridiculous."

?

"Why don't you come out?"

She came into his head again, but without ice water and spiders. He was abruptly flooded with *her* sensations. She could see him, and so he could see himself. Brown hair well streaked with grey falling across a high wide forehead, a very erratic nose, a smallish mouth over a stubborn chin, grey-blue eyes that still were not focusing too well, his anorak and jeans covered with bits of grass, his lower lip taped where the stitches pulled. He was a mess. And yet he had the distinct impression that she *liked* him. He was . . . oh. On top of everything else, he had forgotten the obvious.

She was a woman.

She wouldn't come out because her face was dirty.

His amusement must have come across because he received the sudden and not very pleasant sensation of being . . . flicked . . . across the brain. He was not to laugh at her, apparently. She could laugh at him, of course, but the reverse was unacceptable.

"Look, I've no intention of continuing to sit here and talk to a bush," he said to the bush. "Either you come out or I'm going to come in and get you."

Negative, fear, negative, fear.

"There's nothing to be afraid of. I'm a doctor, Annie, I'm not going to harm you. I work with people like you—and like me. I'm trying to find out—well, look for yourself." He began to loosen his mental locks but again received that . . . flick . . . and paused. "What is it?"

There was a full minute of silence both aural and mental.

Then the bushes shook a little, and she stood up. So did he.

Her face *was* dirty. As far as he could tell, she was filthy all over. Not very big in herself, her shape was enlarged and made amorphous because of the layer upon layer of old and grimy clothing she had wrapped around herself. Dresses, shirts, skirts, cardigans, shawls—all put on haphazardly and all weathered to a hazy grey, with every edge frayed and torn. They were what had given her that strange furred silhouette the previous night. Beneath the topmost shawl she was clutching something to her chest, also grey and shapeless. All this was secondary to Elliot's overwhelming first impression of her face, and particularly, her eyes. The eyes were enormous, golden-amber, with the dilated pupils of myopia, and their stare was inward as well as outward, as if double-vision were her only vision; she saw, she saw through, she saw within, and more. He had seen something similar in the eyes of epileptics about to undergo a seizure, the gaze over inner distance. But she went into no seizure, there was no release from that all-seeing stare, golden and blind yet not blind.

He forced his eyes away from hers and tried to take in the face as a whole. She was thin, to judge by her cheekbones, which were high. Aside from the eyes, her features were delicate and slightly slanted, almost fox-like. That was it, he decided, taking refuge in familiar analogies. She looked like a vixen, startled from her den. A vixen with eyes of timeless knowledge, a vixen who recognized the hunter, and knew his name. Her hair helped the analogy; it was deep fox-red, thick and matted, networked with brambles and—here and there—a wild flower, wilting. The first was neglect, the second the woman in her, sad and strange and shy. Under the veil of dirt-streaks, her skin was translucent. He found another refuge in visual diagnosis: malnutrition, some anaemia, probably, possibility of TB, parasitic infestation certainly. But her teeth, when her lips parted, were white and even and, again, almost feral. The canines were slightly lifted, the effect was . . . disturbing. Which of them was really the hunter?

He took a step towards her, and she took a step back, pressing against the branches. Like electric eels they faced one another in silence, wary, alert to the danger but unable to deny the fascination.

"Please don't be afraid, Annie. I understand you far better than you think. Please trust me." He took another step forward.

Negative, fear, negative, fear, fear.

"Please . . . Annie . . ." Another step.

FEAR, FEAR, FEAR, STOP STOP STOP

Another step. "But—I won't hurt you."

And then she spoke, her voice strained and thin with lack of development. "I . . . canna . . . hold . . . on . . ." She struggled to say, and then lost control completely.

Annie had not been afraid of him. She had been afraid *for* him.

Even as he went down under the flow of energy from her unleashed brain, he realized she had been protecting him. When she had entered his mind, she too had experienced interface and realized just how severely her powers were affecting him. And she had also realized, perhaps without understanding exactly why, that what she had done as a simple defence against others whose sensitivities were not as developed or as raw from constant abrasion, was far worse for him. He was certain she did not want to cause him this much pain. She was not evil, only afraid. Too late, she had discovered his lack of defence was total.

He went into convulsions, *grand mal* this time, felt the searing pain of rising interface, and just before blackness claimed him, picked up a faltering sensation—her despair—following him down the long corridor to oblivion.

Sorry, sorry, sorry

When he came to, a few hours later, he was alone again. But it didn't matter.

4

Talbot Hall did not look like what it really was.

Built in the early 1800s, it had been a country retreat for generations of a family that had come to an abrupt end during the First World War. Shaped like a C with its long back to the circular gravel drive, the central semi-enclosed area at the rear had been flagged over, making a courtyard onto which opened one of the labs, the kitchens, and the magnificent two-storey library that had somehow survived the rabbit-warren proclivities of the Government departments that had been housed there over the years.

Talbot Hall's rosy brick façade was trimmed in gleaming white, and it still looked like something out of a feature in *Country Life*. There was nothing to indicate that it was anything other than what it seemed, except for the large gravelled car park to one side, and the mammoth auxiliary generators behind the kitchens. Digital and analogue computers, among other items, do not plug in and run like washing machines.

The panel on the gate still read "Talbot Hall." It was only the staff who affectionately referred to it as Elliot's Nuthatch.

It seemed appropriate to Elliott when he first took over

the building that British research into parapsychology should be thus housed. In America he would have been part of the Pentagon's Advanced Research Projects Agency, and suspended in some modern glass and chrome cube. In Russia, it would have been the grey mausoleum on Bezukhov Street, which many entered but few left. In England, it was statuesque oaks, clipped lawns, and Georgian listed buildings set in the rolling hills of Berkshire. Parapsychology, like stamp-collecting and butterfly-chasing, was still considered a dilettante interest here, and if the dilettante in question was the Defence Department, it made little difference to the attitude. We are doing it only because "they" are doing it; and he blessed the categorization. There would have been too many noses poking over his shoulder anywhere else.

His personal team had been assembled gradually over the years, and his personal dictum had been consistent from the beginning—you do not intentionally eavesdrop on friends or colleagues. He treated his staff with scrupulous fairness, listened carefully to every problem and complaint, and invariably put his people before himself because it seemed to him the only logical way to treat those you expect to work their guts out for you. He assumed, correctly, that they respected him, but he assumed no more.

He would have been astonished, therefore, at Ted Holbrook's remark when he put down the phone the next afternoon. "That damned idiot's coming *back*. We'd better get in touch with Longjohn."

Janet York stared at the man behind the desk. Heavier and darker than Elliot, he had a habit of taking over Elliot's office in his absence that annoyed her. "But *why?* We only got him out of here a few days ago—he can't be ready to—"

"Oh, he's not. He sounded just as tight and nervy as he was when he left—more so, in fact. And I simply do not *believe* these instructions." He stared down at the six pages he had covered in frantic, ever-accelerating notes while Elliot shouted over the crackling line from the north.

"He's got hold of something, or someone, as far as I can tell, who's sent him off on another hysterical bender."

Janet sank down onto one end of the cracked leather chesterfield and looked morosely at Holbrook. "Oh, *no!* Oh, Ted!"

He stared at her helplessly.

"Couldn't you have talked him into a few more days, at least?"

Holbrook shrugged, half in anger, half in bemusement. "Janet, have *you* ever been able to talk him out of anything when he gets like that? Ever?"

"No . . . dammit."

Gathering the notes together, Holbrook laid them in the centre of the blotter, peered at them, and pulled over another blank page to try to organize the priorities. "We'll have to go back to slipping tranks into his coffee, I suppose. I can't tell you what that does to my ethical self-image."

"I can imagine," she said wryly. "It doesn't do much for my coffee, either."

He grinned up at her. "He did seem to think it was getting a little strong there, towards the end, didn't he?"

"I think he was on the verge of accusing me of poisoning him, especially when nobody else complained. Why *does* he drive himself the way he . . . ?" She shook her head despairingly.

"It's a good thing I know you're in love with Vanderhof," Ted said, going back to the notes. "Otherwise I'd say you were too fixated on your boss to be your normal efficient self."

"Who said I was in love with Danny?"

"I did," Holbrook muttered, shifting the pages around in irritation. "Do we have enough copper mesh to build a full screen-room at the end of Lab One?"

"I don't know," she said distractedly. "I'll have to check with Cragg."

"Ah—no. Don't do that." She looked puzzled. He continued. "Instruction eight thousand and six was no mention to

Cragg. Very clear on *that* was our favourite crusader. Cragg stays absolutely out."

"And how did he suggest we manage that?"

"He didn't. Mark of an executive, delegate all the insolubles to the menials. That's why I suggest you get Longjohn back from Edinburgh. Born scroungers aren't that easy to come by around here."

"What on *earth* is he onto this time?"

"He says"—Holbrook leaned back in Elliot's chair and smiled winsomely at Elliot's administrative assistant—"he *says* it could be the answer to everything."

"Oh, my God," Janet moaned. *"Again?"*

Hawkins stared at the mess in Laboratory One with a disbelieving eye, then turned to Janet. "And he wants it ready for *when?"*

"This afternoon, late this afternoon. He's bringing whatever it is down by helicopter—I gather he pulled some strings and Air-Sea Rescue are handling it."

"He's got more strings than the viola section of the LSO," Hawkins muttered.

"Longjohn, can you give me a minute?" It was George Lomax. He had spotted the psychologist from the far end of the lab and left the construction work to wander down.

"Problems?"

George followed Longjohn's nod towards the nearly completed screen-room, and shook his head. "Not with this. Got something to show you upstairs."

"Upstairs" was the electronics lab. George escorted a puzzled Hawkins through it to his own glassed-off cubbyhole in one corner. After rummaging in one of his desk drawers for a moment, he drew out a small cardboard box and lifted the lid. "I've taken up a new hobby. Bug-collecting."

"Wow! With a net and everything?" Hawkins asked sarcastically.

Lomax tipped the box over his blotter and the contents

rolled out to lie winking in the light from his desk lamp. "These don't crawl *or* fly." On the blotter were seven small mesh-covered metallic buttons with rubber suction discs on the back. Hawkins stared at them and then at Lomax.

"Where did you find them?"

"Four in Lab One when I started running the new wiring in for the screen-room, the other three in his office."

"Any idea how long they'd been there?"

"No. Lab was painted two years ago, could have been then. Or last week. They don't exactly write dates of installation underneath them, you know."

"Russian?" Longjohn sank down onto a straight chair and pulled one leg up to rest it on the seat, his chin on his knee as he stared at the listening devices on the blotter.

"Japanese, which means they could be anybody's."

"Have you checked anywhere else?"

"Haven't had time. Didn't want to make a fuss, so after I found the first one, I rigged a detector together and came back when everyone had gone home. I think I cleared his office, but I'm going to go over it again tonight."

"Do it now, George." Longjohn paused to look angrily around the room. "Goddammit, we haven't had anything like this before. What the hell is going on?"

George sat down on the edge of the desk and prodded one of the buttons with a stubby forefinger, making it roll in a circle. "I don't know. But I didn't mention it to Security. Should I have?"

"Security means Cragg."

"That's what I thought. I also thought it might *be* one of Cragg's little operations. You know he hates the Doc's guts because he never tells him what's going on."

"It's none of his goddamn business what's going on."

"Well, somebody thinks it's *somebody's* business."

George got up and went over to pick up a cardboard box from the corner. "Do you want me to do your office, too, while I'm at it?"

"No. Just make sure Phil's room is safe. Can you make some kind of interference thing just to cover all the bases?"

"No problem."

"Do it, then. Soon as you can—before he gets back, if possible." Lomax nodded and started out. Gathering up the bugs and putting them back in the little box, Longjohn spoke again. "George?"

"Yeah?"

"You done good. Thanks."

"My old man always wanted me to take up a trade. Exterminator's as good as any."

Elliot gave no indication of surprise at seeing Longjohn standing next to Ted Holbrook when the helicopter set down on the lawn behind Talbot Hall. He helped them transfer the stretcher to the trolley, then went back for his cases. Almost immediately after he'd emerged again, the big Wessex lifted up and away, its red roundels showing bright against the dark blue curve of the fuselage. They began to push the trolley across the grass under its diminishing shadow—Longjohn at the head, Ted at the foot, and Elliot trotting alongside, his fingers on Annie's wrist. A frown was beginning to appear between her eyebrows and she was restless under the restraining straps. Longjohn peered down at the small pinched face under its amateurishly clipped cap of freshly washed red-gold hair.

"What is it?"

"It's a girl."

"Congratulations."

"Just because you go for big busty blondes doesn't mean everything smaller should get thrown back," Elliot snapped, concerned with her rising pulse rate and growing discomfort. "She'll need 10 mg of Haliperidol stat, Ted. I couldn't get as much as I needed from the hospital on Lewis."

"Okay," Holbrook said soothingly as they lifted the trolley over the sill of the French windows and pushed it between the computers in Laboratory Two. "Let's get her bedded down, first."

After they had settled Annie in the high hospital bed, Elliot glanced around the hastily erected screen-room with approval. Cutting off the end of Laboratory One, the inner side of the hardboard partition and the other three walls were faced with fine copper mesh which carried a low-Herz charge. It prevented or weakened most unconscious brainwave transmissions from outside, and would provide a continuous shell of interference which, though imperfect, would give Annie some mental peace.

Ted administered the hypo and within moments her small body stiffened as the strong anaesthetic brought every muscle into rigid order.

"George did a good job on this room, remind me to thank him," Elliot said to Longjohn. He was beginning to relax as she went deeper into sedation. He turned to Holbrook. "Ted, I want you to list her as your patient, not mine." Holbrook started to ask why, but had no time as Elliot continued listing what he wanted. "Do a complete blood screen, RFTs, LFTs, serum proteins. Put her on full parenteral feed, aminosols and intralipids in dextrose-saline, she's badly malnourished. If you can get a specimen, I think you'll find intestinal parasites present. Also check—oh, for God's sake, you know the damn routine better than I do. Then get in touch with Slough and see if we can get a couple of hours on the Phillips scanner. We'll want skull X-rays, too. Build up as complete a physical status picture on her as possible. Oh—and when you do that blood screen, check her monoamine, catecholamine and cortisol levels, too."

Ted turned to stare at Annie's face. "My God, is she psychotic?"

"No, I just want control levels to check against later on. I think that's it for now. Keep her completely under until I say otherwise, all right?"

"But—"

Elliot started out. "I'll be in my office when you've got those blood screen results. Do them yourself, I don't want anybody else in on this. Just the three of us, and Janet. She can handle whatever nursing is needed."

Holbrook nodded curtly and they parted at the double doors of the lab, Longjohn slouching after Elliot down the long linoleumed corridor. He almost crashed into him when Elliot turned abruptly and called after Holbrook.

"Ted?" Holbrook stiffened, stopped, turned around, and waited for his next instruction. Elliot gazed down the long space between them and suddenly gave one of his rare boyish smiles. "Do your gentle best with her, all right? She's only a little one."

Holbrook started, then slowly smiled back, his spine losing its resentful line. "Kid gloves."

"Thanks."

Longjohn continued after Elliot, shaking his head and smiling to himself. He was so caught up in his inner amusement at Elliot's unfailing ability to charm subordinates that he almost tripped over him again just inside the office door.

Elliot had two havens—his home and his office. He looked around, then sighed with deep relief.

The corner room was big, but not because he needed the status. He didn't like the lines of control to show any more than they had to, so he'd made sure the "office" was well filled with old comfortable chairs and couches, plenty of low tables, large ashtrays, and a constant supply of coffee on tap. His door was always open. As a result most of the talking at Talbot Hall took place there, in an atmosphere as relaxed as an undergraduate seminar. It was a simple method of keeping track of what everyone was doing, how they felt about it, and how they felt about one another. The habit of sprawling out with your problems in Elliot's room had grown over the years. Before the discovery of the electronic bugs, Hawkins had always considered the room a good place to kick your shoes off, scratch your armpits, and wonder what the hell to do next.

Which was exactly what Elliot was wondering.

As he went over to the percolator, however, he noticed that something new had been added. He raised an eyebrow and looked at Longjohn.

"Termites?"

Hawkins glanced at the side wall where a gaping hole about six inches in diameter had been smashed into the plaster.

Longjohn shook his head. "You tell me your story, then I'll tell you mine. Come on, who is she, what is she, why is she? From the top, preferably."

"Shut the door." Elliot busied himself pouring out two mugs of coffee. He handed one mug to Longjohn and carried his own to his chair behind the desk. "Her name is Annie Craigie. As far as I can ascertain, she is a full-power telepath with virtually unlimited send/receive capacity—and absolutely no control over it worth considering. I brought her here to help her *get* control and to find out how she does it."

"You're kidding," Longjohn breathed.

"No," Elliot said, evenly. "I am not kidding at all."

"How do you know?"

"You'll simply have to take my word for it. I *know*."

Hawkins stared at the hunched figure behind the desk. Elliot's collar had begun to overlap his jacket and his tie was slightly askew. He was the kind of man who looked immaculate for the first seven minutes after dressing, then slowly disintegrated during the day. Every suit he put on ended up looking as if he'd slept in it. In this case, Hawkins supposed, he probably had.

"Love you, Phil," Longjohn demurred. "Great guy and all that—but it's not good enough."

Stalling, Elliot outlined how he had found Annie, her medical history as far as Baines had been able to give it, and the conclusions he had drawn.

"Still not good enough," Hawkins countered.

Swivelling his chair to face the window and the long line of willows that edged the river at the far end of the lawns, Elliot spoke so softly that the Canadian had to lean forward to catch his words. "I've communicated with her. She's been in my head."

"Communicated *telepathically?*"

"Yes."

There was a long, uncomfortable silence. Finally Longjohn spoke again, hesitating slightly because he could not see Elliot's face, just the top of his head over the back of the big leather chair. "Formal symbols . . . auditory exchanges . . . eidetic imagery . . . words?"

Hidden by the curve of the chair, Elliot put his hands up over his face, bent his head down, and rested his elbows on his knees, concentrating hard. After a moment, he began. "You've got a date tonight with somebody called Joanna. You met her last night at Skindles, she was with a couple you know called Trace. Joanna . . . Baxter? About five foot ten, blonde, brown eyes, and was wearing a red dress. You took her home but only got as far as the front door. You expect to get inside both the door *and* Miss Baxter tonight, if you play your cards right. Your left foot itches, you wish I hadn't put so much milk in your coffee, and you're pretty sure I'm trying something on or I've finally snapped. You think you should put somebody named . . . Mathers? . . . Manvers? . . . onto me because I need—you need—a second opinion." He paused. "Yes?"

"What the hell?" Longjohn gasped.

Elliot's voice continued to come over the back of the chair, unemotional, formal, clinical. He outlined his own medical history over the past twelve years, concluding with the mysterious "fading" he had been experiencing in his own telepathic powers. "Annie's attack, for some reason I don't quite understand, obviously has heightened my powers again, but it's only temporary. I can feel it sliding away again, hour by hour."

This time the silence was distinctly unpleasant. Longjohn finally broke it.

"You bastard."

Unseen by his friend Elliot nodded, dropped his hands, stared at them. "Sorry."

"Why . . . didn't . . . you . . . tell . . . us?" Longjohn's words were spaced out by rage. Elliot dropped his head back against the chair and closed his eyes once more, his hands gripping the arms on either side until his knuckles showed white.

"What would you have done if I had?"

"Why, tested you, of course. Put you through the—"

"Using who or what as a control?" Elliot interrupted.

"Simply the standard."

"What standard?"

"We could have evolved—"

"Who could have evolved? Who between us knows the most about ESP, including how to cheat at it?"

"You, of course. But—"

"And who would you have been testing?"

"You. But Phil, you wouldn't cheat . . . we . . ."

"How do you know? You thought I was *crazy* a minute ago, you were going to set a psychiatrist onto me, right?"

"Well, only because you sounded . . . a little loopy . . . but . . ."

"I sounded a little 'loopy' because I said I could read Annie's mind? Even though you *know* I'd never lie about something like that? What about all the other scientists, the ones who don't know I wouldn't lie?"

"We could have found a way."

"What way?"

"I don't know, but . . ."

"You see?" Elliot turned his chair to face him and

smiled wryly. "I don't know, either. After all these years the only thing I'm sure of is what *not* to look for in that girl's head."

"You could still have told me."

"I'm telling you now."

"Because you have to," Longjohn stated in a flat voice, his eyes cold.

"Yes."

"*Only* because you have to."

"Yes."

"Didn't you trust me?"

It was difficult to say, but Elliot said it. "No."

"Why not?"

Elliot felt a weary impulse to burst into childish tears. He realized he hadn't eaten since breakfast and leaned down to get a packet of digestive biscuits out of his bottom drawer. As he struggled with the wrapper it burst, scattering biscuits all over the desk top. He began to stack them up, letting the silence stretch to breaking-point.

"Are you reading my mind now?" Longjohn suddenly demanded.

Elliot smiled at him. "That's why," he said, softly.

"Then you *are*—"

"No. No, Longjohn, I'm not. Until a few minutes ago I had never, ever, *ever* gone into your head or Ted's or Janet's or anyone else's on my staff. Now that you know I can, it's not a matter of me trusting you, but the reverse, isn't it? Will you ever be certain, now, that I'm *not* reading your mind?"

Longjohn digested this, watching Elliot break up a biscuit into smaller and smaller pieces. "But you *have* used it?"

"Oh, yes. Yes, indeed," Elliot admitted. "Many times. But only on strangers. I used it to get this position, and I've used it in other ways. When I had to. *Only* when I had to. For one thing it's hard work, and for another I don't think I really want to know what you think of me after a long hard day." He tried to keep it light but it fell heavily and lay between them.

"That's probably wise," Hawkins said icily.

Again, Elliot felt an impulse towards tears. Oh God, he thought, looking at the stranger staring at him out of Hawkins's face. Can't he see how bad it is, how lonely it is, how frightening it is to see him watching the freak?

Hawkins blinked. "I heard that," he said in astonishment.

"What?"

"Freak. I heard that."

Elliot waited for him to work it out. "You know you have latent Psi-abilities," he reminded him. "Your test scores—"

"I *heard* it," Longjohn repeated.

"I felt it," Elliot said bleakly.

Hawkins leaned his head against the back of the sofa and regarded Elliot thoughtfully. After a while he began to chuckle, then laughed aloud. "You're right, you know. I *would* have put you through the hoops, no mercy shown."

Elliot grinned. The stranger had disappeared from Longjohn's eyes. For an instant he was almost tempted to probe the façade to verify whether his friend *did* trust him or whether—but there it was, the problem itself. And there was no breaking his law. He had to function according to his own ethics and take friends as friends took him, on surfaces and actions alone. He began to eat one of the stale digestives as Hawkins continued to laugh.

"Man, I'm sure glad I never played poker with *you.*"

"You should be," Elliot said through a mouthful of crumbs. "You don't *really* think I bought that plane on a bank loan, do you?"

Hawkin's laughter ceased abruptly. "What?"

Elliot was trying to push the wayward biscuits back into the remnants of the wrapper but they seemed to have multiplied. "You don't really think I inherited money from my grandfather's trust, do you? We weren't a rich family. Country GPs never made money even before the NHS came along."

"Gambling?" Hawkins asked, appalled.

"Oh, it's no gamble. I cheat." Elliot smiled. "I cheat like merry hell. Or I did when I was able to. I haven't been able to for some time now, unfortunately, as I said before." He stopped playing with the biscuits and stood up. He wasn't proud of this, but it would make the point quickly. "Look, what were my alternatives? I needed money to finance my research, for equipment. Good God, you've seen the bills from IBM and EMI, haven't you? I could have set up as a fortune teller, of course, but I'd look damned silly in sandals and a turban. I could have gone round begging contributions for medical research—certainly. I would have got a cheque for two hundred from one millionaire, five hundred from another. They would have felt very generous about the whole thing, and set it against their taxes. But I needed a lot more than that. I still do, or I wouldn't be here at Talbot working for His Majesty's Government, I promise you. And so . . ." He was wandering round the room, avoiding Hawkins's eyes, touching the books and the filing cabinet and pausing at the coffee maker to refill his mug. "So I put on a well-cut dinner-jacket and my grandfather's gold cufflinks, assumed a well-bred air of not giving a good goddamn, sat down at the poker table with well-heeled gentlemen of finance—and skinned the living day-lights out of them. They loved it, it eased their consciences about grafting an income off the backs of the sweated poor."

"The great and ethical Philip Elliot cheats at cards," Longjohn marvelled, staring at the back of Elliot's neck.

"Mmmmm, I do indeed." He returned to his desk and hid behind the flare of his lighter. "But I didn't take money from anyone who wasn't in a position to lose it, I didn't take too much at one time, and occasionally I lost, just to keep them interested. I am not a greedy man, I am a gentle man. With the fingertips, Longjohn, the fingertips only." His voice hardened. "And one good night at the Colchester Club paid for a Pedersen rig, or a new digital keyboard, or that coffee over there. Not *all* your bills find their way to Cragg's office. I have to stay in budget, remember?"

"You must have had quite a reputation at the tables."

"Oh, they loved trying to break a 'lucky' man. They loved it."

"And you hated it." Longjohn's statement was flat. Elliot didn't try to contradict the empathetic leap his friend had made. Nine years is a lot of familiarity.

"I detested every boring, iniquitous, shameful minute of it, yes."

"How much?"

"What?"

"How much do you have stacked away in Switzerland? I presume you *have* been prudent over the years?"

"Do you really need to know? I wasn't bragging. I'm trying to make a point if you'll give me the chance."

"Sure, fine, make your point. But . . . how much, Phil?"

Elliot leaned back in his chair and looked at the Canadian, a slight smile on his lips. "I've been lucky with investments, and tight on myself. At the moment, about eight hundred thousand."

Longjohn whistled appreciatively.

"I don't suppose you give lessons?"

"I'd give every bit of that eight hundred thousand to be able to find a way. It only *sounds* like a lot. If Talbot Hall closed up, it would buy another year or two of private research at the most. No more."

"And is that the point you're trying to make?"

"Not at all. I'm trying to make a point about abuse. *My* end is simple, even if my methods are less than savoury. I want to find out what it is in my head, and in that girl's, that gives us powers of telepathy. I *had* to come here to Talbot Hall because no matter how much I made at the tables, it wasn't enough. Now, if my ability were known to the people who run Talbot—Cart Curtiss, say, or to just about anybody else in power—do you think I'd be allowed to pursue my goal in peace? Do you think I'd be here at all?" He stubbed his cigarette out in the big pottery ashtray, clasped his hands in front of him, and leaned forward. "No. Oh, no. *I* use me, that's my choice and my responsibility. But I don't want to be used by anyone else. And I don't want that girl used, either."

"That's a very thin line you're walking, Phil," Longjohn said slowly, as the full implications of what Elliot was saying hit him, and he extrapolated from the fact of telepathy to applications other than poker.

"Longjohn, you have no idea just *how* thin it really is," Elliot's voice wavered, but held. "That is why I've told you about me. And that is why we have to keep every blessed thing about Annie Craigie to ourselves. There was nowhere else to take her, except into this bloody lion's den. It stinks in here. It stinks of wanting to win, no matter how it's done, and no matter who does it. She shouldn't be here, I shouldn't be here, but there's no other place to go. No other way of finding out except by using *their* tools, and *their* money, and *their* facilities. I need your help, your trust . . . and all the time we can get."

Hawkins stared at the desperate, earnest eyes that blazed at him across the blotter, took in the clenched hands and suppliant attitude, the tired lines of the face, and the husky prayer in the hoarse voice.

"I'm afraid we may have run out of time before we even start," he said regretfully.

Elliot straightened up, startled. "What do you mean?"

Longjohn raised an arm and poked a finger into the edge of the hole in the plaster over the sofa. "George did this." As Elliot continued to stare at him, puzzled, Hawkins outlined George's "bug-hunt," and the trophies he had gathered. As he went on, Elliot's face became whiter and whiter, until the only colour in it was the dark blue of his angry eyes.

"Why the *hell* did you let me talk?" he finally whispered.

"Oh, don't worry, they're all out. George made sure of that this afternoon. *And* he set up a little gizmo . . ." Hawkins looked around the room until he located it on one of the shelves of the room divider and pointed it out. "That's putting an electronic blanket around this room so nobody ain't getting nothin' out or in. Kind of like Annie's screen-room, George says. It's crude, but it does the job for the moment. He has plans for something more elaborate, using tapes that will supply normal conversation for those who are fans of normal conversation, while we say what we damn well please underneath it. George is a born sneak. We've only been using him around the edges. He's got real possibilities, Phil."

Elliot realized he was shaking and took hold of the edge of the desk.

"You think he's right about it being Cragg?"

"Nope. I think you said the name already, kiddo. I think the name is Curtiss. You once paid me the compliment of saying I had the best instincts for people you'd ever come across, despite my training. I take it as a bigger compliment than ever, now, but I've been thinking about it all afternoon. Our own security set-up is too tight for it to be Russians or any other nasties under the bed. I happen to play golf with a few of those Security bastards; they do regular sweeps of the premises for listening devices as part of their routine. How come they missed all these, hey? Because they were told to miss them, buddy, they were *told*. Not by Cragg, he's too small. By your good friend and superior, Carter Hooks Curtiss. How come you never read *his* mind while you were at it?"

"Oh, I used to," Elliot said quietly, staring at the little device on the shelf. "Sometimes it took all my willpower to smile, get out of his office and down the hall to the loo before I threw up." His face tightened. "My God, we've got to get her out of here . . . we've got to!"

"And just where do you plan on going?" Longjohn asked, curiously. "You already said there isn't anywhere else. Unless you'd like to take her back to Mhourra?" He watched Elliot's face go through all the permutations and finally settle stubbornly, mouth thin, chin squared. Longjohn sighed softly. "No —I didn't think that would appeal to you, somehow." He picked up his mug and drained the last of the cold coffee. "Anyway, they know she's here. That helicopter was hardly the kind of thing you can pass off as everyday routine. So it's Us and Them, with that girl in the middle, hey? Great. Everybody line up and wait for Starter's Orders. You don't happen to have Clark Kent's phone number, do you?"

"I left it in my other suit," Elliot growled.

"Pity. Of course, we *could* try being honest right from the start and hand her over like good little—"

"Never," Elliot's voice had a vicious edge Hawkins had never heard before, serrated, cutting. "She's mine. *Mine.*"

Hawkins nodded and looked away from the taut, white face opposite. For the moment, old buddy, he thought to himself. For the moment.

5

The lab was dark except for the lights over the computer console where Hawkins sat, and the grey oblong of the television monitor screen. Elliot kept his eyes fixed on the latter, watching Ted Holbrook moving around Annie's bed, checking her progress. They had begun the reduction of the Haliperidol dosage the following afternoon, and she was now becoming restless and distressed, her face twisting into little grimaces of distaste, like a baby given its first taste of spinach.

"What are you getting?" Elliot's voice was quiet as he kept his eyes on the monitor just above his head.

"Steady Alpha when she stops moving for a minute, otherwise just a lot of splodge."

The "splodge"—high-frequency waves from muscle reactions—was obliterating the EEG read-outs with maddening regularity. It made no sense. The slowest brain waves measurable were those of Delta—deep, dreamless sleep—which ranged at 1 to 3 cycles per second. Theta waves—indicating deep meditation or creativity—ran at 4 to 7 cycles per second. Alpha waves—occurring in relaxed pre-sleep state—had a rate of 8 to 12 cps. And Beta waves—those of normal wakefulness —had a pattern of 13 to 30 cps. Over and beyond that were the waves of brain activity monitoring the involuntary nervous system and muscular systems, followed, at the highest level of up to 70 cps, by those of the voluntary systems. What was awkward for the Talbot researchers was the fact that all these waves ran concurrently in the brain, and had to be separated out in order to be properly monitored. The digital computers at Talbot, like all used in conjunction with electro-encephalogram readings, had filters in them to cut out the high cps frequencies governing physical activity. But in this instance, even with those filters in operation, Hawkins was having a hard time getting more than a few seconds "in clear" at one time.

He leaned forward to the mike and spoke to Holbrook. "Can't you tie her down or something?"

Elliot leaned forward, too, switching the monitor to the whole-room camera, and caught Ted as he turned to address his invisible partners.

"Seriously?"

"Seriously."

"Phil?"

Elliot switched on his mike. "Go ahead, I don't think it will matter."

"Okay." Holbrook turned back to the bed, brought up the restraining straps that were hanging down from the frame, and proceeded to fasten them across Annie's agitated body as tightly as possible.

"Is that helping?" Elliot asked Longjohn.

"A little. Only a little."

Elliot sighed and lit another cigarette, ignoring the signs that were plastered all over the walls of the lab.

"Please no droppa da ash inna computer," Hawkins groused.

The grey computer was chattering to itself, throwing ever-changing read-outs onto the small screen in a bright green electronic rainstorm. Hawkins tapped out a few instructions on the keyboard. There was a pause while the tapes spun, and then the green rain started again. Inside the screen-room, Annie was festooned with a network of electrode leads that splayed out around her head and body. There was a sudden continuous tone from the computer on two of the channels, and Longjohn cursed under his breath.

"She's knocked off four and five again, Ted."

Holbrook leaned over and replaced the electrodes, smearing fresh gel onto Annie's scalp and pressing a second strip of adhesive over each one. The computer resumed its chatter.

"Secure her head, will you?" Pulling some gauze strips from the tray beside the bed, Holbrook ran a couple of turns under her chin, tying them back onto the bedframe behind her head. It was still no good.

"Splodge, splodge, splodge," Hawkins muttered in disgust. "Bloody hell—can't you freeze her up with Novocaine or something?"

"Sorry," Holbrook said over his shoulder in the general direction of the camera as he tried to restrain the girl.

Elliot sighed and reached again for his coffee mug. They had erected a heavy lead screen borrowed from the Radiography Unit at the local hospital and he was sitting behind it, hoping it might make a difference. It didn't. Suddenly he was hit with pain that virtually welded him onto his stool, then nearly pitched him from it physically. Annie's mental scream was reinforced by an audible echo.

"NO NO NO NO NO NO NONONONONONONONO-NONO."

The sounds ripped from her throat and into Elliot's brain, draining the blood from his face and leaving him pale with shock. He was transfixed by the television screen, and as he cupped his hands to his temples he saw Holbrook back away from the bed, his mouth open.

"ELL . . . I . . . OT . . . PHIL . . . IP . . . NONO-NONONONONONONONO."

"How does she know you're here?" Holbrook shouted over her protests, turning and standing so close to the camera that all Elliot could see was the blurred side of his face. Be-

yond it, in sharper focus, was the thrashing, struggling shape of
Annie fighting the restraints. The computer was choking and
spluttering and Hawkins's hand flashed over the keyboard trying to regain some semblance of order.

"She . . . hears me . . ." Elliot tried to explain through
a mouth that was fighting him because it wanted to scream,
too. "You'd better get out of there . . . you're hurting her."

"I'm not anywhere *near* her," Holbrook argued.

"Doesn't . . . matter . . . Come *out* . . . for God's
sake!"

There was a flash of brighter light in the lab as Holbrook
came out of the screen-room and over to stand by the computer. The twisting figure on the bed seemed to settle a little,
but not much.

"*HURT . . . PHIL . . . IP . . . GO . . . WAY . . .
AWAY . . .*"

"Get down to the other side of the lab," Elliot ordered
brusquely. "Hurry."

"But the readings . . ." Hawkins protested.

"Forget the damned readings," Elliot gasped. The other
two moved quickly down the lab and stood against the far
wall, some forty feet away. The computer continued its manic
staccato chatter. The ten-inch read-out screen looked as though
it was picking up Hurricane Hannah. It was covered with a
coruscation of flickering dots in ever-changing patterns, em-
erald electronic hysteria.

*Annie . . . Annie . . . it's all right . . . you're safe
. . .*

You . . . not safe . . .

I'm all right . . . you won't hurt me . . .

Can . . . would . . . sorry . . .

A bolt of fire ran through Elliot's skull, and he went off
the stool and hit the floor on his knees, grabbing at the computer console as he fell. Holbrook started forward, but Hawkins held him back.

Sorry . . . sorry . . . sorry . . .

Elliot looked up at the television monitor, now several feet above him. Annie was awake. Her eyes were wide open, rolling wildly as she twisted and turned to look around the room. Haliperidol compresses time, and he realized that to her it must have seemed as if she had fallen asleep in the cottage on Mhourra only to reawaken minutes later in this strange white and chrome world where she was unable to move, caught in some terrifying trap she couldn't comprehend. She screamed again, in rage this time, and even louder. Her piercing cries came through the thin partition as pure animal torment, and both Hawkins and Holbrook stepped back against the wall behind them, horror wiping their faces and eyes clean.

"LONG . . . JOHN BAD . . . HURT ME . . . NO . . . AWAY . . . PHILIP . . . STOP THEM . . . THINKING . . . LOUD . . . LOUD . . ." He was getting feed-through from her head too, now—static from the other men's reactions. Panic and shock reverberated through him like gongs.

"Blank yourselves, can't you?" he shouted down the lab.

"Blanking" was a term used at Talbot for trying to wipe the mind clear of everything except a single concentrated image. Difficult ordinarily, almost impossible now. But they had all done it so often during telepathic test transmissions that it was almost a reflex, and they responded to his order.

"AHHHH . . . hurting . . . still hurting . . ." But she was less active, struggling less frantically against the restraints, trying to get some kind of control over herself. The others were only getting her verbal agony, but Elliot was getting all of it. What random and marginal control he had accumulated over the years since his accident was useless now because his compassion for her lowered all his defences. It could have been him in that bed, *was* him as he had been twelve years ago. When he'd been faced with similar torment he'd immediately retreated into unconsciousness, but she was waging a fight against her own terror. Her effort filled him with admiration—and pain. She was trying, trying so very hard, for *him*.

Oh . . . Annie . . . little one . . . try . . . try . . .
No . . . don't . . . love . . . hurts . . . hurts more . . .
She was crying, now. He could see the grey image of her
face on the monitor as he crawled past it and dragged himself up into the chair Hawkins had vacated. The computer
screen still read green splodge, and the clicks and chatters were
becoming syncopated as the tape reels spun, stopped, spun,
stopped, dutifully taking down the meaningless green rain.
"ROSES . . . ROSES . . . ROSES . . ."
Roses were Holbrook's standard image, his "identity" for
ESP tests. Elliot glanced over his shoulder. The minute she had
called out "Roses," Holbrook had lost his control, so startled
had he been to hear her recognition. Annie moaned again.
"Stay blank . . . for God's sake . . . I told you she
can . . ." Elliot shouted. Holbrook's face twisted in concentration, but it was no good. The gongs were starting to ring in
Elliot's skull again. For a last desperate moment he tried to
make the computer see sense, but it wasn't having any, and he
didn't blame it.
"BALLS . . . BALLS . . . BALLS . . ."
He might have smiled at what seemed like sudden vul-
garity on her part, but it wasn't—baseballs were Hawkins's
standard image. *He* was coming through, too.
"It's no good," Elliot called in despair. "You'll have to
go back in there and put her under again, Ted." Still his hands
flew over the keys, hoping for something, anything, that would
tell them what was happening in her head.
"How can I?" Holbrook shouted back as Annie's shrieks
began to rise again. On the television monitor she was just a
blur of arms and legs flailing the sheets and blankets, frantic
with pain and fear.
Elliot was shaking so badly himself that he could barely
whisper. He began to slump forward onto the computer keyboard, his hands jerking convulsively in a pattern that was
strangely synchronous with Annie's. When her arms lifted, so

did his, when she turned, his body turned, when her legs kicked, his hit against the base of the computer console. Where her movements were wild and total, his were fainter echoes, yet they seemed locked in a complementary dance of torment. Hawkins watched in fascinated horror as Holbrook ran down the length of the lab, past Elliot, and into the screen-room. Annie's reactions intensified savagely as he came near the bed, and Elliot's became stronger, too. Moving as if the girl in the bed and the apparatus were somehow burning hot, Holbrook finally managed to get the hypo into the IV tube that led down to the cannula in the back of her hand, strapped to the flat board beneath it. Within seconds she was quiet, and within a minute she was regaining the rigid immobility characteristic of Haliperidol sedation.

The silence was absolute. Then Elliot moaned and began to slide sideways off the chair and onto the floor again. Hesitantly, then more quickly, Hawkins came up the lab, his footsteps echoing. He dragged Elliot away from the computer, reaching blindly behind him for a couple of lab logbooks to shove under his feet. Elliot slumped like an empty scarecrow, and Hawkins almost lost his hold on him. "I think Phil could use some help, too, Ted."

Holbrook stumbled out of the screen-room and came over to hunker down next to Elliot's semi-conscious body, automatically reaching for the wrist. His face was as white as Annie's sheets, and there was a film of sweat over his skin. Leaning forward he spoke hoarsely, trying for a response.

"I'd like to talk to you about your medical insurance programme."

"Go to hell," Elliot groaned, weakly. Holbrook managed a grin.

Hawkins stood up, relieved, and went over to the computer. He started flicking the switches off, one by one, rewinding the tapes and pulling out the leads. He glanced at the monitor. Annie was lying absolutely still, the sheets and blan-

kets tumbled over her. There were bloody welts on her arms
and body where the restraining straps had cut into her flesh.

"So much for round one," he said, softly.

They let her sleep for forty-eight hours and then Elliot tried
it on his own. Towards dawn, after trying repeatedly to phone
the lab without a response, Longjohn drove back. He entered
the lab to find the computer chattering madly to an empty
chair, a long shaft of light cutting down the aisle like a sword
from Annie's room. Her screams were hoarse, as if they had
been going on for a long time. The soundproofing of the lab
had prevented them being heard by any of the outside guards.
When he reached the room, he froze. Annie was a blur of
movement on the bed, but even so he could see she was literally
foaming at the mouth with rage, fear, and desperation.

Halfway across the room, Elliot lay on the floor, terribly
still and white, the smashed hypo still in his hand. He had
never got to her, although Hawkins could see marks on the
floor where Elliot had struggled and crawled until he could
take no more.

*PUT ME OUT . . . TURN OFF . . . GIVE ME
. . . HELP HIM . . . HELP HIM . . .*

Startled by the clarity of his first full telepathic contact,
he stared into the wild spinning torment of Annie's golden
eyes. Somehow he managed to locate the ampoule of sedative,
extract the dosage into a fresh syringe, and get it into the IV
tube.

Seconds later there was silence again.

He knelt beside Elliot and touched the square line of the
jaw, eventually locating a pulse. It was thready and racing, but
already beginning to stabilize. His own was probably the
same. To Hawkins, the slightly older man had always been
the strong pivot of their relationship around which he himself
circled with zany unpredictability. Together they made a
good team. Now Elliot lay for a second time like a wounded
child, his face lax with deep unconsciousness, whatever lacera-

tions he had suffered bleeding unseen within. After a moment Longjohn caught his breath in a sob, shook himself and spoke aloud.

"This don't get no potatoes peeled, Hawkins—move your ass."

Struggling with Elliot's inert form, he got him over his shoulder, then started down the length of the shadowy lab. Even though the sun was rising outside, it looked like they had a long dark time coming.

George Lomax's assistant was Frances Murphy, a small, dark, quiet girl who wore wire-rimmed granny glasses and dressed consistently in smocks and jeans. She was one of the most self-contained women Elliot had ever encountered. Brought in on the problem out of sheer necessity, it was her suggestion that they try to make a "head-set" for Annie. Something she could actually wear that would be a more sophisticated version of the screen-room concept. What she and George produced, in the end, was a simple silvery band that encircled Annie's temples and fastened at the back with a small flat box. It was very pretty and it worked for fourteen minutes before it burnt out and precipitated Annie back into the screaming agony Elliot knew so well.

They made more bands.

He longed to test them himself to spare her some of the ordeal, but he and Longjohn had decided that his abilities— or what vestiges of them remained—should continue to be a secret for the time being.

In the burst of consciousness the bands provided they learned a little more about Annie Craigie, and it was not encouraging. Without her telepathic ability to fall back on, her spoken vocabulary was woefully inadequate. With the band on, it was impossible for her to explain exactly what it did to or for her: without it, she was impossible to reach. Little by little they were able to explain to her where she was and what they were trying to do, but every time they got close to conversation the bands would short-out and they would lose her.

"I just don't understand it, Doc. Look, here," George said, prying open the control box on the last one. There was a black arc running between three or four of the minute components. "She literally burns them out. You measured her DC level, didn't you?"

"Yes."

"And it was normal, wasn't it?"

"Yes, perfectly normal."

"So, what's she doing to make this happen?"

"How can *I* tell you?" Elliot cried in frustration. "If I don't even understand how that thing works, how can I tell you why it *doesn't?*"

"I wish somebody would," George muttered. "What does she say?"

Elliot turned away and hit his knuckles lightly against the edge of his desk, again, again, again. "She says she doesn't do anything; it just . . . goes. Without any warning, without any sensations at all. One minute it's fine, the next minute . . ."

"Bang?"

"Bang." He continued to hit the edge of the desk, harder and harder until the pain made him realize what he was doing. Absently he raised his hand to suck at the raw knuckles, staring out of the window at the sunny stretch of lawn that sloped down to the river. "Look, George," he said, after a minute. "Can you set up some kind of remote control to let us run the EEG computer from a distance?"

"How much distance?"

"At least half a mile. More if possible."

"Yes, if you don't mind a hell of a bill for wire."

"Then do it." Annie had been in and out of her suspension for over two weeks, mostly in, and it was not doing her physical condition any good at all. Her intestinal tract was riddled with parasitical infestations that needed medication carried in solid food to push them out. Her blood protein levels were up, but she was not gaining much weight. Janet and Frances were now having to turn her every two hours to relieve the bed-sores that were developing because the sedation kept her so rigid she did not even make the normal sleep movements that would have varied the pressures. Mentally she was at rest, but physically she was deteriorating, and that would hardly qualify as good medical management, no matter what the cause. He might excuse failure to make her better, but he found it hard to face the responsibility of making her worse. They had to find out *why*, even if it hurt her.

"George?"

"Yeah?" Lomax turned at the door.

"Have you found any more of the listening devices?"

"No. I check every night before I leave, come in early every morning. So far they haven't been replaced. Maybe . . ."

"What?"

"Maybe they were old."

"You mean maybe they've found *another* way to get their information, don't you?" Elliot asked.

"If they have, it's got to be some*body*, not something. I'd find it, if it was."

"Okay. Thanks." Elliot leaned back in his chair and closed his eyes. After looking at his boss with a worried expression, Lomax went out. Elliot seemed near breaking-point, as if the wires holding him together were resonating to some note outside himself. The struggles of the past weeks had left dark circles under his eyes. He lit one cigarette after another only to leave them burning in ashtrays all over the place. He was living on coffee and digestive biscuits and almost never went home except to feed his cat and change his clothes. George was worried about him, they all were, but Elliot was simply not the kind of man you could fuss over or lure into going out for a drink and a steak. He just looked at you and the impulse died in your throat. The work was everything, or in this case, the girl was. George wished he had never gone to that goddamned island.

Alone in his office, teeth clenched, hands convulsively grasping the arms of his chair, Elliot was trying to reach out and locate the mind that belonged to the betrayer. Because there was one, of that he was now sure. Not a particularly neat man by nature, he was obsessive about one thing—his desk. He knew to the inch where everything was in every drawer. It had been built to his specifications and he had the only key. Three days after bringing Annie to Talbot, he had opened one of the drawers and known at once that someone had been through his notes on Annie. They were not extensive notes, he had been too busy with the practical side of things to take time over them, but they were not in the order he'd left them. After that he'd taken them home with him and locked them in his safe. It would have been so easy if he still had the powers he'd had before—but his telepathic capacity was well and truly dead. Whether it was a result of his encounters with Annie or natural decline he didn't know. All he knew was that, try as he might, he could only see with his eyes and hear with his ears. The rest was silence. Not for the first time, he ended the attempt with frustration and exhaustion shaking him into childish tears. He almost wished George had never gone to that goddamned island.

It had been unseasonably hot all day, and even now in the dead of night the temperature inside the caravan they had borrowed from one of the technicians was at oven-heat. There wasn't much room to move inside once the equipment had been installed. Elliot was hunched on a bench seat with his chin on his knees, staring at the television monitor, while Ted was on the far side of the computer deck trying to find room for his elbows in order to make notes on Annie's progress. She was not as restless coming out of the sedation, probably because she understood more about what was happening to her,

Elliot reasoned. It had been like that for him, too. Understanding a pain is halfway to fighting it. Eventually her eyelids fluttered open. He switched on the microphone. "Annie?"

"Yes?"

"How is it?"

"I still . . . hear . . . pain."

He closed his eyes for a moment. "Yes, I thought you might. Is it too much for you?"

"No . . ." But she wasn't too sure, he could see. "You . . . thinking . . . *to* me. Could go near people . . . if they didn't . . . know. Sometimes . . ."

"Sometimes what?"

"Sometimes . . . look in the . . . windows? At night . . . see they . . . happy . . . all close . . . no hurt . . ."

"Oh, Jesus," Longjohn whispered softly, and Elliot dropped his forehead onto his knees, feeling his eyes sting. She'd had so many kinds of pain. He sighed, cleared his throat, looked up again at the monitor. There was a fine film of perspiration on her face, evident even with the grainy resolution of the TV picture.

"Annie, we're going to turn on the computer now. Do you remember what I explained to you, about staying very, very still?"

"Yes."

Elliot gestured to Longjohn and he activated the panel. The screen began to flicker, its green dots changing and flowing as the computer chattered its way through the initial programme. After a minute, Longjohn cursed. "Tell her to stop moving, will you?"

Glancing again at the monitor, Elliot saw that Annie was almost rigidly still. "She's not moving. Look for yourself."

"The read-out screen says she's leaping all over the place. *You* look."

Elliot followed the green impulses for a while. "Splodge."

"Yep."

"Annie, could you blink your eyes for us, please?"

She did as he asked. The channel for the needle electrodes over her cheekbones dutifully registered on the screen
—three eyeblinks. "That's enough." She stopped, and he
leaned forward to check the readings again. There was definitely a difference between her physical movement and the
rest of the readings. "Now move your right hand." This time
the "splodge" registered right across the range. "Okay, now
stay very still. Even hold your breath." But it was no good.
While they were still getting basic Alpha patterns from her
when her eyes were closed, there was an overlay of high-
frequency waves that spiked through disruptively. As he
watched them, something began to nag at him. They were
almost—regular?

"Okay, love, you can breathe again. Just lie there for a
minute." He clicked off the microphone and stared at his knees.

"This isn't going to be any good either," Longjohn finally
said.

"No, wait a minute. Let me think." Elliot turned his eyes
to the beer cans that littered the fold-down table at the end of
the caravan. He pushed up the microphone switch with his
thumb. "Annie?"

"Yes?"

"You said you can still hear our heads, is that right?"

"Yes . . . but . . . not . . . very . . ."

"No, listen a minute," he interrupted gently. "We're going to try something at this end. Just be quiet until I talk to
you again."

"Well?" Longjohn asked as the microphone clicked off
once more.

"Set the programme for continuous run. I want all of us
to blank ourselves as much as possible, cut down everything
in our heads, stick to single images. Right?"

Hawkins and Holbrook exchanged a glance, then nodded.
When the computer was set, they closed their eyes and played
the blank game. After a moment Elliot spoke again. "Okay,
that's enough. Run the tapes back and let's see what we picked

up from her during that."

Longjohn punched the keyboard, the tape reels spun back, then started forward again. "Hey," breathed Longjohn after a moment's screen time. "That's almost a clear Alpha, Phil, look."

Elliot looked, then looked again. "Dear God, that's *it*," he whispered. "Why the *hell* didn't we ever look at that end?"

"That's what?" Ted asked.

"Those high-frequency waves aren't coming from her muscles. They're coming from her *brain!*" Elliot almost shouted.

"Oh, come *on!*"

"Longjohn," Elliot directed. "Pull the filters."

Hawkins swivelled in his chair and stared at the man hunched tight with excitement on the bench behind him. "That will only make things worse."

Elliot hit his knee with the base of the microphone. "No, no, *no,* don't you see it? Dammit, pull the filters!"

Hawkins shrugged and leaned down to the bank of filter controls that cut out everything above 70 cycles per second. Instantly the screen was flooded with practically solid "splodge."
"What did I tell you?" he pointed out.

"Wait. Wait—now reverse the filter programme to cut out everything below seventy," Elliot demanded, hardly able to contain himself.

"Below?"

"Yes, *yes.*"

Still sceptical, Hawkins shrugged and turned to tap out the new programme on the keyboard. The computer chattered its way through the instructions, then paused humming reflectively to itself.

"Okay, now K that through."

Hawkins hit the K button for a cross-channel reading. All channels showed intense high-frequency activity.

"Right," Elliot breathed. "Now, cut out the brain-wave activity below eighty cycles per second."

When the readings came up they were still heavy.

"Cut them out below ninety."

Clearer still.

"Below one hundred."

Waves were now slowly and steadily taking shape on the screen, a shape none of them had ever seen before. They were all starting to sweat, and nobody had eyes for anything but that small grey screen with its rising and falling green lines.

"Below one hundred and ten."

Suddenly the channels all read straight across the screen. Just flat green lines and a steady monotone.

"Below one hundred and nine."

Still nothing.

"Below one hundred and eight . . . seven . . . six . . ."

There it was. Right there, right across the screen, a steady mountain range at 105 cps.

They had found the "thing" in Annie's head.

A cold chill ran up Elliot's back, raising the flesh on his arms and scalp. Totally isolated from the rest of her brain activity there was a separate wave cycle pattern, unlike anything they had ever seen, heard about, or recorded. Strong, clear, unmistakeable.

"Q it."

Longjohn hit the key that converted the wave frequencies to a graph of amplitudes. The long vertical green lines made it even more definite. Annie's brain was running a second-string operation, parallel with her normal brain function, contiguous with it, high above it, and constant.

With a shaking hand, Elliot flipped the microphone switch. "Annie."

"Yes?"

Her mouth movements extended one of the frequency spikes upward. When her mouth was still, it dropped again.

"Annie, we're going to all think *at* you for a few seconds. It might hurt—it will probably hurt quite a lot. Will you try to . . ."

"Okay." It was one of her new words. She was trying very earnestly to be what he wanted. He swallowed, hard, as the splodge of her involuntary muscle tension at the thought of expected pain sent another set of verticals upward.

"Right," he said to Longjohn and Ted. "Make it friendly, for God's sake, but think about her as hard as you can to the count of ten."

Almost instantly two things happened. Annie cried out in pain, and the green vertical for 105 cps nearly went off the screen. Automatically Longjohn reduced the ratios, but still the vertical was almost out of sight at the top of the screen.

"Okay, that's enough. Are you all right, Annie? Do you want us to put you under?"

"Yes . . . please . . ." His hand was going toward the relay that would release the sedative dose into her bloodstream when she spoke again. "Philip?"

He hesitated, his hand over the relay. "Yes?"

"What . . . you thinking . . . me . . . was . . . true?"

He was puzzled. "I wasn't thinking anything special, Annie, just thinking about you." He had, in fact, been remembering what she had looked like when she had first worn a headband, sitting up in bed and not getting any "pain"—the way her golden eyes had filled with glittering relief. "Why?"

"No . . . not . . . sleep now . . . please . . ."

"Of course. It will be all right next time, Annie. I promise." His hand descended to the relay and within a minute the computer screen was reading deep Delta. Annie was asleep and safe from them again.

There was a long silence. They were all staring at the television monitor, looking at a very small girl lying rigid in the middle of a very high hospital bed, breathing slowly, the overhead lights casting a shine across her cheekbones. Elliot's voice was quiet. "Can Algernon get a location on the foci, Longjohn?"

"Yeah, I think so." He responded absently, his hands

flickering over the keyboard while his eyes remained on the television monitor. When the read-outs came up, Elliot nodded.

"Electrodes four and six," Ted said. "Those are over the parietal lobes, aren't they?"

"Yes. Are the readings symmetrical?"

Longjohn punched the buttons for a return to frequency readings. The shape of the waves from Annie's left and right parietal lobes was almost identical during the "blank" run, far more disparate during the run they had done while thinking intensively about her. "Stronger on the right," Longjohn observed. "More sensory than linguistic."

"She doesn't have the words, remember?" Elliot whispered, staring at the screen. "She doesn't know the words yet."

While the other two ran the tapes back, Elliot turned away and lowered his forehead onto his knees. If we know little about outer space or the depths of the ocean, nobody is surprised, he thought. But the little we know about ourselves exposes the greatest of all our ignorances. The uncharted reaches of the human mind are on a scale so vast as to be almost incomprehensible. The neurons in a single brain are as numerous as the molecules in our solar system. In a *single* brain. And every one of those neurons has an individual and infinite capacity for function and adaptation. How could we have known? How *could* we? He recalled one of his professors saying that whenever a physicist steps into a laboratory he has to work hard simply to find an unexplored problem, but every time we step into a neurological lab, we have an even harder time not tripping over something new, every day. And yet this was here, all the time.

He rocked his head slowly from side to side against the rough cloth, fighting his exhaustion. The great physiologist Sherrington had written at length about the human brain, long before they had today's sophisticated electro-encephalographs and digital computers to look at. He called it "an enchanted loom where millions of flashing shuttles weave a dissolving pattern, always a meaningful pattern though never an abiding one . . . a sparkling field of rhythmic flashing points with trains of travelling sparks hurrying hither and thither." It was a description Elliot had always loved, one of the few romantic interpretations of a very functional science, one he tried to remember whenever things went bad on him and he needed a little magic.

Now they had just found, with the help of modern electronics, yet another of the cryptic patterns running through the brain's enchanted loom.

He raised his head to stare at the black glass of the caravan windows, and smiled, ruefully. He had always considered it one of the shames of mankind that to reach the level of "civilization" at which they stood (remote-control electronics from a caravan in the middle of a field at midnight, for example) had required the use of only a fractional 5 per cent of the brain's potential. Nature does not waste. If they had come this far using so little—what about the rest? What is that other 95 per cent *for?* Most damning of all, *why* weren't they using it? He stared at his own hazy reflection.

Does the human brain know something it's afraid to tell us yet?

Or have we simply been refusing to ask it the right questions?

6

Elliot spent the balance of the night as he often did, stretched out on the leather chesterfield under a couple of blankets. Just before dawn he was racked by a nightmare and awoke to find himself on the floor beside the sofa, tangled in the blankets and breathing as if he had been running for miles. Shreds of the nightmare still clung to his brain and he remembered it *had* been about running . . . running down the beach on Mhourra chasing Annie, trying to reach her before a great dark thing that hung over and between them dropped and took her in its glinting claws. She had been running happily, not seeing the dark wings above her, and he had tried to scream a warning only to find his throat locked in silence. It was a perfectly straightforward nightmare, the symbology was clear enough, but knowing that did not quite overcome the emotional miasma that still hung around him. Crossly he shook himself and started to get up, only to freeze where he sat.

The dark thing was still in the room.

He had a sense of long slow breathing near him, turned his head towards the window, and felt ice touch his body. A dark shape was hunched behind his desk, unmoving, strange. It took two or three seconds for him to realize it was only his own high-backed leather chair, but the sense of menace remained. He did not want to look behind him, but did so, and found nothing.

Yet he could still sense the breathing. He was sure the "thing" was somewhere nearby listening and watching.

Philip.

His powers of telepathy were gone, but he heard his own name and knew it had not been spoken aloud.

Philip.

Annie . . . my God, it was Annie, it had to be. She was in trouble, something was wrong. Forgetting his own fear, he leapt up and almost fell as his feet caught in the blankets. Kicking them aside with a curse, he staggered to the door and out into the dim hallway. A few steps took him to Laboratory One and he pushed the doors in so violently he nearly burst the catch. There was only the night-light at the far end. Annie's door was closed. He ran down the length of the lab between the tables and fought with her door until he remembered it opened in, not out. Panic was making him forget everything.

His hand slapped the wall beside him until his fingers found the switch and the room flooded with light, making him blink. Annie lay as she always lay, utterly still, rigid under the blankets. He went over to the bed and checked her pulse, respiration, and the readings on the gauges they kept attached to her in a minor version of intensive care.

He wiped his forehead with his sleeve, dropped her wrist back onto the blanket, and then leaned forward. Almost in duplication, her own forehead was filmed with a faint sheen of perspiration. In the corner of the room the EEG they kept permanently monitoring her brain waves was still writing its spidery traces. He went over and pulled some of the tape out of the basket beneath, moving back until he reached the time when he must have been having his own nightmare.

She'd had one, too.

Or, at least, she had shown some rapid-eye movement and a burst of wave activity over a ten-second period at roughly the same time. Lacking a record of his own brain waves, he had no way of being certain there was a real correlation. Letting the folds of paper drop back into the basket, he turned to look at her fine-boned face on the pillow.

Of course it was coincidence. Of course he was still reacting emotionally to his own bad dreams. Everybody dreamt more often toward morning, it was one of the peak periods for dreaming. He and Annie had both dreamed, but there could be no connection. He had heard no telepathic call. There had been no dark thing in his office. There was no dark thing in this room with Annie.

Yet he had the distinct impression it *had* been there.

Just before he opened the door, it had been there, hovering, its claws at her throat.

He awoke to the sound of a pile of papers being dumped onto his desk. Opening one eye he saw Janet turning away toward the coffee maker, and quickly closed it again.

"That won't do any good, I heard your breathing change," she observed mildly, bending down to take out the coffee can and sugar bag.

With a groan he pulled the blankets up over his head and curled into a foetal position, only to slowly lower them again and stretch out as he remembered what had happened last night. He squinted at the bright light pouring in through the window behind his desk.

"We found what we were looking for, Janet," he said, as much to himself as to her. "We discovered what's different about Annie's brain."

"So Longjohn said," she responded, measuring coffee into the percolator.

"He's in already?"

"He likes to put in an hour or so before lunch."

"Lunch?" He struggled up and looked at his watch. "Why the hell didn't you wake me? It's after eleven."

"I am paid to answer phones, type letters, organize files,

make gallons of coffee, tell people you're not in when you are, lie to Cragg, and remind you to be polite. I was *not* hired as an alarm clock."

"You're mothering me again," he groused, swinging his legs off the cushions and standing up, only to waver and sit back down again abruptly.

"Looks like you could do with a little coffee," she observed, glancing briefly over her shoulder. "Or have you been sneaking the medicinal brandy again?"

"I don't have to sneak it, it belongs to me."

"So it does, so it does. She's fine, by the way."

He grinned, then said, "She's more than fine, she's wonderful."

"She's too skinny to be wonderful, fine will do," Janet said briskly, switching on the coil under the glass pot and walking back to the desk. "Meanwhile, in addition to making the greatest scientific breakthrough the Western World has ever known, you have a few other problems."

"Piss on them," he said, getting up and going over to the file cabinet where he kept a set of shaving things.

"I'm not equipped for it," she said. "Aside from the correspondence and the monthly reports and two requests for lectures, Cragg is asking for you."

"Piss on him, too." He pushed the file drawer shut and went across the hall to the Men's lavatory.

"Don't think we all wouldn't like to," she murmured, looking after him and smiling slightly. The lines of strain were still evident in Elliot's face, but she had seen something more there. Not triumph, he was not the sort of man to consider anything a triumph. It was confidence, she decided; he looked confident for the first time since she had known him. She picked up the blankets he had tossed aside and began to fold them neatly.

Janet York was twenty-nine, petite, blonde, efficient, and she was *not* in love with her boss. She had been attracted to him when she first came to work at Talbot Hall, but only briefly. There was no denying that Elliot was a good-looking man, although he wasn't conventionally handsome. It was more a matter of expression, the way he had of listening with total absorption to whoever was addressing him, the intensity of the blue eyes that were so startling in a face which was otherwise monochromatic, and the grin that appeared suddenly and without warning, making him look like a boy of sixteen before he got it under control again. Most women found him very attractive, and it was obvious that he liked women. But he was unreachable. In the end, always unreachable. She shrugged and took the blankets over to the closet, jumping up slightly to slide them onto the shelf over the hangers.

Maybe she did mother him. It was about all he would let her do, aside from running the office. She knew he liked her or he would not have kept her as his assistant for all these years. He didn't suffer people for long if they grated on his nerves, although he was always polite about it. But there was a line she could not cross, and she had quickly accepted it. It would have been a waste of time and energy to pursue Philip Elliot. She hoped she was going to be more successful with Danny Vanderhof, but she was beginning to doubt it. Pushing the thought of Danny from her mind, she checked the coffee, turned down the heat under the percolator, and returned to her own office.

Elliot was peering at himself in the cracked mirror over the basin, one arm cocked high as he drew the razor under his chin. Of course Janet was right, as usual, he acknowledged. There was very little whooping and celebrating done over scientific discoveries these days because they were so hedged with further complexities. He had not heard a genuine "Eureka!" for years.

There would be plenty of routine work to attend to. Annie would have to remain sedated while George and Frances made a new band. Now that they knew precisely what had to be done, there would be no more burn-outs, he hoped. The tapes would have to be processed, *and* they would have to bring Danny into the circle to do it. He rinsed the razor under the tap and dried his face on the roller towel. There was really no reason why he should not spend the day catching up on all the junk that had piled up while he had been so immersed in Annie's problem.

Except that he didn't bloody well feel like it.

He looked at himself again. Insufficient reason, he diagnosed. No matter how high you feel, you'll have to forget it. Just for now, "Eureka" would cost too much.

The door opened and Longjohn stuck his head in. "Phil, Cragg stopped me in Reception an hour ago."

"I hope you stepped on him," Elliot said, gathering up his things.

Longjohn came all the way in and let the door swing shut behind him.

"No, I'd just cleaned my shoes. He wants us to move Annie out of here."

"What?" Elliot spilled half his tackle back into the basin and met the Canadian's eyes in the mirror. "He *what?*"

"He says we're not a National Health Service establishment, we're not set up to handle residential medical problems, and he wants her moved to a hospital or nursing home by the end of the week."

Elliot leaned forward, gripping the cold hard edge of the basin. "Oh, he does, does he? We'll see about that."

Hawkins had rarely seen such fury in Elliot's face, and it made him uneasy. "Well, he has a point, I suppose."

"Yes. Right on the top of his little bald head," Elliot said, turning and brushing past the psychologist. "Janet— Janet!" he called as he crossed to his office, slamming the door shut behind him.

Hawkins caught the lavatory door before it swung shut and went out into the hall himself, whistling tunelessly under his breath. He suddenly felt very sorry for Anthony J. Cragg, RN (Ret.), Administrative Director of Talbot Hall, Curtiss's puppet, and all-round drag. Very sorry indeed. He caught himself grinning at one of the new lab assistants, who stared back at him for a moment, then smiled too. She was pretty, and he spent the rest of the trip back to his office trying to remember her name.

Cragg invariably went to lunch at twelve-thirty, so Elliot arrived in his office at twelve-twenty and announced that he had no other time to spare. Cragg could either see him then or wait until another opportunity arose. He was very polite about it. And very firm.

Cragg was a small man, in every sense of the word. He propagated details the way other men bred rare orchids, hovering over them, adding nourishment where necessary, bringing them along until they were ready to show in the full splendour of their finest blossom. He and Elliot had been doing their ritual dance around petty details for many years now. Elliot was fed up with it, but Cragg was not and never would be.

"You wanted to see me?" Elliot asked blandly, dropping into one of Cragg's reproduction Chippendale chairs and dangling one leg over its delicate arm. The small man's pale eyes were like over-poached eggs, and they narrowed momentarily.

"Indeed, Elliot, I have wanted to see you for several days, now, but have been told repeatedly that you were 'tied up.' "

"And you prayed fervently that it was true, I expect."

"The image did attract me briefly, yes." Cragg leaned back in his chair and began to turn his gold fountain pen end-over-end. "However, it would have been counter-productive. There are a number of items that require your attention. The monthly reports, which are now two weeks overdue . . ."

"Let's start having bi-monthly reports, then," Elliot suggested helpfully.

"They are not complex. Two hours once a month hardly

seems overburdensome to a man of your energy and ability, surely?"

"To a man of my energy and ability two hours a month spent on repeating myself is not only burdensome, it is a pain in the neck."

"Mmmmm. Perhaps if you came up with some new results the exercise would be more amusing?"

"Perhaps."

"Then why don't you try it?" Cragg was forced to finish.

"I tried it once, but I didn't like it."

"And have been living on it ever since."

"Indeed. Much like yourself." Elliot's smile was very friendly.

Cragg's pen halted momentarily, then resumed its revolutionary progress. It seemed very apt to Elliot that Cragg would choose to keep something going around in circles that never got it anywhere.

"Then there is the matter of the *annual* report."

"My goodness, is it Christmas already?" Elliot asked, glancing out of the window in amazement. "I haven't even finished paying for *last* year's gifts."

"Your *last* annual report."

"Finally finished having someone read it to you? Well done."

Cragg put his pen down with deliberation, leaned forward, and clasped his hands together on the blotter. His fat little fingers reminded Elliot of chippolata sausages overlapping on a grill. "It was not satisfactory. Not satisfactory, not impressive, not designed to inspire confidence in any direction."

"Oh . . . well . . . Win a few, lose a few," Elliot said easily. "I can't manufacture success—it's a funny area we're into here. We don't get cures and breakthroughs in this field." (Don't we, hell, he added to himself.) "It's a very wishy-washy thing, ESP research."

"I couldn't have chosen a better adjective," Cragg snapped. "Not only wishy-washy but a total waste of the tax-payer's money."

"Our allocation also includes your salary. How about that?"

"*I* pay my way in efficiency."

"Yes. I noticed the toilet paper was thinner this year. How much did we save on that?" Elliot brought his leg down off the chair arm and faced Cragg. "Look, you are here to see that things run smoothly so that I can do what I am paid to do. Ostensibly, anyway. Anybody could do your job, Cragg, but *not* anybody can do mine, so why don't we leave all this fancy fencing—which *is* counter-productive—and get down to it. Tell me what you want."

"I want to know who that girl is in Laboratory One, what she is doing here, and when she is leaving."

"She's not leaving."

"I beg your pardon, she *is* leaving, and by the end of the week. Who is she?"

"Her name is Annie, and she's not going anywhere by the end of the week. She is a rather pathetic girl I found in Scotland, with a very interesting brain malfunction that Dr. Holbrook and I are studying with a view to easing her discomfort."

"You and Dr. Holbrook no longer practise medicine."

"True. We're through practising—we're actually doing the real thing, now. But our credentials are unchanged."

"You know perfectly well what I mean."

"You mean you hate not knowing every damn little thing that is going on here whether you understand it or not. Paper-clips you understand, but sub-cortical brain anomalies remain beyond you even though you won't admit it. If I were you I'd stick to paper-clips and leave our work to us."

"You forget that I am also in charge of Security in this establishment. I do not like having unauthorized people in Talbot Hall, and it is within my responsibility to verify every person who enters. Surely she has more of a name than 'Annie'?"

"She may have. Annie is all I know for the moment. She doesn't eat much, she won't dent your budget."

Cragg's colour began to rise. "Whether she eats or not is immaterial. We are *not* an NHS establishment. If she is ill, she should be in a hospital, not in a laboratory."

"She's not ill."

"You said she was."

"I said she was 'uncomfortable.' So would you be if every time you stood up you threw up and then fell down into your own vomit." As Elliot expected, Cragg immediately demonstrated his unique qualification for administering a medical research establishment—he hated sick people.

"Spare me the gruesome details," Cragg said, the rising colour suddenly retreating.

"As you like." Elliot began to stand up.

"But she *is* leaving by the end of the week," Cragg continued.

"No, she isn't." Elliot stepped towards the desk and smiled. "Really, you know, she just isn't going anywhere, Cragg. She is staying here for as long as I say, and there isn't a damn thing you can do about it." As Cragg started to speak, Elliot raised a hand slightly. "And before you begin to list chapter and verse, I suggest you look at my contract. It would be under E for Elliot. Ask your secretary to read you Section Four under the Clause of Requirements. It states quite clearly that I am empowered to bring in any organisms I deem necessary to further my research, to keep them on the premises for as long as I require them, and to treat them in any way I require to aid my investigations."

Cragg looked startled, then sneered. "That refers to laboratory animals and you know it."

"It doesn't actually specify. It says 'organisms,' that's all. Annie is an organism. So are you—although the similarity ends there."

"That's ridiculous."

"No, that's legal detail. Something of a hobby of yours, I believe. Is there anything else?"

"There is a great deal—"

"Ah, pity," Elliot said with heavy regret, looking at his watch. "I can't spare you any more time today. Perhaps you'll send a memo to my secretary outlining all the 'anything else's' and then I'll have her send a memo back to you saying thank you for *your* memo." He began backing towards the door. "And then you can send a memo back, and she can send another, and it will all be very pleasant for you, because you don't take enough exercise, you know, Cragg. Your colour is very poor indeed. I'm speaking medically, now, of course. You should look after yourself—or somebody should."

As soon as he was in the hall, Elliot began to berate himself. Cragg invariably had a bad effect on him. He was not normally a man given to baiting another, but the simple sight of that ferrety little face and those ghost-grey eyes triggered his worst instincts. Knowing that in a crunch his authority slightly exceeded that of the administrator made it all the more reprehensible, but he could not help it. It was for Cragg's own benefit, really. Indulging in verbal abuse had stopped him from hitting the little man in the face more than once.

Anyway, his point had been made. It had taken Janet all morning to find the loophole, but it was wide open. Cragg would probably find a way to close it, but it would take him time. Time was the first priority, still, for Annie.

Four days later they had a band that George said would work. As far as Elliot could see, the only difference was that the control box was slightly bulkier. Electronic theory had never been his strong point; all he knew was that when he put it on it gave him a headache. So for the last time, they hoped, they sat in Laboratory One in the middle of the night, waiting for Annie to come up from the dark trough of her sedative sleep. Elliot leaned against her door and said, softly, "Hello."

"How . . . long . . . minutes?" Annie stammered nervously.

"We think this one will last for good," he assured her. The others came into the room behind him, and they stood there gazing at her until, incredibly, she began to blush.

"Annie . . . bad?"

Ted laughed suddenly, and crossed to the bed to take her pulse. She had grown so used to his being in charge of her physical welfare, whenever she was conscious, that she automatically lifted her hand. "No, love, we're just three men staring at a very pretty girl."

The blush deepened and she looked down at Agatha, the doll from which she refused to be parted. Janet had made the pathetic one-eyed thing a new dress, and she fingered it tentatively with pale fingers. Annie's fox-red hair had grown while she slept, and had now begun to curl gently over her ears and forehead, making her look like a cherub recovering from anorexia nervosa. Her translucent flesh was still drawn tight across cheekbones and jaw. Then, when she looked up again, all resemblance to angels ceased, for the eyes were golden whirlpools of unreadable knowledge, inner-aware and infinite. Longjohn shivered involuntarily, but Elliot stared deep into her face, unable to look away.

"Agatha . . . pretty . . . thank you," she said with careful, small-girl politeness, again modifying their perception of her.

"Janet made the new dress, not us." Elliot smiled. "Needlework isn't our strong point." She looked puzzled. "Never mind. You'll meet Janet tomorrow. How do you feel?"

"Her pulse is good," Ted commented. "A little racy, but strong."

"This . . . hurt thing . . . bad . . ." She indicated the cannula for the IV that was still inserted into the back of her hand. "Take . . . no?"

"Take, yes. Tomorrow," Ted said, patting her shoulder. "After you've eaten a good breakfast."

She shook her head. "No . . . empty . . . inside."

Elliot chuckled. "You're very empty inside. You just don't know it yet because your blood is full of . . ." He paused, still unsure how much of what he said aloud was comprehensible to her. "You'll be hungry in the morning."

Sudden suspicion clouded her expression. "What . . . eat?"

"Anything your little heart desires, love," Ted said expansively. "And as much as you can hold."

The suspicion changed to sly hope. "Chocolate?"

"I'll personally bring you the biggest bar of chocolate you've ever seen in your life," Ted promised. She gave a little excited bounce in the bed, clutching Agatha tightly to her breast. Elliot glanced at Longjohn in amusement and found the lanky Canadian regarding the girl very thoughtfully.

"What's the nicest thing you know, Annie?" Longjohn asked, suddenly.

"Chocolate," she said instantly.

"And what else?"

"What . . . else?"

"Make a list," he suggested, leaning against the wall with his arms folded. She looked confused. "Tell me one nice thing, then tell me another nice thing after that," he explained patiently. Elliot stared at him, as confused as Annie. What the hell was Longjohn doing?

She understood, finally, and began to count off on her fingers. "Chocolate. Agatha. Granny . . ." she paused, then added resolutely, "Granny . . . deaded. Red flower . . . running . . . splosh water sand . . . brownbirds."

"What about stories, Annie?" Longjohn interrupted. "Do you like stories?"

She looked blank, then her face lit up. "Granny . . . make . . . stories."

"And playing games. Do you like playing games?"

She glanced at Elliot in some confusion. "What is games?"

"What *are* games," he corrected her, automatically.

"Not . . . you know, either . . . Philip?" she wondered.

"No . . . yes. I meant . . ." he trailed off helplessly, looking towards Longjohn who smiled ruefully at him, then crooked a finger. They went out into the lab proper, leaving Ted to talk to Annie about Agatha's new dress. She watched Elliot slowly follow the tall skinny man out of the room, but Ted was talking about Agatha, so she talked about Agatha for him.

Longjohn reached over and pulled Elliot's cigarettes out of his jacket pocket, shaking out two. Elliot was surprised, for Longjohn rarely smoked cigarettes, but he flicked his lighter for both of them.

"You see the problem?" Hawkins asked.

"What problem?" Smoke filled the space between them momentarily.

"Our *next* problem. You got rid of the noise in her head, fine. What do we have in there now, though?"

"Just Annie," Elliot smiled, looking through the open door at her head next to Ted's dark one.

"And Annie, my good friend, is a blank page. Just listen to the way she's been talking."

Elliot looked disgusted. "Oh, for Pete's sake, that's just because she doesn't have much of a vocabulary yet. I told you, she relied mainly on images before. What she sounds like is somebody feeling their way through a foreign language . . . and doing a lot better at it, I might point out, than you or I would with Russian or Urdu at such short notice. English is not the easiest language in the—"

Longjohn was shaking his head. "I wasn't referring to her words, or lack of them, Phil. That young woman has the emotional range of a four-year-old child. You're so busy gloating over the potential of her brain, you're overlooking her limitations. She's never had any continuous contact with anyone except her grandmother, and that was probably very rudimentary. She's spent her whole life without *any* kind of restriction or education. She's never had to accommodate herself to the wishes of another living soul. Remember what she said about looking in the windows?" Elliot nodded, dumbly. "What do you think it looked like to her in there? How could she comprehend the complex subtleties between human beings —things like companionship, social conventions, word-play, manners, morality?" He settled himself on the edge of a bench, while Elliot stood listening. "I don't think you've actually thought about Annie's life too much, Phil, because it hurts you to think about it. It hurts me, too, but I've got a little distance between her and me. You haven't. For my sake, think about it now. Forget the pain in her head, think about the rest of it. Other children, for instance. Maybe she watched them in the schoolyard . . . maybe she even crept up and tried to join in their games. *Once.* Can you imagine the reactions of the other children when they caught sight of her? When she tried to talk to them? Or the reaction of the locals, or tourists if they caught her spying on their picnics, for instance?"

"Oh, Jesus, Longjohn, don't," Elliot begged, turning away.

"I have to, Phil, it's my job, remember? If that band George and Frances made holds, she won't be troubled by the noise of other people's heads any more. But she *will* be troubled by other people. And they'll be very troubled by her, unless she learns what any four-year-old has to learn—how to deal with the world around her. It isn't easy for a four-year-old, and it sure as hell isn't going to be easy for her. Or us, for that matter."

"What are you saying?" Elliot stared across the lab, the cigarette smouldering unnoticed between his fingers.

Longjohn shrugged. "I'm saying that you'll have to turn her over to me for a while. I know you're eager to begin testing her, but if somebody doesn't help her get her head together, you won't get very far. Fortunately she seems eager to please. I'd better lay in a big supply of sweets."

"Don't be so damned—" Elliot flared.

"So damned what? Cynical? I'm not being cynical, *or* cruel, although I can see you think I am. She's a child, Phil, a *child*. Never mind what she looks like."

Elliot took a moment to regain control, then turned, flicking the long ash off his cigarette. "Look, Longjohn . . . I appreciate what you're saying, but I've been in contact with her head, with what's *inside,* and I promise you, it's not childish. Not in the least."

"Isn't it?"

"No—*no*. Her mind is quick, supple, brilliantly imaginative, she has a highly developed sense of humour. She can play structural and interactive *games* with imagery that would make you reel, she comprehends total thoughts with accompanying sensory and memory echoes instantly. She can—"

"She can also blow the back of your head off," Longjohn reminded him mildly.

"Not with the band on," Elliot countered.

"And with the band on, where is that lovely mind of hers?" Longjohn went on. "Hmmmmm? Can you get at it? Can she get at you?"

"No, that's the whole point." He stopped. "Ah."

"Yes, 'ah.' I don't give a damn what those big gold eyes of hers are saying, she is now in our world and she's stuck with it. We're stuck with her, too, thanks to you." Elliot's face darkened. "Oh, I know. There wasn't anything else you could do, except maybe leave her alone. But it's just about the same as catching a wild animal, isn't it? Bring *any* wild thing out of its natural habitat where it knows its place and functions in it, chuck it into another world, and you've got trouble."

"You don't like her," Elliot challenged, feeling oddly defensive.

"I don't like or dislike her, she simply scares the hell out of me, that's all. What scares me even more is that she *doesn't* scare you, despite the things I've seen her do to you."

"You don't understand, she didn't *want* to hurt me . . ."

"But she did, didn't she?"

There was a burst of sound from Annie's room. "There you are," Elliot said, triumphantly. "She's laughing. Listen to that. She's laughing."

They looked down the lab to the open door of the screen-room and saw that Ted was making Agatha dance across the coverlet towards Annie. Longjohn sighed. "Well, it's a start, anyway. She *has* got a sense of humour. Maybe that's where yours went."

A chastened Elliot got home just before dawn, and let himself in with a sense of intrusion. Drawn by the sound of the car, Joseph appeared through the cat-flap in the kitchen door and regarded him quizzically, as if he remembered the face but not the name.

"No, it's not Mrs. Purdey, it's actually me for a change," Elliot informed the cat. "Surprise, surprise." Joseph didn't seem particularly surprised, just hungry. Elliot opened a tin of salmon as a treat, and watched him wolf down the pink meat eagerly. He made himself a sandwich and coffee and carried it into the sitting room, flicking on the gas log fire and settling down in the big double chair. The house was his special retreat, even though he had spent hardly any time there since returning from Mhourra. He had scouted the area shortly before starting work at Talbot Hall, and had quietly bought up enough of the land surrounding the site to ensure that his privacy would be permanent. The lady at the top of the lane was an elderly widow who spent most of her time knitting for her grandchildren and looked after Joseph when Elliot was away. He always remembered to bring her back some special wool from wherever his lecture, conference or consultation took place. The arrangement was pleasant but not intimate. The house had been built by labour imported all the way from Manchester because he hadn't wanted it talked about locally.

What was peculiar was not the design of the house—it was simply a nice, white, rather long cottage with a circular room at either end. The problem had been the actual construction of the two circular rooms. His bedroom and his private laboratory were actually two permanent versions of the screen-room in which Annie slept at Talbot. At the time the house was built he, too, had needed protection from mental interference in order to sleep. In between the two screened rooms lay the kitchen, living room, and bathroom. No guest rooms, obviously. The décor was simple and comfortable, with lots of books and the few pictures he liked hung against neutral colours and textures. The last thing he needed was a house that fought him back every time he came home. Most of the women he brought there thought it too "bland" and had visions of all the improvements that could be made in it. He caught those visions from time to time—everything from bright chintz to chrome tubing. None of them had been his idea of home—none of the women had been, either.

Before his accident, Elliot had been as normal as any man. He still was, so far as his physical reactions were concerned. He liked women who were attractive, witty, intelligent, loving, warm. Once in bed with any of them he thoroughly enjoyed himself and he hoped they did too. But, and it was a big exception, if he became too involved in lovemaking, occasionally the controls in his brain would slide a little and he would find himself riveted by the woman's thoughts.

Not: "My God, this man is beautiful, fantastic, wild." Oh, no. More like: "I wonder if I should have my hair done on Thursday?" or, "Do you put two cloves of garlic or three in that casserole?"

It was, he had informed Joseph one grey morning, enough to put any man off his stroke.

Elliot knew very well everyone was like that, thinking on a dozen levels at once and compartmentalizing themselves. Women were better at it than most men because they had to be. But he didn't like to get slapped in the face with it. His brain might have altered, but his ego remained as tender as anyone else's.

So, since the accident, he'd kept his pleasure in women strictly visceral. No emotional involvements, *ever*. Because, unfortunately, along with casserole recipes, he would occasionally pick up other gratuitous information—how he compared in bed with Fred, Charlie, or Sam, that his taste in literature revealed a bourgeois middle-class outlook, that it was a shame he wasn't taller but he *was* rich—and so on.

He and Joseph led a very simple life by the river.

Each had his pursuits. Each respected the other's domain.

And Elliot knew how lonely Annie had been.

Longjohn had set to work the next day to bring Annie through her necessary stages of emotional and intellectual development. The first thing he did was to lock Elliot out. He gave no explanation, merely issued orders.

Annie, now safely banded, was to be looked after by Janet and Ted, no one else. Adapting his battery of intelligence tests to solely non-verbal evaluations, he found that Annie's IQ was far far above the norm, giving her a mental "age" of approximately fifty-five, in functional capacity at least. Her brain was a big bucket, but an empty one so far. Further tests verified his initial casual estimate—emotionally she was about six years old, but ageing at a rapid rate because of her desperate need to be "normal." It seemed to him logical, given those parameters, that she be given a primal family structure within which to evolve, so Janet and Ted became her surrogate parents.

Now, many weeks later, Longjohn had reason to be pleased with his programme. Annie was developing at an amazingly accelerated rate. Sitting in his office, in the midst of his daily report on her progress, he leaned back in his chair and looked out the window. Ted and Janet were having a picnic with Annie on the lawn. It was a charming scene,

Annie laughing as Ted tried to juggle three hard-boiled eggs without much success. Then a movement across the courtyard caught his eye. Elliot was standing behind the French windows of the library, also watching, his stocky figure alternately tense and dejected as the picnic proceeded. Hawkins sighed.

"It's for your own good, buddy, I promise you," he whispered. "I've known you long enough. If I read you right, it might hurt now, but it could hurt a lot worse later on."

He picked up his pen again and continued the report, translating Annie's progress into the cold, technical verbiage he hated. "MMPI and AVL test procedures (modified, see Appendix D) show she is still both paranoic and hypomanic, with strongly developed theoretical, aesthetic, and religious capacities. On reaching emotional puberty, subject showed signs of high sexual awareness, with episodes (see Appendix E) that have caused temporary rift in familial structure: active expression of Electra complex, deferred to Vanderhof from Holbrook who rejected, with complications arising from surrogate mother. . . ."

He grinned over that one. In other words, Algernon, he thought, when you get all this crap into your memory banks, what you'll have is a startling little drama of human passion in which girl makes pass at stepfather, is spurned, turns to alternate male figure, Danny, is also spurned, and then is turned *against* by Janet who is also hot for Vanderhof.

Elliot had gone berserk, of course. Halfway between laughter and despair, he had stormed into Longjohn's office and demanded to be told what the hell was going on?

"She's having trouble relating her hormones to her head," Longjohn had said in an effort to calm the pacing figure who was treading a new path into his already well-worn carpet. "Perfectly normal."

"Did I get it right from Danny? She went into his head and gave him an erection, then tried to get him to—"

"You got it right," Longjohn chuckled. "I think we ought

to cut down on her calorie intake, by the way. She's got too
damn much energy."

"When is all this going to end? When do I get her back?"

"I don't think you'd *want* her back right now, Phil. Unless you want her in your bed as well as your head. She's
quite a handful, in more ways than one." He watched Elliot
closely as he spoke, and was satisfied that his original instinctive evaluation of the other man had been correct.

"It *is* just a—what do you call it—a 'phase,' isn't it?"
Elliot asked anxiously, pausing to look at Hawkins.

"That's all it is," Hawkins said easily, wishing he was
sure. "She'll be through it as fast as she's been through the
rest. She *wants* to grow up, Phil, that's our biggest asset."

Released from immediate contact with Annie for the time
being, Elliot tried to distract himself by dealing with the back-
log of paperwork and the increasing interference from Cragg.
He watched Annie's development from behind a wall of pointless activity, knowing that most of the research going on at
Talbot would soon be more or less obsolete.

And the nightmares continued.

He had asked Longjohn to include some questions about
dreams and nightmares in his analytical sessions with Annie.
She did report "bad dreams" but was unable or unwilling to
describe them. Pressing her for details only brought anger
or tears, so Longjohn told him to forget it for the time being.
It was obvious to Elliot that whatever it was arose from his
proximity to Annie—he never had the nightmares at home,
only when he slept over at Talbot. Several times he had repeated his charge of the night brigade down to the screen-
room, only to find Annie sleeping peacefully. They no longer
monitored her brain waves, so he had nothing other than
her words to go on. But she refused to speak about the dreams.

In fact, Annie was beginning to refuse to do a lot of
things. Once Janet had taught her to read, she had started on
the extensive Talbot library. Psychological texts had soon

given her a clue to what Hawkins had been doing, thereby rendering the process useless. There wasn't much point in continuing anyway, Hawkins said with a shrug—she had reached an emotional level that was roughly equivalent to her chronological age, taking into account her limited background and experience. She still had a great deal of difficulty relating to others, but it was now a product of her personality rather than previous emotional deprivation. She hated talking because, apparently, it was frustrating to limit her communication to mere spoken words. She became moody, withdrawn, and hostile to almost everyone except Elliot, with whom she was now allowed regular contact. Their antagonism was on a totally different level.

Many of the staff found her frightening and strange, even though they did not know about her abnormal mental capacities. It was her eyes more than anything, the strange golden eyes that seemed to eat into you, suck you dry, turn you round, and kick you out as if you didn't measure up. Well, Hawkins mused, they didn't measure up in a way, because they couldn't do what she *knew* she could do. She was becoming arrogant, conscious now that her abilities were power rather than weakness. Elliot had never been like that— at least not so far as Hawkins knew.

But Elliot's almost obsessive insistence that Annie wear the band at all times was becoming a nuisance. From being desperate to explore and define her abilities, he'd now gone to the other extreme, insisting that they put her through all the old tests and measurements they used on ordinary subjects. Almost as if he were afraid to release her from the band, afraid to bring her into the light. Reverting to his usual method for releasing tension, Hawkins kicked his wastepaper basket across the office. They had discovered Annie and what made her brain different. Keeping her at this level of experiment was rather like Madame Curie slaving over radium all those years and then locking it in the coalshed against a rainy day. Despite his protestations about security and exploitation, was it possible that Elliot was being *coy?* What the hell was he waiting for?

He kicked the wastepaper basket again, denting it.

Passing Hawkins's office on the way to his own, Elliot heard the familiar clunk and clatter rebounding off the walls, and smiled briefly. He wished he could deal with his own frustrations as easily as Longjohn did. But two of them requisitioning new wastepaper baskets every week would send Cragg into orbit.

He opened his door and found Annie sitting on the chesterfield trying to smoke a cigarette. Suppressing his amusement at the awkward way she held it between her thumb and forefinger, he closed the door behind him.

"Hello."

She didn't greet him, merely turned her enormous eyes in his direction.

"Would you like some coffee?" he asked, stopping to pour himself some.

"No . . . thank you." As always the hesitancy, the reluctant use of words when she would have preferred a richer exchange of images.

"I've got your photographs here, would you like to see them?"

"Which . . . photographs?"

He settled himself at the other end of the chesterfield, put his mug down on the low table, and proceeded to open the large manila envelope he had brought back from the dark room. "The ones we took this morning."

"Fingers . . . pictures of my . . . fingers?"

"No. Pictures of your aura. I thought Longjohn explained?"

She shook her head. "Just . . . took the . . ." she left the phrase unfinished. It was another habit she had, going just so far with a sentence and then leaving it up to the listener to complete.

"Okay, then I will. These are Kirlian photographs. The technique was developed in Russia a long time ago. You see, around every living thing there is an 'aura' of energy we simply don't understand. We don't know what it *is,* we don't know how it *works,* we aren't even sure what it's for, but we can take a picture of it. All right?" She nodded, not deeply interested but keeping her eyes on his face as she always did, unsettling him. He leaned back and rested his head on the leather cushions, staring up at the ceiling as he gently lectured on one of his favourite subjects. "It's easy enough to do. The subject places a fingertip onto a standard photographic plate, and we pass a very slight electrical charge through the plate to the finger. Then we develop the plate in a perfectly normal way, and we get a picture of the Kirlian 'corona.' In ordinary people, it's no more than a quarter of an inch or so and, if they're in a restful state, light to dark blue. If they're excited or aroused, the halo brightens up to red and white, with fine hairlike spindles flaring radially, like the sun. Yes?"

He sensed her nod rather than saw it and continued. "All right. Now, psychic healers exhibit much larger coronas than ordinary people, much more intense and colourful. They start out bigger, and during their healing state it looks like a picture of the sun during a period of sunspot activity—great flares and blotches of light like licking flames of hot yellow tipping to red-orange. If we take a Kirlian photograph of a healer and a patient before and after treatment takes place, we get a very interesting correlation. Before treatment the healer's corona is large, the patient's normal. *After* treatment the patient's corona has grown, and the healer's has diminished, in a directly measureable ratio. In short, this energy, whatever it is, has actually been transferred from the healer to the patient. We don't know how or why, but it happens every time."

"Aspirin . . ." Annie observed.

He turned his head. "What? Oh, I see. No, we don't know how aspirin works, either. Quite right." He smiled. "Very good, Annie."

She didn't smile back.

"So . . ." he leaned forward and turned over the pictures. "Here are *your* Kirlian photographs." He watched her look casually at the prints, then lean forward and inspect them closely. He didn't blame her, he'd been staring at them for some time already, unable to believe what they showed.

"Bigger," she finally said. It was a typical understatement. They were incredible. Her at-rest corona was a full inch in depth. Her aroused corona was nearly off the plate, yellow-white to blinding orange, with enormous royal blue blotches that were a consistent feature in the coronas of all psychic healers.

"Yes," he said softly. "Why do you think that is, Annie?"

She shrugged and kept her eyes on the pictures, reaching for her cigarette only to find it burned out in the ashtray. He pulled out his packet and offered it, casually. She hesitated, then took one and waited for him to light it and his own, her eyes still averted.

"You *can* heal, can't you, Annie?" he said after a minute. When she did not reply, he went on. "Baines said he thought you had healed some people on Mhourra. Did you?"

Still she would not look at him. He reached out to touch her arm, and she stiffened, then lifted her face. He was stunned to see the golden eyes swimming with tears that she was trying vainly to blink away.

"Not . . . evil."

"Of course it's not evil. Whoever said that it was?" he asked in astonishment.

"Granny . . ." One tear escaped and ran down over the freckles that were now partially concealed by the make-up she wore. It annoyed him that Janet encouraged her to try to look like any other damn red-head on the street—she wasn't. She never would be. Abruptly she reached up to the band as if she wanted to wrench it off.

"No!" he said, sharply. "No, *tell* me, Annie. *Say* it." He resolutely ignored the pleading in her eyes, and waited. Slowly her hand dropped back down into her lap, and she stared at it.

"Yes," she admitted in a shamed whisper. "It . . . me
. . . . healed."

"Even the cancer?" he asked softly. She nodded, then
swallowed and looked up at him.

"But . . . not always." She took a deep, ragged breath.
"Not . . . always . . . possible . . . Sometimes only pain
. . . taken away . . . but death . . . not always." Another
tear escaped to join the first in symmetrical sorrow.

Now he saw it. It wasn't the use of the power that disturbed her so deeply, but its failure. He reached again for her
hand, then let his own fall short onto the cool leather between
them. "I understand."

"*Not* . . . understand," she said, angrily. "*Not* understand without . . ."

Again, the reaching toward the band.

"No. *No,* Annie. Someday, but not now. Please."

"Why?" She looked into his face. "Why?"

Abruptly he turned away to gather up the photographs,
sliding them back into the manila envelope and standing up
to carry it over to his desk. "I have my reasons."

She stood up, too, tossing the still-burning cigarette into
the ashtray on the coffee table. "Bloody hell," she said clearly,
and went out, slamming the door behind her.

Not sure whether to laugh or cry himself, he stared at the
blank wooden panel, then sank down into the chair behind
his desk.

Because I'm hiding, Annie, he told her silently.

Because I'm hiding from you.

7

Elliot pulled his car up to the entrance to the underground car park and displayed his credentials to the guard on duty. After a phone call upstairs the guard waved him through, and he drove into the murky shadows to find an empty space between the big black limousines and other equally expensive cars that lined the walls. Slamming the car door behind him, he made his way across the gritty concrete to the lift and waited while it hummed down to him.

He hated this place with such intensity that coming into it invariably knotted his stomach into double-reefs. But it had been a summons he could no longer ignore. Knowing that Cragg had instigated it did not make the attendance any less distasteful, quite the reverse. He could handle Cart Curtiss on the squash court, but in his own office not so well. Being here reminded him all too forcibly of just who he worked for, and why.

Although he had punched Cart's floor on the panel, the lift automatically stopped on the ground floor, and the doors slid back to reveal yet another guard who pressed a hand against the protective rubber strip and looked in.

"Dr. Elliot?"

"Yes."

"Could I see your . . . ?"

Patiently, Elliot drew out the leather folder again and
flipped it open so the guard could compare the photograph
on it with his own face.

The guard took his time studying the photo, then nodded,
thanked him, and stepped back, removing his hand from the
safety strip and allowing the lift doors to close. As he continued upwards, Elliot tried to decide how he would handle
the interview. He had been considering and rejecting attitudes
and approaches all the way in on the M4, and was still un-
satisfied. Any explanation had to be good and complete for
Curtiss. He couldn't think of a damn one that would be convincing.

Except for the truth, and he was *not* going to hand that
out unless he absolutely had to. Not yet.

Carter Hooks Curtiss had a large corner office in one of
the upper floors of the modern white oblong that cut upwards
over Whitehall. The building had a number, but no name.
Those who needed to know what it was knew what it was,
those who didn't, didn't. The office was rather luxuriously
furnished for a civil servant, but then Curtiss had money of
his own (or his wife did), so that was all right. Everything
about Curtiss was "all right." Background, breeding, education, ability, ambition. As long as you ignored the contents,
the Curtiss package was a charming and attractive addition
to the Service.

Elliot had never been able to ignore the contents.

"Ah, Elliot," Curtiss said with what sounded like genuine
pleasure. "At last I've got you down here for a chat. How long
has it been?"

"Not so long."

"No? Seems it." He waved Elliot into one of the comfortable chairs and poured him out a scotch without asking
whether he wanted one or not. As it happened, he did, but
he ignored it.

"Well . . ." Curtiss sank into a chair beside Elliot rather than returning to the one behind his desk. (Standard protocol, indicating friendly relations, indicating this was to be a communication period between equals, so nice, so nice to see you again, Elliot, old chap.) "How are things down at Talbot Hall, then? Cheers."

Elliot nodded but did not raise his own glass, leaving it on the low table between them. Curtiss paused for a moment, sipped his own, then placed it on the table, too. "Everything going along all right?"

"As always, we make haste slowly."

Curtiss chuckled and drew out his cigarette case, offering it to Elliot and using the table lighter. "You haven't practised medicine for years, but you still keep your mouth shut, don't you? Bad habit, and pointless. One way and another, I know quite a lot about the things you work on."

"I'm sure you do. You always did like to keep informed."

"Exactly. Tell me about her, Elliot. Your little mind-reader."

Elliot was deeply shocked, but didn't allow it to show. Ninety per cent of the explanations he'd prepared were suddenly useless, and he gazed out at the hazy vista of buildings obscured by the falling curtain of rain.

"What do you want to know?" And who told you what you know already, he wondered to himself? Not Cragg. Definitely not Cragg.

"All of it. Please." Curtiss added unnecessarily. He could have made a flat demand, but for the moment, he was being polite.

"It's a little too early to call her a 'mind-reader.' What she has is a potential, no more."

"But an incredible potential, nonetheless."

"If we can make it work, I suppose so. Potential for what, I couldn't say."

"Or wouldn't." Curtiss tapped his ash into the large glass oval on the coffee table. "I know your attitudes, Philip. I heard you express them often enough over beers at the Union, remember?"

"And I know yours. You always talked more than I did."

"Yet you were happy enough to ignore them when I was in a position to offer you Talbot Hall, weren't you?"

"Not happy. But I ignored them."

"And you feel . . . compromised? Still, I've let you have a pretty free hand down there, you must admit. Haven't made many demands, haven't laid down many hard and fast rules. Which it now seems was a mistake."

"I'm no magician."

"Which leaves the corollary of a rabbit out of a hat fairly inevitable, under the circumstances. You still haven't told me what I want to know."

"You still haven't told me what you want to hear." He picked up his drink.

"I want to hear that after all this time and all this money spent you actually have something to give me that I can use," Curtiss said. "I want to hear that all your expectations of ESP as a functioning possibility are now a functioning reality. And I want it to function for me. That is to say, for us."

No, Elliot thought, you were right the first time. For you.

"I'll need more time before I can give you that."

"How much more time? You've had years already."

"I only found Annie a few months ago. Obviously you know something about that."

Curtiss leaned back in his chair gracefully, his dark, immaculately cut suit settling into equally immaculate lines of repose. He and Elliot had been on the same staircase at Cambridge, although Elliot had been two years senior to him. They had begun as friendly enemies, wrangling from their opposing philosophical viewpoints, but only once coming to half-hearted and slightly drunken blows over it. After Elliot's accident they had lost track of one another, but when he went to Whitehall to seek research backing, he'd found Curtiss there, firmly entrenched as a young White Hope. One brief mental

encounter with the Curtiss below the impressive exterior had
been enough for Elliot to realize that the views he'd argued
against at university had now become almost a messianic code
for Curtiss. Subsequently he'd used every defence at his disposal to avoid touching Curtiss's mind again, so distasteful did
he find the feverish mania of its contents.

Soon there was another reason to avoid it. Within months
of their reacquaintance, Elliot had begun an intense but short-
lived affair with Madeline Curtiss, Carter's beautiful and sex-
ually voracious young wife. She had homed in on Elliot like a
sleek silver barracuda sensing fresh prey in the water. Purely
physical in nature, the affair began and burned out in weeks.
Elliot only belatedly learned that this was Madeline's habitual
pattern. From some things that she had said, he knew that
Curtiss was aware of his wife's proclivities and had been forced
to accept them or lose her, because he was unable to satisfy
her needs. Elliot might have pitied Curtiss if he hadn't begun
to suspect that Carter occasionally even used her to make
vulnerable certain men who might be useful to him in their
guilt. It soon became apparent, however, that her affair with
Elliot had cut more deeply than the rest into Carter's pride.
Nothing was ever said, but the quality of the sparring between
the two men had taken on a more savage undertone. The
problem was that he and Curtiss had always respected one
another's ability, if not each other's views. Diametrically op-
posed in almost every way, they continued their peculiar relationship because Elliot needed Curtiss as a sponsor, and
Curtiss believed that Elliot might one day bring him the power
he so single-mindedly sought.

Elliot had always wondered whether Curtiss regretted
committing himself to the future of his "worthy adversary."
He often regretted it, but the simple fact was that there was
very little alternative for either of them. Curtiss ranked highly
in the one Department that could fund Talbot Hall, and was
now too far along to withdraw his support of Elliot without
raising a great many eyebrows and calling into question all

his past expenditure. It was in his interest to continue to tolerate and even encourage Elliot's progress. And so, with gritted teeth and an effusive charm that no one but Elliot suspected, he had continued to do so. Now, it seemed, he was about to demand a little payment towards the debt Elliot owed him.

"I know that somewhere, somehow, you discovered a girl with rather spectacular mental capacities," Curtiss said. "That you brought her back to Talbot Hall and have spent some time getting her under control. She *is* now under control, and you have begun exploring her potential. I know that she is quite a pretty little thing, that she is not particularly liked there, and that you have done your damndest to conceal all this from everyone. That's what I know."

"The 'control' you talk about isn't all that positive," Elliot said, stubbing his cigarette out firmly, pursuing every spark to extinction. "We've developed a 'damper' that keeps her from getting out and blowing everyone else cockeyed, but it's burnt out once, and could do so again. Any time." He still felt sick when he thought about the occasion when Annie had been brought back to Talbot in an ambulance, rescued from the hospital at Slough where she had been taken after collapsing in Boots on a shopping expedition with Janet.

"What do you mean, 'blowing everyone else cockeyed'? Does she attack people with this power of hers?"

"She did, at first, when she was still reacting childishly to opposition or disapproval. Unless you know how to deal with it, it's a very distressing experience to have someone else's thoughts running through your head. Particularly when they're angry and painful thoughts, intended to wound."

"You know how to deal with it?"

"I've had quite a lot of experience with telepaths over the years."

"*Latent* telepaths, you mean. She's hardly latent, is she? And I thought it wasn't so much a matter of her getting out as of others getting in."

Damn, Elliot thought, he *has* been keeping himself informed. "Look, Cart," he began, turning to face the horn-rimmed glasses and the famous crest of blond hair the cartoonists loved to caricature. "If you had waited a little longer I'd have been able to tell you a lot more. I meant what I said. We simply don't *know* what we've got down there. Until I've established parameters, until we can get some kind of understanding of the thing, I *can't* give you what you want with any degree of certainty."

"And what do you think I want?" Curtiss said with a mildness that in no way deceived Elliot.

"You want some kind of super-spy."

"Just like that?"

"Exactly like that. I *know* what you're after, what you've always been after. What I don't understand is why you're so impatient *now*." He was trying desperately hard to "read" Curtiss, but nothing was coming through. Apparently he was into one of his blank phases again; there was no power at all in his head when he needed it most. There was a time when he could have peeled Curtiss like an onion.

"Well, I'll tell you why. Does the name Kossetz mean anything to you?"

"You know damn well it does. He's the leading Russian parapsychologist, head of their Institute of Advanced Behaviourism. Why?"

"He's recently been given a massive increase in funding. My sources say it's indirectly from the budget of the KGB. That's why."

"You think Kossetz has got something?"

"I know bloody well he has. What it is, no. But *something*, definitely."

"He is also a monster. Do your sources tell you that?"

Curtiss stared at Elliot in amazement, startled by the intensity of his tone and expression. "A monster? That's a pretty emotional word for you."

Elliot stood up and went over to the window, looking

down at the glistening pavements far below, the hurrying black mushrooms of umbrellas, the occasional unprotected pedestrian dashing from doorway to doorway.

"Sorry. I met him once, at an International Conference of Neurological Sciences. He is totally without any feeling, except ambition." *A lot like you, my well-dressed friend,* he added silently. "He has published some absolutely terrifying material on experiments no Western scientist would consider, much less condone. He's been after the same thing I have, but his methods are . . . different."

"I see. All the more reason for us to be worried, then."

"Perhaps. But not a reason to follow his example."

"I'm not asking you to follow his example. I'm just asking you to help us be prepared for whatever he's up to."

"Assuming he's up to something that would affect us, you mean."

"I said the money came from the KGB, didn't I?"

"You said you had reason to believe it did. Indirectly. Maybe they're just shuffling their money around. As we do."

"Oh, Philip." Curtiss sounded deeply disappointed. "You and I might not agree on politics or anything else, but I've never thought you were naïve."

"I'm not naïve, just hesitant to jump to conclusions in my work or in your interests."

Curtiss sighed. "What *are* Kossetz's ambitions, anyway, just out of curiosity?"

"Funnily enough, not so very far removed from yours," Elliot said quietly. "He believes that people should be controlled, that they would be happier, healthier, and all the rest of it if their impulses towards natural aggression and rebellion were curbed and channelled into productive outlets. That creativity and invention grows from those same roots is irrelevant to him."

"Do *I* believe that?"

"I seem to remember knocking you flat after an argument

along those lines in the Union, yes. Oh, you couched it more attractively, and you expressed it more benignly, I agree, but you said it."

"You can hardly call me to account now for undergraduate maunderings."

"I'm not calling you to account. You asked me what his ambitions were. That's what they are."

"His control would be under communism, presumably."

"Presumably. What does it matter?"

"It matters quite a lot, in my opinion. Doesn't it in yours?"

Elliot shrugged. "One economic system is much like another when it's run that way."

"Well, not to me, it isn't. Anyway, this is off the point. When can you give me what I need?"

"How much time do I have?" His breath misted the window briefly.

"Let's just say you have no time at all, and work to that, all right? Delivery yesterday, if possible. You're already running over your deadline."

Elliot turned, his square body set stiffly within the rumpled tweed suit. "And if I refuse?"

"I wouldn't recommend it."

"Ve haf vays of making you vork?"

Curtiss smiled genially. "Oh, Philip, we have lots of ways. *Lots* of ways. Don't make me use them. Please, don't. Things would be very dull around here without you. And I'm sure Annie would miss you, too. Wouldn't she?"

8

"Well, I think it damn well stinks." Longjohn was so angry he was eyeing Elliot's wastepaper basket with a view to drop-kicking it straight through the window.

"As a matter of fact, so do I. It's *exactly* what I was hoping to avoid." Elliot was pretending to look at the lawn, but was seeing nothing. "But that's actually what we're here for, what they've been paying us to find."

"But not what they pay Annie for. Annie's not their property."

Annie stirred restlessly in the rocking chair, watching Elliot's back. "Not . . . pay me . . . what?"

Elliot sighed and turned to face her. She was wearing a pale blue sweater and skirt, and sat with her legs tucked up on one side. She was still slender, but her figure had filled out as a result of all the good food they had been pouring into her, and was now rounded and womanly under the light material. He thought she was easily the loveliest thing he had ever seen and was grateful she could not read his feelings for her. They weren't making this conversation any easier.

"Annie, I've explained what Talbot Hall is, why we're

here, what they want from us. Do you understand what I've told you?"

"Oh . . . yes. But . . . they don't . . . pay *me*. I must owe . . . someone . . . for the clothes . . . and the food . . . and—"

"Don't be silly," Longjohn interrupted brusquely. "You don't owe anybody anything."

"I'm . . . never . . . silly," she protested, turning her big golden eyes on him in reproach. "Not . . . any more, any . . . way."

It was true, Elliot thought, sadly. She rarely laughed now, rarely even smiled at any of them. The silvery band was apparently a heavy burden. It seemed to drain all the life out of her.

"Anyway . . ." she continued, "if they . . . want . . . this . . . thing . . . from me . . . it would pay them . . ."

"The question is purely academic in any event," Elliot interrupted. "You couldn't *do* what they want. To 'read' someone you'd have to take off the band, and if you take off the band—"

"Oh . . . no problem?" She almost smiled, using one of Longjohn's favourite phrases. "Easy . . . to . . . learn."

"Easy to learn what?" Elliot sat on the edge of his desk and looked at her in puzzlement.

"To control . . . Omega." That was the somewhat poetic name they had chosen for the new wave pattern they had discovered in her brain.

"Easy?" Elliot demanded. "It took me a year just to get an edge on it, and even then—"

She was shaking her head in what looked almost like pity, he was irritated to see. "Didn't . . . think it . . . through. All *here*. I was talking . . . to Frances . . . She says . . . yes." She paused. "Yes . . . maybe," she amended carefully.

"What are you talking about, Annie?" Longjohn asked, curiously.

"Bio- . . . feedback."

Elliot and Longjohn looked at her, then at one another, stunned.

"Not . . . right word?" Annie enquired anxiously. "I mean . . . the . . ."

"We know what you mean, Annie," Elliot said.

"Jesus wept," Longjohn breathed. "Jesus bloody wept."

"What on earth made you think of that?" Elliot asked.

She shrugged. "In the books. Alone . . . all night. In that . . . room." There was a bitter undercurrent in her voice that made Elliot wince. "Don't *like* depending on the . . . band. On the . . . cage. Looking for a way . . . like you . . . Philip . . . to get out."

"Out?"

"Out of *your* . . . cage." Even trapped by the band she saw too much, he decided.

"Would it work, Phil?" Longjohn asked.

Elliot managed to drag his eyes away from Annie's and looked over at the lanky Canadian sprawled on the chesterfield. "I don't know," he said thoughtfully. "It works on blood pressure and bladder control and fairly simple things like that. But on something as complex as Omega—"

"Not complex. Omega is . . . very simple, Philip. Yours is very . . . simple, too. I can hear it."

"Hear what?" he asked, startled.

"Your Omega. It has a . . . noise." She turned to Longjohn. "You, too . . . only . . . not so loud. Philip . . . very loud, even through the band."

"Are you telling us you can actually *hear* Omega?"

"Oh, yes. Of course." She seemed surprised that he should question it. "It makes a . . . hum? Like a waterfall . . . like a river . . . flowing . . . running . . . all the time."

"Not from me."

"Oh, *yes*. From you. All the time."

"And in me?" Longjohn demanded. "In *me?*"

"In . . . everybody. Philip is strongest . . . but yes, in everybody." She kept looking from one to the other. "I thought . . . you knew."

Longjohn had sat upright, and now leaned forward, his hands clasped tightly in front of him. "Wait a minute, let me get this quite straight, Annie. You can actually hear Omega, even through the band?" She nodded. "And you can hear it in *everybody?*"

"Some . . . very soft. Some . . . better."

"But I can't read minds any more," Elliot said.

"Still there . . . you won't use . . . but . . ."

Elliot stood up and walked over to the coffee maker, but his hands shook so much he could hardly get any into the mugs, and spilled most of it over the table-top. He bent down and got one of the towels out to mop up the mess, while Longjohn went on questioning Annie in growing excitement.

"Then, theoretically, anybody could do what you do?"

"Don't know. Everybody has legs . . . not everybody can dance," she said succinctly. "Not everybody . . . would . . . *like* to dance, perhaps."

"Phil, do you realize what she's saying? We've been wrong about this from the start. We assumed it was a freak development, genetic mutation in Annie and the result of physical trauma in you. We've been putting off checking out our other ESP subjects because . . ."

"Because we thought we could move faster by concentrating on Annie," Elliot finished for him. He was staring at the puddles of coffee that had escaped the towel. So simple, he was marvelling. So simple that I couldn't accept it. It *is* a natural evolutionary development, it *is* there in normal brains as well as psychics. I was right, yet even I thought it was only a dream, was never really convinced by my own theory.

"Then Omega is normal," he said, softly. "Everyone could be like Annie and me—"

"*No,*" Annie said, flatly. "There is a . . . difference. Some . . . differences . . . but I can't tell . . . with this—"

She meant the band, the hated band that encircled her temples.

"Well, *are* we different or aren't we?" Elliot demanded, turning around with the towel in his hands.

"We're the same . . . but different from some . . . and *they* are different from . . . another . . ." Words were failing her again, and he wasn't surprised. They obviously needed a whole new vocabulary for this.

"You mean there are *kinds* of Omega? Different *varieties* of Omega?"

She raised her hands helplessly. "Different . . . noises . . . yes. But you . . . something else I don't . . . understand."

"What do you mean, I'm 'something else'?"

"I don't . . . *know*," she wailed, tears forming in her eyes and running down over her cheeks.

He dropped the towel and came over to kneel beside her. "I'm sorry, Annie. Don't cry, please. It's just that—" she stared at him, the golden-amber depths of her eyes making him feel as if he were drowning, sinking, losing himself over and over again in some kind of strange and alien sea of light. He looked down at his own hands gripping the arm of the rocker. "It's just that *I* don't understand either. And I want to. I need to."

Hawkins watched as Annie hesitantly raised her hand to touch Elliot as softly as a moth, to touch his head and smooth the strands of grey-brown hair back from his temple. All the way, he thought, they've gone all the way and they don't even know it yet. It seemed that if he could get out of there, they might—but he couldn't think of a way to remove himself without distracting them, so he sat still and wished he could stop watching. A little ability for teleportation would be a handy thing to have right now, he decided. I don't belong here.

Elliot stood up abruptly, and if he saw her hand jerk back to rest in her lap he gave no indication of it. "Anyway, you're right, Longjohn. We'll have to start running everyone through the mill tomorrow. And we'll have to see if we can work out some kind of bio-feedback apparatus that Annie can use to control this thing." He walked towards his desk, then turned. "Also, if she's right, and there are kinds or degrees of Omega, it stands to reason that the place to look is in some of the psychics we've had through here over the years, right?"

"Yes, that seems reasonable enough," Longjohn conceded, carefully keeping his eyes away from Annie while she recovered from Elliot's sudden rejection of her, or what she probably saw as rejection, damn it. "Yes, that seems very reasonable. I'll get Danny to start programming Algernon tomorrow."

"Yes. Yes." Elliot suddenly looked relieved. "You see, if we can find *others,* then they wouldn't have to use Annie for their dirty work."

"I . . . don't mind . . ." Annie started to say.

"Well, I mind. I don't want them using you, Annie. I'm damned if I'll let them use you."

That's better, Longjohn approved silently, seeing the glow come into Annie's eyes again. That's better, Elliot, you dumb cluck.

"I can think of better things for *you* to do," Elliot continued. "More important than finding out yesterday's code."

Oh, hell, Longjohn despaired. "What he means, Annie . . ."

"I . . . know what . . . Philip means . . . Longjohn. Thank you." And she turned her golden eyes onto him, shrinking him down to six inches of adolescence. I am out of my league, he acknowledged. Band or no band, the lady is way ahead of me. And she's very very lonely out there.

Elliot left at about seven that night, but returned some time near midnight to a dark and empty building. Empty, except for the guards and Annie. He was relieved to see a line of light under her door, and tapped gently.

"Who?" came her voice, startled, frightened.

"It's Philip, Annie. I have to talk to you. May I come in?"

"Yes . . . come."

He opened the door and nearly shut it again. She was sitting up in bed wearing a lacy nightgown that hid everything that needed to be hidden, and was for that reason all the more revealing. He had never understood how women's clothes could do that.

"You'd better put on a dressing gown or something," he muttered, handing her what looked like one from the chair. She wrapped it around her shoulders with some amusement, while he settled himself gingerly on the end of the bed.

"Annie, I need your help."

Her face suddenly shadowed. "You . . . want me . . . heal . . . Omega?"

The possibility had never occurred to him, and for a moment he was thrown off his original intention. "No. Could you?"

"Not . . . with hands."

"Ah." He nodded. "Well, anyway, thank you for thinking of it." He made a wry face at her. "I don't really know how to put this," he confessed.

"Just say," she directed him calmly, and he felt as unhinged as a boy by her strange gravity. It was always catching him unexpectedly. In its way it was as distracting as those casserole recipes he used to get from ordinary women.

"When I went in to see Mr. Curtiss—I told you about him . . ." she nodded encouragingly, "well, he knew a great deal about you that he had no right to know. Things he could have known *only* if he'd been told by someone here at Talbot Hall. Someone who had no right to tell him. Do you understand?"

"Traitor."

"Oh, nothing as dramatic as that. Just someone who can't be trusted, that's all. Now, it could have been Cragg getting lucky and putting a lot of things together. It could have been."

"No."

He made another face, unaware of how appealing she found it to see him so perplexed, twisting his mouth that wry way. "No, probably not." He looked around the room, suddenly seeing it as she must have. So stark and bare, all the more so because of the small vases of flowers she had put out and the open rack that held the few items of clothing she had acquired. He cleared his throat. "When you get control of Omega, if you do, do you think you could find out who it is for me?"

"You . . . can't?"

He shook his head, miserably. "It's all gone, Annie. I don't care if you can hear it or not, *I* can't hear anything. It's worse than going deaf in a way because . . ."

"Because . . . so much more . . . lost . . . than ordinary. Band . . . the same . . . only . . . *grey* . . . words."

Staring at her, he gradually realized just what bringing her to Talbot and confining her in this room night after lonely night had been like. He had been so concerned about easing her pain that he had not considered what else he was taking from her. Now that he could no longer use his own power, he knew. This cheerless sterile room, this "cage," in addition to everything else—no wonder she never smiled, never laughed, seemed so bitter now. He made a sudden decision.

"Annie, get dressed. I'm taking you home with me."

"Why?" She was astonished.

He had so many answers, suddenly, that he could not sort them out. Most of them he couldn't admit, especially to her. "Because, this is a lousy place for you to live. It's just one big . . ."

"Zoo."

Had it been that bad, then? He suddenly saw that it had, and felt like kicking himself. Bad enough to be deaf now, worse to be blind, especially to her.

"You can have my bedroom. It's screened like this one, only permanently. I can move into my lab. It doesn't matter where I sleep now. It's not a very beautiful house, but it's better than this, God knows. I don't know why I didn't think of it before." He knew very well, and it was still a bad idea for the same reasons, but he could not bear the thought of her trapped in this white sterile place a minute longer. "I have a case in my office—you can bring your things in that." He got up, being as firm and practical about it as he could manage. "Can you cook?"

"Don't know."

"Never mind, neither can I, but I haven't starved so far. We'll manage." He grinned, suddenly. "We can toss for who does the washing up."

"Toss?"

"It's a—just get dressed. I'll be right back." They could talk about the informant later, when he had taken her away from this specimen box of a room.

Joseph thought she was the greatest thing since sliced sardines.

"What's his name?" she asked, stroking his back while Elliot watched.

"Joseph."

"Funny . . . name . . . for a cat."

"His coat of many colours. It's from the Bible." It did sound a little silly when he said it out loud, he decided.

She inspected the house from end to end while he moved his things out of half the wardrobe and cleared some drawers in the chest for her. She opened every cupboard, gazed long at every painting, read every title on the bookshelves, poked curiously at the knobs and controls of his elaborate stereo system, kicked off her shoes to wriggle her toes in the carpet, and seemed to hold a steady communion with Joseph who followed close on her heels the entire time, purring with proprietary contentment. Hate to see you go, Joe, Elliot smiled to himself when the cat ignored him for the tenth time.

"It's . . . a perfect house . . . Philip. Thank you."

He paused, his arms full of shirts. "Well, I suppose you'll want to make some changes. You do whatever you like, I don't mind."

"What . . . change? What's . . . wrong?"

"You don't think it's . . . ?"

But she was shaking her head emphatically. "Nothing . . . wrong. Oh, yes . . ."

"What?"

"Need . . . new jar . . . of bay leaves. Need to buy . . . butter."

And that was how he learned that Annie had not wasted her time at Talbot Hall. While they had been absorbed in her tests and her brain structure, she had spent her free time talking to the cook in the kitchens. While they had been writing reports and feeding facts to Algernon and the other computers, she had been asking the maintenance man about plumbing and washing windows. In between texts on algebra and geography, she had perused *Vogue, House & Garden, Motor,* and *Which?* She had been wide open to every kind of information and had absorbed it all, without pause, totally curious. The delightful thing as far as he was concerned was that Annie reading was one thing, Annie experiencing was another. She could probably have told him how to get ten more miles to every gallon from his car because she had read about it, but the sensation of speeding through the dark country lanes on their way home had been new and exhilarating for her. The learned child he had rescued was not quite the helpless refugee he had thought. She was a visitor from another planet, come to stay.

The only thing that baffled her was the stereo system. After an hour's questioning, he had discovered the full extent of her accumulated knowledge and was reasonably sure she could probably take it apart and put it back together again. She clearly understood its structure and its function. But she didn't know what it could do.

"Tapes . . . like Algernon . . . your work?"

"No, Annie. For music. Listening to music." Then he saw that there was actually something he *could* give her that she had never known before. Nowhere in Talbot Hall was there even a transistor radio because the electronic equipment set up too much interference. Her one trip into town had led to the burning out of the band, so she had never gone back. Everything had been brought to her from outside. Everything, no matter how new, had been second-hand for Annie.

He went over to the long rack of tapes and selected one. In his solitude Elliot fed on music, every kind of music. He needed it as much as food and air, it was the main reason this house had been his special haven. It was always filled with music, and so had needed no other decoration. To welcome Annie, he chose what was to him the purest, clearest, most triumphant definition of hope ever composed.

After the first few bars she dropped to her knees on the hearthrug, amazed. "What *is* it?"

"It's called a symphony. It was written by a man called Vaughan Williams. They don't have names too often, mostly numbers. This is his Fifth."

"But . . . it tastes . . . blue . . . green . . . see them . . ."

"Can you? It wouldn't surprise me," he said softly, smiling at her rapt expression. Synaesthesia was the technical term for it, and the way her head was put together made it quite possible, he conceded. The composer Alexander Scriabin had been the same—sounds always had colours for him. For others they might have textures, flavours, all kinds of things. When the strings began their accelerating run up to the trumpet top note and beyond to the exultation of the first climax, she shivered.

"It . . . like . . . running . . . in skygold . . . free."

"Is it?" He sat down on the edge of the big chair and watched her. The small high-boned face was tilted back, and with her eyes closed she was unaware that his absorption in her was as great as hers in the music. She laughed when the brass blatted derisively in the second movement, wept when the theme of the third finally rose clear and complete, sighed when the final notes of the fourth whispered away into silence. She was the only person other than himself that he had ever seen simply *listen* without feeling compelled to comment. When it was over she turned to him, shining.

"Is every . . . music . . . so?"

He chuckled. "Oh, no, there are all kinds."

"Put . . . on . . . all . . . hear . . . everything."

"It would take you days . . ."

"Yes . . . *please,* Philip . . . Days . . . and days."

Annie listened to Sibelius—"silver lemons"; to the sensual tenor sax of Paul Desmond—"slippery red"; to Bach and more Bach—"Algernon laughing."

Towards morning, while Elliot was replacing Woody Herman with Ravel's *Tombeau de Couperin,* he again brought up the subject that had taken him back to Talbot earlier that night.

"Annie—about what I asked you to do . . ."

She was in a haze of satiety, the glow of her eyes softened and unfocused, the music still running through her. It occurred to him, not for the first time in the past few hours, that even without having touched her he now knew how she would look after making love. It took several attempts before he could get the cassette into the opening. "If you don't want to do it—don't. I understand it might be . . ."

"Don't . . . mind . . . If good . . . better for you."

He was not even sure why he wanted to know who had let the secret out, since whoever had done it might well have had prior loyalties, and theoretically he himself should have been the one to report his discovery.

He stared down at the switch that activated the playthrough. "If we do manage to give you control over Omega without your band, there's something else I want to say. It's very important, Annie."

"Yes?"

"You are never, never, *ever* to come into my head without

my permission. Do you understand? I want you to promise me that you won't."

"Not . . . hurt you . . . Philip."

"It's not that. Just take it as a . . . ."

"Why . . . hiding? Afraid . . . of *me?* Couldn't find . . . anything . . . to make . . . unlike . . . in your head . . . never."

Even limited by what she called the "grey" words, her concern for him came across, and he was grateful for it. He realized she simply meant that whatever she found out about things he had done, whatever animal drives or fears or hungers rose from the miasmic swamp of his unconscious, she would understand it was no more than the filth that accumulates in anyone's mental filtration system. He was not worried about that, either; what was there was there, he could do nothing about it. Everyone was the same. What he had to hide was his own vulnerability, his own fear of not being loved where he had finally come to love. He admitted it humbly to himself. He loved her, but it would place too much of an obligation on her if she discovered it. If she responded with love, he could never be sure, in his mental deafness, whether it was anything else *but* obligation. The possibility was unbearable. Loneliness was better; it had to be. It was a strange reversal, he acknowledged, to be a man and to fear penetration. Was this how they felt, women on their backs? No wonder it was always such a struggle to make them trust you enough to let you in, or want you enough to disregard what was ultimately, even in the deepest love, a violation of their own sense of entity.

"It's not that, Annie. It would simply confuse matters. I'd find it very hard to exert my authority when all the while you knew about the time I stole a fiver from my father's wallet," he said lightly.

"Did you?"

He pushed down the switch and watched the tape begin to unwind beneath the clear plastic cover. "Did I what?"

"Steal . . . a fiver."

He turned to regard her warily. She was smiling impishly at him from the hearthrug, Joseph asleep in a circle on her stomach. "Oh, sure. Lots of them. I was a really awful child."

"No . . . Can see you . . . very serious . . . very solemn? . . . Wanting to be . . . doctor . . . reading . . . dreaming."

Tempted to counter her image with the truth—that he had broken his own nose and several others on the rugby field by the time he was fourteen and had been generally considered to have the foulest mouth in the school, he suddenly decided he preferred her version of things.

"Ah, yes, I was a sweet boy."

Never in his wildest imaginings had he dreamt she could laugh like that, jolting Joseph into wakefulness and getting his claws into her skin as her reward. "Ouch . . . wicked boy," and more laughter, lifting the cat away and putting him unceremoniously onto the floor beside her. Elliot wasn't sure if she meant him or Joseph, they were both equally chagrined at her merriment. "Liar . . . liar," she finally managed, clarifying things.

"I *told* you not to read my . . ." he began, hotly, forgetting the band.

"No . . . no . . . fingers . . . fingers," she pointed, her hoots of joy descending into giggles. He looked down. Automatically, as every good child should, he had crossed his fingers while telling a lie. Do we never grow up, he wondered, flushing, and then looked at Annie who was wiping her eyes and reaching again for a hold on Joseph. If she was very very lucky, maybe *she* never would. He hoped not. He hoped he would never see Annie's magic disappear.

When he walked into his office the next morning, Longjohn was waiting.

"Bloody hell, Phil—we thought she'd run away or something! I was just about to call the cops when I saw you drive up. Where did you take her?"

"If you'd looked in the logbook you'd have seen where I took her. Home, with me." He exchanged his jacket for the pullover hanging from the back of the door, and emerged from the neck to see Longjohn grinning.

"Oh?"

The grin irritated Elliot. "What do you mean, 'Oh'?" He went over to the percolator and felt the glass, then crouched down muttering to pull the coffee can from the cupboard.

"Nothing. Just—oh."

Elliot glanced up from measuring the grounds into the filter. "She was unhappy here. It's an awful place to be, day after day."

"Night after night."

Elliot put the coffee can down with a clatter. "No, Longjohn. *No.*"

"No?"

"No. I told you my bedroom was built with screening in the walls. I'm sleeping in my lab on a camp bed and she's sleeping in my bedroom. With Joseph." He pushed the lid down onto the can. *"Just Joseph."*

"And you expect me to believe that?"

"As a matter of fact I do."

Longjohn looked into Elliot's face and decided he did believe it, after all. But he didn't think anyone else would, and said so.

"You know, for a scientific establishment we get more like Peyton Place every day," was Elliot's exasperated response.

"I can't help the conclusions other people will leap to," Longjohn said mildly. "She's turned into a pretty girl, and you're not married and you're not queer. What else would they think?"

"They can think what they damn well like, as far as I'm concerned."

"What about as far as she's concerned?"

Elliot switched on the coil under the percolator and returned the coffee can to the cupboard. "I don't think it matters to her one way or another."

"Then you're an idiot."

"Okay, I'm an idiot, and we've got a lot to do so let's get off this rather irrelevant subject and onto how we're going to get things organized." He went over to the filing cabinet and began going through the first drawer, pulling a folder out every now and again, stacking them haphazardly on the top. He paused, momentarily, a red-stickered file suspended over the rest. "Have you ever listened to Stockhausen?"

"Who?"

"Stockhausen."

"The composer?"

"Mmmmmm." Elliot extracted two more folders.

"Once, I think. Why?"

"Did you like it, his music?"

"Not particularly. Too . . . angry."

"That's what she said. Too angry—and strangled."

"Annie? She's a music critic, now?"

"Among other things." Elliot smiled to himself, closing the drawer and opening the one underneath it. "Among other things."

Elliot sat on the edge of his desk and looked around the room. Longjohn, Ted, Danny, Janet, George, Frances, and Annie looked back at him.

"Okay. I'm pulling you all off whatever else you're doing for the moment and we're going to concentrate on two things only. First of all, I want George and Frances to work out a bio-feedback rig that Annie can use to control her Omega waves. She seems to think it's simple." He hesitated. "It also seems she knows more about it than I do, so maybe she's right. She'll work with you on building it."

Frances smiled across at Annie, and Annie smiled back. "We've already made a start," Frances told him. "I'm not *quite* as optimistic as she is, but maybe."

Elliot rubbed his face, then said, wearily, "Nobody ever tells me anything these days. I *thought* I was in charge, here."

"I broke my fountain pen, yesterday," Janet offered.

"There's a bird's nest in the gutter over my office," Longjohn added.

"I soldered forty-six connections yesterday before lunch," George told him. "And Algernon's busted a sprocket on his left—"

"All right . . . all *right!*" Elliot laughed. He looked around at them again, and his amusement faded. They sensed something had changed, and settled, waiting. "We've all worked together for a very long time here at Talbot, and it's all been very nice and very friendly and very pleasant. Now, it's not going to be so pleasant any more."

He got up and began to walk around the room, his hands deep in his trouser pockets, his head down. "Theoretically, we all knew that we were working for the Government, but we all assumed that was just another way of getting someone else to pay for our own individual research. It wasn't, because we aren't as easy to categorize as ingrown toenail research, for example . . ." He trailed off, banging a fist gently against the side of the filing cabinet. Bang. "The Pentagon, the Kremlin . . ." Bang. "They've all got Talbot Halls." Bang. "Compared to them we're small-time—even in this country we're an indulged fringe operation because we're considered too crazy to count. Conversely, we're also considered too dangerous to leave in the realm of pure medicine. As a result, as in Russia and America, we come under 'Defence' and then under 'Intelligence.' Not because of what we're working on, but because of what the enemy is doing in the same field. All right?" Bang. "Now, we might have gone on forever just as we were, but *I* made a mistake." He left the filing cabinet and went over to the potted plants that lined the shelves of the room divider, looking closely at them one by one.

"When I found Annie and brought her here, I had no

intention of doing anything other than helping her find a way out of her pain. Then, maybe, with her permission—finding out more about that pain. One by one you've learned about Annie, about what she is, about what we've discovered." He plucked a dead leaf off the grape ivy and laid it carefully on the shelf beside the pot. "Unfortunately, our employers have found out, too. They want to use Annie. They want to use her —as a weapon, I suppose. That's a nice euphemistic way of putting it. As a weapon."

"Ready, aim, fire," Annie said, unexpectedly, startling them all. "Boom!" she added, and grinned.

"Shut up, Annie," Elliot said absently. That startled them too, and a few eyebrows went up. "It isn't really funny, I'm afraid," he went on, finding another brown leaf on the ivy and struggling with it. "Annie thinks it's funny because Annie has never met the people we work for. Some of you have." One of you certainly has, he added to himself, finally breaking off the leaf and putting it down beside the first. "They have made the options clear. Either we supply what they require, or they'll close Talbot down for good. Maybe you think that makes it a simple choice between this job and working somewhere else. I think it's more important and complex than that. I think it's a choice between whether you think the development of Omega is vital enough to go whoring for it, or whether you'd rather preserve your scientific virtue intact. It's up to you. I've made my decision and Annie has made hers. If you want out, this is the time to go."

He waited for a while, then picked up the two leaves and carried them over to his desk, dropping them into the waste-paper basket before sitting down again. When they all continued to stare back at him without commenting, he was surprised to feel a flush spreading across his cheekbones, and ducked his head finally to grin at the blotter. "Well—now we know what we are. I draw the line at black lace Y-fronts, but you may set your own parameters." He found it very difficult not to say thank you, not only because they all stayed where they were, but because no one even made any comments on the entire question. He had not realized their loyalty went that deep, but on the other hand, thank you would be unprofessional. They would not expect to be thanked; just informed. He took a breath, held it, let it out.

"So." Lighting a cigarette helped. "Annie, who I discover is a veritable fund of information these days, has now seen fit to inform us that she isn't the only one with Omega. She can, she tells us, hear it humming all over the bloody place. How about it, Annie? Any strong ones here?"

"Danny. Frances. Longjohn. Others . . . not so . . loud."

"Excellent. Then Danny, Frances, and Longjohn are the first we'll put onto Algernon's EEG. Followed by the rest of you, as time permits. I have also pulled out the files on some of the best psychic subjects we've worked with over the years, and I want Danny and Janet to process their EEGs again, this time looking for Omega indications. We'll be bringing them all back in so we can test them fully, once we know *how* to test them. What I'm after, you see, is to develop a group. A group of weapons, if you will, to keep our employers busy and happy and *off our backs*. All right?"

"Weapons to do what?" Danny wanted to know.

"I'm not sure," Elliot admitted. "But it will probably be nasty."

9

For Elliot, the main advantage of the new order of things at Talbot was that Cragg stayed away from them. He remained silent as their requirements escalated, as they requisitioned more equipment, space, and power, apparently held firmly in check from above by Curtiss. But as the equipment flowed in and Elliot's new Omega Group project gained momentum, it became apparent that Talbot Hall's facilities were inadequate. By the end of the first month, they realized they either had to make numerous basic and functional changes or move somewhere else. Finally Curtiss himself came down, rendering Cragg nearly speechless. Elliot couldn't decide whether it was awe or anger; on Cragg they looked much the same.

Curtiss was taken on a tour, flanked by Elliot and Longjohn. Watching them move through the halls, Janet murmured to Frances that they looked like the last three pipes on a church organ. Finally ensconced on the leather chesterfield with a mug of coffee, Curtiss seemed enthusiastic about everything he had seen.

"That cybernetic apparatus," he marvelled. "I still can't believe you weren't pulling a fast one. He *really did* activate that series of relays by *thinking* the orders through the computer?"

"Oh, sure," Longjohn said, stretching his legs out and resting them on the low table. "That's *old* stuff. What we'd like to do is cut out the computer, eventually. We've had two of the recruits show up with very strong telekinetic potential, so far, and there may well be more of them. Trouble is if they're moving things around physically with mental energy it takes their concentration off *why* they're moving them, or what the end result should or might be. It will take a lot of control development. We're trying to find ways of patterning or channelling the various abilities, or setting up two subjects in tandem."

"One to provide the power, one to focus and apply it," Ted amplified from the rocker.

"Incredible," Curtiss murmured. "And this thing about distance?"

"With Omega, distance will never really be a consideration," Elliot said from behind his desk. "We're not working with conventional concepts here—interdimensional, subdimensional, supradimensional, if you like. It's a different frame of reference, even different temporal parameters. *If* we can make it work. We still don't know that."

"When will you know?" Curtiss was quick to ask.

"When we know whether Annie can control Omega without depending on mechanical devices," Ted said.

"Ah, yes, the miracle girl, Annie? That's her name?"

You know damn well that's her name, Elliot said to himself, looking across at Curtiss lounging comfortably next to Longjohn. "Yes," he said, aloud. "Annie."

"And when do I get to meet her? Or did I, somewhere along the line?"

"She's not here," Elliot said. "The method she's using, bio-feedback, like that rig we showed you upstairs, only far more complex, means she must work in total isolation for the time being." She was, in fact, at his house, probably bellowing back at the tenor in *Carmina Burana*—it was her latest hobby. They had found that the bio-feedback would probably work, but it took such a lot out of Annie that she had to limit her sessions each day. George and Frances had taken the components to the house and assembled them in Elliot's lab, forcing him to move his camp bed into a corner and his clothes back into the wardrobe to hang in friendly proximity to Annie's. At least my clothes get to touch her, he thought. "Meanwhile, we're lining up people who show the greatest potential and subjecting them to all kinds of tests and investigations. Then we'll be ready when she is. If she ever is."

"Why so pessimistic?" Curtiss asked.

"Well," Elliot leaned back in his chair and balanced his mug on his knee, "as far as we can tell so far, the ability is probably quite natural, just a matter of practice, like learning to ride a bicycle. That part is easy. But sorting through what a fully functional telepath would pick up, that's hard work. I suppose you could say it's like hearing a full symphony orchestra but only listening to the piccolo. It helps, too, if you know what you're after in the first place, obviously."

"How do you mean?"

Sighing, he leaned his head back against the chair and looked at the ceiling. "All right, let me give you a word. Any word. Candle, say. Instantly, right now, in fact, your head is filled with candles. The smell of them, their heat, their light. *All* the candles you've ever seen in your life. Your first birthday cake, your last trip to church, maybe you once burnt yourself on one, perhaps you fell in love by the light of another, lit your cigarette on another, knocked one over or saw someone else do it, saw boxes of them displayed in shops, and so on, and on. Yes?"

"Yes . . ." Curtiss allowed, hesitantly.

"Ah, but that's not all, you see. While you're thinking your candle thoughts, you're also thinking thousands of other things. The couch is too hard or too soft, you're hungry, your nose itches, why hasn't so-and-so returned your call, what's that noise, where's your wife right now, have you enough in the bank to cover some cheque, on and on and on. Add to that your *unconscious* thoughts, memories you've buried, movements, sensations, emotions, questions, rationalizations, hates, fears, facts, the total physical running of your body and keeping it in balance, and so on. Echoes of echoes of echoes." He took his eyes from the ceiling and turned his chair so that he could face Curtiss directly, leaning forward a little. "Now, tell me, where do I, *if* I had the power to enter the murmuring, roaring, flashing, throbbing, working city of your brain, where do I find the right candle burning? What window is it in, and how do I recognize it when I find it?"

"Good grief," Curtiss said.

"And one last thing," Elliot added carefully. "Do you *want* me to find it or will you try to stop me?"

They stared at one another across the office. "No wonder you want to make some changes," Curtiss finally said. "I don't think I . . ."

"Quite," Elliot said, finishing his coffee.

Longjohn watched Elliot tilting his head back. He had been speaking from experience, he thought, not creating a textbook teaching aid. That's how it was for him, when he could do it. Never mind candles, how the hell did he locate all those *aces*? It can't be very nice, that "city of the brain" he described. It must have a lot of back streets and sewers, cops and criminals, fires and floods, rats and garbage, museums and concert halls, and one hell of a lot of people past and present. We don't need a laboratory, we need a monastery to get this thing together.

"I suppose what I'm asking is that you let me make Talbot Hall into a kind of monastery for the moment," Elliot said, putting his empty mug down onto his blotter and catching Longjohn's startled expression. What did I say, he thought, momentarily, we've talked this all out before, haven't we? He returned his attention to Curtiss. "As you know, our computer came up with a list of some five hundred possible subjects, which we turned over to your people. They came back to *us* with a list of fifteen who would be acceptable in terms of Security. Some day you might tell me if it was blue eyes or left-handedness they objected to. Anyway, if we are eventually able to turn those fifteen people into functioning telepaths for you, I would earnestly suggest that they be allowed to live together, apart from the outside world, at least initially."

"Sounds like a priesthood all right," Curtiss commented disapprovingly.

Elliot ran a hand through his hair. "Not really. You see, you're actually asking me to create 'freaks,' aren't you? Oh, they'll eat and sleep and itch and scratch and sulk and laugh and all the rest of it, just like you and me. But once they're into their power, they'll be very aware of their . . . of being outside the normal world. In addition, they will undoubtedly develop a kind of *Gestalt* among themselves and, if we're not very careful, it might grow into a kind of arrogance. That could be negated somewhat by their being only among equals. Much as a bright child in a class of bright children isn't given the automatic opportunity to shine that he would be in a class of dullards. His or her brightness among equals is not a passport to superiority; he has to succeed on other levels, such as adaptability, honesty, appearance, humour, and so on."

"I suppose it makes sense."

"You might also prefer to know where they all are at any given time. It isn't only enemy minds they'll be able to read. They'll be able to read yours, too."

Curtiss stared at him appalled. "What's *that* supposed to mean?"

"Hmmmmmm?" Elliot looked up from a note he was jotting onto his telephone pad. "Just what I said. Once they develop the power, it's in *their* hands. You can't tell them not to use it with any certainty that they won't. That's why I accepted your high wash-out rate. You'd better be damned sure you're keeping them happy, Curtiss. One of them might get it into his head—if you'll pardon the expression—to tell your wife about some blonde, or the Minister about some expense-sheet irregularities."

"But . . . *no,* we can't have that. Do you realize what the hell you're saying?"

Elliot put his pen down gently, then reconsidered and picked it up again, drawing concentric circles on his blotter. "Well, of course I realize what I'm saying. I'm surprised you hadn't seen it for yourself, Cart."

"Well . . . but *I* thought . . ."

He looked around at them, not flustered, Elliot decided, you could never catch Cart being flustered, but disturbed certainly. "I thought it would be some kind of device—some kind of mechanical device like that needle-electrode helmet you showed me. Something they could turn on and off, under supervision."

"Why should it be something like that?" Longjohn asked curiously. "We're talking about *mental* powers, not the internal combustion engine."

"But all the literature, they're always in screened rooms, wired up . . ."

Ted laughed, comfortably, rocking back and forth. "Screen-rooms are to keep things *out,* not to keep them in. Or to prevent cheating. Anyway, all that was, well . . ."

"Old hat, Cart," Elliot said, kindly. "We're not talking about dribs and drabs of a circle and a star and a rectangle picked up fuzzily and by chance. We're talking about—what's that phrase you always use, Longjohn?"

"The whole schmear," Longjohn said. "Omega is the big one, Mr. Curtiss, the whole power, not a game, and not a stab in the dark. Hiroshima, if you like, *and* all that that implies. You still want to push the button?"

Curtiss blinked behind his glasses for a moment, then reached for his cigarette-case and extracted one, remembering only belatedly to offer it around. He sat there, his cigarette in his hand, staring, until Longjohn leaned forward and lit it for him, breaking his reveries.

"You can't have that, Elliot," he finally said.

"Fine," Elliot said with some relief. "We'll cancel the whole thing before it gets too far."

"No, we can't do that, either. It's too . . . we have to go ahead."

Elliot sank back and watched Curtiss, wishing fervently that he could get inside that smooth blonde head and find an edge to use. Curtiss continued, more firmly.

"No, what you'll have to do, Elliot, you'll have to find either a way to control these people, or a way that we can protect our own side from them. That's what you'll have to do."

"I see," Elliot said, slowly. "And how do you propose we do *that*?"

"My God, man, *I* don't know. What about some kind of reward thing? I read about something like that—some kind of brain stimulation that gives intense pleasure sensations? Better than any . . ."

Longjohn nearly choked on his coffee, and lowered the mug to stare at the man beside him. "Jesus, Mr. Orwell—I hardly recognized you without your moustache."

Curtiss looked at him in bemusement. "What?"

"Cart," Elliot said, shaking his head in despair. "These are *people* we're talking about, not rats. Ordinary people— with something like an extra thumb, perhaps, or a second set of eyes—but people nonetheless. Not stupid people, either. We've found some correlation already between what we've been measuring as IQ and Omega. You aren't going to bribe them with *sweets*, for heaven's sake."

"All right, I can see that was silly. Sorry. Well then, some kind of protective device thing will have to be made."

"Just like that," Ted said.

"I'm afraid so," Cart said, flatly. "Just like that."

Longjohn was stirring his remaining dregs of coffee with a pencil. "And who gets them?"

"What?"

"Who gets these protective devices we're supposed to make? Everybody, or just some bodies?"

"I don't get the—"

"Who gets immunity, Cart? Who will have the right to say, 'Keep out—I know things you can't be told'?" Elliot asked.

There was a pause, and then Curtiss grinned. Elliot had seen that look before and was not happy to see it again. Cart was about to be charming in order to buy time. "Well, *me* for a start. There are at least *two* blondes I don't want Madeline to hear about, thanks very much."

Elliot could grin, too, and have it mean just as little. "Well, before we start working out an allocation rota, why don't we just see if we can make the whole thing a reality, all right? And, if you like, I'll turn our technical people loose on your side of the problem at the same time. When it becomes a question of 'yes' instead of 'maybe,' I'll throw it back in your lap and you can make up your own mind. Again, pardon the expression."

Curtiss took a deep drag on his cigarette. "Fair enough. Fair enough. Meanwhile . . ."

"Meanwhile you'd better get out your little pad and pencil," Elliot said. "I've got a list for you."

A week later, glad to escape the constant noise of hammering, crashing, thumping, and the all-pervasive stink of paint that was now a part of Talbot Hall, Elliot parked his car in the lane outside his house and wondered why it was dark. Annie usually liked to turn the lights on at the first shadows. He had grown used to the glow of a house that was alive, waiting for him to come home and make it complete. He unlocked the front door and stepped inside.

The stereo was on, he could see the dull green glimmer of the radio tuner on the far wall, but there was no music pouring from the speakers. Alarmed, he called out.

"Annie? Where are you? Annie?"

Glancing to his left he saw that there *was* a light on in his laboratory. The curtains must have been drawn. Quickly he hurried across the sitting room and opened the door.

Annie was lying on the floor in front of the bio-feedback rig, the long leads trailing from her head. Joseph looked up from the camp bed where he was sitting, peering at her fallen figure, and mewed plaintively at Elliot.

"Oh, God! Annie!" Elliot breathed, moving across to rip the leads from her head and lift her in his arms. Hardly daring to consider what might have gone wrong, he sat down next to Joseph and held her cradled in his arms. "Annie, darling, Annie!" He rocked her back and forth, smoothing her hair. It curled and feathered round his fingers. The cat mewed again and bumped his head against Elliot's arm, finally extending one paw in the only trick he knew, shake hands before dinner. Impatiently Elliot shook off the tentative touch and Joseph retreated to the far end of the camp bed, his tail flicking in reproach. Elliot pulled her closer to him, still rocking her, seeing the slow regular pulse in her throat, counting her respiration, judging the pallor of her skin, and making all the rest of his diagnostic evaluation automatically, almost subconsciously. He could see what was right, but not what was *wrong*.

His eyes went to the rig and again, automatically, he took in the position of the controls, the settings, the power still humming through the amplifier. Nothing wrong there, either. It was even, he saw, set lower than usual. She stirred slightly in his arms, murmured, and then was silent.

Puzzled, he drew back a little to look down at her. Slowly it dawned on him. He reached up once more to smooth the damp red curls away from her forehead. He'd seen nothing *wrong* because nothing was wrong.

Annie was asleep. She wore no protective band, she was not under sedation. She slept in his arms as deeply and naturally as an exhausted child. It had worked. She was safe.

Joseph mewed again and Elliot glanced at him. "I suppòse you think *you* did it," he choked. The cat just blinked his lime-green eyes. Elliot lowered his head, pulling Annie in against his shoulder, pressing his lips against the warm satin of her throat, whispering her name. She was asleep. She'd never know.

IO

"Okay, Ari, let's run it through again," Longjohn said into the mike, rasing a hand to make a circular gesture through the glass of the control booth. The big red-headed Irishman nodded, and turned towards the other man in the chair opposite, saying something Longjohn couldn't make out through the soundproof double glazing. "Robin, this time I want you to try to freeze the trigger and let Ari try to unlock it if he can."

The other man, a thin fine-boned figure with pepper-and-salt hair cut neatly to his head, smiled to show he understood. Longjohn flicked the mike off for a moment.

"Tuckwell's looking a little tired, Phil, what do you think?"

Elliot had his feet up on the control panel, making notes on the clipboard in his lap. He glanced up briefly, looked through the glass, then turned back down to the board. "He'll do for another run, then we'll let him get some sleep."

"He *is* over sixty, you know."

"And a lot tougher than he looks. Go on."

Shrugging, Longjohn hit the lever to his left and watched as the two men inside the room began to go through their inter-lock countdown, holding up their fingers in sequence so that he could tell how deeply they were going. On a table some six feet in front of them lay a network of simple mechanically triggered relays that went nowhere, simply A to B to C to D. After a moment, he spoke.

"They're in synch. That's faster than last time."

"Who took the lead?"

"Ari."

"You'll have to talk to him—dominance isn't going to get him anything but a headache."

"It's instinctive—damn!" Abruptly the relays clicked over like a series of dominoes, and Tuckwell slumped slightly in his chair, a fine film of perspiration glistening on his high domed forehead. Longjohn switched on the mike.

"That's pretty good, Robin, don't look so defeated. Or is that the Lear in you coming out again?"

The older man smiled before opening his eyes, and lifted his left hand in a two-fingered opinion of Hawkins's comment. Longjohn chuckled. "Okay, you two *Wunderkinder* . . . go have some supper and get some sleep. We've got a new recruit coming in tomorrow and from what I hear, he's nervous as hell. You'll have to hold back for as long as you can on him, *please*, Ari?"

Even through the glass they could hear the bulky man's laughter. "Every head for himself, Hawkins!"

"And yours," Longjohn shouted, releasing the doorlock so the two men could leave the screen-room. He swivelled his chair and looked over at Elliot, who was still writing on the board. "You look a little pooped yourself, buddy."

Elliot nodded, and kept writing.

Hawkins sighed and reached for his own clipboard, writing down the dial settings that had been frozen the moment Ari overcame Robin's lock on the relay trigger, noting the time from his wristwatch. Then he reached for his coffee mug, grunting when he found it empty.

"Where's Annie?"

Elliot shifted in his chair, reaching across to scratch his

shoulder. "She and Frances and Sandy are working with Janet in Room Six, I think. Why?"

"How's Janet doing?"

Elliot raised his head to meet Longjohn's eyes, his own unreadable. "Annie says what she hasn't got in power she's making up for in determination. She's coming along, coming along." He dropped his attention to the clipboard again, turning his pencil around to erase something, and blowing the rubbings away.

Longjohn lit one of the small cigars he had taken to smoking, watching Elliot through the bluish haze he created. "Phil?"

"Mmmmm?"

"When are you going to let us open you up?"

The pencil stopped, then hurried on again over the paper, filling in the spaces. "No rush. We've got plenty to work with for the moment. You need me out here, not in there."

"But *they* need you in there more."

"Rubbish."

"Annie says they need you in there, Phil. They haven't got a focus, she said."

"Oh?" Elliot sighed and laid the clipboard on the panel. "When did she say that?"

"She's *been* saying it for months."

"Not to me, she hasn't."

Maybe not so you could hear it, Longjohn thought, watching as Elliot rubbed his face wearily. He himself was avoiding the opening-up process because it involved such a complete loss of privacy. The thought of another mind totally inhabiting his, even for only a few minutes, made his skin crawl. That it was as impersonal as a surgeon's knife as far as the operating telepath was concerned made no difference. He knew, also, that after the Omega function was activated (a process Annie had described as roughly equivalent to a light coming on in a dark room and an exclamation of, "Oh, why didn't I see that before?"), the members of the Group went to scrupulous lengths never to intrude on one another. Ostensibly there was no privacy between them, but they always sought permission before entering with a kind of coded mental knock at the door, or performed the mental equivalent of averting their eyes and ears should someone else's mental exchange be in danger of being "overheard." They simply "looked at" the one they wanted to hear, and tried to ignore all the rest. But it wasn't easy, and the sensation was rather like being trapped at a crowded party that never ended, where everyone was talking at once.

Sometimes they collapsed with the effort, and many of them used the bands or drugs to seek the peace they could not gain otherwise. Indeed, barbiturate addiction had already threatened a few, and would probably increase unless they found another way out of the mess they'd voluntarily gotten themselves into. What puzzled him was that Annie kept insisting that Elliot *knew* a way out, but wouldn't share it. She thought he was testing them, still.

The only thing that was keeping them all sane, apparently, was a kind of euphoric pleasure in the exercise of their Omega powers, and an abiding sense of humour—the black, often cruel and defensive humour occasionally found in hospital wards for the physically disabled. There were personality clashes and arguments, but they were within the Group. Like a family, they could attack one another, but woe betide a critical outsider. Stubbornly, Elliot remained such an outsider, and not even Annie could convince him or lure him or help him to "change his mind."

"How is it with the two of you?" Longjohn asked, noting Elliot's drawn features and the increased grey in his hair.

"What do you mean, 'with us'? How should it be? The same as always."

"Why hasn't she moved into Talbot with the rest of them? How come she's still living at your place with you? Or should I draw the obvious conclusion?"

Elliot glanced at him in annoyance. "If you're asking

whether we're sleeping together, the answer is no. I suggested she move here, but she says she's happier 'at home'—from which you can deduce what you damn well like."

"All right, all right, no need to bare your teeth," Longjohn said mildly.

Elliot shrugged. "She and Joseph have a very intense thing going on. She doesn't want to leave him and she doesn't want to bring him here, either. I think she's trying to develop his Omega, but all she gets is the smell of salmon." He smiled, briefly. "A *strong* smell of salmon."

"I see. Nothing to do with you, then."

"Nothing at all to do with me." Elliot stood up, glancing at his watch. "I'm just the man who takes out the empty cat-food tins."

"Oh." Hawkins tapped the ash from his cigar. He had never known Elliot to be so strung-out. He had always been open and ready to laugh at himself. No more. Lately, he was irascible and defensive, refusing to face what to Hawkins seemed pathetically obvious—that he wanted Annie. Why he hadn't done anything about it was inexplicable to Hawkins, because Elliot had never before been reluctant to bed a woman. Far from it. But Annie, apparently, was untouchable. It was almost as if Elliot could not believe she could ever care for him, or that he feared her refusal so greatly he wouldn't even risk asking the question. "Just a nice father and daughter relationship, is that it?" Longjohn suggested lightly, and then actually drew back when he saw the warning in Elliot's eyes. He was about to be hit. "Joke, joke . . . ha, ha," he said quickly.

"Stay out of it," Elliot rasped. "Just keep your damn psychological rubbish off my doorstep, all right?"

"Forget I spoke."

Elliot grunted and turned away. "I'll try. Is that the last of the work for today?"

"The last formal work, yes." Longjohn tried to ease the

tension that had suddenly flared out of control. "God knows what they'll be trying out after dinner. Two nights ago I found four of them in the library playing bridge for money."

"So? What's wrong with that?" Elliot paused at the door. Longohn grinned. "No cards."

Elliot allowed himself a soft apology of laughter, then went out, raising his hand in a vague farewell. As he went down the hall he saw Annie, Sandy, and Janet coming towards him, laughing. It was an eerie sight they'd all grown used to— people conversing silently but reacting audibly to the inner exchange of images and words. All the non-Group staff were now required to wear bands so as not to overwhelm the telepaths with extra input. Those who did not know the true situation were simply told that it was a protection against a new kind of electronic equipment being tested. Those who did know the nature of the Group wore them gladly, for their protection was two-way, and it eased their relationships with the telepaths.

George Lomax, however, had no compunction about expressing his feelings. He'd taken to calling the place "Zombie Manor" in great disgust, and insisted that Frances talk to him *out loud*. He would become infuriated when she used Omega kinetics to bring a screwdriver or a wiring diagram from the other side of the room, instead of having to fetch it as he did. At least once a day you could hear him shouting, "A man could get killed like that, Frances!" as yet another piece of equipment sailed uncomfortably close to his head on its way to her. She would just look at him sadly from behind her granny glasses, hiding her feelings along with everything else. George was another one, like Longjohn, who had refused what he contemptuously referred to as "high-voltage conversion," although his Omega potential was excellent. Elliot's rule prevailed—nobody should be forced to join the Group, no matter how promising. Including himself.

"Evening, ladies," Elliot said, as the trio of women drew

closer. Automatically they raised their eyes, but there was a split-second pause while they altered their telepathetic greeting to a verbal one.

"I built a tree . . . all on my own," Janet said gleefully.

"How big?" Elliot challenged.

"Three feet, two and a quarter inches."

"Very good," he said, approvingly. "Very good indeed."

"She was *trying* to build a horse," Sandy said, wryly.

"Big mares from little acorns grow." Elliot smiled, then looked at Annie. "Do you want to drive home with me or are you staying on?"

She smiled. "I'll come now," she said. "I'm absolutely pooped."

The other two suddenly laughed, and he knew that she had accompanied her words with an overlay of visual images to them. "Fine," he said. "Get your coat and we'll go."

The phone was ringing in the house as they drew up, and Elliot rushed in to answer it, afraid as always that something had gone wrong at Talbot five minutes after he left.

"Elliot? Cart Curtiss."

Annie came in slowly and raised an eyebrow at him. He mouthed the name "Curtiss" at her while shrugging off his coat and settling himself on the edge of the table.

"Yes? Why call me here?"

"Listen, have you got anybody ready, anybody you can really trust? *Really* trust?"

"What do you mean, *really* trust?" Elliott said with some misgivings.

"To read who they're asked to read and *nobody* else?"

"I can trust them all," Elliot said tersely, angry at having the whole thing suddenly put on a personal basis. "You should put the request through the way we—"

"No, listen, *listen,* will you? This is . . . separate. I really need your help now, Phil. I've been doing a lot of giving lately. Now I want some back. For *me.*"

Elliot sighed. He didn't need any of Danny and Ari's clairvoyant ability to have predicted this kind of request. The minute anyone knew . . . "Spell it out."

"I'm giving a party on Saturday, a really big do, the way Madeline likes to splash out . . . remember?"

"I remember," Elliot said, patiently.

"There's going to be a man there, I won't tell you his name yet, but he knows something I badly need to know before anyone else at the Ministry knows."

"We agreed no politics."

There was a silence from the other end of the line, broken only by the susurrus of Curtiss's breathing and the slow ticking of a clock in the background. That meant he was at home; Elliot remembered the massive ebony longcase clock in Curtiss's study. "Don't make things difficult," Cart said, softly. "This isn't big, it isn't important to the world, it doesn't matter a damn to anybody but me. It's only a small piece of information . . if they're anything like you say they are, it will be a snap for them. Just a date and a name, nothing else, a date and a name. That's all I want."

"Or else what?"

Again, the silence. And again, the soft voice. "There are so many 'or elses' I hardly know which to choose. I started it and I can stop it, simple as that. You don't want to stop now, do you?"

Elliot took a savage kick at the table leg, making Joseph, who had come over to say hello, jump back in alarm. Annie walked slowly across and picked up the ruffled cat, holding him to her and rubbing beneath his chin while she watched the play of emotions on Elliot's face, none of them happy.

"What time does this party of yours start?" he finally said.

"I appreciate this. Eight o'clock. Formal dress."

"And who is the man?"

"I'll point him out when you arrive."

"Very well." He hung up without saying goodbye, staring down at the phone as if it had bitten him. After a while he became aware of the patient regard of two pairs of eyes, one amber-gold, one lime-green, and reached over to scratch an apology between Joseph's ears. Briefly he told Annie what Curtiss had asked him to do.

"Lovely . . . lovely. Party, Joseph," she said into one of the cat's ears, making it flick back. Elliot looked at her stonily.

"Party Philip, party maybe Robin, not party Annie," he said, mocking her gently.

Her face went very still, very quiet. "Party *Annie*, Dr. Elliot," she said just as stonily. After a moment he had the grace to laugh, just a little.

"No, Annie, really. We'll just be in and out and it won't be particularly pleasant. There will be lots of people there and lots of noise. Madeline Curtiss's parties are the most dreadful . . ." She was not convinced, he realized. He thought he knew why. Longjohn had put it succinctly enough. "Annie, in addition to Omega, has a fine mind. She's highly intelligent and insatiably curious. Intellectually she can appreciate that that makes her special, and she enoys her mind. But Annie doesn't really *want* to be special. Annie's deepest emotional need is to be ordinary. Her greatest dream, whether she consciously realizes it or not, is to be *exactly* like every other woman. While she wants to help us, all her struggles to conquer Omega have really been directed towards that end—to make herself acceptable as a woman and to have her acceptability demonstrated. After twenty-four years of ostracism and rejection I don't think I'd be much different."

Several times in the past few weeks he had caught her mooning over the glamorous autumn collections in *Vogue* and *Harper's*. Now Annie, quite simply, wanted a new dress and somewhere to show it off. He regarded her, amused at the defiant set of her features and the stiffness of her spine. "I see," he said, seeing too much. "Annie, you have never been in a room with more than ten people at one time. Never. And these are sophisticated people, they're . . ."

"Ashamed."

Oh God, he remonstrated with himself, have you forgotten everything about handling a woman? "Annie, no man would *ever* be ashamed of you," he said gently. "I simply meant that they'd overwhelm you, not because they're so marvellous or anything like it, simply that there will be so many of them, and few would be what I would term 'nice' in the emotional sense of the word. Cart's parties are full of people in power, people who are used to money or position, people who—"

"Zoo games," she interrupted. "Robin . . . Ari . . . Sandy . . . James . . . Brian . . . I know . . . zoo games, Philip."

"What do you mean . . . 'zoo games'?"

She turned away for a moment, then turned back, her face entirely altered. "Why, Mrs. Paddington-Smythe, how *charming* you look, I've *always* loved you in that dress, and how is your adorable daughter, still seeing that *sweet* Freddy Appleton? Isn't he the one who had all that *amusing* fuss with the police about the cannabis resin in his underpants? Such fun, didn't you know? We all nearly died laughing . . . Well, hello, Commander Barclay, and how are all those sailors of yours? *Bonjour, matelot* . . . and Mr. Cuthbertson . . . Wasn't that your wife I saw in Asprey's the other morning? Do you know, for a moment I could have sworn she was *selling* that brooch rather than buying it . . . isn't that *ridiculous?*"

Elliot stared at her in amazement. "Annie," he said weakly, watching her circle the room gracefully, speaking to all kinds of invisible victims.

Suddenly she turned on him and advanced. "I *know* zoo games, Philip. Group . . . shares . . . Group . . . blends . . . all experience . . . one experience . . . all together. *Annie* party. Annie party with *you*, Philip. *Not* afraid."

He had to admit that Annie was a smash hit in Eaton Square.

The new dress flowed over her like the shallows of the Aegean Sea in August, her hair was a cap of fox-red magic, her eyes glowed with amber fire. She made all the men her slaves. The women were less susceptible, eyeing her with guarded speculation, some of them trying to make her look and feel out of place. When that happened she simply moved away with a smile and left them steeping in their own gall.

Elliot took advantage of the opportunity to renew some old acquaintances and mend some social fences, avoiding the eyes of a few ladies who had made him jump hurdles of their own devising, long ago. They were the ones who gave Annie the most difficulty, and the worst of them was, not surprisingly, Madeline Curtiss herself. As sleek and beautiful as ever, Elliot had to admit, but his approval went only skin-deep. He greeted her, said the proper things with the proper smile, and removed Annie from her vicinity. The second time he was forced to do this, he noticed Madeline suddenly put a hand to her head and wince.

"What did you do?" he asked Annie, when they were out of earshot.

"Do?" Annie asked, innocently.

"Just now, to Madeline?"

"Nothing."

"Annie . . ." he said, warningly.

"She's not a nice lady," Annie said with disdain. "I let her know what I thought of her, that's all." Her tone was totally unrepentant.

"That's breaking the rules, Annie."

She looked up at him, her eyes oddly bright. "You broke them first," she said, and walked away before he could answer. She'd been like that all evening, arch and elusive, slipping away from him at every turn. It had started a few moments after their arrival.

"So *this* is Annie?" Cart had said with gallant amazement at the door, leading both of them to one side of the long hall and taking in her appearance with an appreciative smile. It was something he did very well.

"Annie, may I present Carter Hooks Curtiss," Elliot said, and only the flesh of his arm beneath her grasp told him how she fared; he could feel her nails right through the heavy broadcloth of his dinner jacket.

"Suddenly some of the things I've been hearing recently fall into place, Phil," Cart murmured.

"Oh?" Elliot asked, coldly.

"You have a lovely home, Mr. Curtiss." Annie's voice was soft. "Isn't that a Correggio on the far wall?"

His look followed hers. "Ah, yes, some of the benefice from my wife's ancestors. Your eyes are very acute. And unusually beautiful, may I add?"

She smiled at him. "Add as much as you like, Mr. Curtiss—I'm never averse to flattery from *any* source." Elliot managed not to smile.

"If you'll point out who you want and tell us what you want to know, we'll get on with it, Cart," he put in, brusquely. "We'd like to get it over with, if you don't mind."

"Of course." Curtiss briefly outlined what he needed to know and indicated the man whose head held the knowledge, a rather nondescript octogenarian who leaned heavily on a silver-headed cane while talking to several of Curtiss's minions from the Ministry. "Will you actually need to talk to him?"

"Only for a few minutes. Introduce us, and work the conversation around to the general area you're interested in," Elliot told him. "If his decision is as vital as you say, whatever's worrying him about it should float near enough to the surface for Annie to fish it out. She'll let you know when she's had enough."

"Excellent. Wonderful. Meanwhile," he summoned a butler with a tray of glasses, "do you like champagne, Miss Craigie, or would you prefer something else?"

"Champagne would be perfect," Annie said, taking a glass and smiling over the rim as she sipped. "Particularly *this* champagne."

Elliot allowed Annie her precious hours of proof that she was what she most wanted to appear, but by the time the sumptuous buffet had been reduced to a condition even a ravenous crow would reject, he could see that she had used up the last of her meagre reserves. Her eyes were too glittery and, under the make-up, her skin was pale with fatigue. He rescued her from the clutches of a damp and eager representative of the Foreign Office, drew Curtiss aside briefly to relay the information he had asked for, and firmly conveyed her out of the door and into the fresh night air. She managed to make it back to the car on the far side of the square before she started to shake.

"Philip . . ."

"It's all right, just relax. Here." He reached in and drew a headband out of the glove box, putting an arm around her and easing her into the car. George and Frances had made a small monitoring device and disguised it as a hair ornament, so that Annie could withstand the onslaught of the many raw minds round her at the party. When she had faced the man she was to "read," she'd simply made a pretence of adusting it in her curls, switching it off momentarily, and then replacing it.

Under the extra protection of the band she was asleep within minutes, and Elliot drove back to the house alone with his own reproaches. She stirred when he went over the level crossing in Bourne End, but didn't speak until he had locked the front door behind them and flipped the switch to set the electric kettle grumbling on the kitchen counter. She paced restlessly from kitchen to sitting room and back again, unable to settle or stand still. He watched her from where he was leaning against the refrigerator, wishing his mother had drowned him at birth. She tried to help by getting the teabags out of the cannister and upset the whole lot over the counter.

"Annie, go to bed. We'll talk tomorrow."

"No . . . no . . . I want to tell . . . now."

He sighed. "All right, but sit down, for heaven's sake, before you fall down."

She turned and stood in the middle of the room, the overhead strip light settling a strange mask over her features, throwing her eyes into shadow.

"It was Ted who told him about me." She swallowed and then went on. "Ted works for Mr. Curtiss . . . he . . . has . . . for a long time . . ."

"You went into *Cart's* head?" he asked, appalled. He hadn't noticed her touching the hair ornament when they entered, but she must have. And other times, too.

"Yes. I had to . . . find out . . . for you."

He stared at her, unable to speak, horrified at what she must have encountered. No wonder she was so upset. She forced herself to continue, jerkily, helplessly, spilling it all out for him. "Longjohn said . . . you were . . . too trusting . . . wouldn't face facts."

"If he meant I wouldn't face Curtiss, he's right. I've tried to make sure nobody did. If any of the Group realized the kind of man . . ."

"*Somebody* should realize . . . Longjohn said . . ."

"He had no right to tell you . . . to ask you . . ."

"Didn't ask. Only said. *I* decided. For you. That man . . . Stein?"

Elliot nodded. He had been surprised to see Zal Stein at the party, and had presumed he was another of Madeline's "trophies." A popularizer of things technical, he had been a BBC guru, then had branched out into writing expensively illustrated tomes on science for the masses. Recently he had had a best-seller about ESP research that made it all look one step from the witch's cauldron. The book had made Elliot's blood boil with its glib overstatements and under-verifications. The man's intelligence was unquestioned, but his motives were suspect. The book before the ESP opus had been openly contemptuous of Western scientific methods and goals, which in Stein's opinion were too "hesitant" and narrow-minded, too bound by convention and considerations of safety. That alone should have made him the last man you'd expect to see at the Curtiss party, and yet, there he'd been.

"Curtiss . . . letting him . . . vet? . . . your reports

. . . and Ted's. Stein has . . . very strong Omega potential. Philip . . . *very* strong . . ."

He had noticed Stein trying to charm Annie with his quick white smile, his eager long fingers touching her more and more frequently as he talked. "You mean . . . ?"

She shook her head quickly. "He doesn't . . . know . . . his own . . . mind." She almost smiled. "He's not what he seems . . . not Curtiss, either . . . something else between them . . . bad . . . something together and lying . . . pretending . . ."

He started pacing back and forth, trying to work out what it all meant. Was she trying to say there was some kind of homosexual thing between Curtiss and Stein? Was *that* why Madeline had to seek her sexual partners elsewhere? He'd never suspected it, but perhaps it had been latent . . . He came to an abrupt halt in front of Annie, focusing on how miserable, how tired she looked standing there.

"You don't have to say any more. I'm sorry, Annie, I'm really so sorry." Stupid word, sorry, he told himself, stupid bloody useless word. "You've read the books, you know some men . . ."

She hit her hands against her sides in frustration. "No, *no* . . . not that. Stupid, Philip. Hate . . . I mean . . . *hate*. In Curtiss . . . in Stein . . . mostly Curtiss. Wishes you . . . dead. Hates you so . . ."

"He has his reasons"

"Not just . . . *her*." Her mouth twisted as if Madeline's name was too bitter to put on the tongue. "More . . . after that. Wants to break you . . . physically . . . tear you apart . . . destroy everything . . . you . . . *everything* . . ."

He decided he didn't want to hear any more. "Forget it, Annie. Forget it ever happened. I should have warned you about Cart and me. There's always been a war beween us."

"War . . . yes. Enemies . . . lying to you . . ."

"I should never have taken you there, you weren't ready. Maybe you should go back to Mhourra."

"No! Won't . . . leave you. Too late, now. You did warn . . . how bad . . . you did . . ."

"It can only get worse."

"Animals!"

"Yes, animals. But only little animals. The higher up you go, the more savage they get. Men who rule don't get to the top of the pack by taking bites and nips—they go for the throat and they're full of what you only glimpsed in Cart's head."

"*She* . . . was worse . . ." Annie said, pointedly.

He turned and poured the boiling water into the teapot, watched it swamp then sink the teabags, watching the stain spread. "I'm sorry."

"I'll learn . . . Philip," her voice was becoming desperate now. "Get stronger. *Must* get stronger to help you. Curtiss . . . so much trouble . . . so many bad things . . . Every time he looked at you . . . smiling . . . but inside . . . saw you lying there . . . smashed . . . torn . . . screaming . . ." Her voice broke and her shoulders slumped. He took her in his arms and cradled her head against his shoulder, as one does with any child when the nightmares come. Her breath was ragged, her words half-sobbed.

"Stein didn't want you . . . just to find out . . . planning to tell . . . to tell . . ."

He stroked her hair, her shoulders, the delicate bones of her spine. "No more, Annie. It's over, now."

She was choking it out, he couldn't stop her. "*Not* over . . . only the beginning . . . I won't let him . . . hurt you . . . Philip. I love you. Always loved you. Kill anybody that . . . kill them . . . love you."

He covered her words with his mouth. Her lips trembled, then parted, her fear and torment suddenly forgotten in the urgent response of her body, lifting and arching against him. He felt the hot sweet tip of her tongue touch his and knew he could not hide or pretend any longer. Nor could he stop what was happening. Nothing on earth could have stopped it.

Annie was not a child in his arms any more. She was a woman, and she was his.

They lay on the bed, naked, quiet now that the first frenzy of their hunger had been satisfied, shadows following the lazy tracings of their slow tender fingertips. He lifted himself slightly and moved his head down to her breast, his tongue circling the aureole of her nipple, his lips brushing warm and soft over the silken flesh as his hand cupped the rich weight up to them. "Come into me, Annie," he whispered, moving up to her throat, sliding his fingers into her hair, resting the length of his body against hers. "Come into me."

She drew her breath in like a sob. "I . . . can't . . ."

"Yes . . . yes . . . *yes,*" he insisted, kissing her eyes and tasting salt. "I want all of you . . . I want you to have all of me . . . *all* of me. Not just this . . . but everything—"

"But . . . can't . . . have been . . . always . . . trying . . . trying . . . to reach you . . . touch you . . . but you won't let me . . . in . . ."

"I will . . . it's all right . . . Come into me—" he touched her mouth with his own, the shadow of his head darkening her face, hiding the tears and the wide eyes—"Please . . . come into me . . . now!"

And again, the sound of a sob, her body convulsing against his until he drew away, puzzled, not understanding her anguish. "What is it? Darling . . . little love . . . don't . . . What is it?"

"Can't . . . come in . . . The wall . . . the wall—" She was really crying now, her hands clutching at his shoulders, turning her face against the pillow. The sound of her despair tore at him.

"Annie . . . there's no wall—"

She turned back and lifted her arms to press her hands on either side of his face, her fingers as deep into his hair as his were in hers, and they lay like that for a moment, everything touching but what needed to touch more than any other part of them.

"In here . . . in your head . . . A wall . . . smooth . . . all around . . . smooth . . . Can't get through, over, under, around . . . keeping me out . . . keeping me out *now* . . . Knew you loved me . . . always . . . from the beginning . . . from first time . . . when you thought at me from the caravan . . . But now . . . you stop . . . behind your eyes . . . even now . . . Locked out . . . locked out . . ."

He stared down at the pale triangle of her face in the darkness, as she struggled to explain. "We thought . . . new thing . . . waiting to teach . . . when we were . . . ready . . . But not . . . see now . . . only the Wall . . . locking me out . . . keeping me away . . . smooth . . . all around . . ." And she wrapped her arms around him, clinging to him.

Elliot lay against her, stricken, screaming unheard within the trap he had built for himself in his head. Locking her out. Locking himself in. Still alone.

Alone. Alone.

II

He could see the eye of the fly. It hung, inches away, the facets reflecting his thousand eyes, returning his stare, multiplying the fear and the loathing. The fly moved its massive hairy head, and the long curled tongue began to travel towards his face. The end of the glistening black tentacle was sticky with viscous acid. The fly's eye was melting, too, melting into the acid that was running down over his face faster, faster, covering his chest now, sloughing the skin away and burning the bones, exposing the moist pulsing mass of his heart, purple and crimson, it lifted away and left him hollow, bleeding streamers of scarlet into the whirlpool that was sucking him down, down, down . . .

Danny Vanderhof clapped his hands over his ears and cursed. "God, why is he screaming like that?"

Longjohn glanced at his watch, then at the panel in front of him. "He's right on schedule; after four and a half hours, hallucinations beginning." He made a tick on his chart, and wrote in the time next to it. Through the glass panel of the monitor room he could see the big Sensory Deprivation chamber, the eerie green light of the water outlining the outstretched bat-shape that was Philip Elliot, suspended in a no-world, lost, isolated.

Danny's hands were shaking as he checked the computer for the tenth time and swivelled his chair to read over the telemetry. "I still wish he hadn't sent Ted up to Birmingham. I'm no doctor. I can't read these things."

"Anybody can read them."

"All right," Danny snapped. "I can't understand them, let's say that, okay?"

"Okay," Longjohn said mildly. "Don't worry about it."

Danny looked up. He was an unusually handsome man, but so intensely shy that he always hid his features behind massive spectacles and a drooping moustache. "I also wish I knew why he thought this would work."

"Nothing else has. None of you in the Group could get to him, the drugs didn't unlock him, I couldn't even get him into a *light* hypnotic trance, so we have to destroy him."

"Wait a minute," Danny protested, looking even more pale, "you never said anything about destroying him before."

"Well, I guess that's a sloppy word for it. Basically SD removes the personality, and it's his personality we're fighting here. It's a psychological block, I'm sure. There's nothing physical about it."

Danny's eyes went to the big window, saw Elliot's shape twisting and thrashing in the water, in silence now that they had turned off the speakers. "That scares the living hell out of me, going into that thing."

"Him, too. Like you, he's a little claustrophobic. The thought of being sealed into that suit—so he sees nothing, hears nothing, feels nothing, smells nothing, tastes nothing—and then to be suspended weightless in that blood-heat bath. I always said he had guts, but now we're sure—he spewed them up twice before we started. I've been through SD myself, a long time ago. We don't use it much any more."

"What's it like?" Danny asked, more to distract himself

than out of genuine curiosity.

Longjohn leaned forward to check the telemetry readings —blood pressure, respiration, eye movements, pulse, EEG. "Oh, it's quite pleasant at first. You float there, thinking about your life, your future—like when you're dropping off to sleep —nice Alpha rhythms making you feel good. But gradually you lose interest, it doesn't seem important. So you start remembering things to pass the time. Nice things at first, why not? But little by little you can't control the memories and they *all* come at you—good and bad. And strong—you are reliving them instead of just remembering. Then *that* goes. You lose the desire or ability to think in any organized way whatsoever. You're in blackness, nothingness, emptiness. You are nothing, you are no one, you just *are*. And that's when the hallucinations start. Or what we used to think were hallucinations, anyway."

"Aren't they?" Out of the corner of his eye Vanderhof could see that Elliot had quietened down again, was lying there spread-eagled, still rising and falling gently as the waves of his previous agitation slowly ebbed.

"Hell, no. When the mind can't get any sensory stimulation or feedback from the body, it starts looking around outside the body, desperate for something to relate to. Extrasensory perception replaces normal. Omega takes over . . . only up to now we didn't know it was Omega, did we?"

Lights, shapes, colours, movement, patterns forming, unforming, re-forming. The fly came and went. Shards of glass fell gleaming. Ice glazed him, flames burned him, the wind blew and blew and blew. Then, abruptly, he was in the monitoring room with Danny and Longjohn. And could see himself beyond the glass floating like a big black bat. Hazy, gauzy, melting and changing, but he was there. Out Of Body Episode, OOBE, okay, he could handle that. Now what? Back inside himself again. Hello, me. You ought to get a load of yourself out there, you look bloody ridiculous. You look . . . and the

*glass shattered again, and the fly attacked . . . screaming
. . . screaming . . .*

"Oh, Jesus, there he goes again," Vanderhof complained,
flinching.

Longjohn looked over at him with concern. "You getting
any spill-over from him in there, Danny? If you are—"

"No, no, it's okay. He's still locked up behind that Wall
of his. I can just *see* he must be screaming, struggling like that
against the restraints."

"You'd better start giving me regular readings now.
How's Annie?" Annie was in an adjacent room in minor SD,
darkness and quiet, waiting to try reaching Elliot when he
was no longer Elliot but simply a thing that existed. Others
of the Group had volunteered, but both she and Longjohn
knew that only she could motivate Elliot to come out, or to
allow her to enter.

Vanderhof's eyes flickered shut briefly. "She's okay—
fine."

"Give me her readings, too."

"Right." Vanderhof dropped into a monotone with some
relief, finding numbers, as always, a hedge against emotion.
"Channel 1—pulse: Phil 108, Annie 73. Channel 2—BP—
Phil 160/120, Annie 119/80. Channel 3—respiration: Phil
28, Annie 16. We've got REM on Channel 4 for him, none for
her. Channel 5—EEG—Phil Alpha, Annie Alpha/Omega
. . . she's trying to get to him."

"Yeah. I wonder what he's seeing that's giving him such
fits?" He watched Elliot's black figure jerk and twist in agitation, then found himself relaxing as the movements slowed,
only realizing then that he was fighting, too. "He's settling."

"Right. I get pulse rate dropping, in the 90s and going
down. BP is 140 . . . sorry, 130/110, respiration 20, and
he's stopped moving his eyes. Still Alpha dominants, but slow-
ing—approaching Theta configuration."

"Annie?"

"Normal vital signs. Pushing Omega."

"Keep tracking them, something might start happening soon."

"What makes you say that?" Vanderhof kept his eyes on the telemetry.

"Time. Just time—nearly five hours, now. SD has most people pretty well empty by then. Most people."

Longjohn reached forward to flick on the speaker for Elliot's mike, and picked up a low uvular moaning, half choke, half despair. After a moment it regulated to a gutteral negative repeated over and over . . . "nononono nono . . . nono . . ."

"What does he read now?"

Danny ran through it again. "Pulse 94, BP 120/80, respiration 18, no REM, into Theta some peaking Alpha."

"And Annie?"

"She's—*very* strong Omega reading. Wait a minute—her pulse is rising, now, up to nearly 90. BP going up, too. Respiration . . . 20, no REM. She's pushing hard."

Still Elliot's voice choked out of the speaker, refusing all. "nonononononono . . . please . . . no no no . . . please . . . please . . ."

The entreaties began to break up the negatives more and more, and the voice began to rise as his demands grew. "Please . . . please . . . please . . ."

Longjohn found himself whispering, too. "Please, Annie —please . . ."

Suddenly, out of another speaker that had been totally silent, another whisper began. Annie's voice: "Yes . . . yes . . . yes . . . in . . . out . . . in . . . yes . . . yes . . ."

Danny, incredibly, was blushing "That sounds like . . ."

"Yeah, I know, but it isn't," Longjohn said. "You've got a dirty mind, Vanderhof."

"So Janet says. Hey—what's this?"

"What?"

Danny had his back to the glass window. "Is he moving . . . ?"

"No, why?"

"I got some—just for a minute—a burst of Omega. Gone now."

It was dark in the cave, and the walls were swelling toward him, pulsing, moving, and across the entrance lay the Wall . . . he beat his hands . . . bleeding . . . behind him the cave was growing smaller, smaller, pushing him into the Wall, squeezing him . . . no breath . . . and then he drew in one long breath of light . . . and then . . . gone . . . darkness . . . darkness . . .

Philip.

?

Philip

?

Need you . . . Philip . . . empty, alone . . .

?

"His pulse dropping . . . hers, too . . . BP going down even . . . faster . . ." Danny's voice was tight with apprehension. "I don't . . . everything is dropping except . . . there's another burst of Omega from him . . . hers . . . broke . . . still losing their BP . . . my God!"

He wanted to cry out because the light was drowning him . . . but like a man suddenly turned into fish . . . he breathed the light . . . breathed the light . . . and it flooded and burned without pain . . . and saw the light split the Wall . . . split the Wall . . . and . . . someone . . . someone . . . Annie . . .

"Longjohn . . . Look . . . look!" Danny's voice was triumphant.

Hawkins turned from staring at the totally still figure in the glowing pool of water and went over to stand behind Danny. "She's done it!"

Danny took refuge in the numbers again.

"Channel 1—pulse—Elliot 71, Annie 71. Channel 2—blood pressure: Phil—119/79, Annie 119/79. Channel 3—respiration: Phil 13, Annie 13. Channel 4—eye movements: . . . duplic . . . no . . . wait a minute . . ." He hit some keys—the computer chattered for a moment. "Not quite duplicated . . . seeing the same thing, but from a few feet apart . . . that's what Algernon makes it . . . is that right?"

"Look at the EEG," Longjohn said, softly. And their eyes went to the green waves on the small screen. "Total synchronization . . . absolutely total synch, full Omega."

"I never saw that before . . ." Danny choked. "'Synch, yes, sure, but not—"

He could see her . . . she was there . . . she was here . . . she was . . . he was . . . they . . . are . . . will be . . . always . . .

Take me home Philip.

Annie of the soft mouth of the sweet hands. *The Other Home . . .*

The . . . way in is the way out . . .

And the cave walls retreated faster and faster. Turning he saw that the light was from behind them, now . . . deep deep into the cave . . . far down and far away . . . calling . . . calling . . . calling them Home . . .

"What the hell are they *doing* in there?" Danny asked plaintively after about ten minutes.

"Hmmmmm?" Longjohn looked up from his notes.

"How long are we—I mean—what the hell are they *doing?*"

"I don't suppose even the Greeks had a word for it. You get synchronization in the Group, don't you, on some of those structural synthesis exercises you've been doing . . . ?"

"Yes, but not total—and only for a few minutes . . ."

Longjohn frowned, slightly. "How long has it been?"

"Twelve minutes now." Suddenly Danny's eyes fell on the telemetry indicators, which he had been ignoring in his fascination with the computer read-outs on the Omega wave synchronization between Elliot and Annie. He had blown it up to the most minute increments and still found no lack of correlation. The simultaneous reading was coming from one mind and one mind, only. "Oh . . . no . . ."

Tossing his clipboard on the panel, Longjohn glanced again at the still figure suspended in the warm embrace of the water, then came over to Danny's chair.

"I don't like the look of that at *all*," he finally said.

"Their pulse is down to 41 . . . BP 80/40, only five breaths a minute . . . the REM is way up, way up . . . they're seeing . . . something . . ." Suddenly Danny took hold of the arms of his chair, his knuckles whitening and the cords of his wrists standing out. "They're killing themselves."

"Don't be . . ." Longjohn's voice wavered, trailed away; his eyes fixed on the irrefutable evidence of the telemetry.

"The . . . Lindner experiments . . ." Danny choked out, pulling the facts out of his cache of total recall. "Mutual plenary trance—remember?"

"Remind me," Longjohn said abstractedly, leaning over Vanderhof's shoulder to adjust a couple of the telemetry controls.

"Late fifties. George Lindner put two people, two students, into a mutual trance, and they took each other into just that kind of state through what he concluded was reciprocal reinforcement on a telepathic level—scared the hell out of him. He only did it twice and then, they became . . . wouldn't respond . . . so deep in, like the yogis . . . dropped their vital signs . . . mutual plenary trance . . ."

"But he got them back . . . ?"

"He'd established a call-back procedure before he started, obviously—he forcibly counted them back, but it took hours . . ."

Longjohn saw that his hands were shaking over the controls and he clenched his fists as he straightened, turning to look into the glow of the pool beyond the glass. "Go in and wake Annie, quick!"

Danny knocked his chair over as he got up and it hit Longjohn's shins with a sharp pain he welcomed. *They'd* instituted no call-back procedure—there had been no reason to, Elliot and Annie had not been under hypnosis. He stared and stared at the motionless black figure floating in the shimmering water. They were not killing themselves, exactly. Just refusing to come back. Time would kill them. He stumbled over Danny's chair as he turned back to the telemetry dials. Pulse down to 30 . . . BP 70/30 . . . respiration . . . 4.

He turned back to the SD monitor panel and hit the speaker control with a fist like a hammer. "Philip, *Philip*, PHILIP ELLIOT."

The door crashed against the wall behind him and he could hear Danny's heavy breathing. "I can't—she won't respond! Just . . . cold . . . lying there . . ."

"PHILIP ELLIOT!" Longjohn screamed into the microphone, gripping the edge of the panel, leaning so far forward his forehead nearly touched the cold smooth glass that separated them. "PHILIP ELLIOT. PHILIP ELLIOT!"

"I'll wake some of the Group—maybe we can link and go in after them . . ."

"And get stuck in there too?" Longjohn whispered, then screamed again. "PHILIP ELLIOT! PHILIP ELLIOT!"

Then, from the speaker beside his forearm, Elliot's voice, far-off, hardly a voice at all.

"Go away . . . leave us . . . happy . . ."

"NO. NO! COME BACK. YOU MUST COME BACK!"

"Away . . . away . . . leave us . . ." came the moth-whisper of refusal.

"NO! COME BACK NOW. *NOW!*"

"Going . . . home . . . beautiful . . . home . . ."

Longjohn hit the panel with both fists, making the clipboard jump and slide off onto the floor. Danny was beside him, staring out at the pool and the man within its glowing embrace. "Jesus . . . Jesus . . ." Longjohn sobbed.

Danny straightened. "They're lovers, aren't they?" he said in a strange voice.

Longjohn had his hands over his face, and dropped them slowly to stare at the angry stranger so close to him. "What?"

Danny didn't answer but leaned forward to the microphone.

"Philip, Annie is dying . . ." Longjohn stared at Danny. "Annie is dying, Philip, you'll lose her."

From the speaker: "Annie . . . here . . . with . . . me."

"*No,* Philip, *no.* Annie's body is *here,* and Curtiss is here, and they're taking her, taking her away . . ."

"It won't work," Longjohn whispered.

"It would bloody well work with me if it was Janet," Danny said tersely. "Start that damn pool draining, give him some weight, make his body come back to him. Don't you *see,* he's forgotten he's flesh and blood—because he has no sensations, he thinks it will last forever. Go in there and shake the hell out of him . . . make him *hurt.*" He closed his eyes momentarily. "I've sent Janet in to do the same with her."

"I don't understand you," Longjohn protested. Danny turned to face him, his eyes blazing behind the lenses of his glasses. "If you'd let us open up *your* Omega, you would. There are laws . . . convictions within the Group . . . you cannot, must not deny the body even though the mind is greater. You must not abandon it until you are *called* to go."

"Go *where?*"

"Home." Danny turned back to the microphone. "If they take her away you will lose her, Philip. She won't be with you. Don't let them take her . . ." His voice went on, insistent, demanding, as Longjohn went through the connecting door and into the SD room. Danny could see his long thin figure stop at the pool, open the drain cocks, then climb over the edge to wade waist-high through the water towards Elliot. He risked a glance over his shoulder at the telemetry dials as his voice went on and on and on.

"If they take her the thread will break, Philip, the thread will sever and you'll be alone, she'll be alone—always alone. This isn't the Way. This isn't the Way. Curtiss will destroy. Curtiss will take her. Only *you* have the strength. Don't let them hurt her. Not now . . . not ever . . . only you can save her."

The readings were coming up, he saw with a sudden rush of excitement. Elliot's pulse was rising, Annie's too, and he could see Longjohn shaking him in the water, the water droplets flying around them in great spirals and twists. There was a warning tone from Algernon, and a chatter of the controls . . . and he saw the synch was broken between them.

Thank you, Janet.

You understood . . .

I've always understood . . .

He watched as Longjohn struggled with Elliot, and then, suddenly, Elliot was at Longjohn's throat, his strong square hands tightening with ferocious intent. He was killing what he thought was Curtiss.

It took Danny a long time to drag Elliot away from his victim. To rip off the helmet, force him out of the pool, hold him until his body caught up with his head.

Panting, dripping water, Elliot stood like a black glistening eel beside the low rim of the pool, his face still twisted with rage and fear. Slowly, only slowly, did the confusion leave him.

He stared at Danny, then at Longjohn who stood knee-deep in the draining water, hanging onto the edge of the pool and rubbing his throat.

We went Away. He looked at Danny. *We were nearly free.*

I know. But you belong here.

Why?

I can't see all the way ahead . . . but you're needed here.

The Wall.
We'll need that, too. Didn't you know?
Elliot began to cry. *Nobody told me.*
We were waiting for you to tell us.

PROLOGUE II

Beyond the long French windows the sun was half swallowed by the open mouth of the valley on the Canadian horizon. The heavy oyster silk curtains stirred faintly with the first touch of the cool night air flowing down. It touched the flimsy sheets of paper in the hands of the man behind the desk, bending the corners over and making them whisper another message.

. . . No, I can't tell you where we went.

First of all there are no words for it. Second of all, it's a place that's in you, and in me, and in all of us . . . but you have to find your own way to it, and back. Ours was a path of light and music. Yours could be the scent of lemons or the taste of chocolate or the eye of a needle.

All I can tell you is that you will be happy when you arrive.

If that sounds a little close to religion, so be it.

Religions are about people, aren't they?

People and the promise of something better?

I am no priest, no follower of priests.

But I promise you—it is there. Waiting for you.

It's been there always.

"What is Home?" the man behind the desk asked.

"Home is where you live," said the shadowy figure simply. "It is where you begin, and where you return at the end of your day. Or days."

"And where you are happy?"

"Oh, yes. Until your next Day begins."

Request: 2 O Group
Assignment: Surveillance
Place: London
Object: Verification identity suspected KGB "floater"
Agent(s) supplied: R. Tuckwell. M. Robinson
Assignment completed.

Request: 1 O Group
Assignment: Interrogation
Place: Paris
Object: Suspected blackmail embassy official
Agent(s) supplied: D. Stuart
Assignment completed.

Request: 1 O Group
Assignment: Surveillance
Place: Chicago
Object: Establish relationship consular/staff/private citizen
Agent(s) supplied: D. Vanderhof
Assignment completed, objection noted.

Request: 3 O Group
Assignment: Observation
Place: Geneva
Object: Monitor special extramural SALT discussions
Agent(s) supplied: D. Vanderhof, F. Webb, D. Stuart
Assignment completed.

Request: 1 O Group
Assignment: Interrogation
Place: Belfast
Object: Identification
Agent(s) supplied: A. Grundy
Assignment completed, objection noted.

Request: 4 O Group
Assignment: Observation
Placc: Istanbul
Object: Suspected conference between Turkey/USSR
Agent(s) supplied: F. Murphy, D. Vanderhof, J. York,
    R. Tuckwell
Assignment completed. Expenses noted, form attached, please
    clarify.

Request: 1 O Group
Assignments: Surveillance
Place: London
Object: Relationship (see File S 78-44-61329)
Agent(s) supplied: B. Miller
Assignment completed, objection noted.

Request: 2 O Group
Assignment: Observation
Place: Brighton
Object: Establish power relationships Shadow Cabinet

Agent(s) supplied: —
Assignment refused.

Request: 2 O Group
Assignment: Observation
Place: London
Object: Monitor suspected Arab/Italian meeting
Agent(s) supplied: A. Grundy, B. Miller
Assignment completed.

Request: 1 O Group
Assignment: Surveillance
Place: Cardiff
Object: Establish influence student organization
Agent(s) supplied: B. Dix
Assignment completed, objection noted.

Request: 2 O Group
Assignment: Interrogation
Place: Birmingham
Object: Suspected sabotage, 2 instances
Agent(s) supplied: R. St. John, D. Stuart
Assignment completed.

Request: 1 O Group
Assignment: Information retrieval
Place: Royal United Hospital, Bath
Object: Identify assailant agent, URGENT
Agent(s) supplied: D. Rossiter
Assignment completed. Suggestion implemented. Thank you,
    condition satisfactory.

Request: 3 O Group
Assignment: Information retrieval
Place: Manhattan, UN

Object:See File Purple/S-9971-88-23Tg6551
Agent(s) supplied: **D.** Vanderhof, **M.** Robinson, **D.** Rossiter
Assignment completed, objection(s) noted.

Elliot spread the request forms on his blotter and opened the Assignment Log. "Ummm . . . Danny can do that one, it's a technologist from East Germany . . . Robby for this one . . . Tom Leeson can go with Ari, it will help him get used to multi-reading . . . and Frances can do that, she likes Chinese food."

Janet gathered up the forms and clipped them together.

"Cragg has asked for twenty minutes this afternoon." *rat, cheese, trap*

Elliot smiled. "Why not? I've only got nine million things to do." *snap*

"He's changed, have you noticed?" *teeth, mask, rotten eggs, eel*

"You'll have to learn to go deeper." *snake in hole, foot on neck, Curtiss*

Janet sighed, and glanced at the top request form. "Does it *have* to be Danny? Bonn means overnight."

"Still having trouble with your sending?"

Janet nodded, and Elliot summoned Jackson in the library. *Could you run through distance practice with Janet some time today?*

Patterning Robin on sub-temporal alternates

Sandy? He finally located her by the river.

Sure . . . tell her to bring some sandwiches

She . . .

I heard . . . egg or ham?

Yes.

Janet went out, leaving Elliot to complete the Assignment Log. Then, from halfway down the hall, she sent *Thanks.* Elliot smiled and reached for his coffee mug.

*   *   *

It gave him great satisfaction to see how absolutely ridiculous Cragg looked wearing one of the protective bands. The little man had been moved out of Talbot when the place had been converted to a combined residential and development centre, and now had to spin out his red tape from a small office in Maidenhead. His attitude was far more conciliatory than it used to be, but it was purely a surface alteration. The little man was still little, and hated the changes that forced him from the centre of his web.

"Mr. Curtiss has asked me to discuss these with you . . ."

"Why can't Mr. Curtiss talk to me himself?"

"He had to go to Helsinki."

"*Cart?* That's a little out of his circle of influence, isn't it?"

"It's my understanding the trip was . . . personal. Just a holiday. Now, these—"

"Like some coffee?"

"No, thank you. Thank you all the same. These assignments."

Elliot poured himself some coffee and added a dollop of brandy from the decanter in the cupboard below the percolator, noting it was nearly empty. Again.

"I just made this week's assignments. I haven't got anyone—"

"No, no, these are the assignments you've rejected over the past two months. Twelve of them."

"Oh? Is that all? Twelve?"

Cragg rested the sheaf of forms on his knees and watched Elliot return to his chair behind the desk. "*All?* Between these, and the assignments your people *did* complete with objections, or refused to complete."

"You noted the objections?"

"We always note them."

"I'm glad to hear it. Cigarette?" He exended the box toward Cragg, who hesitated, then took one. Elliot tossed him the desk lighter and made sure it dropped just short onto the carpet. "Sorry."

Cragg ignored the fallen lighter and drew out his own, eyeing Elliot warily through the flame. He let the smoke flow out with his antipathy. "Altogether, we have had a total of twenty-three unsatisfactory operations by your people in the last eight and a half weeks alone."

"And how many satisfactory ones?"

"I'm only here to—"

"I'll tell you, Cragg. In those same eight and a half weeks they have completed over a hundred assignments, and frankly I think *that's* too damn many, as well."

"Even so—"

"Even so nothing. You all seem to think this is a bottomless well we've drilled out here. It isn't. My people are getting exhausted, *and* they're getting annoyed. So am I. They don't mind doing things that make a serious contribution, it's all these piddling little jobs you load in that make the trouble." He slammed his coffee mug down, and leaned forward onto the desk. "Look, less than a year ago this was a medical research establishment, remember? I was a doctor working towards something I thought was important. Now I'm a bloody paper-shuffler just like you. The Group is so busy eavesdropping and all the rest of it we haven't the time or the energy to get any further along with developing their full abilities. And that's stupid, frankly. You're using them too *soon*. It's a short-term view. Oh, hell, forget it."

"I take your point, Elliot," Cragg said with specious sympathy.

"Do you? I doubt it, I really doubt it."

"Perhaps if there were more of them?"

"We haven't got time to develop more of them, damn it. We haven't even fully developed those we *have* got. Frankly, if things don't ease up you won't have twelve refusals, you'll have a solid refusal right across the board. You can't force them to work for you, remember?"

"I'll tell Mr. Curtiss what you say, of course." Elliot just looked at him, then turned away in disgust to stare out of the window. Janet was walking over the grass towards the river. She had remembered the sandwiches—they were on a tray hovering over the grass about three feet in front of her moving somewhat erratically towards its destination. He could see the tension in her shoulders as she concentrated on controlling it. Squinting a little to gauge the distance, he over-rode her with Frances's help and plucked one of the sandwiches skyward, looping it and sending it back to circle her.

Stop that.

You're not supposed to practice where the tourists can see you.

I can't carry the sandwiches and *the enhancer, can I?*

Why not?

Because I've only got two hands, that's why.

Still only two, hey? You disappoint me. He contacted Danny in the computer room and together with Frances, they took the enhancer and the sandwiches and sent them ahead to drop lightly onto the grass beside Sandy, who was asleep by the willows. *You're just too piss-proud to ask for help.*

I want to learn to . . . he saw her hesitate as Danny came back into her and . . . Elliot turned back to Cragg and left them to it, there in the sunlight where nobody could see. The exchange had taken just under seven seconds and Cragg was still blowing smoke between his sentences.

"But you have to understand that Mr. Curtiss is also having trouble with demands. We turn down far more requests than we fill, you know. Far more."

"I thought Curtiss was keeping the lid on?"

"Pardon?"

"I thought Curtiss was still not letting anyone know he has a bunch of tame mind-readers on a leash for rent to all and sundry," Elliot amplified with irritated precision.

"Well, of course he isn't. But the success rate, the results . . ."

"Ah. They think he's a genius and recognize his worth at

last, do they? That ought to make a difference to next year's Honours List."

"Mr. Curtiss is hardly keeping your people a secret for his *own* sake," Cragg protested. "Can you imagine what would happen if . . ." he trailed off under the weight of Elliot's glare. "At any rate, I have also noted that at no time since your Group became active have you used Miss Craigie on an assignment."

"That's right," Elliot said evenly. "Nor do I intend to."

"Mr. Curtiss would like to know why."

Because she belongs to me, Elliot told him silently. "Because she is involved in the small amount of development we are still able to do in our free hours. Because, perhaps only for my own satisfaction, I am determined to continue with my original work, at least some of the time."

"But surely she's the most powerful—"

"Yes," Elliot agreed. "Precisely."

"I see." Cragg leaned forward to put his cigarette out in Elliot's ashtray. "Mr. Curtis would also like to know what progress you have made towards a more viable and less visible protective device."

"Not much." Elliot lied. "But we *are* working on it, of course. Any other little queries you'd like me to ignore before you go?"

Annie? She was in the electronics lab with Frances. Her mouth brushed his with an invisible response, and he smiled under the gentle pressure. *When is Longjohn due back?*

?

I expected him this morning. Can anyone find him for me?

The request echoed through the Group, but nobody could focus on Hawkins.

He frowned. If only Longjohn would let them develop his Omega, there wouldn't be all this damn difficulty keeping track of him. He accepted the Canadian's instinctive revulsion at the loss of privacy and individuality he seemed convinced would be a natural concomitant of membership in the Group. No matter how much they all sought to reassure him, however, he remained obstinately Outside. Just before he'd left for the north to screen four new possible candidates for the Group, Elliot had again approached him on the subject.

"You were always after *me* to do it. Have I changed all that much?"

Hawkins had eyed him with amusement. "Yes."

"Oh." There was no answer to that.

"You smile more."

Elliot had laughed. "Well, then, what's the trouble? I would have thought any psychologist worth his PhD would leap at the opportunity to leave all the fuzzy testing procedures and guesswork behind if he had the ability to actually confront a subject mind to mind with no subterfuges and no confusion. Think how much more you could do, how much farther you could go toward—"

"Think how they could see through all my little techniques," Longjohn had observed wryly.

"But now that we know about the Wall, now that we're learning to open and close it *at will,* you can have all the privacy you want. I always said the conventions would develop with the power, and they have."

"But not enough. Not for me, not yet."

"What's the matter, afraid someone will find out you want to go to bed with Ted or something?" Elliot had said lightly. "I don't care what your kinks might be, Longjohn, there aren't any the Group hasn't encountered and managed to ignore."

"Maybe I want to go to bed with *you,*" Longjohn snapped, and Elliot turned to stare at him, startled, until he saw the glint of derision in the green eyes.

"Okay. I deserved that." Elliot smiled. "But although I sympathize with your reactions to Omega, I still don't really understand why your head can't overcome them."

"Oh, it can. What it can't overcome is what you're letting them make you *do* with Omega. It turns my guts, Phil, all this 'intelligence' work. Crap. Sheer and utter crap, all of it. When you first came back to us from Mhourra and talked about Omega, admitted the truth about yourself, you were so big on making sure it wasn't abused. *You* could abuse it and cheat rich men out of their gold at the poker table, but you didn't want Annie used, remember?"

"She isn't *being* used."

"No, not yet. But the other members of the Group are."

"We're being paid to do a job."

"Oh, Phil," Longjohn had said, softly. "That doesn't track. You've been complaining about the escalation of assignments already. Do you think it's going to *stop*? Don't you see that eventually they're going to get you by the throat? That eventually even Curtiss won't be able to keep the Group under his wing alone? Why doesn't he ever come to Talbot? Hmmmm? Why does he keep agitating for the development of a protective device? I'll tell you why—he's a *bad man*. I could give you chapter and verse about personality development, social pressures, and all the rest of it, but sometimes even we psychologists have to admit some people are just plain *nasty*. He's one of them. It's all going to go bang, Phil. One of these days, it's all going to splatter back in your face. You seem to think Omega will protect you, that it has some magic property like the old Cloak of Invisibility or the Ring of the Niebelungen to make you untouchable. You aren't, buddy, you *aren't*."

There was a knock at the door, startling Elliot out of his reverie.

?

The knock was repeated. One of the staff then, not a telepath. "Come in."

It was Bartlett. Elliot smiled and waved him in. "Don't tell me it's stew for dinner again?"

The smooth face didn't smile, but the dark eyes did.

Bartlett was the best thing and the worst thing that had come to Talbot in the past months. Now that it was a residential complex as well as a scientific one, they had needed a housekeeper. What they got was a butler. Well, Elliot conceded, one could hardly call Bartlett a mere butler, more a Magic Dispenser of Ease and Comfort. With twelve permanent residents of varying temperament and requirements—fourteen if he and Annie stayed over—who were totally isolated from the normal world and totally dependent on a go-between, they needed a little magic to keep things running smoothly. Bartlett was just that, and, unfortunately, a little more.

"No, not stew. A choice of Bœuf Wellington, Turbot Normandie, or Chicken Kiev tonight, sir. Will you and Miss Craigie be staying?"

"With a choice like that we can hardly refuse," Elliot acknowledged. No wonder Annie was gaining weight.

"What can I do for you, Bartlett?"

"It's about Mr. Tuckwell, sir." The band on Cragg had looked ridiculous, but on Bartlett it seemed a part of his uniform, if a perfectly cut midnight-blue suit, spotless white shirt, and discreetly figured red on blue tie could be called a uniform. Elliot always felt more than usually unkempt when Bartlett was in the room, and unconsciously squared his shoulders within the snagged Navy pullover and open-throated blue shirt.

"Robin?"

Bartlet advanced a little closer to the desk. "He's asked for a—"

Robin, what the hell are you after now?

"For a what?"

"For a horse, sir."

Elliot stifled a smile. "I see. To eat or to ride?"

I am a gentleman. Gentlemen require gentle exercise, Robin observed pompously.

You're a foxy old bastard and you were born in Shoreditch, Elliot sent back.

"To ride, sir."

"And that presents a difficulty, does it, Bartlett?"

"Well, sir, I suppose we could find a *place* for it. There are the old stables, but they're being used for storage at present. It's that the Security regulations forbid any kind of—"

"They're afraid he's going to ride off into the sunset?"

Bartlett allowed a flicker of amusement into his eyes. "Something like that, sir."

"Isn't that a little . . . ?"

"I agree, sir," Bartlett said. "But Mr. Cragg has quite simply refused to entertain the idea in any form whatsoever. I'm sorry."

Cragg again. Cragg, whenever possible, in fact. "Kind of breaks your record, doesn't it, Bartlett?"

"Record, sir?"

"Your record of being able to supply whatever anyone asks you for, no matter how outlandish."

"I do my best, sir."

"I know you do, Bartlett." And that's not *all* you do, Bartlett, he added to himself. You also report back to somebody Curtiss doesn't know about, don't you? You also keep such a close and subtle eye on the lot of us that there is hardly a breath we take you don't count, tally, and record. And dammit, Bartlett, I like you.

"I'll explain to Mr. Tuckwell that a horse is unavailable, Bartlett."

"Thank you, sir."

"Anything else?"

"No, sir. I believe that's the only problem at present."

"Carry on, Bartlett." He'd always wanted to say that.

"Very good, sir."

Elliot watched the narrow back retreat, watched the door shut quietly behind it. Bartlett represented the tip of the problem Longjohn insisted was lurking below the surface, waiting to tear them apart. It was true that Curtiss was still keeping the truth about Talbot Hall and the Omega Group to himself, using them secretly to reinforce his own agents, thereby achieving an astonishing record that was beginning to make some of the other Services not only envious but curious. Hence the ubiquitous Bartlett, indispensable, unassuming, and a constant threat.

Love thine enemy. Annie. Always, Annie.
What do we do, little one?
Dazzle them with footwork.
?
Come upstairs. We have some things to show you.

Tossing his pencil onto his desk, Elliot stood up and stretched, rubbing the back of his neck where it had rested against the chair. He reached over to finish the last of his coffee, with its kicker of brandy, then let his hand fall back, empty. Too much of that lately. The heating at Talbot Hall was more than sufficient to deal with the vagaries of the English spring. But even though the days were lengthening once again, and the trees were beginning to haze with green, he felt cold. Every day, every hour; colder and colder.

Frances startled Elliot yet again with the deviousness of the mind hidden behind her serene face and granny specs.

"Any good mother will tell you that if you have an over-inquisitive child it's better to distract than punish it," Frances said, her hands jammed deep into the pockets of her flowered smock. "Preferably with a toy."

"So?" Elliot asked wearily. The littered electronics lab seemed more like the bottom of a wastepaper basket than ever, with scallops of fine wire trailing from the benches, wiring diagrams and scrawled formulae stuck up with drawing pins onto most vertical surfaces, jeweller's tools and encrusted soldering irons propped against overflowing ashtrays.

"So," Frances continued, "if you're so worried about the Group being overworked on these spying sessions, why don't we give Curtiss and some of his friends something more specific to play with? A few toys. We *are* a lot more than just mind-readers now, aren't we?"

They were indeed.

As they had developed Omega in each successive member of the Group, further patterns and abilities had emerged. Telepathy was common to all because the need to communicate was common to all. But Annie could heal. Frances had an astounding capacity for telekinesis. She could lift, without visible effort, something as bulky and heavy as a sofa—very handy, she said, when doing housework. Ari Grundy, the flamboyant Irishman who'd made a very good living with a "mind-reading" act in the northern clubs, had proved to have a very strong clairvoyant power. Objects told him about the people who had owned or touched them. Danny Vanderhof couldn't do that, but he could read the future to some extent. He insisted it was really only a process of logical extrapolation from the present—but that ability coupled with his total recall was giving Vanderhof a hell of an edge. Several local bookies had refused to take his bets recently. Janet had proved to be a superb mental "switchboard operator"—her ability to keep track of and co-ordinate the flow of several minds at once had proved invaluable in the intricate mind-games and exercises.

But Elliot himself had brought the greatest gift of all— the Wall.

The Wall meant that each member of the Group now had mental privacy at will, without resorting to the bands or to drugs. A breach *could* be forced, but it took tremendous effort and concentration. Multiple exchanges were possible by using a technique similar to the mechanical scrambling of telephone lines, and members could "ring" some receivers while excluding others. And even during a multiple conversation, they had quickly worked out and perfected a kind of rapid-fire transmission, which they nicknamed "bullets," so that they could make a private aside while maintaining general communication. As a result, Group exchanges could be on a simple individual basis, or as complex as multi-dimensional crossword puzzles. The brain, with its vast unused supply of neural relays, handled it all easily. Once learned, the facility became as automatic and almost as unconscious an operation as that of a man riding a bicycle while singing a song, working out a thesis on Carlyle, keeping track of his route so as not to miss the second turning on the right, digesting his breakfast, and noticing the spectacular bust on a girl coming towards him along the pavement.

They had finally decided that the Wall was probably the result of a bio-chemical process rather than an Omega trait. Recent research had proved that the human body produced natural equivalents to morphine that deadened pain under stress, enabling a soldier, for example, to keep fighting without noticing his wounds. Elliot, under psychological stress, had produced a high concentration of some other natural body chemical that served to insulate the Omega function when it became unbearable for him. Although they hadn't the time or the facilities to isolate and identify the substance—a long research project in itself—they *had* learned to stimulate its production at will through bio-feedback. Elliot could still build a Wall higher and wider than any, but then he'd had more practice.

Other members of the Group had shown other talents, and it was on this range of abilities that Frances was basing her suggestions. She produced three objects and proposed that Elliot use them to put on a "demonstration" for the various M1 unit chiefs. After twenty minutes of discussion, Elliot had to admit her plan was sound. He looked from Frances to Annie to the rest of the Group who by now had joined them in the laboratory.

"It sounds to me as if what you really want is to show off for an audience," he said in mild reproof.

"Why not?" Ari asked. "Everybody likes applause."

"Some more than others," Elliot observed. Ari shrugged, then grinned.

"We're getting bored, Philip. We don't amaze us, any more."

"You still amaze me," Elliot smiled back. "All of you."

Instantly he was flooded with images of himself as a baby with a rattle, a boy with a butterfly-net, a mad scientist leaping about with a smoking test-tube, a slack-jawed vicar watching a stripper, and other visual comments far more insulting.

Plus one very private one from Annie that was exceptionally amazing and had absolutely nothing to do with butterfly-nets.

It's time we went home, he answered her, simultaneously sending back different images to the others in response to their teasing.

"All right, Frances," he said aloud. "We'll work out the details tomorrow. You're a clever lady." He got an invisible kick up the backside for his compliment, and blinked.

"Don't be so chauvinistic," Frances said. "I'm clever, period. What I do as a lady is quite separate."

"True," Elliot agreed, blandly. "Where *is* George, by the way?"

Frances flushed and looked away. He got kicked again, this time by a number of invisible feet. He folded his arms and leaned against the nearest bench. "You are all getting above yourselves," he began a little pompously, and felt himself being lifted slowly to hover a few inches above the floorboards. *"Stop that!"* he ordered "I'm trying to talk sensibly about—"

They dumped him so abruptly he had to grab hold of the bench to stay upright, deafened him with a mental cascade of nonsense syllables, twisted them into a picture-image of the Tower of Babel, then blew it up into a shimmer of rainbow dust that spiralled around until it re-formed into a caricature of himself and Curtiss in outsized shorts and gloves boxing in a ring surrounded by faceless men in dinner-jackets placing bets.

Summoning what remnants of his dignity that were left to him, he sighed and started for the door. "I am going home. At least my cat appreciates me."

He's not the only one. Annie slipped her hand into his.

As they went out, they were followed by a mental queue of absolutely impossible creaures—the members of the Group each conjuring up a wild version of themselves waving farewell and throwing garlands of equally impossible flowers. Involuntarily stepping over a heap of non-existent blue-striped roses, he smiled and tightened his hold on Annie's hand.

His Group was an irreverent, warm, loyal, and totally incredible bunch of loonies. As ill-assorted as any family, as full of strengths, weaknesses, and complexities as human beings everywhere.

And like no other human beings anywhere. If only . . .

If only it wasn't such a long drive home, Annie interrupted before he could get depressed again.

They began to walk a little faster down the narrow dark hall.

Philip and Annie had been married quietly several months before. The final step in Annie's relentless quest for respectability, Longjohn had laughed, but he'd performed the role of best man with a reasonably straight face. Amused and indulgent, Elliot had participated in the ceremony only to please her. No religious or legal ritual could bring them any closer than they were already, he'd pointed out. But it was difficult to maintain his objectivity when Annie's radiant joy was so evident.

And, to his surprise, it *had* made a difference to him. That night, as they drove home, he realized he now had a sense of home, and it was giving him strength and a measure of peace. He had something to protect, something to cherish, something that was important to him alone. His home. His wife. And, in the autumn, his child.

Later, with Joseph scratching irritably at the closed bedroom door because they hadn't stopped to feed him, Elliot raised himself on one elbow and looked down at his wife. He had been too impatient the first time, too eager for the satisfaction only Annie could give him. Now, gently, he began to re-explore the corners of her mouth with his tongue, feeling her hands flutter down over his body to stroke him, and he rose to meet them. Lifting his head he smiled down at her, his hands touching her face, throat, shoulders, wondering at their new softness, and then moving to her breasts, filling his palm with their ripe, heavy warmth. His fingertips circled one nipple, slowly, slowly.

Hello, woman
Hello

Moving down to taste the sweetness of her flesh, he curved his body so that her hands could still reach him, could still slide up and back, fast and slow, making him wait and then starting again, harder, harder. Suddenly she moved them away to trace his spine, leaving him to ride a while on his own heat. Smiling into her throat he reached around to bring her hand back to where it could play better games, but as soon as he let go she gave him a quick flick with her nails and sent her hand further away to draw patterns on the inside of his thighs. He covered the wayward hand with his and moved it onto her own body, forcing her fingertips between her thighs and deep into her own wet and slippery excitement. She struggled until he let her hand escape. His own remained. She bit him, and he laughed.

Willful piece, aren't you, Mrs. Elliot?
Willing
Willful

Just to remind her he had teeth, too, he bent to nip at her stomach, where it was beginning to round upward.

The baby won't like that.
Let him grow up and find his own woman. You're mine.
But this is mine. Her hands were back where they belonged, on him.
Only when I say you can have it.

Say I can.
Take it. Take it . . . take me in . . .
The phone rang. The private line from Talbot.
"Bloody hell!"
Annie giggled. *Ask not for whom the bell tolls.*
"Hah." He staggered across the bedroom, stepping over
the heap of clothes by the bed. He opened the door, reached
around, and dragged the telephone down the table towards him
by the cord, finally picking up the receiver as he leaned against
the wardrobe, shivering. "Elliot."
"This is Bartlett, sir. I'm sorry to disturb you."
"I'm sorry, too, believe me. What's the problem?"
"I . . . I think you'd better come back, sir."
He straightened and glanced at Annie, alarmed. Bartlett
would call for no small reason. "What's wrong?"
"There are some men here, sir. It's about . . . it's Dr.
Hawkins."
"Are they from the Ministry?"
"No, sir. They're . . . police officers. I think you'd
better come back as quickly as you can. Please."

Elliot sat on the edge of the chesterfield, his arms crossed over
and hugging himself, trying to make warmth where there was
none. Bartlett hesitated, then opened the cupboard beneath
the percolator and drew out the brandy decanter, pouring a
generous measure into one of the empty mugs. He crossed
over and held it out until Elliot took it, swallowed the lot in
one long gulp, then shuddered.
"The records gave this as his home address, we had no
way of knowing it was—" the younger police officer began.
"This was Dr. Hawkins's home . . . as well as . . . as
well as . . ." Elliot's voice wavered, faded away.
Bartlett cleared his throat. "I think I can supply you
with all the details you require."
"Dr. Elliot was listed as next of kin, you see."
"There was no one else—is no one else."

"Gentlemen . . . please." Bartlett stood by the door, waiting. The two men followed him out into the hall, leaving Elliot hunched on the leather cushions, staring at nothing.

"Took it hard for somebody who just worked with the man," the older officer commented as they went down the dark corridor towards the glow of the Reception area.

"They were very old friends as well," Bartlett said quietly.

"Ah."

Bartlett slowed halfway across Reception. "There's absolutely no doubt?"

"The Coast Guard brought back some of the wreckage. There's no doubt it was the same plane Hawkins took off in from Stornoway. No body yet but the currents are very strong in that area, they said. It might take days, even weeks, before it shows up. If it ever does."

"Then until it does . . ."

The police officer was shaking his head. "There wasn't a piece of that plane found more than a foot across. He went down hard and fast. He radioed a Mayday just five minutes before he went off the radar. I'd like to say he had time to jump, but they say he had no chance. They would have picked him up if he had."

"I see. Thank you."

"What *is* this place, anyway? Why did we have to put these things on?" The officer gestured towards the band that sat slightly lopsided on his head.

"This is a neurological research unit. We have some very powerful electronic equipment here. If you don't wear a protective band, the least you'll end up with is a nasty headache."

"The least? What's the worst?"

Bartlett smiled, briefly. "Don't ask. You wouldn't really want to know."

Elliot sat alone in his office, Annie's arms around him. From beyond the room solace reached out to him, cocooned him in a web of love and sympathy, as the Group locked their grief with his. But slowly, slowly, he crawled behind his Wall and shut the door, where his pain hurt only himself and where darkness filled the space in which Longjohn had lived.

13

"Gentlemen, I appreciate your coming all the way down here to see the things we have to show you, but I know you understand Security problems better than most."

Elliot was standing at a table in front of the French windows in the Talbot library. The two-storey room was filled with the scent of leather and newsprint. Vases of bright spring flowers stood on some of the smaller tables, next to ashtrays, boxes of cigarettes, and all the other paraphernalia of hospitality. From the kitchens across the courtyard came the sounds of preparation and the first sharp promise of frying onions and simmering sauces. He was determined to impress *all* their senses, today. It would increase their confusion.

Reaching across, he plucked the silver egg from its silken nest and began to toss it from hand to hand, idly. "You all know we've been working here at Talbot on some rather esoteric areas of psychological and neurological research. Until now we've not had much to show for our efforts because knowing ESP exists and proving it are two very different things. *I* know ESP powers are a reality, but like any other scientist I wouldn't accept mere opinion—even my own—without physical substantiation."

They were beginning to watch the egg. Sometimes he threw it a little higher so that its satiny surface would catch the light from the windows behind him. "But even the most stubborn problems can be cracked if enough pressure is applied . . ." He tossed the egg really high and stood up to catch it. Opening his hand, he held the egg level on his palm, then tilted his hand. The egg began to rock. He knew it was driving them mad, half because they were annoyed with him for playing with it, and half because they could not figure out what the hell it was. He stopped tilting his hand, but the egg continued to rock on its own, back and forth, back and forth, with metronomic regularity. They couldn't take their eyes from it.

"I won't go into a long song and dance about the history of parapsychology and neuro-psychiatry—my secretary will give you each a folder with a reading list and various other items so that when you're in the privacy of your own offices, you can place what you're going to see and experience in a more definitive context. I'll limit myself to demonstration."

Leaning forward he grabbed the hand of the man nearest him, flattened it, and let the egg roll into his palm. Startled, then frightened, the man held his hand rigid, afraid to let the egg drop, not knowing what Elliot expected of him and not wanting to look an idiot. The egg continued to rock—evenly, smoothly, endlessly.

"Have you ever thought you might have psychic powers, Mr. Halliwell?"

"Psychic powers? What do you mean?" the man asked nervously, watching the egg.

"Oh, clairvoyance, for example. Do you do well at the races?" Elliot had already read enough to know the man was badly in debt to several bookies. "Do you find that you're unusually perceptive about the moods and emotions of other people, or occasionally pick up thoughts from loved ones?"

"No. Never. Nothing like that."

"Ah. Then you'd hardly expect to be able to project your

own thoughts to anyone else, would you? Telepathically, I mean?"

"Certainly not. In point of fact, Elliot, I think your whole area of investigation is utter and absolute balderdash—a total waste of time and money."

"I'm so glad to hear you say so. No, you keep that for the moment." Halliwell had extended his palm as if to return the egg that was still rocking, rocking, in his palm. Elliot knew the surface of the egg was beginning to grow appreciably warmer and that it was worrying Halliwell. "Bear with me. I understand you took part in the pursuit of Rommel during the Second World War, have a very distinguished war record, in fact?"

"I served with Monty, yes." Halliwell was puzzled at this apparent diversion from the subject at hand. Or in hand, in his case.

"Yes. Although he wasn't too happy to find you using his private latrine that night after you'd over-indulged in the local version of lamb stew, was he?"

"How . . . what on earth . . .? Nobody but . . ." Halliwell gaped at him.

Elliot ignored his astonishment and smiled encouragingly. "Mr. Halliwell, do you remember how hot it got out there in the desert? I mean, do you *really* remember what it was like?"

"I . . . yes, of course I do. Intolerable."
Annie? Robin?
Ready.

Elliot turned away and strolled back to the table, trailing a finger along its edge, talking softly. "I want you to send your mind back, Mr. Halliwell, just for a moment. Imagine yourself sitting beside your tank in the few inches of shade it provided, the sun high and brassy overhead, no refreshing coolness in the air you're breathing, your clothes binding you, sand irritating and chafing every fold and crevice of your body, flies endlessly buzzing . . . all of it. Close your eyes, think really hard about it. Please."

Halliwell looked a little bewildered, but eventually closed his eyes.

"Hot, wasn't it, Mr. Halliwell?"

"Terrible."

"And it stank, didn't it? The sweat, the melting rancid grease from the tanktracks, the discarded tins of half-consumed rations everyone was too weary to finish . . . not a nice place, the desert at high noon . . . unbearable in fact."

"It was awful." Halliwell was getting into it now, letting it come back under the gentle persuasion of Elliot's soft words. The other men in the room were watching the two of them, their eyes inexorably drawn back to the egg as it continued to rock in Halliwell's palm. Some of them began to shift uncomfortably in their chairs. One ran a surreptitious finger around his collar, another began to furtively scratch his thigh. Gradually, they all began to grow red in the face, and beads of perspiration appeared on foreheads and upper lips. One man clutched his stomach, another looked annoyed and began tilting his head to one side as if avoiding a persistently circling insect. Elliot stopped talking, stopped moving. They were getting very uncomfortable indeed, each unaware that those around him were also suffering, each thinking he was alone in his distress. Elliot waited for a full minute, then spoke sharply.

"Each of you look at the man on your right."

Startled by the sudden change in his voice, they did as he directed, and were amazed to see one another looking so hot and bothered.

"The ambient temperature in this room, gentlemen, is fifty-eight degrees Fahrenheit. Some of you complained earlier, in fact, that it was decidedly chilly in here. Still think so?"

They stared at each other, at him.

"You *aren't* hot, gentlemen, but Mr. Halliwell's memory is. You feel hot, you look hot, but you aren't." He reached over and plucked the egg from Halliwell's palm. "Are you?"

The instant the egg was back in Elliot's hand, their discomfort ceased. *Thank you. Stand by.*

"Good heavens," muttered the one who had been clutching his stomach.

"On his own admission, Mr. Halliwell is a man devoid of any psychic abilities whatsoever. I am not. I have quite a high degree of latent psychic ability." He tilted his hand and set the egg rocking again. "I also have an arthritic knee developed from an injury I sustained as a very eager prop forward during a rugby game against Oxford, far too many years ago. It hurts me quite a lot when the weather changes. As we've had some rain in the night, it's hurting me now."

To a man they all stiffened, grimaced, and reached for their left knees simultaneously—like some chorus line in a Busby Berkeley routine. After a second or two they began to twist in their seats, and some began to sweat—the cold grey sweat of shock arising from severe pain. *A little more, please.* Three of the men cried out and all of them went pale. Elliot let it ride for a moment longer, then rolled the egg off his palm and back into the silk-lined box on the table. Instantly their pain ceased. His had never existed.

"I think you'll agree there was a marked difference in intensity between Mr. Halliwell and myself?"

Halliwell was the first to speak. "What *is* that thing?" he demanded, staring at the now motionless egg with antipathy and fear.

"For want of a better term, we call it a Psi-projector." Elliot touched it lightly with a fingertip. "It can amplify thoughts or sensations to a high degree, particularly in the hands of a trained psychic. Even someone who has no training or ability at all, like Mr. Halliwell, can use it to some effect. *I* used it instead of one of the trained psychics on our staff because we want you to remain conscious, at least until lunch. Any of *them* could have had you screaming with pain or crawling with terror in seconds. Seconds, gentlemen. I'm sure you can see the possibilities." He leaned back a little over the table and picked up the golden circlet and bracelet that were coiled under a vase of purple and crimson anemones. "Now this—"

"Wait a minute, Elliot," one of them began in irritation.

"Why not let me finish my act, gentlemen, and then I'll answer any and all questions you might have. All right?" He smiled at them benignly. You poor bastards, he thought.

Wearing the circlet and the bracelet, he (and the other members of the Group who were stationed outside the periphery of the library) took the men on a journey to the hills of Wales, where they had to climb themselves to exhaustion in search of a way down to the sweet green valleys waiting below. No matter which path they tried, they always came back to where they had begun hours before. Yet, when they returned, frustrated and starving, they saw by their watches they had been "gone" for exactly twelve and a half minutes. Elliot called for coffee and biscuits to be served, but still refused to answer their questions.

Then he brought out the Gauntlet.

Unlike the silvery egg or the highly polished golden bracelet and crown, the Gauntlet looked very unpleasant indeed. The visitors eyed it warily, already reduced by sensory bombardment to a condition of near-pathological sensitivity. It was basically a fingerless glove, made of black, light-absorbing material. As he fitted it over his forearm and fastened the clasps underneath, Elliot asked them to produce the various metallic objects they had been requested to bring along. Then, as they brought out their offerings, he slid the two rings over his middle fingers and clipped them to the links over the knuckles of the glove, effectively forcing his hand to remain open.

"Fine. Now, what have we got? A lump of steel, a couple of fountain pens, a stapler, a . . . shelf bracket . . . a screwdriver, a Dinky car. I hope you'll buy another one of those on the way home, General Porter, your little Timmy won't get much more fun out of it when I've finished, I'm afraid." He smoothed the Gauntlet down over his hand and arm, carefully. "I wonder if you'd place your objects on the rubber mats near your chairs." They did. "Thank you. And step back, please."

Raising his arm, Elliot bent his middle two fingers down, causing the rings to pull at the links in the glove. This produced an audible click followed by a low malevolent hum. Holding his hand out in what was very definitely *not* an accidental duplication of the ancient gesture of warding off evil (index and little finger extended in imitation of the horns of Satan), he flattened the steel into an inch-thick sheet, snapped the two fountain pens, sent the stapler flying against the far wall, twisted the shelf bracket into a knot, and melted the Dinky car to a puddle of cold but seemingly molten metal. "They are *your* objects, gentlemen, I've never touched them," he said, lowering his arm. But Frances and Janet had.

Two of the men immediately pounced on the rubber mats, lifting them away from the soft pile of the Axminster and prodding the carpet suspiciously. "If you'd like to examine the mats more closely, you'll find scissors on the table," Elliot said quietly, walking around to the French windows and looking out at the rose bushes that were beginning to bud in promise.

What do we think of it so far?
RUBBISH!

He winced. *There's no need to shout.* And silent laughter surrounded him, while Annie straightened his tie and kissed him.

I wish you'd wear a suit more often.
No you don't. Takes longer to get out of.

"It *was* the Gauntlet, gentlemen, I assure you," he said, turning back to the room and facing them. "No wires, no secret rays, no tricks. All in the mind, you see. All in the mind. Now, if you'll be seated just for a moment, there's one last thing I'd like to say before lunch."

Elliot came around to settle himself once again on the

front edge of the table, still wearing the Gauntlet, smoothing
it repeatedly and absently over his hand as he talked. "I know
some of you will leave Talbot Hall convinced that what you've
seen was all a product of some kind of mass hypnosis, or a
complicated process of legerdemain. I'm used to that kind of
reception—everyone in ESP research is. And I don't really
blame you, because it does demand a major alteration of your
mental attitudes. The energies involved here can't be measured
or defined because we simply don't have the machinery to do
it. *Yet.* Such machinery will come, in time, as will a new set
of laws such as Newton or Doppler or Einstein formulated to
cope with concepts that once were new to *them,* like gravity,
motion, time, and space."

He didn't look directly at them, but kept his eyes either
on the floor or on the rows and rows of books. At first, because
they were by now totally focused on him and what he might do
next, they didn't notice what was happening. Elliot gave no
indication that he did, either. "None of those energies were
really new, obviously. They were there all the time, working
on us, governing our physical world with consistent, formal,
and precise effects. It wasn't until we found a way to categorize them that we saw they were real and true. While the
world of parapsychology *seems* like witchcraft, it isn't. *Everything* seems like witchcraft when it first goes bump in the night
of man's ignorance. I wonder what a caveman would have
made of atomic energy—we can tell him it's there, but he
can't see it, can't feel it, can't smell it or hear it. Until we make
it go boom! right in front of him and destroy a city in seconds.
It's all in your point of view, gentlemen. All a matter of per-
ceiving reality from a different angle."

And he looked at them.

They were staring down at him like a bunch of astonished
goldfish, eyes wide, mouths gaping, their hands clutching the
sides of their chairs in terror as they hovered some six feet
above his head in thin air.

"Nothing changes, gentlemen, just because we learn more about it. Psychic energy is there. It was *always* there. We just couldn't see it from where we were standing. Perhaps you can see a little of it now. Yes?"

14

Cart Curtiss was nearly hysterical with triumphant glee.

"My God, Phil, you really put it to them! I hear they were nearly fit to be tied when they got back. I wish I could have seen it myself."

"So do I," Elliot said without much enthusiasm. As usual, he had come to London because Curtiss would not come to Talbot Hall, and the atmosphere of the building and this office in particular were having the usual effect on him. He was still concerned about his arrogance during the demonstration, and Curtiss's glee was making him feel even worse. "But you were on holiday, I hear."

"Hmm? Oh, yes, we like to get away early before the rush. Listen, they've been all over me wanting to know when they can get their hands on those things."

Elliot shrugged. "I made it as clear as I could that they were merely prototypes and still had a lot of problems to be ironed out. They seemed inordinately interested in the destructive applications, I must say. Even though I pointed out what a valuable theraputic tool the Psi-projector could be."

"Yes, well, that's their business, isn't it?"

"I suppose so." Elliot got up and went over to the tray

to refill his glass from the decanter. "Anyway, it should help you in getting a budget increase through. And it will strengthen your position, won't it?"

"Yes, and don't think I don't appreciate it. But . . ."

Elliot turned, his glass at his lips. "What?"

"It doesn't really change anything, does it? I mean, it's still the Omega power we're after, isn't it? Developing it so that we can use it to do things, things that need doing."

Frowning, Elliot swallowed some of the whisky. "I don't understand. What things?"

"I've been doing a lot of thinking over the past few months . . . and I agree that using Omega so quickly just to play spies and robbers *is* a waste."

Gratified, Eliot sat back down and rested his glass on the chrome tube arm of the chair. "I'm very glad you see it my way. At last."

"Well, I suppose it was obvious, once the first excitement was past. I get there in the end, you know. No, Omega's potential is far, far greater than that. It could actually change the entire face of the world, couldn't it?"

"That's a little expansionist at the moment. What would *you* do with it?"

"Why, make life better for people. Ease their doubts, remove their worries, help them live more productive lives without, well, without having to fight over everything."

"Seems to me we've been over that ground before."

"Oh, I don't mean—I mean for *good*. If you can use that egg thing to make some poor soldier in the field think he's lost the war before he's even fired a shot, then you can use it to make some poor plumber forget the fact that his wife hates his guts, can't you?"

Chuckling, Elliot shook his head and finished his drink. "There's only a few of them at Talbot. How many plumbers do you think they can work on in a week? And what about the butchers and the bakers and the candlestick makers? Haven't they got worries, too? Come on."

"Only a few *now*, yes. But we can find more . . . your first computer run alone came up with over five hundred potentials, didn't it? And anyway, I'm not talking about dealing with individuals. I'm talking about dealing with whole masses of people at once, not a city or a country, but . . ."

"Today East Croydon, tomorrow the world?" Elliot's voice was sarcastic, but Curtiss ignored it, fired with enthusiasm at his new vision.

"If you like, *yes.*"

"I don't like. Not if I really understand what you're driving at, anyway."

"Oh, it would have to be carefully done, of course. With controls, checks and balances and all that, certainly. I'm not advocating 1984, the way Hawkins seemed to. Oh, I say . . . I heard, Phil. I'm sorry about—"

"So are we all, Cart, thanks. Maybe it just goes to prove that even with all this new potential, we're still as vulnerable to the odd germ or the odd mechanical failure. Or the odd drunk behind the wheel," he added. He didn't like what he was hearing. It was obvious that beneath Curtiss's polished exterior the undergraduate still lurked, and lurked closer to the surface than he had in years. Cart, quite simply, was getting carried away. Maybe it was time to find out what *else* was going on under that blond hair. Elliot reached out to tap into Curtiss's mind.

And found nothing.

Startled, he covered his shock by reaching for a cigarette from the box on the edge of Curtiss's desk. His Omega *couldn't* have failed so suddenly again, without warning. Flicking the lighter, he sent his mind beyond the wall of the office and tapped into a nearby secretary. No, it wasn't gone at all, he could clearly pick up everything she was . . . What the hell was going on? Again, he tried to read Curtiss's head and found it empty, which was patently ridiculous, as Cart was walking and talking right there in front of him.

Without (if Elliot's perceptions were to be believed) a brain to direct him.

Separating out a section of his mind to deal with the continuing conversation, Elliot tried every way he knew of penetrating Curtiss's head and was defeated. It was very like the Wall . . . except that it wasn't. It was stronger, it was blanker, and it was . . . mechanical. Suddenly he was sure of it. Cart's head wasn't keeping him out . . . but something *in* Cart's head was.

Triggering himself into hyper-sensitive visual perception, Elliot focused on Curtiss's skull, slowly, painstakingly, minutely, continuing at the same time to parry arguments that were being thrown at him verbally. Eventually he found it, as Cart turned in front of the sunlight that streamed in the window.

Just above and behind the ear there was a break in the smooth line of the sleekly combed hair. As casually as he could, Elliot got up to refill his glass and Curtiss's, contriving to stand directly behind the other man for a moment. Yes. Recently, very recently, in fact, Curtiss had undergone a little surgery. Where had Cragg said he'd gone on his holiday again?

Elliot paused on his way back to his chair, then sat down, pulling his mind back together and smiling vaguely as Curtiss made a rather outrageous pun.

Helsinki.

And Helsinki, though a lovely and ostensibly neutral spot, was very near to . . .

Suddenly it all snapped clear, like a lens focusing in his head.

This wasn't new, this change of Cart's.

It hadn't been his idea alone to put the "bugs" in Talbot, to set a watch on Elliot and the work they were doing there. This was no sudden defection—it was the natural progression of a liaison with the Russians that had to go way back in Curtiss's career. You don't arrange for surgery with the Soviets by dialling the Kremlin and saying, "Hello, you don't know me, my name is Curtiss and . . ."

Oh, no. The net had been closing on Talbot Hall long before this.

And he'd brought Annie right into it, as neatly as a trout for the table.

Kossetz? Probably. Knowing Elliot was his closest rival in the field, knowing it was an even chance one of the two of them would get the answers first. When had the Russians first approached Curtiss? After Talbot Hall had been set up, certainly, otherwise he would have read the signs in Curtiss's mind years before. He had stayed out of Curtiss's hair and his head once he'd got Talbot going because he hadn't needed him any more. That had been a bad mistake.

When Annie appeared on the scene, Kossetz had put on the pressure. Through Curtiss, *using* Curtiss. He'd let Elliot do all the work, waiting for the right moment.

The nightmares had been perfectly real. Probably the result of attempts by some telepathic protégé of Kossetz's to establish contact with Annie, to gain control of her before Elliot could. It had failed—but only because of Annie's loyalty. No wonder she had refused to talk about her "bad dreams." Not knowing anything about foreign powers or spies or even hate, she had only been aware of a brush with something evil. She had tried to shield him, thinking it some failure within herself, some "wickedness" of her own. Oh, Annie.

How much did Kossetz know at this point?

The Wall was now keeping him out of the Group, that was certain. So the Russians were building a Wall of their own, using implants. God, they were quick off the mark. Elliot knew what was going on behind *his* Wall.

What were they doing behind theirs?

The sun was beaming through the window, the girls down on the street below were in their summer dresses, he and Curtiss were wearing lightweight suits. Flowers were blazing in all the gardens behind all the houses of all the towns and villages in the land.

And it was getting very, *very* cold.

"I'm telling you, Danny, the bastard has an *implant* of some kind in that skull of his."

Danny and Janet sat in the double chair opposite his in front of the fireplace, while Annie poured coffee into cups on the tray that was beside her on the carpet. Joseph was waiting patiently for his saucer of cream, and she supplied it, making him shake hands first. After handing around the cups, Annie curled up next to Elliot's legs, resting her head against his knee. Automatically his hand began to stroke the cap of red curls as he continued to speak.

"Somehow, somewhere—and I could just about guess when—he had something put in there that totally blanks him. I just *couldn't* get inside."

"But Curtiss is no traitor, surely?" Danny protested, clinking his cup back into the saucer.

"Listen, you should have heard him. He's begun to think way ahead, and he's begun to think big. All the way, in fact. Omega, to him, is a chance to have all the eggs *and* the basket. Things like borders and borderlines become invisible to a man like Curtiss when he can see his way to power. Real power. Traitor? No, he wouldn't see it that way. Making use of the available alternatives, that's how he'd rationalize it. He's gone over the top, Danny. He's talking about using Omega, using *us,* to eventually control the population. The *world*."

"But we wouldn't do it. And he couldn't force us to, either."

Spit in his eye.
Laugh in his face.
Shut up shop.
Close the shutters.

Hide behind the Wall.
Never come out no more.

"That's no answer either," Elliot said, quietly. "Maybe some of the others in the Group would agree with him."

Which was why they were at Elliot's house, and why they were confining themselves to primarily verbal exchanges. A social evening, two couples having a little light supper away from the office. Maybe.

"How can you possibly think that?" Janet demanded. "You've *been* in their heads, you know what they're like."

"Not completely. You forget, I brought the Wall with me when I joined the Group. We've all been able to maintain privacy since then—I was never wide open to Total Mesh as you all were in the beginning. We can make a reasonable assumption that most mystics throughout history have probably been people with high Omega function, and granted that most mystics throughout history have been benign, you'll still have to accept that some weren't."

"Well, *our* mystics are," she insisted stubbornly.

He glanced down at her hand, resting on Danny's knee, and his mouth quirked. "They're also the randiest bunch I've ever come across."

We follow the leader.
I'm only depraved because I was deprived.
Not me. I just like it.

Danny was still considering Curtiss and ignored the exchange, although he covered Janet's hand with his own as he spoke. "What are you going to do about him, Phil? Blow the whistle?"

"How can I do that without saying what I am and how I found out? All *he* has to say is that I'm crazy. His record is perfect. Impeccable, in fact. Whereas Elliot is the original Mad Scientist, or could be made to look it."

Friends . . . do you suffer from Credibility Gap?
Sounds like a place in Wyoming.

"You need hard evidence, in other words."

"In any words. The trouble is, he's sealed off so I can't get it from him. And our movements are so proscribed by his damn Security set-up that I can hardly take to following him around wearing a trench coat and dark glasses—even if I knew how to do it without him realizing I suspected something."

"Okay, he's been to the Russians, therefore the Russians know about us. They wouldn't like being readable any more than he does; they'll be implanted, too. So they'll have to make contact physically, somehow."

"Obviously. Know how to tap a phone?"

"Sure, don't you? What I *can't* do is get into his building to do it."

Set a thief to catch a thief.

Elliot looked down at Annie, startled. She had been silent on every level up to this point, listening and playing with Joseph and a piece of string . . .

What?

Set a thief to catch a thief, she repeated.

"Well, my darling, I don't know what kind of life you think I've led up to now, but if you assume that gaming clubs are automatically underworld haunts, you're sadly mistaken. I wouldn't have any more idea of how to contact criminals than the local baker."

Not all thieves are crooks.

We haven't time for a moral discussion right now.

I wasn't talking about morals. I was talking about occupations.

"You don't *have* to be enigmatic when you're pregnant, Annie," Janet chided.

"Your trouble is, you're all too scholarly," Annie said, lightly, drawing the piece of string along the carpet until Joseph pounced. "Schopenhauer isn't worth much in a fight. You should put your faith in little old ladies."

"Little old ladies?" Danny faltered.

"Mmmmmm, wasn't Agatha Christie a little old lady?"

Annie's eyebrows arched in mock innocence, and Joseph pounced again as the string trailed past his paws.

There was a silence, then Elliot started to chuckle. "You know, there are days when I feel a definite sympathy for Dr. Frankenstein." He reached down and tugged a curl of her hair gently, pulling her head back so he could look into her face, upside down. "A very definite sympathy."

"Sit down, Bartlett." Elliot waved him to a chair and the butler perched on the edge of it, prepared to take instructions. When they came, they were not what he had expected. "I'd like you to remove your band, Bartlett."

"But . . . the machines . . ."

"Screw the machines, Bartlett, they're a myth and you know it as well as I do. Tell you what else I know. I know who you are and what you are. The only thing I'm not sure of yet is who pays you."

"His Majesty's Government, of course."

"Are you sure you haven't a second source of income, Bartlett? In yen, perhaps, or roubles?"

Bartlett stiffened, gave Elliot a very hard stare, then abruptly leaned back in his chair. "Stuff you," he said, mildly.

Elliot grinned, and took a sip of his after-dinner brandy. It had been a long day and it had every promise of being an even longer night. He detested what he was planning to do, it went against every principle and instinct in him. He was still hoping he could get Bartlett to volunteer, and to that end he was listening as Danny sent him the telemetry readings of the monitors they'd put into the leather chair in which Bartlett was now taking his ease. The band cut out EEG and Omega readings, but there were still the old physical stand-bys of blood pressure, skin conductivity, heartbeat, and so on, to give them an indication of Bartlett's reactions.

"Then you consider yourself a loyal man?"

"Of course."

He's telling the truth, Danny sent.

"Loyal to Mr. Curtiss?"

"Certainly not."

Truth.

"Loyal to whom, then? Who sent you here?"

"The Office of Administrative Assistance—they're part of the Ministry, but quite separate from Mr. Curtiss and his Department."

Partially true.

"And who sent you to them?"

"I'm not sure what you're getting at, sir."

He knows damn well.

Elliot sighed. "You're too good, Bartlett. They wouldn't waste someone of your caliber out here at a minor research facility unless you were useful to them as well as to us. Perhaps you don't report to Mr. Curtiss, but you report to *someone* about us, don't you?"

"I have to submit monthly reports on the catering and other services, of course, plus reviews of . . ."

Bullshit!

"Bullshit, Bartlett," Elliot echoed. "Are you on your own, or are there more of you in the woodwork?"

"We have a full staff of . . .

He's good, but he's lying.

"Are you on your own, Bartlett?" Elliot persisted.

Bartlett was as immaculate, as calm, as quiet as ever, but there was a different man behind the eyes now. Wary, and ready to defend himself. And Elliot didn't have to be able to read his mind to see that he was assessing the situation and Elliot himself with great care and intelligence.

"Quite alone, sir."

Truth. Ask him why.

"Then you must be even better than I suspected. Why just one of you?"

Amusement flickered in Bartlett's eyes. "Because no one

thought the assignment important enough to warrant expend-
ing more than one salary towards it. It's a watching brief,
nothing more."

"I see. And who are you watching?"

Again, the flicker of amusement. "Curtiss."

Is that the truth, Danny?, Elliot asked.

Amazement came back at him. *Yes, by God, it is.*

"Why are you watching Curtiss? And why here?"

Bartlett shrugged. "Whitehall is a battleground, Dr.
Elliot. Each sub-section of each Department of each Ministry
in competition with one another. Not everyone thinks Mr.
Curtiss is the new Messiah."

"Thank God for that."

"Indeed." Bartlett's tone was dry.

"You haven't asked me why I'm confronting you with
this," Elliot observed.

"Because you're desperate, I presume."

Elliot raised an eyebrow. "It's that obvious?"

"Yes."

"Do you know *why* it's that obvious to you?"

"I've seen desperate men before."

Elliot knew perfectly well that outwardly he was evincing
no sense of desperation or fear, he'd had too much experience
in hiding his feelings for that. "You have a very high Omega
potential, Bartlett. We can pick it up, you know, even through
the band."

"I find that hard to believe."

"Nonetheless, it's true. And hardly surprising in a spy, of
course. You'd need such a capacity to survive, wouldn't you?"

"I think the term 'spy' is a bit extreme. I'm merely one of
the many bureaucratic cogs in the machinery, an efficiency
expert, if you like. There are some who would like to know
why Mr. Curtiss has suddenly become so very efficient, you
see. Jealousy, a concern about the distribution of departmental
appropriations, that sort of thing."

Lies, bloody LIES!, Danny bellowed.

"Then it won't surprise you to know that I, too, am worried about Mr. Curtiss," Elliot said, slowly.

"It would surprise me if you weren't," Bartlett replied, mildly.

"Before I tell you why I'm worried, I'm afraid it will be necessary for you to remove your band."

"I think not, if you don't mind."

"I do mind. I have to have you on our side as quickly as possible, you have expertise we need."

"Your side? Of what, exactly?"

Elliot sighed. They were wasting time. He would have to break his own rule. *I guess you'll have to take it off him, Frances, he won't volunteer.*

The band around Bartlett's temples suddenly flew up and off. He grabbed for it, but it clattered to the floor six feet away. Elliot put his glass down and went into the man opposite him as fast and as hard as he could, hating himself for it. Bartlett's eyes widened, and a gasp escaped him as the struggle began. Elliot closed his eyes because he didn't want to see the outrage in Bartlett's face, or the panic. The Group watched, ready to help, but he told them to stay out. He had to be alone with his quarry in the dark city of the mind.

It seemed to Elliot an endless city, a sprawl of crisscrossing streets and alleys, footsteps running, the sound of his own breathing loud in his ears as he chased the personality of Adam Bartlett this way and that, trying to back him into a corner. But Bartlett eluded him, and Elliot had no taste for inflicting pain. There was no doubt about it—the man was exceptional. So exceptional that Elliot came to a reluctant decision and called out defeat. When the phantom of Bartlett turned in the dark street, Elliot faced him squarely and dropped his own Wall.

Bartlett came in, was drawn in, and stayed.

After a long time, Elliot spoke, his voice startlingly loud in the silent office. "I'm sorry—but you see the problem."

Bartlett's own voice was shaky. "Yes. I understand, now."

He opened his eyes and stared at Elliot across the expanse of the desk. "Why are you speaking aloud?" Then he answered his own question. "You've taught me how to build the Wall."

"Yes. I couldn't have lived with what I just tried to do without giving myself the satisfaction of ensuring it could never happen again. I'm afraid you're stuck with having your Omega function put 'on line,' but at least you can defend yourself from now on."

"Thank you."

"Your grasp of your own identity is amazing; it would have taken me hours to break you. Where did you learn to hide so well?"

"I was once held for quite a long time in a small cell in the basement of a very large institution in Smolensk," Bartlett said. "It was a matter of protecting my ego or going insane. Presumably you understand the process—I don't. I only know I remained sane. Eventually I was exchanged, and demoted at my own request. I only wanted to do simple work after that." He gave a wry chuckle. "The last easy assignment they offered was to come here."

"I'm sorry."

Bartlett smiled. "I don't think I am. Not now."

"You don't have to join us, you know."

"I realize that."

"But we would be grateful if you'd help us. If you have your network to fall back on . . ."

"I don't think that would be a very good idea, under the circumstances," Bartlett interrupted.

"Oh? I was rather counting on it."

"Indeed, I'm sure you were. I'd better explain." Elliot was amazed to see a faint flush suffuse under Bartlett's cheekbones. "And I'd prefer to do it verbally, rather than . . ."

"I told you, you don't have to lower your Wall for anyone, until and unless you're ready," Elliot said gruffly, knowing only too well the rawness and the sense of vulnerability felt by the newly invaded.

"Thank you. The title 'Intelligence' is often a misnomer, I'm afraid. Very few of my superiors could be described as more than averagely bright. With a few exceptions, most of the brains in my branch of the Service are at the bottom—or so we agents would tell you. When Mr. Curtiss's Department began to chalk up so many inexplicable successes, my superiors presumed it was because of some kind of electronic gadgetry your technicians had developed. They think very conventionally in Whitehall, and more often than not tangle themselves up in their own red tape."

"But you've told them there's no gadget."

"Actually, no—I haven't. I've told them very little."

"Why?"

"There seemed to be plenty of time. On reflection, I think now that I must have sensed some . . . fellow feeling. Is that possible?"

"You mean you had an impulse to protect us, even before . . . ?"

"It sounds foolish, put like that. I merely kept procrastinating, telling myself I needed to know more before I did anything concrete. I knew what would happen, you see."

"What?" Elliot's eyes narrowed.

Bartlett took his time. "Whatever Curtiss's moral failings might be, he *does* have the guts to take a chance on something as—worrisome—as the Group. Perhaps he feels confident enough of his own position to think he can keep it under control. My superiors have no such delusions. They would take no chances, because there is an inbred inclination in Whitehall to preserve the status quo at all costs. The cost to you would be total destruction—the cost to them, negligible. Despite your protestations of benign intent, which I now know personally to be valid, they would see you as insupportably dangerous. They're too accustomed to suspecting one another to ever trust you. It would be a case of baby and bath-water, I'm afraid."

Elliot slumped in his chair. "Then you can't help us."

"I didn't say that, exactly. What I said was that I thought it would be risky to tell them what was going on here and expect *them* to help you."

"What do we do, then?"

"Oh, we use them, we most definitely use them. But we don't tell them why. I suggest a broad programme of deception. By the time they sort out the loose ends from all their inter-office red tape, we can only hope to be in a position to bargain with them. If what you suspect about Curtiss is true, they may see him as the greater threat and accept us as allies. Of course, in the long term. . . ." He paused.

"In the long term, they may have second thoughts about us."

"I'm afraid so. But . . . we'll have to think about that later on. Right now, our first priority is to manufacture a story I can give them that will force them into extending a few helping hands. They are still happy with the idea of electronic gadgetry, you know. They still think you need it to do what you do."

"Then we mustn't confuse them with facts, must we?" Elliot grinned.

Bartlett grinned back. "It would only upset their digestion."

I feel bloody ridiculous, Elliot complained peevishly.

I can authorize general surveillance and I can authorize mechanical surveillance, but I can't instigate actual intrusion without having to answer a lot of questions.

Elliot glanced at Bartlett's shadow beside him.

But why me? Why not Dave Stuart or Ari? They were both trained as commandos. I'm pushing forty and a devout coward.

They wouldn't know what one looks like.

I'm not sure I would, either.

Even so, your guess would be better than theirs. And you're not watched as closely as they are, remember?

Bloody hell. Elliot ducked his head down again to look at the house on the opposite side of the street. *It just looks like an ordinary house.*

They rarely erect neon signs, Bartlett commented drily.

It *was* an absolutely ordinary house. In a row of absolutely ordinary houses in an ordinary street in West Ealing. There were a number of quite ordinary cars scattered down the curb under the twisted fingers of the few plane trees. A man walked past with a Jack Russell terrier on a length of cord and turned in at the gate three along from their objective. Light flashed across the garden briefly from the open door, then was gone.

Funny how all the dogs come home when the pubs shut. Elliot rubbed his face and ran his fingers through his hair. *How many are in there?* Bartlett was so calm it was making him nervous, not that he needed much help in that direction.

There's no way of being certain, if they're implanted, is there? My people have counted four regulars, and a number of visitors. I have myself observed two visitors in the past week who went in wide open and emerged the next day implanted. The conclusion is obvious.

So there could be an extra twenty or so in the cellar who never come out?

There could be. The contents of the rubbish bins says otherwise.

Unless they're religious fanatics on a fast.

In which case they'll be too weak to give us any trouble.

You don't know many religious fanatics, do you?

Only you. Are you going in or not?

I want my mother.

You want one of those implants, too.

Yes, he did. They couldn't get around the implants if they didn't know what was in them, and only turning George and Frances loose on one was going to answer that. Bartlett had been keeping Curtiss under observation for over a fortnight and there had been absolutely no Russian contacts observed of any kind. Only picking up the pattern from the Kensington end had led them to this house in which they were certain was the surgical unit that was placing the implants in the Embassy staff. And in some others who were definitely not Russian, but tying them into the pattern would take even longer and they did not seem to have that much time. Curtiss was getting a little more demanding each day, a little more excitable, too. It was a set of symptoms Elliot found all too easy to diagnose.

Okay, what do I do? Go up and ring the doorbell?

It has a certain novel appeal, but I wouldn't recommend it. We'll break in through the back when we're sure they're all asleep.

Wonderful. How will we be sure?

When we're reasonably sure, I should have said, Bartlett amended.

Elliot turned away from the window and nearly knocked over the telescope that was focused through the lace curtains of the upper bedroom in which they waited. He had found it inexplicably annoying to discover that a real surveillance operation was mounted in *exactly* the way they showed in the films. Where was the insouciant charm of the British amateur, he mourned. There wasn't a white hat among them. They were all as calm and efficient as Bartlett and made him feel as rumpled as a laundrybag, even in his neat dark pullover and trousers. He gazed down. And sneakers. At his age.

Two hours later they circled the street and came up the alleyway behind the houses opposite, stopping at the one they wanted. It looked just as ordinary from the back. Bartlett leaned down to inspect the latch on the gate set into the high wooden fence, then slowly lifted it and pushed inward. There was a slight protest from the hinges, no more. They passed through into a bleak garden that was mostly planted in concrete and oil stains, crossing to the back door as quickly as they could. Elliot felt his imitation of a shadow left something to be desired, but Bartlett moved as silently as a bat.

You're enjoying this, aren't you?, he challenged as they reached the small overhang above the back door and stood in its thicker darkness.

Haven't been on a field operation for four years.

And you're having fun.

Not enough to want to make it last. Bartlett squatted down and began to pick at the lock on the door with a small tool that looked like a crochet hook. There was no need for a torch, as they had adjusted their optic nerves to compensate for the darkness. As Ari had often pointed out, if all else failed they could make a reasonable living robbing banks for the rest of their lives, thanks to the new depths Omega gave to their sensory perceptions. Nothing had changed in the outside world, it was simply a matter of what you did with stimuli once they entered the brain. And every drop of water *was* an ocean.

Frances could have opened that in two seconds.

Perhaps. But would it have locked again afterwards?

Bartlett stood up and pushed the door inward silently. Now that's stupid, Elliot thought. If I was a spy, I'd make sure all the hinges on my doors were as noisy as hell. Then, as they crossed the kitchen, he realized this bunch depended more on loose floorboards.

Where would it be?, Bartlett enquired.

What?

The surgical thingy.

I'm no bloody interior decorator. Could be anywhere. Depends on how complex the implantation procedure is. If it's just set into the mastoid bone, it wouldn't take much. If it's deep inside the brain itself, it would be very complex indeed. Did you say they walked out the next day?

Yes.

Then it could be done virtually anywhere, I suppose.

Downstairs or up?

Anywhere.

They paused inside the door that led to the rest of the house. As Bartlett raised a hand to push it open, it was sud-

denly pushed at them from the far side, hard. Elliot's elbow
caught a pile of dishes that started to slide off the counter,
but as the door pressed him further back, his body prevented
them from crashing to the floor. The only noise was a dull
clatter and the wheeze of the air going out of his body across
Bartlett's shoulder.

Whoever had opened the door obviously realized fairly
quickly that the glass of warm milk or whatever he'd been
seeking had suddenly escalated into human form, for just as
suddenly the door was released and they heard footsteps moving quickly away. Bartlett pushed the swinging door outward
against its hinges and squeezed through, taking four running
steps after the shadowy figure and bringing it down with a
heavy thud. Elliot caught and held the door in time to see
Bartlett's elbow move back and forward in a short arc. After
a moment, the double form on the floor separated and Bartlett
stood looking down.

He should have yelled. I'd have yelled.

*We'll arrange a lecture tour for you next week. Now
what?*

Now we wait to see what happens.

Nothing happened.

Elliot wasn't sure if he was glad about that or not. The
sudden burst of activity had set his adrenalin flow into high
gear, and he would have preferred doing something, anything, rather than just standing there like a statue. He scratched
his leg as a poor alternative.

Well?

I'll do a tour down here—we might get lucky.

They had used up their luck. All the downstairs rooms
were just downstairs rooms. Bartlett returned and stood looking down at the man he'd knocked out. *If we leave him, he's
going to tell them somebody was here as soon as he wakes up.
If we take him with us, they'll also know.* The original idea
had been a quick in and out to steal one of the implant devices
and hope that there were a sufficient number there to have

the theft go unnoticed for a few days at least.

So? Elliot had by now accumulated so much adrenalin in his system through sheer terror that he was ready to start jumping up and down and screaming Ya boo sucks to anyone who was interested. *So so so so so?*

So we might as well take him and forget about finding their spares. If I get you to a suitable place, can you remove his implant as a viable alternative?

I imagine so. Surgery was never my speciality but it shouldn't be difficult.

Right. Let's go.

Between them they got the unconscious man through the kitchen and across the yard into the alley, but he was big and his inert weight had the curious quality of increasing with every step.

We sound like two hippopotami in heat, Elliot observed, gasping and letting the two legs drop to the rough broken concrete of the alleyway. Bartlett lowered his end more slowly, but with as great a sigh of relief.

I'll watch him—you go get the car.

Are you sure you'll be all right?, Elliot asked.

I'll be fine.

But Bartlett had over-estimated himself or under-estimated the Russian. Elliot was just nosing the car into the entrance of the alleyway when his headlights picked up Bartlett and the Russian struggling together. Elliot killed the engine and leaped out, running down the alley towards the writhing combined shadows with no very clear intention of what to do, but hoping he'd think of something positive by the time he got there. What he did was to jump onto the Russian's back and try to drag him off Bartlett, precipitating all three of them onto the filthy concrete of the alley in a tangled heap. As his ear slid across a rotten orange, Elliot decided he should have tried a more intellectual approach, such as kicking the Russian in the balls. He was obviously not cut out for this kind of work.

He lay there, trying to drag back the oxygen that the impact of the other two on top of him had removed from his lungs, blinking as his eyes refused to focus. There was a lovely sky overhead, pale pink as the light of the city reflected off the underside of the clouds. A few feet away he could hear the struggle continuing as first Bartlett and then the Russian took the advantage. Surely there must be *something* he could do? His body didn't agree. He managed to roll over and got onto his hands and knees, only to discover he was facing the wrong way. Turning on all fours like a dog, he saw the Russian had broken free from Bartlett and was coming towards *him,* one arm up and back. He heard a choking gurgle start in his throat, the best he could provide as a protest, as Bartlett grabbed the Russian's arms from behind. There was a long moment of stasis, then Bartlett forced the Russian's arms forward, following the motion with the weight of his own body. The Russian collapsed and Bartlett ended up on top of him with his face between his opponent's knees.

Elliot started to crawl forward. Bartlett gave a sudden heave and rolled off the other man. When the Russian didn't show any signs of moving, Elliot crawled a little closer and saw the hilt of a knife projecting upward from a spreading stain on the chest. His elbows gave way and he laid down next to Bartlett in order to contemplate the universe.

Had a knife, Bartlett commented.

So I see.

Sorry about that.

We can't leave him here.

No.

And we can't take him to Talbot, now.

No.

Bit of a problem, isn't it? Elliot wiped his face with his sleeve and saw that what he'd felt trickling down his neck was partly sweat and partly blood. On top of everything else, he seemed to have broken his own nose.

I have an idea, Bartlett offered.

Will I like it?
I doubt it.
So do I, Elliot mourned.

Bartlett stopped the car halfway down the lane leading to Elliot's house, pulling over to the side and turning off the headlamps. "Let's get him down to the water."

Elliot had been half asleep and turned his head to stare. "That's just a shallow stream. He won't even be a foot under."

"I don't intend to leave him there. Come on."

Bartlett opened his door and got out, leaving Elliot to follow suit. They met at the back and Bartlett took hold of the Russian's feet, pulling the body towards them. "Keep him face up so he doesn't bleed onto the deck." Elliot was too weary to keep asking questions so he simply helped Bartlett drag the dead Russian across the thick grass of the verge and into the deeper shadows under the trees. When the body was alongside the edge of the stream, Bartlett said, "Strip off."

He had his pullover halfway up before it occurred to him to ask why. Bartlett was busy pulling the knife out of the chest, and didn't answer immediately. When he did, Elliot just stared, and then started to pull his sweater back down.

"I can't."

"You know where to cut, I don't. You did anatomy presumably?" He held out the knife. "You can stay dressed if you're the modest type, but personally I'd rather wash blood off skin than clothes."

When he had finished, Elliot staggered through the water and sank down onto the prickly grass at the edge of the sluggish stream. Bartlett held the body shoulders down in the water, having settled himself comfortably against the base of a tree. "Aren't you going to pull it out?" Elliot said, still trying not to vomit. Anatomy class had been a long time ago, and he hadn't enjoyed it then, either.

"I think he'd better drain for a while. I've got a friend with a pig farm—they'll eat anything if it's ground up. You'd better go home and stitch that chin of yours together. I don't think anybody's going to believe you cut yourself shaving, though. Maybe you'd better stay at home for a few days."

"Maybe I should." Shaking with fatigue and reaction, Elliot hauled himself the rest of the way out of the water and laid what he had been holding on the grass. The sky was beginning to lighten in the east, and a few birds asked sleepy questions from the branches overhead. Gathering up his clothes from the bank, he rolled them into a bundle then leaned down to pick up the rest of his burden. Without saying anything further, he turned and started back towards the road. Bartlett wedged the body more firmly between his knees and watched him go, the square stocky figure glimmering white in the pre-dawn mist. It was just as well the lane had no houses other then Elliot's on it, he decided. Otherwise some early-rising householder might step out onto the doorstep for the milk and be a little unnerved by the sight of a nude man walking down the road, his clothes in one hand and a severed human head in the other.

Taking a firmer grip on the wet hair, Elliot padded along the edge of the tarmac, hardly feeling the gravel under his naked feet. The head swung heavily beside him, occasionally bumping into his leg, and he held it away slightly. The half-opened eyes looked blankly at the morning, and the blue-grey lips were drawn back from the teeth in a rictus that seemed almost cheerful. Every few steps another drop or two of blood fell from the half-stem of the neck onto the road, glittering for a moment before it sank into the dust.

Your face . . . your beautiful face.

You always said it was a rumpled face. Now it's a little more rumpled.

After dissecting out the implant, Elliot had used the kitchen cleaver to smash the head into fragments small enough to shove down the waste-disposal unit in the sink or put into the incinerator. Then he had taken a long, slow bath. It hadn't made him feel any cleaner. The implant was now sitting on the bedside table, and Annie was leaning over him, her eyes filled with sorrow.

It's clotted itself together. I'll stitch it up later.

No, let me.

He felt her hands on his face, light, gentle. As exhaustion dragged him down into darkness a tingling warmth spread from her fingers. The last thing he remembered was the touch of her mouth on his while her hands cupped his chin, and then there was nothing. Blessed, silent nothing.

When he walked into the electronics lab the next afternoon and handed the implant to George, Bartlett was there. He stared at Elliot's face. It was still the same face it had always been. Nowhere on it was there a sign of either wound or scar. Elliot had even shaved. When he saw Bartlett's expression, he smiled crookedly and referred him to the file on Kirlian photography and healing.

Annie?

Annie. Always, and forever, Annie.

15

The storm had been building since after lunch. By four o'clock the air had a sullen yellow cast, and no breeze lifted the heavy heads of the old trees that surrounded Talbot Hall. Low black clouds rolled up from the south-west, harried by a high wind that brought no relief to the meadows and hills below. The atmosphere pressed down, silencing even the birds. Everything waited, waited, for the first mutter of thunder and the first breeze that would finally turn the leaves back and expose their silvery bellies to the scowl of the sky.

Lights were already on in the bedroom overlooking the lawns to the rear. The curtains hung limply in front of the wide-open window, the figures within indistinct behind the gauzy folds. Two men stood on either side of the bed, each bending forward to observe what lay between them.

"This is the worst one yet, Phil," Ted said through his mask, looking down at Ari's twisting body as it rolled around on the bed, grabbing for and finally capturing a wrist as it flailed past. "Can't one of the Group get inside him and find out what the hell's wrong?"

Elliot wiped his forehead with his sleeve. "Tried it when

Danny went. Robin got in, then had a hard time getting out again."

"And when they come around again, what are they saying?"

"Nothing. They don't even remember it happening."

"But Danny was like this for more than two hours!"

"Yes, I know."

Ted dropped Ari's wrist and made a note on the clipboard. The big Irishman continued to writhe as if in the grip of some great and terrible pain, his face wet with perspiration and his lips drawn back from the mouthful of big white teeth Elliot had never been able to reconcile with the shape of his jaw. There had always seemed to be far too many in there, all his own, all healthy. Suddenly Ari arched upwards, his spine lifting from the bed, and then his sphincter control went and the bed was darkened with urine and faeces.

"They all did that, too," Ted said, putting down the clipboard and matter-of-factly starting to strip the sheets from the bed. "But only once. They just let go, like babies."

Elliot turned to the stack of linen he had placed by the side of the bed and shook out a fresh sheet to replace the one Ted was now shoving in a plastic bag to go to the pathology lab. Between them they cleaned Ari up and re-made the bed.

From outside came the low conversation of distant thunder, and a cool breeze began to explore the curtains, pushing them into the room, dropping them, then lifting them again.

Elliot slowly reached up and removed his mask. "We're not going to find any bacterial or amoebic traces on those sheets, any more than we're going to find any viral source in the blood samples. This isn't a disease. This is Omega."

Ted stared at him across the bed. "I was wondering how long it was going to take you to admit it."

"The correlation is obvious, isn't it? They're dropping in the same order. First Danny, then Frances, then Janet, now Ari. By that criterion, Robin should be next, then Dave Stuart, then Brian Miller."

"And why not Annie? She worked with the bio-feedback first."

"Only for control, never for enhancement. Her strength was natural, theirs has been pushed up."

"And now it's backfiring, is that what you're thinking?"

Wadding up the mask, Elliot walked over to the waste-paper basket and dropped it in, staring down at the litter of papers and orange peel. "That's one of the things I'm considering, yes. It might be a one-time thing—a mental belch, if you like. Or . . ."

"Or the attacks might recur. A new epileptic order—Omegalepsy—how about that?"

"Not very funny."

"It wasn't really meant to be."

Lightning briefly challenged the lamps and a few seconds later a deep thud of thunder shook the window in its frame.

The "attacks" had started three days before. The symptoms had all been the same, starting with Danny: a sudden "screech" or whine of Omega clearly heard by all members of the Group, followed by unconsciousness, feverish agitation but without an accompanying rise in temperature, a gradual drop in pulse and blood pressure levelling at just above the danger point, then a series of sudden dysfunctions—one by one heart, lungs, and so on went terrifyingly off-line for several minutes, then just as abruptly resumed normal activity. Each patient had exhibited outward signs of deep physical shock. Each had recovered without after-effects, and without any memory whatsoever of the experience.

"If Robin goes next, we'll be sure."

"All I can say is I'm glad I never let you open up *my* Omega," Ted said.

You would be low on the list, my friend, Elliot thought, watching Ted trying to wrap a sphagmomanometer cuff around Ari's arm. I'm generally a forgiving man, but I have a long memory for betrayals.

Ari came around an hour or so afterwards when the rain was streaming down the windows. Like the rest, he could remember nothing. A few hours later, while sitting in the kitchen with Bartlett, Robin Tuckwell succumbed. Just before midnight Dave Stuart went under and they nearly lost him, having to use electro-shock to restart his heart when it showed no signs of picking up on its own, as the others had.

They had initially assumed Danny's attack was caused by some illness, but when Frances repeated the pattern, Elliot immediately cancelled all assignments until further notice, recalling all his people to Talbot where he could keep an eye on them. So it was with some irritation that he heard Curtiss's voice on his telephone the next afternoon. No one had had an attack all day, but he was far from assuming the thing was over.

"I'm sorry, Cart. No to whatever you want. We've got some problems at the moment."

"So I heard. I'm sure it isn't anything permanent."

"I appreciate your diagnosis, I wish I could be as certain."

"Never mind, you'll manage," Curtiss said soothingly. "Meanwhile, I want you to give me two or three of your best people next week. Including your lovely wife, please."

"Absolutely out of the question."

"It's important. Probably the most important thing you've had to do for me so far."

"I'm sorry, nothing is important enough for me to risk Annie, much less any of the rest of the Group until I find out exactly what—"

"Then perhaps *you'll* do it for me."

"I beg your pardon?"

"You haven't fallen prey to this mysterious little bug. You take the assignment."

"How can I? I'm not one of the Omega Group."

"Oh, but you are. And don't bother saying otherwise, Phil—I *know* you are."

"What makes you think that, for heaven's sake? I haven't had time to get my hair cut lately, much less turn myself into a—"

"Don't waste time, please. I will require you and two or three others to be at my disposal for several days next week to monitor the Little Summit."

"The what?"

"Do you *only* read the newspapers while you're having your hair cut? Next week there will be a number of Heads of State here for—"

"Oh, that. What's the matter, suspect the President of the United States of being a KGB agent or something?" Elliot said with a bantering tone that was only tongue-deep. How had Curtiss found out? How?

"Hardly," Curtiss said drily. "But it will be a golden opportunity for gleaning information of the highest possible order, don't you agree? Every one of those men knows more than we could possibly acquire in years, no matter how many lower-echelon people we—"

"No." He was certain it wasn't Curtiss alone who wanted the information.

"I beg your pardon?"

"It didn't seem all that complicated to me. *No.* I will *not* give you any of my people to do anything of the kind."

"In addition to the gathering of information, I will also require you to do a little social work on my behalf. Build an attitude of—how shall I phrase it?—acceptance in regard to the future? You could do that quite easily, it seems to me. Sow the seeds of hope for a better world in the minds of some of the more sloppy liberal thinkers among them?" Curtiss had simply ignored his refusal, brushing it aside as if it were meaningless. Elliot decided he had not been specific enough.

"Fuck off, Curtiss," he said venomously.

"Not just now, thank you, Philip," Curtiss said with great good cheer. "Never this early in the morning. I'm not talking about anything massive, I'm a patient man, really. Just a little 'softening-up' of the front-line troops, as it were."

"I can think of a little softening-up I'd like to do to you, preferably with a crowbar. I'll say it again. NO!"

"I really think you should reconsider that, you know. If you wish to reduce this to the level of threats, I can oblige. I would very much like to continue our working relationship, Philip—you have so much more to offer than you've given. But make no mistake, I don't need you any more. *You* are not important. What you've discovered and developed at Talbot Hall is, of course, but not you."

"I think you'll find it a little difficult to run an Omega Group without me."

"All for one and one for all? Touching, but a little out of date. It might be that they wouldn't have any choice, you know. Any more than you have any choice about next week. You *will* do as I ask, or suffer the consequences. And in case you imagine that nipping out of your office and taking that crowbar you mentioned to all those pretty bits and pieces you've built down there will make any difference, I'll save you the trouble. I have copies of every record, every chart, every wiring diagram, and every item in your inventory. I also have people who can duplicate everything. *Everything.* However, I don't want to be heavy-handed about this. I'd far prefer to keep you than to lose you, after all. You and Annie *are* the most powerful Omegans at my disposal, so far. So you just think about it."

"I don't have to think about it." He glanced at his wrist-watch. "As of four-fifty-five on the afternoon of Friday, August Twelfth, you just lost yourself the whole Omega Group. I *know* who your 'people' are, Cart, and I'm not interested. If you—"

"Let's call it five o'clock, shall we? Five o'clock. I'll give you just forty-eight hours to accept the inevitable. If I haven't heard from you by five on Sunday afternoon, you'll hear from *me*. And you'll regret it."

Elliot stared at the humming phone in his hand. Slowly

he replaced the receiver. Wiring diagrams? Records? How could he have got those? They kept a close eye on Ted Holbrook, never let him get near anything like that, *never*. There had been no point in getting rid of him, he was still a highly useful member of the medical staff. It had simply been a matter of containment, no more. And Holbrook didn't know Elliot had regained his powers, either. Yet Curtiss had sounded too sure of himself to be merely guessing. So there was someone else. . . .

After an hour's brooding he decided he'd had enough. The whole thing had become dirty and pointless. His people were falling ill, they were being pushed too far. He had started it and he was going to finish it. Curtiss could ring back all he liked on Sunday afternoon, there would be nobody at home.

He set off for the dining room where most of them would be starting on the soup. He would tell them everything, explain the position, then . . .

There was a new guard on duty in Reception, one he had never seen before. And even before he got close, he realized the man wore an implant. They all recognized the sound it made now.

"Good evening, Dr. Elliot."

"Who are you? Where's Baker?"

"My name is Porter, sir. Can I help you?"

"Why are you wearing a sidearm, Porter? Baker never wore one."

"No, sir. But the directive clearly states that—"

"What directive?"

"I'm sorry, sir, I understood you'd been informed. No one is to enter or leave Talbot Hall until further notice, and we have been directed to enforce that order by whatever means necessary. Because of the quarantine, you see. The danger to—"

"What bloody quarantine?"

"The quarantine the Ministry has placed on this institution until the disease has been identified and measures have been taken to—"

"What bloody *disease*?" The man just stared at him, and he realized it was useless to go on. There was nothing quite as stringent as a Department of Health Quarantine, *if* they cared to enforce it to the full. And he was absolutely positive Curtiss would find it very convenient to make them do just that. He reached for the phone on the desk.

"I'm sorry, sir."

"You can send flowers by phone, but not germs. I simply want to call my wife."

"Oh. But your wife is here, Dr. Elliot. She arrived about twenty minutes ago. She even brought your cat. Wouldn't come without it apparently."

He stared at the guard, aghast. "Who brought her?"

"We did, sir. She has been exposed to the disease, you see, and so she has to—"

"Where is she?"

"I believe she's upstairs in your room. She was very . . . tired."

Elliot turned and ran for the stairs, pounding down the hall and bursting into the corner room that was kept for Annie and himself whenever they stayed over. She was there, all right, sound asleep on the bed with Joseph beside her. Very soundly asleep. Looking down he discovered, just inside her elbow, the unmistakable mark of a needle. No wonder he had heard nothing from her, no call for help, no warning.

Curtiss had been absolutely and totally serious. Without even going to the window he knew there would be new guards all around the place. Implanted guards they could not attack with Omega. Armed guards who, whether they knew why they were really there or not, were under orders to shoot to kill if necessary. What had Curtiss used to invoke it—rabies? plague? transmuted virus strains? *He* knew what went on at Talbot Hall, but the Department of Health didn't. They believed what they were told, acted fast, and would only require explanations later.

Curtiss had obviously been prepared for Elliot's refusal, because it had only taken the time between the phone call and the changing of the guards to implement the Quarantine Order. Assuring the authorities that proper medical supervision was available at Talbot would keep the Inspectors out for a while, anyway. No doubt Curtiss had an explanation ready for just about everything, in fact.

And Elliot had no answers ready at all.

Annie awoke little the worse for her nap, although surprised to find herself back at Talbot. Elliot waited by the bed, watching her face, holding Joseph in his lap and stroking him absent-mindedly. The cat put up with it. I remember you, he seemed to say, but I'm hers now. When she wakes up, forget it.

Even knowing that her sleep was simply a matter of sedation and not an Omega attack, he still felt a great rush of relief when her eyes fluttered open and she turned her head on the pillow until she saw him there.

Hello, perfecto, she sent amiably, sleepily.

Hello, fox.

Joseph was dumped unceremoniously as Elliot rushed to the only sanctuary he trusted, Annie's arms and Annie's body and Annie's mind. He held her against him so tightly that she began to laugh and struggle—the laughter going and the struggle ceasing as she read the turmoil in his head.

The minute my back is turned you get into trouble.

Oh, Annie, no jokes.

They lay there together, their minds interlocked as they tried to unravel the web of Curtiss's deceit and faced his no longer concealed ambition, his determination. And his weapons.

Whatever they are, he's sure enough now to go ahead.

He'll take the baby . . . he will . . . they will . . .

You know what I'll do if they try.
You might not have time.
Then you'll have to do it . . .
There was a long silence.
This is the darkling plain, isn't it?
Yes, I think so. He remembered it was one of her favourite poems. Only in poetry had Annie found that the greyness could be removed from simple words. *Except the armies that are clashing by night aren't ignorant. They know too damn much.*

The weekend dragged its hours reluctantly past them. Elliot haunted the electronics lab where George and Frances still laboured to break the secrets of the implant device. Three more of the Group were hit with the mysterious attacks, and he and Holbrook watchdogged them through, learning no more than they knew already. The quarantine meant that not only could none of them leave, but no auxiliary staff could enter either. Meals were put together anyhow, under Bartlett's supervision.

It rained all day Sunday, steadily and without a single break. The empty halls of Talbot were damp and gloomy, and Elliot paced them constantly. The guards were certainly much in evidence; every corner he turned seemed to bring him face to face with yet another blank head with a gun on its belt and "orders" from the Ministry. It had occurred to Elliot, briefly, to simply call for help, but every number he dialed was abruptly disconnected with a long flat tone. Except Cragg's. He didn't have anything to say to whoever it was answering Cragg's phone. Omega hardly seemed necessary for Curtiss to institute a police state, for he had already created one here at Talbot. It was not a big place, after all—just big enough to start a kingdom with.

He had told the Group, finally, what the alternatives were. As he had suspected, not all of them were quite as horrified as he at Curtiss's ideas for implementing a "better world" through mass mental control.

"All very well if you're doing the controlling, is that it?" he had challenged them. "What makes you so damned sure you would be? We gave you the choice when you came to Talbot, we didn't just sock you in here and turn you on. Or off. Doesn't everyone deserve the same choice?"

Apparently not. Apparently bigotry and suspicion and convictions of superiority could survive even Omega, despite all he had tried to do. That depressed him more than anything else. Curtiss might have an easier time of it than he had thought. Perhaps I was wrong, he thought. Perhaps my parents brought up a soppy kid, after all. Telling me that virtue was its own reward and pain was to be endured and people mattered and turn the other cheek and love thy neighbour. But they had been happy, and he had been happy, too, living like that. It had never been terribly difficult, being "decent." Far more effort seemed to be required for treasons, stratagems, and spoils. In the end, an understanding of the pleasure of evil was simply beyond him.

And that, friends, is how I got where I am today. He bowed to an invisible audience. You see before you, in living colour, the world's first telepathic horse's ass.

At five o'clock he was in his office. Danny, Janet, and Annie were with him, and Bartlett joined them at two minutes past the hour. Nothing seemed to be wrong, he said. Everything was fine.

Three minutes later, nothing was.

Three minutes later, Annie stopped.

She had been rocking gently, smiling at Elliot behind the desk, using Omega against his orders to tell him he was extremely beautiful in every way despite his big ears and the wrinkle between his eyebrows, and then they all picked up a high keening screech from her brain, and then she just . . . stopped.

He went over the desk, not around it, and he and Danny

reached the rocker together, almost knocking one another over.

Annie wasn't dead. She simply sat in the rocker, her hands in her lap, staring straight ahead, breathing evenly, locked behind a new kind of Wall so impenetrable it made their heads ache to be near her.

Ninety seconds later the phone rang.

Elliot backed away from the rocker, horror in his eyes as he stared at the doll-thing that had been Annie. Fumbling behind him, he picked up the receiver as he watched Danny and the others trying to reach her.

"Can we talk now, Elliot?"

"The attacks . . . *you* caused them," he accused in a choked voice.

"Practice runs, that's all. Mere practice runs. I can make them much more effective now—as you see."

"Let her go, Curtiss. Let her go *now*."

"The very minute you finish doing what I've asked, dear boy. Oh, the very minute, I do assure you."

"No. NOW!" His voice cracked like a boy's.

"But she's perfectly all right. She won't die. Nothing will happen to her at all. She'll simply stay like that for as long as it takes. She'll even eat nicely when you feed her, stand up and sit down if you help her, and do all the things she needs to do to stay fit and healthy. She can go on like that forever, in fact. *Forever.*"

"Please, Curtiss. Please," he whispered. Danny turned to look at him with pity, as helpless as any witness to an accident where the agony of a survivor surpasses that of the loved and maimed.

"Tomorrow at nine o'clock you will be taken . . ." there was a rustle of paper. "Miss Murphy, Miss York, Mr. Vanderhof, Mr. Grundy, and yourself, of course, will be taken to a place where you will do as you are told."

"Please."

Curtiss's voice continued inexorably. "I suggest you all have a good night's sleep, because we expect you to work hard and work well tomorrow. If you do, we might even let her have a few minutes off for good behaviour. *Your* good behaviour, that is. She can't do anything else but behave well, can she?"

And he was gone.

Elliot felt a cleavage in his mind. As neatly as a blade, shock severed his emotions from his intellect. The part of him that cried out in anguish at the sight of Annie trapped and beyond his reach cried out in silence. What was left spoke quietly and coldly.

"Danny, where were you when you had your attack?"

They turned from Annie to look at him, appalled by the sudden clinical tone of his voice. Danny, who had worked with the medical profession long enough to recognize a symptom when it addressed him, recovered first.

"I was in the computer centre."

"Janet?"

She looked from Danny to Elliot. "In Medical Records."

"And Frances was in the electronics lab? Ari the components room? Robin in the monitoring section?"

"Yes." Danny, again, coming towards the desk. "Why?"

Elliot's eyes hazed briefly, then cleared to glitter with an overlay of clear ice.

"I wonder what the Russian word for vacuum-cleaner is?" he asked softly.

"Pylyesos," Danny supplied automatically.

"Pylyesos," Elliot repeated. "Thank you."

16

He lay in the dark for a long time, unable to sleep or to find comfort in Annie's presence beside him. It was like lying next to a shop-window dummy, except that her chest rose and fell regularly and he could hear the breath flowing softly between her parted lips. Somewhere inside was his Annie, his wild red fox, hopelessly caught. That the trap was invisible did not decrease the strength of its jaws, nor their cruelty. His was the pain.

It was obvious that the Russians had now passed something more than implantation devices over to help Curtiss circumscribe the Omega Group and force them to his own ends—and ultimately theirs. That all the victims of the attacks had gone through *exactly* the same pattern would have told him as much if he had been less subjective in his attitude. Guilt had been his guideline, not clinical diagnostic procedures.

He remembered, suddenly, something Annie had once said about Algernon. She had looked at the computer sadly, hoping to find in its functional logic a security that randomly factored human minds could not provide. "You can reason with a machine," she had said. "But you can't scare it, you can't love it, and you can't make it love you."

And now a machine held her in its loveless grasp.

Turning onto his side he reached over to touch her face, warm marble under his searching fingers. He knew he would do what Curtiss asked. In the end his altruism had a limit, and Annie marked it. Slowly he slid his hand down her body and let it rest on the gentle swell of her belly. Annie's slimness had kept the baby secret from any outside the Group, but if Curtiss knew everything else, he doubtless knew of the baby's existence, too. The child of two powerful Omegans had to be a prize the Russians would try hard to take from the beginning. All their joy about the baby had been overshadowed by their fear for it. It was barely possible that it would emerge as average as any, but genetically the odds were for an intense Omega strength. Algernon had said as much, and Elliot knew it was true because he could hear, faintly, even in this sixth month, a tiny Omega hum from the still-forming brain.

Moving closer, he pressed his body against Annie's un-responsive side, burying his face in her throat and dreaming, finally, that she turned to him, alive, open, his.

He awoke suddenly to darkness.

Someone was crying.

"Annie?" Sitting up hastily, he switched on the reading lamp over the bed. "Annie?" But she lay as before, precisely as before, motionless except for her breathing. Still the crying continued, and he looked around the room. The light above the bed was not much illumination in the large area, but he could see enough to know they were alone.

He went to the door, opened it, and looked into the hall. Darkness there, too, except for the faint moonlight patterning the carpet below the long windows that looked out over the drive. Just to make sure, he padded the length of the hall, listening at the various doors. Out here the crying was faint.

He returned to their room and closed the door. There, it was louder. Definitely, definitely in this room. Feeling more puzzled by the minute, he looked into the wardrobe, behind the curtains, even behind the chairs, then returned to the centre and concentrated. It was definitely an audible sound, nothing he was receiving telepathically. His ears told him someone was crying in deep and helpless despair, but every other sense said it was a lie. His eyes went to Annie again, seeking some explanation, but her parted lips supplied no answer. That is . . . looking at her throat he saw movement, minuscule fluctuations in the bulb of the adam's apple. Reluctantly he approached the bed, unable to reconcile the noise with such a miniature source. And yet, he could not deny that the closer he came, the more audible the crying grew.

Leaning over, he put his ear close to Annie's mouth— and the hackles rose on the back of his neck. From between her lips and teeth the sound of grief was flowing out on the warm river of her breath.

For one insane moment he imagined that it was their baby crying.

He straightened abruptly, staring down in horror at her waxen features, as the infinitely tiny wail slid out into the room. Then he turned away and looked at the scatter of scent bottles on the top of the chest of drawers. Taking several deep breaths, he tried to steady himself.

After a moment, he turned to face her again, and leaning forward on his locked arms, he once again placed his ear close to her barely open mouth.

And heard words.

A thousand ants swarmed across his skin, and he felt the muscles of his arms tremble and go lax, but he pushed against the coverlet and kept listening. None of the words made any sense to him, but words they unmistakeably were, breaking the sound of sobbing into definite syllabic rhythms. He sank down onto the edge of the bed, half turning away from her, staring at his own hands now in his lap, every ounce of concentration directed towards his hearing alone. And while he listened, he remembered all the myths of speaking in tongues, possession, the dybbuk, knew them for superstition—and could not reject the fear he felt there in the shadowy room.

Then he caught a word he *did* know. And it was a Russian word.

"*Matushka.*" Little Mother.

He clawed his fingers deep into the muscles of his thighs until the pain gave him a focus. Then he summoned Danny.

It was like holding a three-way conversation with a moth.

"Can you hear me?" Danny asked in Russian.

And the crying ceased.

Lifting his head, Danny stared across Annie's recumbent form. The light from the head of the bed flashed across the lenses of his glasses, and then Elliot saw the wide eyes behind them, startled.

"Go on," he urged. "Go on."

"Who are you?"

There was a minute susurrous in the stillness.

"Valery . . ."

"Who are you, Valery?"

There was another, longer whisper.

"He says his name is Valery," Danny translated.

"He?"

"Apparently. What . . . ?"

Elliot shrugged elaborately, helplessly. "Ask him why he's in Annie's throat. That is . . . how he's . . ."

Danny nodded and spoke again towards Annie's unmoving face. And again, a response fluttered out of her parted lips.

Danny removed his glasses and rubbed the bridge of his nose.

"Well?" Elliot demanded.

"It's not easy . . . my Russian is mostly technical and . . . it's distorted by the fact her lips aren't being used—there's so much glottal distortion."

"Did you get anything?"

"I think he said he's in the machine. Something like that. 'In the machine.' With Annie."

"My God." Elliot stared down and then back at Danny. *He went ahead with it.*

Danny caught the reference. *Kossetz?*

Elliot nodded, slowly at first, then firmly. *Those papers he published in '47—the Psi-series on the theory of the cybernetic automaton. Did you read them?*

I've read everything of his. But he didn't do anything with it.

No. Elliot went over to the window, parting the curtains to look out over the drive. There was a car parked across the gate, and he could see the glow of a cigarette within. *They stopped him. Then.* Elliot's jaw clenched. The theory of cybernetics was basically to augment the brain with electronic machinery. But Kossetz had taken a more radical view. If, he postulated, the brain was intrinsically more efficient than any computer that could ever be built, then how much more "sensible" to use the brain *as* a computer. He'd suggested integrating a living brain permanently into an electronic matrix, a concept Hollywood would have clutched to its horror-film bosom. Except that Kossetz had seen nothing horrible about it. It was, he maintained, simply the most logical thing to do. He'd tried it, too, using "volunteers" from prisons and mental hospitals. Elliot had to admit he'd achieved impressive results. But eventually even the hardened sensitivities of the Kremlin had drawn the line, perhaps with memories of places like Auschwitz still too real for comfort. For the "volunteers" had, without exception, died or eventually succumbed to total insanity. Kossetz had been "re-directed."

Danny was pulling the papers out of his incredible memory, flipping the pages rapidly, sending what he found across to Elliot. *Yes, that's it.*

Danny started and looked down. The crying had begun again. "He thinks we've gone away."

"Tell him . . . ask him . . . what's wrong?"

"I can damn well imagine what's wrong if you're right about this."

"Ask him anyway."

As Danny spoke again, the crying broke up into a rush of words he had to lean forward to catch. After a moment he straightened and stood there silently until Elliot turned. "He says . . . he says he's lonely."

"How long has he been in the machine?"

After another exchange, the tiny whisper growing more eager, more excited, Danny told Elliot, "Nine years."

"Nine *years*?"

"That's the number he gave. Nine."

"Why is he using Annie to actually speak for him?"

"The machine controls her outward actions," Danny translated after a moment. "It controlled all of us in turn, through or around or using him—that part isn't too clear, either. He's using a word that roughly translates as 'function' but he doesn't really know what the function is. Only how it feels."

"How does it feel?"

"Well, the closest I can get between his limitations and mine is like a water current . . . rushing . . . pulling . . . something like that."

"Or like a vacuum-cleaner?"

"Maybe." Danny stared at him. "Is *that* what it meant?"

Elliot nodded. "I think so. Each member of the Group was "taken ill" in a particular place, remember? That's what made me suspicious, finally. You were in the computer centre, Janet in Records, and so on. You were each taken over in turn, used to cull all relevant information without realizing it, and then—discarded—when that particular bag of the vacuum-cleaner was full. That's how Curtiss got his information. He knows everything about us, now. *Everything*. Or Valery does. From our lists of potential Omega candidates to George's wiring diagrams for all our instruments to the strengths and weaknesses of each member of the Group. If Curtiss doesn't understand all of it himself, he has his Russian friends to explain it. And use it." Elliot let the curtain fall back into place and sighed. "Why is Valery using Annie? Why not you, or one of the others?"

This time Danny conversed with the invisible Valery for some time before stopping to translate. "He says the machine was never used this way before, not on people like us. I gather we were some kind of revelation to him, because our minds are now structured differently from others he'd touched. He wanted to make direct contact with us right away, but at first he couldn't—override, I suppose you'd say—the machine. And he says Annie is different."

"How 'different'?"

Danny tried to smile. "She's the only one of us who's pregnant. He keeps calling her 'Mother' . . . or 'little Mother.' He says he felt . . . welcome . . . within her. Or maybe it's closer to love. These aren't terms you run up against too often in computer journals."

"No, I guess not." Elliot looked down at Annie, the harsh lines of his face softening momentarily. Endless Annie. Little mother. Not *his* image of her, but—nine years isolated within the soulless gut of some damn machine? He supposed it would be understandable the man should be more interested in comfort than excitement.

"What does he want?"

Danny asked. "He wants to get out. He seems to realize what we are. I'd say he was an Omegan although they couldn't have known the term. High Psi-ability, anyway. He recognizes that capacity. The machine must be incredibly crude or painful. The words he uses . . . hate . . . loathing . . . fear . . . terror, even."

"I can imagine. Kossetz was never interested in subjective emotions, only results. Can't he refuse to co-operate? Is he in it *all* the time? How do they feed him, reward him, get him to . . ." he trailed off as he saw that Danny's face was streaked with tears. Tears, from Danny?

"It's long-term SD, Phil."

"Nine *years* in SD?" Elliot asked, horrified.

Danny nodded, then turned away. His voice came over his shoulder, choked, rough-edged. "If he's good, they give him—flowers."

"Flowers? *Flowers?*"

To die of a rose in aromatic pain, Danny quoted.

And Elliot saw it all. We never pushed sensory deprivation longer than a few hours, he thought. We like keeping our volunteers sane, whole. And even at the end of hours, the only thing left was fear. Unfocused, total mindless fear. Anything, they would do anything, just to hear a human voice. *Say* anything, *be* anything—even welcome pain because pain was real and they no longer were. He supposed this Valery had gone far beyond that, and some indestructible core of his special mind, perhaps Omega itself, had given him a focus so he had retained a few remnants of his personality, survived, lasted. And, by lasting, ensured his continuing imprisonment. To this man, the scent of a rose would be a cascade of sensation so intense that they would need no more elaborate device to secure his co-operation. To this man floating in his dark and endless hell, the mere touch of a petal would flood his entire being with such overwhelming ecstasy by now that. . . . He looked down and saw that he had drawn blood from his own palms, so tightly had rage clenched his fists.

Painfully he forced his hands open, flexing the fingers one by one. "Ask him how we can help," he said, hoarsely. "And ask him—ask him if he can help *us.*"

The next morning, promptly at nine o'clock, an ambulance came through the gate. The five of them rode in the darkened interior, unable to see their route through the covered-over windows. They drove for about twenty minutes or so, then were decanted at the entrance of a perfectly ordinary two-storey house. They had a momentary glimpse of a white-fenced garden and large trees before they were hustled into the hall and then to a rather bare sitting room.

Elliot had expected Curtiss to be there. He was not prepared to encounter the long straggling hair and pale eyes of Zal Stein, who lounged comfortably in the only upholstered chair.

"Ah. Good morning, good morning," came the plummy ex-BBC tones. "So glad you've decided to help us in our little experiment, Elliot. It should be extremely interesting, extremely exciting." He stood up with courtly alacrity when he saw Frances and Janet behind Elliot. "Ah, ladies, welcome, welcome." Stein's habit of repeating words had been one of his most irritating traits when he had run his popular pseudo-scientific programmes.

Bustling with hospitality he drew up the straight chairs for the women, settling them with a gracious smile they did not return. Elliot and Danny found their own places, eyeing with some misgivings a series of leads and crude headbands that were lined up on a table against the wall.

"Ah, interested in our hardware, are you? I know it's not up to your chrome-plated standards, but function is all, as they say. Function is all."

"What particular function did you have in mind?" Elliot asked.

Stein gave a short bark of laughter. "What it must be like to have a choice! Elliot, Elliot, you're standing on the edge of paradise and balking at the entrance fee. Really, I don't understand you at all. Curtiss told me you were an anarchist, but I thought it was his little exaggeration. Can you really think that Everyman would be a suitable recipient for something like Omega? I don't believe it. Just don't believe it."

"Believe what you like."

Stein's eyes narrowed behind his half-rimmed glasses. "Come now, come now. Something as powerful as Omega has to be *administered,* man. Used responsibly. Not just handed out like sweets on the corner. It is up to those in power to protect those who are not. 'The wolves should be fed and the sheep kept safe.' Otherwise it would be chaos—chaos!"

"Only because no one would have anything to hide behind. We could judge one another on substance—we'd know the truth of every man."

"And the truth will make you free? Good God, you *do* believe it. I'm amazed, amazed." Stein shook his head. "I can see it now—a world full of humming hippies and nobody to collect the rubbish."

"I doubt it. Omega doesn't destroy common sense. But it might mean that eventually man would step up onto the next rung of the ladder and find a new way to live, a new purpose, new goals. Maybe even why he exists."

"If he exists at all, by then."

Elliot just shrugged. If he could get inside Stein's head perhaps he could show him . . . but Stein was implanted like all the rest. In more ways than one.

"I never said it would be easy, just preferable to what you propose."

Stein looked at him for a long time, then glanced at his watch. "What I propose would obviously take weeks to explain to someone like you. Weeks. And we have only a few minutes before . . . ah, well. Perhaps later we can take some time to talk. You interest me, Elliot, you interest me. Such an ordinary background, such an ordinary man in so many ways, and yet this thing in your head. Incredible, incredible. But I suppose the common man in you is the source of these nonsensical idealisms and beliefs. The world is *hard,* you idiot, hard and real. Man is a destructive creature."

"The world is very young," Elliot said softly. *"Man* is very young."

"Spare me, please. Ah, come in, come in."

The door to the hallway had opened and a man entered. With a sense of shock Elliot recognized him. Konstantin Kossetz, the son, and so like the father it was like meeting an echo bounced back and only slightly distorted. He was wearing a long white coat over dark trousers, and had eyes only for Elliot.

"Good morning, Elliot," he said with a slight bow.

"Academician Kossetz," Elliot responded neutrally.

"You recognize—I am honoured."

"You are like your father."

Kossetz's eyes flickered momentarily, and then he smiled, his thin dark lips stretching without humour to show small, even teeth. "And these others, you will introduce also?"

"Miss York, Miss Murphy, Mr. Grundy, Mr. Vanderhof."

After each name Kossetz bowed and murmured his three-syllabled "Honoured." Glancing at Stein, who sat somewhat impatiently through this show of manners, Kossetz thrust a hand into the pocket of his white coat and brought out a small notebook. "The schedule has been given, now. This morning will be good time as is social only, very relaxed, not anger or controversy to intrude."

"Ah, splendid," Stein said heartily. "I am very eager to see this in action. Getting second-hand information is never satisfactory, never. All the reports in the world lack flavour, Elliot, especially yours. No adjectives, no zest, no enthusiasm."

"You prefer the sizzle to the steak," Elliot replied mildly. "I'm a scientist, not a circus performer. Adjectives can be misinterpreted, never facts."

"And facts are what we're here to get, aren't they?" Stein concluded brightly. "Lots of lovely facts plucked like feathers from chickens."

"And stuffed into whose pillow?" Ari gravelled from the corner.

Stein swivelled in his chair to look at the bulky Irishman. "Grundy, isn't it? Why, whoever needs an easy sleep, I suppose. Would that be you?"

"I sleep very well. Better than you should."

"Elliot," Stein crowed. "I detect a little chauvinism in your group."

"We're very tolerant," Janet commented. "We even sit down with traitors."

Stein's face darkened, more at the twitch of a smile in the

corner of Kossetz's mouth than Janet's attempt at insult. "Categories bore me," he snapped. "Let's get on with it, shall we?"

"As you wish." Kossetz turned to the others. "You will wear these, please." He nodded towards the headbands on the table. "Move the chairs to a line along front, and we will begin."

"What are they?" Danny asked.

"They are . . . connections. We intend amplification of your power, you call this Omega?"

"Yes."

"Yes. We use neural reinforcement system . . . give you—what is—reach? Distance? Without fatigue, no fatigue because mechanical support takes the strain." He finished triumphantly with this colloquialism.

Elliot and Danny knew this to be a lie. From Valery they had learned that the Russian technology had a limitation that had been exhibited in the "attacks" it had induced among the Group. They could draw information from a brain, it was true, but to do so they had to take over the body. Which would hardly go unremarked in the middle of a conference. Elliot could just imagine the reaction if the President of the United States was suddenly turned into a twitching baby for several hours. What Kossetz wanted to try was putting the Group under the control of the machines, and then using their ability to enter a mind undetected in order to extract information without anyone realizing it was being done.

"Will it hurt?" Frances asked nervously.

"No pain, no discomfort," Kossetz assured her earnestly. "Better really for you, effortless, easy."

"I don't want to," Frances wailed, on cue. "I don't want to, Philip."

Kossetz was absolutely nonplussed at the sight of her imminent tears and rebellion. He looked from her to Elliot and then to Stein, who was also a little startled. "I . . . we . . . understand you agreed . . . you . . . ?"

"Remember Annie," Janet said, going over to Frances and comforting her. "Remember we said we'd do this for Annie." Frances only sobbed more, burying her face in her hands.

"Your wife," Kossetz said stiffly to Elliot. "I am sorry this was necessary, but . . ."

"But it was necessary," Elliot said frigidly. "I quite understand."

Kossetz looked relieved, if a little doubtful. "You are not distressed. She is not harmed but . . ."

"But it was necessary," Elliot repeated.

"Unfortunate, unfortunate, of course," Stein soothed. "But you would *not* see it our way, would you? I really should have thought your scientific curiosity would have impelled you to co-operate, if nothing else."

"Are you married, Mr. Stein?" Janet asked over Frances's head.

"No, actually, I'm not."

"Then shut up."

"I suggest we start without Miss Murphy," Elliot said quickly. "Perhaps when she sees that none of us is uncomfortable using your system, she'll be more ready to help."

"We would prefer—" Kossetz began.

"Oh, for God's sake, get on with it, get on with it," Stein exploded. "It's well after ten o'clock already. I have to be in London by one."

"We'd hate you to miss anything on *our* account," Janet said sweetly. "Lovely lunch laid on, have you?" Stein just glared at her.

Kossetz accepted the dictate and helped them move the chairs over to the table. One by one, with the exception of Frances who was still crying, they put the headbands on.

As Elliot's leads were connected, he felt a cat's claw run through his body, and then felt himself held rigidly erect, his muscles locking him into his seat as Valery had warned would happen. He saw Stein's eyes widen, and then a strange expression of content entered them. Apparently he found it immensely satisfying to see Elliot under someone else's control.

Hello, Valery.

Hello, Elliot. The barrier of language was no barrier to images, although Elliot found Valery's "vocabulary" strangely limited without sensory referents.

Are you ready?

Affirmative.

Annie? And briefly, fleetingly, Valery allowed Elliot to touch Annie.

He was filled with a flood of warmth and love, and detected a small echo within her, the child, reaching, yearning for the light. And then they were gone.

There was a rushing sound in his head, but Elliot could make out Kossetz's voice clearly enough to understand that he was attempting to contact the American President during the experiment. Elliot nodded to show he understood. Kossetz moved down the line, assigning each of the others a target mind. Instead of waiting for the signal, Elliot sent his mind out in a widening circle, attempting to locate his own choice first. It was true, the Soviet technology *had* produced a reinforcing technique that gave him a boost for his Omega abilities, for he had never before been able to send or read over any distance worth mentioning.

He felt his mind running over other minds, like pebbles at the bottom of a shallow stream, and then he was in a large drawing room—long and narrow, with a bay of mullioned stained-glass windows at the far end. There were men there, drinking coffee, chatting, and he recognized all the famous faces from countless newspaper photographs. He found he was examining them through the eyes of someone serving coffee, and hesitated until he came face to face with his intended contact. Gently, he flowed into the mind he sought.

He/the Other looked down at the coffee and thanked the server quietly, wishing He/the Other were still in bed instead of sitting here wasting time. Why couldn't He/the Other and the rest of them get on with the business at hand instead of pretending they were all such good friends?

As gently as he could, Elliot knocked at the mind's door, and saw the hand holding the cup and saucer jerk, spilling the creamy liquid over the edge. *You are not insane You are not insane You are not insane* he soothed. *Do not speak, move, cry out. Just listen. Please, please, listen.* He reinforced this with a flood of comfort and reassurance until he saw the hand relax slightly. *Soon, very soon, others will enter the minds of the men around you, as I have entered yours. When that begins, I will be unable to talk to you directly. If you understand, please drink some coffee.*

It was extremely good coffee.

I hope to avert what is intended. There may be some pain, some discomfort if I am successful. If that happens, will you try to fight me as strongly as possible, I will tell you how? And he taught the mind the Wall as best he could with the seconds ticking away. *If you can do this, you will be able to help the others. Please try.*

With his own eyes back in the other room, he saw Kossetz getting ready to give the master signal, and with He/the Other's eyes he saw the Heads of State still talking and chatting easily. *Any second now. Please try. Please.*

He had chosen his man well, based on what he had read and heard about him. The mind he was inhabiting was clear and clean, with a tremendous sense of identity and a solid strength that held rock-hard against the impossibility of what it was experiencing. It had absolutely no idea how to answer him, but somehow reassurance was conveyed back and he knew there was a chance.

Now he drew in, racing against the fall of Kossetz's hand and the pressure of his thumb on the relay. As he saw the thumb begin to tighten, he made the leap into Frances's mind and thrust the full power of his own and Valery's Omega into her.

The relay clicked home and he felt a surge of rising

mechanical exaltation possess him, wrenching his mind into a blur. Part of him was with the Other, locked in a struggle against an imperfect wall, and part of him was with Frances in her familiar territory, on ramparts and battlements he had often walked, and on which he had always been welcome.

He felt the kinetic dimension of her Omega and it was strange and new, for he possessed none of this object-controlling capacity of hers. It tasted yellow.

A shrill whine of terror came from Stein as Frances lifted the headband that had been intended for her and sent it across to twine its trailing leads around him, tightening until his eyes bulged. Nearer the door, Kossetz whirled and ran out after finding the relay control no longer worked.

First the guns. And the guns were located and made useless.

Now the locks. And the locks were melted down.

Now the house to break the machine's connections. And the house began to shake.

From far off, through the Other, he could see that coffee cups were being put down, and puzzled expressions of pain were beginning to appear on the famous faces. He/the Other got up and began to speak, not easily, but trying to explain as the pain increased. Distantly, through Valery, he heard Ari, Janet, and Danny struggling against the machine. Trying not to do what they were helpless not to do—and information spilled from them into microphones that spun the stolen facts onto tapes whirling silently somewhere else in the house.

The room shook again. There was a smell of electrical burning, acrid and biting. They could not attack the machine itself without harming Valery, so they had to break the lines between. In Frances he was shaking the house and in Elliot he was watching her face agonized with the effort they were making and in the Other he was struggling against his own Wall and speaking to men who trembled white-faced and afraid.

Dust filtered down from the ceiling and rose from between the floorboards, and in one corner a fine crack shot crazily up the plaster like a spider running over the wall. There was, even through the throb in his head, a sound of splintering and crashing as the house vibrated and objected to this inner earthquake. Then a sharper crack came to him, partly through his ears and partly through his head, and he screamed at Frances.

Now now now now now.

With a final wrench she severed the connections that held them immobile in their chairs and their minds returned with a crash to their own skulls. Elliot got up and staggered to the door through which Kossetz had fled moments before —only moments before—and behind him came Ari and Danny. Janet went to Frances and held her while the real tears came.

Kossetz was at the top of the stairs, and Elliot followed, aware of the others struggling with strangers who appeared to stop them, still unaware that their guns were useless and all locks were open. Kossetz ran down the upstairs hall and through a door like all the rest. Elliot's body felt heavy, leaden, as if something were trying to drag it through the floor. When he got to the door Kossetz had entered, he followed, and found something he spent the rest of his days trying to forget.

The room was dark, lit by red bulbs of which only one still burned. All the walls were lined with heavy felt padding, and in front of that, small portable computers and other less familiar mechanisms. Flickering monitors now displayed a jumble of erratic nothing from connections that had been broken or altered. The floor was thickly felted, too, with a semicircle cut out to allow the door to swing inward. On his right was the frame of a brass bed from which the mattress had been removed to accommodate a deep container filled with dark liquid. Kossetz was bent over it, doing something with frantic haste.

"No! Leave him!" Elliot shouted, and Kossetz fell back a step, banging into the frame of the bed. The liquid in the container, jarred by the impact, began washing back and forth, lifting and dropping the shape that floated just beneath the surface. Tubes and wiring led from it in all directions. The boxes to which they were attached still whirred and clicked and muttered.

"Leave him. He belongs to us, now," Elliot said more quietly. Kossetz just stared at him. Walking slowly over to the container, Elliot looked down. Looked down and began to shake. Danny had got it wrong. Valery hadn't been in the machine for nine years—he had been alive for nine years.

Valery was a child.

No . . . no . . . no . . .

Hello Elliot! Go home now? Home to little mother?

He was very small, even for a nine-year-old boy. Encased in a rubber suit, floating in the warm liquid, supported from beneath, blind, deaf, dumb, numb, unformed. He could see Valery's head was abnormally large, the body limp. The muscles would be entirely flaccid, unable to support any weight because they had never known weight. The bones would never have fully calcified, nor would the heart have developed sufficient strength to power a body in a normal environment. In fact, any attempt now to change his environment to something approaching "normal" would mean subjecting him to physical and mental torture beyond imagining. There was *nothing* they could do. Valery was where Valery would always have to stay.

"Leukaemic," Kossetz volunteered suddenly. "Not long to live—We thought to try before . . . unique opportunity, you understand? Interesting cephalic development . . ." The voice droned on and on while Elliot stood looking down.

Hello Elliot. Go home now?

The hopeful little voice echoed in his brain, and he felt Valery's yearning for a new life, a real life of wholeness and freedom. The normality that Annie had hungered for, a normality that was totally impossible for this half-child who had never really been born. Valery had existed in darkness with only the echoes of what he could never have, fed by other people's sensations but never never his own.

What do you want, Valery?

To run . . . to be free . . . you will make me free. Elliot? Make all better?

Elliot felt his breath catch in his throat as he watched the glistening featureless black helmet, wondering if the face beneath it was smiling. To remove the helmet would be to flood Valery with sensory agony, so he could never know what Valery looked like. He remembered the faces of children he *had* known, eager, wide-eyed, laughing. And knew that Valery could never laugh, either. Never run, never touch, never reach out, never feel Annie's arms around him or see a smile that was meant for him alone.

No love Valery? No take Valery home? Valery good—be very very good.

He could give him nothing. Nothing. Except . . .

Love Valery, yes. Go home now. No pain. Many flowers.

Many many many many many many many?

Kicking off his shoes, Elliot slowly climbed into the liquid. It washed knee-high against him, then waist-high as he knelt in the embryonic warmth and put his arms around the small dark shape.

Elliot Elliot Elliot hold hold hold hold yesyesyesyes!!!

He could feel the tiny bird of Valery's heart fluttering against his chest, and he tightened one arm around the small ecstatic body while, with the other, he reached out and began to disconnect the leads, one by one.

Many flowers, Valery. Many many flowers forever I promise.

Home, Elliot? Going home?

Yes, my little one. Going home.

And when the last life-support connection was severed, there was a space of silence while he cradled the blind softness against him tightly and waited.

Hold tight, Elliot. Warm, hard, strong. I understand. Not afraid with you.

Valery . . . Valery. He watched the needles on the monitor dials dropping, their images blurring and wavering until he could read them no more, and closed his eyes.

Many flowers, Elliot? I have many many many many?

Yes.

Wait for you come Elliot? And little Mother come?

Yes.

I see Elliot! I see I see I SEE SEE FLOWERS FLOWERS FLOWERS FLOWERS FLOWERS.

And Valery ran into the Light. A tiny figure, arms outstretched, running, running away.

The Russian scientist was still standing against the machines and watched uncomprehendingly as Elliot eventually climbed back out of the water.

"Is finished?" Kossetz asked, then shrugged. "Soon finished, anyway."

Elliot moved.

He was aware that Ari and Danny came to stand in the doorway behind him. Stood, watched, and finally pulled him off.

But they didn't hurry.

17

They stared at him as if they expected him to detonate.

"Gentlemen, my name is Elliot. There are some things you must know."

Not a big man, but a solid man, and certainly an angry man.

His trousers were soaked, there were shreds of felt clinging to his jacket, plaster dust in his hair, and quite a lot of blood on his knuckles. He had refused to wash it off. He liked looking at it.

None of them were that concerned with appearances. Their heads were still throbbing, several of them had spilled coffee over themselves, and they were very very frightened. One a little less than the others.

Elliot met the grey eyes across the room and nodded slightly, so slightly only the other man saw it and accepted the recognition. When told there was a madman demanding admittance to Chequers, the Canadian Prime Minister had been the one who opened all the doors between them. It was, after all, his turn.

Extending the reels of tape he carried, Elliot said, "On these is a great deal of information that you do not want known. Frankly, *I* don't want to know it, either." Slowly he went over to a wastepaper basket and began unreeling the long ribbons of tape. They coiled like silver snakes into the open mouth of the basket, and as they dropped and twisted, he told them things *they* did not want to know.

Finally understanding, the grey-eyed man walked across the room and held out a folder of matches from the Château Frontenac in Montreal.

"Thank you," Elliot said.

"Thank *you.*"

Theirs were the last smiles exchanged in that room that day.

18

"I'm sorry, Philip."

"But it's 'necessary.' Is that it?" Elliot's voice was bitter.

"Look out there—don't you think they make it 'necessary'?" Bartlett countered gently. "Protective custody means just that. Or did you never hear of a witch-hunt?"

Elliot stared out of the window, then turned away Beyond the closed gates of Talbot Hall stood a cordon of police and vehicles. And beyond them, a surging mass of people. Hastily lettered placards bobbed above the heads of the constantly increasing crowd, and he could see others coming across the fields and down the quiet road to add their stares and shouts. "I see the spelling hasn't improved overnight." He paused by the low table and pushed a knee against the already-sliding stack of newspapers.

WHO IS THIS MAN?

Beneath the headline, a blurred photograph of himself being hustled out of Chequers between two very large Security guards. Beneath that, the story of the sudden confusion that seemed to have gripped the Little Summit, changing what had been a perfectly straightforward conference into a madhouse. The evening papers had him variously as an "attempted assassin," a "dissident," a "mysterious figure," and so on. But by morning they had done their homework, and the headlines had taken a new turn.

ARE THE RUSSIANS READING OUR MINDS?

WHAT ARE THEY DOING AT TALBOT HALL?

MIND-BENDING—ARE WE GUILTY?

Suddenly everyone was all too interested in what had seemed up until that moment just a pleasant country house in Berkshire. It was, of course, the silly season—all the editorial writers were bringing out the adjectives reserved for such things as flying saucers, little green men, mad scientists, and other late-summer inexplicables. They had sold a lot of newspapers the next morning.

And scared a lot of people.

Elliot had never cared for the iron fence around Talbot Hall, but he found himself grateful for it now.

"*Why* won't the PM make a statement?" he demanded suddenly. "Surely he could say *something* that would ease the situation?"

"I think they're still discussing it."

"But I destroyed the tapes in front of them, what more do they want?"

"It's not the tapes that are worrying them."

"It's me."

"You and the others, yes."

"I didn't *have* to tell them anything, you know."

"I'm sure they're taking that into consideration."

"Into *consideration*? You make it sound like a judgment."

"It was hardly the best way to tell them a bunch of mind-readers were privy to all the State secrets in the world."

"Perhaps *I* should have tried a little blackmail?"

"Perhaps."

Elliot sank into the chair behind his desk. "What does Curtiss have to say for himself?"

"Nothing."

"Nothing?"

"They haven't located him yet."

Elliot's eyes widened. "My God, he's made a run for it?"

"According to his office he is on a short leave in the country. They're trying to contact him."

"Oh, *really?*" Elliot said sarcastically. "May they find him swinging from his old school tie."

"Oh, come now—"

Elliot slammed a fist onto the desk. " 'Oh, come now'? What possible reason do they think *I* could have had for lying about Curtiss? And Stein—he's a known friend of dear Cart these days—haven't they made *that* connection either? Are your people total dunces in these matters?"

"I'm afraid neither the Government nor the laws of the land are as impatient as you are, you know. All they actually have is a mass of Soviet technology they're still trying to figure out, a dead child, a Russian scientist who is too badly beaten to speak, and a minor cult figure who refuses to speak. Against that—just you."

"But I demonstrated what I am, what we can do."

"Yes. Exactly. Do you think they found that reassuring?"

"It isn't protective custody, is it?" Elliot said slowly. "It's imprisonment, not so pure and not so simple. You're no longer the 'butler,' you're the jailer."

You should be grateful it's me. I'm glad your honesty didn't extend as far as it might have.

I had my reasons for concealing your part in all this.

And I know what they were.

If it comes to . . .

Look as deep as you like. I belong to Us.

Elliot sighed and closed his eyes. *Thank you for that, anyway.*

I hope it's enough.

This time, when he turned to Annie, it was not a dream. She was there, she was his, and there was nothing to keep them apart, except her grief.

It was the only thing I could do.

I know that. She clung to him, afraid he, too, would run away into the Light, leaving her alone. *But he was . . .*

He wasn't afraid.

Then why are you?

Because I'm still alive. And so are you.

You said once there was no such thing as death. Only change.

That doesn't make dying any easier.

But it should . . . why doesn't it?

He sobbed suddenly, convulsively, and tightened his arms around her, his face buried against the soft warmth of her breasts. "Because I'm not sure," he choked. "Don't you see? I'm not *sure.*"

"Ted's here."

"I don't want to see him."

"I think you should," Janet insisted. "There's something wrong. Margery had to bring him over herself."

Elliot turned away from the library windows and the line between his eyebrows deepened. "What do you mean, 'had to bring him'? Is he ill?"

"You'd better see him for yourself."

"How did they get through that bunch of loonies outside?"

"Margery called Bartlett. She's not a complete fool, no matter what you think of her, you know."

"What's wrong, Janet?" Elliot asked gently. Her eyes, he saw, were empty and sad. For the first time in the years they had known one another he realized she was not in complete control of herself. *What's wrong?*

Nothing. Everything. I'm just . . . weary.

It feels like more than that.

"Will you see him?" she repeated, looking past him to

the lawns outside where uniformed guards patrolled the daisies and the poppies.

"Yes, all right." *I'm sorry . . . please . . . I'm sorry.*

"I'll tell them." And she went out. *Not your fault.*

He looked after her for a moment, then wandered down the length of the room to the globe and set it whirling slowly, letting his fingers slide across the continents, tracing patterns over the changing colours as it turned, clattered, stopped.

Margery Holbrook came in with Ted and stood just inside the door looking round the room. When she finally spotted Elliot, her mouth tightened and she left Ted where he was to walk between the large polished tables and leather chairs.

"Do you want to read my mind or shall I tell you out loud?" she enquired in her piercing voice. It seemed to screech even when she spoke quietly.

"What is it, Margery?" He looked past her and saw that Ted had stayed exactly as she had left him, perfectly still, perfectly quiet, staring at nothing.

"Ted's lost his mind," she snapped. "Look at him, he won't talk, he won't answer me when I speak to him, he won't say anything except your name. What have you done to him?"

"I haven't done anything to him, Margery. Nothing at all." Elliot began to walk towards Holbrook, puzzled.

"It's this place, then," she shrilled after him. "This place and the things you do here. I never liked it, never. He should have stayed in London. He was doing so well—making a name for himself. And then you—seduced him—talked him into coming here."

"I hardly seduced him," Elliot argued mildly, looking into Ted's blank face. "He *applied* for the job. I'd never even met him before he was recommended as a suitable candidate for the General Medical position on the staff." Recommended by Curtiss, he remembered, suddenly. Ted didn't *look* as if he'd lost his mind—merely misplaced it. "When did this start?"

"This morning. He was sitting at the breakfast table,

going through the post, and suddenly he just went funny. I suppose it's something to do with that card. He won't let go of it." She was following after him now, her voice scraping at him and the walls. "All I can say is it's lucky the boys had gone off to school. I wouldn't have known what to tell them."

Elliot was pulling at the postcard Ted held in his right hand. "Give me the card, Ted," he instructed. Holbrook let go of it suddenly.

"Well!" Margery exclaimed. "That proves it!"

Elliot was turning the card over. It was a perfectly ordinary picture postcard, addressed to T. Holbrook, and the message section was blank except for a row of circles. The postmark was illegible because it was stamped over the legend describing the picture on the reverse side. The photograph was of a Golden Eagle. Elliot felt a sudden surge of disbelief and joy.

"I think you'd better leave him to me, Margery. Wait outside."

"I certainly will not. I'm not going to let you start doing funny things to *his* mind. For all I know, you . . ." she faltered under his glare.

"Get out, Margery. *Now*."

Her defiant look disintegrated into nervous apprehension. She got out.

Elliot took a deep breath, and moved to stand directly in front of Holbrook. "Tell me about the Golden Eagle, Ted," he said quietly.

Holbrook blinked. "The Golden Eagle flew high," he said flatly.

Elliot nodded, his suspicion confirmed. Omega was no use, here, he had to get it out the way it went in. Backing up slightly, he settled one hip on the edge of a table and held up the postcard so that Holbrook could see the photograph.

"The Golden Eagle flew high," he said to Holbrook.

Holbrook blinked. "Lock door."

Elliot glanced at the doors, which were closed. He got off

the table, went over, locked them, and came back to the table.

"The door is locked, Ted."

"Lock door."

Elliot frowned momentarily, then his face cleared. "The Golden Eagle flew high, lock door."

Holbrook blinked. "The Golden Eagle flew high, lock door, stay out of the dark."

"The Golden Eagle flew high, lock door, stay out of the dark."

Holbrook blinked. "The Golden Eagle flew high, lock door, stay out of the dark, fifty up and down."

"The Golden Eagle flew high, lock door, stay out of the dark, fifty up and down." Elliot repeated.

Holbrook blinked. "The Golden Eagle flew high, lock door, stay out of the dark, fifty up and down, bring beer."

Elliot sighed. "The Golden Eagle flew high, lock door, stay out of the dark, fifty up and down, bring beer."

Holbrook blinked. Blinked again. "What?"

"The Golden Eagle flew high, lock door, stay out of the . . ."

"What the hell are you talking about, Phil?" Holbrook demanded, peering first at him, then around the room. "How— why are we in here?"

Elliot folded his arms. "How do you feel, Ted?"

"I feel fine. Perfectly and absolutely fine." That clinched it. "How do *you* feel?" he added, irritably.

"Much better, thanks," Elliot smiled. "It's all over now, Ted. You feel perfectly and absolutely fine, you can forget all about it."

"I can forget all about it," Ted echoed in the same hollow tone with which he had given the other responses. Then he grinned. "How about a drink?" He turned and went over to the library door, tugged at it, turned the lock, and began to open it. "Expecting burglars? There's not much . . . oh. Hello, Margery." His grin disappeared abruptly.

"Ted? Are you all right?" Elliot could see Margery

standing amazed just outside the library door.

"Of course I'm all right. Why shouldn't I be?"

"But . . ." she stared past his shoulder at Elliot, who smiled briefly.

"Ted was worried because he'd forgotten to tell me what he'd done with the keys to the drugs cupboard . . . we have a lot of pretty volatile stuff in there. No problem."

Holbrook turned to stare at him. "What?"

"I wouldn't bother him about it if I were you, Margery," Elliot said with what he hoped was enough emphasis to penetrate her suspicion. "Just forget the whole thing. Ted's always been a stickler for procedure."

"The hell I have," Ted objected. "Are you two crazy or something?"

"No," Margery said. "Just me. Come on, we have to get back to the house before the boys come home from school . . . and I left a pie in the oven. Come on, Ted."

Holbrook started to follow her, then turned. "About all this fuss outside, Phil—it's a damn shame. They going to let us get back to normal eventually?"

"Oh, I imagine so. Eventually."

Gradually Margery eased a confused Ted out of the library and Elliot closed the doors after them. He stood still for a moment, then went along the shelves until he located an atlas.

Then he summoned Ari and Danny.

"You can't be serious," Ari said, staring at the postcard Elliot was waving under his nose.

Take it. Tell me.

Reluctantly, Ari took the postcard and closed his eyes. Elliot watched him intently for a while, then turned to Danny who had his back to them and was staring out across the lawn. He started to speak, then closed his mouth, somehow warned by the set of Vanderhof's shoulders that his questions would not be answered. Then he heard Ari's sharp intake of breath and turned back. The big man's eyes were wide open, staring.

"He's alive . . . the bugger's alive!"

"Yes," Elliot breathed triumphantly. "Yes."

Ari's eyes focused on him suddenly. "And you knew it all the time?"

Elliot shook his head. "Not consciously, no. But half the reason I grieved so long, so deeply, was because I didn't simply feel a sense of loss over Longjohn's death. I felt—deserted. I thought he'd killed himself, I thought he'd turned his back on me. On us. Deliberately."

"He had," Danny's voice came from the windows. "He opened up his Omega, did you know that? I was checking the logs on the bio-feedback some time ago—there were some blanks in the week before he . . . left. I thought it might be that, too. I thought it was too much for him." Something in his voice stopped Elliot from turning to face him, and he kept his eyes on Ari.

"What do you get?"

"Not much. He didn't send this card, someone sent it for him, but he wrote it. He wrote it, all right. Now, I just get hills . . . emptiness . . . an open window . . . pains."

"Is he sick? Hurt?"

"No . . . it's Omega pain."

"Is he alone?"

"Yes." Ari's expression was sad. "Very alone."

"It's starting now," Danny said, his voice hollow and defeated. And Elliot knew he was going to say things none of them wanted to hear. Ari's clairvoyance had to do with objects and people, but Danny's was wider, more far-reaching, and had to do with tomorrow and tomorrow and tomorrow.

"It's bad, isn't it?" Elliot asked, still not turning to face him.

"It's very shadowy, very unsettled."

Tell me.

"I can't. Part of it is that you mustn't know what you're doing. You have to trust your instincts."

"But it's big. Far bigger even than I've imagined."

"Yes."

He turned then to look at Danny, who was still facing away from them, his shoulders hunched and his arms crossed protectively across his chest. "And it scares you."

"Yes." Very softly.

"And Longjohn? Going away, waiting, sending this card *now*, that's part of the pattern?"

"Yes. Longjohn, and you, and . . . yes. All part of it."

Something in the melancholy deadness of Danny's voice suddenly took Elliot by the throat, made his heart thud painfully. "We're going to lose someone, aren't we?" he whispered.

"Yes."

Elliot felt his entire body clench into one tight fist. "Who?"

But Danny shook his head.

"Who?" *Who, who, who? Not Annie, please God, not Annie.* He tried to charge into Danny's mind, to rip out what he wanted to know, but Danny simply put up the Wall. It was solid, but his voice was thin.

"It all centres on you, Phil. It's all up to you. It always has been."

Elliot stared at the back of Danny's head.

He had never felt so helpless in his life.

"I'm sorry, Philip."

"I wish to hell you'd stop SAYING that!" Elliot shouted. "Where have they taken them? Why?"

"I don't know. The man who came merely had orders to deliver them to an accommodation address in Slough. They'll be moved on from there."

"A blind against Omega?"

"Presumably. They're getting smart." Bartlett looked worried.

"They always were. They just never demonstrated it."

An hour before, all the members of the Group except

Annie and the five directly used in the Russian attempt to read the minds of the men at Chequers had been taken away in cars to an unknown destination. The cars had run the gauntlet of the die-hard core of picketers who still remained outside Talbot Hall. This followed the removal, earlier in the day, of all the technical staff who had remained to do caretaker duty. They were no longer needed because most of the equipment they had been looking after had been removed along with them. Again, to an unknown destination.

"I don't like it, Philip."

"What you don't like is that they've lumped you in with us all of a sudden. Haven't they?"

"Either that or they don't think I'm important enough to consult."

"But you *are* imporant enough." Elliot's voice was suddenly quiet. "Or you were."

"Yes," Bartlett said reflectively. "I think I'll make a few calls."

"And if nobody answers?"

"Then I'll make some more." He passed Danny on his way through the door. Elliot turned back to the table where he had been assembling some sandwiches, getting as much mayonnaise and mustard on his thumb as on the bread. "Welcome to the mess tent. Hungry?"

"No, not really." Danny took a few slices of bread and began to spread them with butter. Elliot saw his hands were shaking slightly.

"You ought to keep your strength up."

"I'd be glad to keep my strength up if I could keep my food down," Danny said, reaching for the plate of ham and cheese. "I'm beginning to feel more like a prisoner every minute."

"Maybe I'd better break some tranks out of the drugs cupboard," Elliot offered, slapping another sandwich haphazardly onto the pile.

Danny put the knife down and sank onto a stool next to

the kitchen table. "Where have they taken them?"

"We don't know. Adam is trying to find out."

"We can always make contact if they don't take them too far. I arranged a call-time with Robin before they left. Every fourth hour . . . Annie or Frances can take turns listening."

Elliot sucked the mustard off his thumb and grimaced. "Why did you do that?"

Danny shrugged. "Bad idea?"

"Not at all. Good idea. I just wondered why, that's all." *What do you know . . . why won't you tell me?* But the Wall only made it echo back at him.

"It seemed . . . sensible. I know they aren't really part of this thing, but they're part of us. I just want to keep track, that's all."

"And Longjohn?"

"What about him?"

"Look, it's all very well saying you know what's going to happen and that telling me would . . ."

"I *don't know* what's going to happen. It's like coming to a crossroads. You're going along one way, and the road splits into a number of alternative routes, all right?"

"Yes."

"And you can see quite a way down some of them, and hardly at all down some others, but you can never see the end. You pick one, go along, and then the road splits *again*. And again you've got alternatives."

"How do you know which one to choose?"

"That's just it, you don't. You *feel* one is a little better than the others, maybe, but not always."

"And what's that got to do with me?" Elliot persisted.

"Something in me says you're the man with the map, that's all."

"Ah, then there *is* a map."

"Oh, Jesus, Phil, there are *hundreds* of them. You know you said that Frances's kinetic power tasted yellow to you?"

"Yes."

"Well, it smelled purple to me. And yet for her it doesn't have any taste, smell, *or* colour, it's just there. So how can I explain clairvoyance to you? It's just there. I wish it wasn't."

"And Ari's clairvoyance is different again?"

"Yes. If it's any consolation, he can't explain *that* to *me.*"

"You know what I wish?" Elliot said, putting the ham back into the refrigerator.

"You wish you'd left Annie on Mhourra."

"Not exactly. But I wish I'd stayed on Mhourra with her."

Danny smiled. "Either way she'd have given you trouble."

"Probably. But at least we wouldn't have passed it on to everyone else."

"You did the right thing. Took the right road."

"So you can look backwards as well?"

"Can't everyone?"

Tell me . . . help me . . . please . . . help me.
I can't even help myself.

"I'll take the sandwiches in, you bring the drinks," Danny said aloud, picking up the plate and grabbing as one of the sandwiches started to fall. "Them that eats together can keep an eye on one another."

"You know, I'm beginning to feel like the next act at a pop festival," Ari commented, looking out at the field beyond the fence. Here and there campfires sparked the darkness, and shadowy figures could be seen moving between the tents. Occasionally shouts of laughter came through the night, along with guitar music and a faint and occasional whiff of pot.

"At least this bunch is the friendly section of our following," Janet said. "It's the ones who pull up in the morning slavering for our blood who give me the creeps."

"What do they *want*, Philip?" Annie asked curiously. "I can feel them wanting something from us, but they don't seem to know what it is themselves."

"Who? Our peaceful friends or our hungry enemies?"

"The ones out there now. There's such a . . . *wanting* . . . coming from them. And they're all kinds of people . . . different kinds of people . . . different ages . . . different . . . but the same wanting."

"They want the Answer, my darling," he said, ruffling her hair, twining a strand around his finger. Annie's hair drew his hands constantly, her hair and the long flowing line of her throat. He stroked her, she stroked Joseph, and everybody purred. "They want us to tell them Everything Will Be All Right."

"Nobody can do that," she objected.

"On the contrary, *anybody* can do that. They do it all the time," Frances said. "But they never give a written guarantee."

Philip? Bartlett, from a distance.

Yes, Adam?

"Well, I don't know why they think *we* know any more than they do," Ari said, going to the percolator. "Just because they've been told we can read minds. We can't read anything else."

I've found somebody who will talk.

What does he say?

"That's funny coming from *you*," Frances told Ari, passing him her mug.

He says we're . . . you're . . . going to be moved tomorrow.

"Ouch," Annie exclaimed. "That hurt." She pushed Elliot's hand from her hair and turned to look at him. "Petting is one thing, pulling *quite* another."

Where?

London.

Where in London?

University College Hospital.

Together?

No.

Elliot stood up. "I'll be right back." Annie slid into the space he had left on the settee, shifting Joseph to a more comfortable position on her lap. There was a little less room for him every day.

Elliot went out into the dark hallway. *Where the hell are you?*

Kitchen.

He went through Lab Two, strangely empty now that the computers and other equipment had been taken away. Across the courtyard he could see Bartlett standing in the kitchen, lighting a cigarette and throwing the match into the sink. He had never seen him smoke before. The night was cool as he crossed the flagstones and approached the service entrance. The dark sky was spangled with a sprawl of stars. Just as he reached the door, a shadow moved at the edge of the lawn. The beam of a torch suddenly blinded him.

"Oh, sorry Dr. Elliot. You should stay indoors, sir."

"I didn't fancy walking through a mile of corridors just to get the salt," he said easily, raising a hand against the light. "Next time I'll whistle the Londonderry Air, all right?"

The shadow chuckled. "I don't know that one. Try 'Yellow Submarine.' "

"Whatever you like. I'm not choosey." He opened the door and went into the kitchen.

Bartlett turned as the lock clicked. "I also found someone else with a different tale to tell," he said.

"I didn't like that first one at all. What's the other version?"

"You'll like it even less. They plan to let the picketers escalate into a riot and tear Talbot apart. Talbot and everything in it. And then say 'oops'!"

"Everything or everyone?" Elliot asked, swallowing a rugby ball that had suddenly been punted into his throat from below.

"What do you think?"

"And which story is true?"

"Both of them. Everybody's got a different way to settle the Omega 'problem.' According to my first source, they're fighting over you like Alsatians in a dog-food commercial. Those at the top want you eliminated because people who know too much make them nervous. Those in the middle want to take you over because they don't know enough but would like to. Those at the bottom . . . are waiting to see who wins."

"I see. Can *we* make any suggestions?"

"No. But I'd like to make one."

?

"Get the hell out of it while you can."

"Uh-huh. That's a *good* suggestion. Is there any more to it?"

"Not yet."

Elliot glanced up at the clock over the refrigerator. "And meanwhile Curtiss is running around loose somewhere with more information than he knows what to do with . . . sorry, I take that back. He knows just what he wants to do with it." He lit a cigarette of his own and paced from the dishwasher to the cooker and back again. "My father did *not* tell me there would be days like this," he muttered.

"Did you expect anything different?" Bartlett asked, tossing his half-finished cigarette into the trashbin and letting the top flop back.

"Yes, funnily enough, I did."

With great deliberation Elliot picked up a cup from the draining board and smashed it into the sink.

Danny. Janet. Frances. Ari. Annie and the baby. Especially Annie and the baby. They were his own. They would not go gentle into that good night.

19

Elliot hung onto the edge of the bank and lifted himself out of the water slightly to see how things were coming along. Then he sank down again next to Annie and started composing a few letters he would write one day.

"Dear East Berks Fire Department: You are not only speedy, you are efficient, smooth, and very, very noisy. Dear Maidenhead and Slough Police Departments: I love your shiny cars and sirens, and all those angry-looking constables who spill out of them. Dear National Health Service: I'd like to commend your Ambulance Division, they are ready for anything and come like a shot when called. Dear *Reading Chronicle, Maidenhead Advertiser, Slough Evening Post:* Your night staff reporters and photographers are a nifty bunch, on their toes and full of persistent questions like "What the hell is going on *now?*" and, "I'm from the Press, officer, how do you spell that name?" Dear Bunch of Grapes Darts Team and the boys from the Goldenrod Social Club: Wasn't it fun to get out at closing time and have somewhere to go? Dear South-East Gas Board: sorry about leaving the cooker on like that . . . we *really* thought it was a gas leak when we phoned. Dear Windsor Fire Department: You, too?

Of course, the Chief of Security wasn't stupid. As soon as the guards popped out of the front door he sent them straight back in to find us. It wasn't their fault that Ari's and Bartlett's home-made bombs began to go off just then, and the halls were full of smoke from the fires in all the wastepaper baskets in our bedrooms, and Bartlett shot a few of the guards and then himself in the arm and ran out onto the front lawn to roll about and scream like that for the reporters, and the firemen ignored the guards and drove their apparatus through the front gate and right up close to the building and began tripping over each other in the dark because by then we'd pulled all the fuses out of the box and Danny managed to sling a chair into the colour telly on his way through the library and glass was everywhere and Frances kept the air full of flying objects and all the taps were on so the water pressure was low and some of the floors were wet and the cook's three chickens got loose just before the cooker blew up and it was very touching to see how everyone tried so hard and I appreciate it, I really and truly do. Yours sincerely, Philip John Elliot, BSc, MD, PhD, FRCP."

It was very quiet in the river under the willows. Very quiet, very wet, and very cold. Invisible fingers of weed clutched at their legs from below and the muddy bank smelt of decay. The next time he risked a look over the edge, he saw that somebody had replaced the fuses and all the lights in Talbot Hall were back on. Through the long French windows in the library he could see figures rushing to and fro through a thin haze of smoke, while other figures appeared and disappeared in other windows both upstairs and down. Some of the guards were coming down the lawn, their torch beams crossing and re-crossing as they searched. Somebody had obviously done a head-count and found no heads at all, Elliot concluded. He slipped back down quickly. Annie's teeth were chattering from the chill of the dark water. They took some long deep breaths and went under. He opened his eyes and caught the glitter of torch-beams flickering over the surface of the water above them. Suddenly one of the guards slipped on the edge of the muddy bank and his foot came down through the water, connecting with Elliot's hand where it gripped the roots of a willow. They could hear him cursing as he struggled back up the slope, and then there was darkness again. They hung on. And on.

Several times more the beams illuminated the water, and then they sensed the guards moving away, the hum of their implants fading. The implants had necessitated the burlesque routine of their exit. They had had no weapons at their disposal except Bartlett's telephone.

They allowed themselves to rise slowly, taking grateful breaths of the night air when their nostrils cleared the surface. Elliot sucked his knuckles where the skin had been scraped away.

Has Ari found a car yet?

Yes. They found one in a garage up the lane. It's a two-car garage and the people have obviously gone away. There are several newspapers jammed into the letterbox.

Let's hope they aren't due back tomorrow. Can he start it?

He always said his father was one of the best car thieves in Belfast.

Useful.

Janet and Danny are about a mile away crossing a field.

Danny's sprained his ankle but it's not too bad. Ari says if we get upstream to that little bridge on the back road he'll pick us up, then go around for Janet and Danny.

Right.

Bellying up the slope, Elliot retrieved the airline bag he'd hidden under the thickest willow. In it was all the cash he'd had in the office safe—not much—plus a few odds and ends he'd swept together before the excitement began. Holding the bag high, he slid back into the water.

You just had to bring Joseph, didn't you? The holdall kept fighting him.

If we drop him near Mrs. Purdey's, he'll be looked after.

They began working their way up the feeder stream, catching themselves on roots and rocks and getting progressively more tangled in waterweeds as the banks closed in. The water began to muddy and shallow beneath them, and eventually they could go no further. The last few yards to the bridge were mostly a matter of moving like otters along the bank. They huddled underneath the bridge, hanging onto the thick baulks and keeping as close as possible to conserve what little warmth they had left once the breeze had passed over their sodden clothing. It seemed like hours . . . and it seemed as if it was rush hour on the narrow back road overhead. Car after car rattled over the loose boards of the bridge, some of them carrying guards widening the search, some of them carrying ordinary people on their way home now that the latest excitement at Talbot Hall was dying down. Eventually a car slowed just short of the bridge.

Hurry up, there may be someone along any minute.

They scrambled out and pulled themselves up to the road holding onto the undergrowth, flopping in through the back door Frances held open and struggling upright as Ari started off again. Frances started passing things over the back of the seat.

What's all this?

Towels, dry clothes.

You burgled the house?

Ari kept his eyes on the road. *Listen, they had so much in there they probably won't notice anything missing for a month except the car. I'm sure they believe in helping the needy.*

Perhaps. But not in the needy helping themselves.

Phil, you are the tight-arsed product of a conventional middle-class upbringing, you know that? Stealing the car is fine, but not the clothes?

Ari . . .

?

Thanks for the clothes.
You might not be so grateful you see them in daylight.

The surface of the lake was corrugated by a soft wind that skimmed between the low hills, and the even grey of the sky was reflected with a metallic sheen unbroken by a single glint of light. Beyond the far edge of the water the hills folded themselves against the sky, purple-green, brown, misting into the distance with only a single square of carefully planted firs to break the endless rolling line. Occasionally a bird would start up a hesitant song, the few notes like a handbell rung against the ear, and then silence would spread across the heather like the fog that was drifting closer and closer as the afternoon cooled.

"I have to hand it to your ancient ancestors, they certainly knew how to name things."

"Loch Dour . . ." she whispered, mesmerized by the infinite horizon.

Elliot fished in the front pocket of his cagoule for his cigarettes, balancing himself on the fence cautiously, then bent his head to his cupped hands to catch the flame of his lighter. The wind stirred his hair, and the dry blond strands fell across his forehead, annoying him as usual. He thrust them back impatiently and blew smoke at his knees. A few feet away the engine of the Honda pinged as it cooled on its kickstand at the edge of the road.

The wind rattled the map in Annie's hands and she smoothed it carefully, turning it so she could correlate the curling brown lines with the scene before them. Last night in the bare splendour of their bed-and-breakfast house he had marked the limits of their search with a black felt-tip pen, laying a corridor from the loch to the eastern coast. "Lock door" was actually Loch Dour. "Stay out of the dark": dark equalled sinister equalled left, so stay to the east of the Loch. "Fifty up and down": fifty miles either side of the flight plan Longjohn had registered in Stornoway before taking off.

"So much . . . why so much?"

Elliot shrugged and removed a loose bit of tobacco from his lip. "When he left he couldn't know exactly where he'd settle, I suppose. Sutherland is the least populated area of Britain; it was the best place to go. The only place where we'd be able to pick him up blind. All he could do was indicate an area, then stay in it, somehow."

"But the postmark . . . didn't you work it out as Basingstoke?"

"His solicitor is in Basingstoke. He must have known. Longjohn probably rang him the minute the story broke. Told him to post the card."

"Then he can't be too far from civilization—to get the papers or reach a phone box."

"It was on the radio, love. They had my name in time for the six o'clock news, remember?"

"Why not just tell the solicitor to phone us . . . tell us right out?"

"Blinds and double-blinds. In case the phone was tapped, in case Ted was overheard. Preparing it that far in advance, he couldn't know exactly what the situation would be, except bad."

"But he put it all in Ted's head—post-hypnotic suggestion, you said."

Elliot smiled. "Ted's a survivor and Longjohn was one of the most powerful hypnotists I've ever seen in action. Omega, I suppose, plus his strong personality. And Ted's a natural subject, easily pushed, easily influenced. Longjohn knew as soon as I saw the postcard I'd make the connection, and he always used the same technique. Simple enough."

"Because your plane was called the *Golden Eagle?*"

"Yes."

Annie began folding the map. "But you might have still thought he was dead . . . he couldn't know Ari would . . ."

"Longjohn knew me even better than I knew him, Annie.

He was counting on my curiosity, my compulsion to find answers for everything."

"And now all you have to do is find him."

"No, all *you* have to do is find him. Your ears are bigger than mine."

She smiled. "Impossible."

He jumped down off the fence and reached up for her. "Anyway, Ari and Frances will be working towards us from the coast, and Janet and Danny will be listening, too, from wherever they are. It shouldn't be all that difficult. They call it triangulation, I think."

She held onto him, once down, and looked up into his face. "Who?"

He kissed her nose. "The people who know how to do it."

But during the night the wind began to rise and the next day broke like a water jug over the hills. In his heavily-accented and broken English he told the woman who ran the bed-and-breakfast house they'd chosen in Clannach that his "Frau" was not too well, and that if it was all right he'd leave her to sleep while he went out for the day. The woman looked duly sympathetic and promised to look after Annie for him.

He went out and started the Honda, looking up at the window behind which Annie still slept. They had bought the motorcycle in Inverness and already he was a convert. It was a far cry from the old Indian he'd had at university, this gleaming fully transistorized many-geared technical marvel. Nearly into her seventh month and healthy with it, he had judged the vibration of the bike a reasonably safe risk for Annie to take, and he thought it unlikely that the hunting packs who were after them would suspect a leather-jacketed pair on a motorcycle to be one consultant neurologist and his lady. He hoped so, anyway.

The vibration of the bike hadn't tired Annie, but the exhilaration had. Fastening the crash helmet, he smiled. Everything was still so new for Annie, and it was one of the reasons she still fascinated and delighted him. Old in knowledge, a child in experience. The red hair was now dyed to a dull brown, but she was otherwise unchanged. Except by the fear that had changed them all. A day of rest would do her as much good as anything would, now.

He began to cover the roads. Just after noon the rain stopped and the heather started to steam gently under a clearing sky. A lot of his time had been wasted while he tried to match what he saw with Ari's mental picture of hills. The trouble was that all the hills looked exactly alike in this featureless lunar landscape. He missed the softness of Berkshire, the masses of old heavy-headed trees, the red brick houses, the rippling wheat meadows and the hedgerows. Berkshire fed the eyes—this drained them.

He was riding along a dirt track leading to a place with the unpronounceable name of Achnaluachrach when something hit him in the back of the neck like a cricket bat. He jammed on the brakes too suddenly and skidded about twenty yards on the muddy surface, nearly ending in a ditch. He cut the engine and pulled off his crash helmet.

There was absolutely nothing to see except more low heather-covered hills, a few exposed rocks, some sheep, and the slick grey surface of the road curving away ahead of him. He wrestled the front wheel of the bike out of the ditch and dropped the stand. Then he slowly went back down the road to the spot where he'd heard it—or felt it—he wasn't sure which.

Nothing came. After a while he waded through the heather and sheep-droppings to the top of the nearest hill. Two sheep rose from their rest and sauntered off at his approach, resentment in every line of their dirty woolly bodies. One made a comment to the other but he let it pass, although it was obviously far from complimentary. Settling himself on a low rock on the far flank of the hill, he opened up the shutters in his head. His sending ability was still weak, but his "read" was steadily improving. It had certainly improved sufficiently for him to bankroll their escape with a night in the gaming clubs of Coventry. Nothing like having a trade to fall back on, he'd told Annie, after coming back to the hotel and showering her with notes and silver. He'd purposely asked for a lot of silver and small notes when he cashed his chips at the last club. Not only because it was more spendable but because he knew Annie would love playing with it. In fact she had, to his amazement, developed some very interesting games to play with it, towards morning. He remembered telling her she was turning into a dirty old lady, but it had not been a complaint.

The cricket bat descended again, and had his name on it. Or in it.

Philip Elliot the cricket bat said, in a Canadian accent. It seemed perfectly natural to him, seconds later, that a blow on the back of the neck with a cricket bat would make one's eyes water.

YESYESYESYESYESYESYESYESYESYESYESYES YESYES

No response. He finally managed to light a cigarette, but it was another eight minutes by his watch before the cricket bat came again.

Philip Elliot

It was not only loud, it was painfully loud, and had a ragged desperate quality that would have been like hoarseness in a throat.

LONGJOHNLONGJOHNLONGJOHNLONGJOHN YESYESYESYESYES

But again, no response. After another ten minutes . . .

Philip Elliot

Although the sensation hit him on the back of the neck, he had the definite impression that Hawkins was in front of him, somewhere, but it was impossible to say at what distance. It also seemed that he was operating rather like a lighthouse, gathering his energy to send one regular burst every ten minutes or so, and it was hurting him as much as it hurt Elliot. Rubbing his cigarette out on the rock, Elliot got up and went back to the bike. According to the Ordnance Survey map, there was another road that ran parallel to the one he was on, about ten miles to the north, but because of the terrain he would have to go all the way back to Clannach and skirt Loch Dour to pick it up. If he could definitely locate the source of the call as being between the two, it would help a lot. Then he could bring Annie out and they'd find him. Together, they'd find him.

"Did he sound ill?" She had thrown the hood of her cagoule back and the wind was whipping strands of dark brown hair around her face.

"No, he sounded strained . . . and tired."

"Well, he doesn't sound anything at all, now." She turned a full 360 degrees with her eyes closed. "I don't hear anything, Philip."

"Well, I did." He looked across the emptiness. "He's somewhere in there. Try sending something."

"I have," she said gently, coming over to where he was perched on yet another rocky outcrop, some ten miles north of the one he'd sat on the day before, but otherwise indistinguishable from it.

"Oh." He leaned over and picked up the backpack, swinging it around until the aluminium frame was in position. "Then I suppose we'd better start walking."

She fastened the straps on one side while he did up the others. He looked down at her as she concentrated, the pink tip of her tongue between her teeth. When she had finished, she looked up and smiled. "We'll find him," she promised brightly. "It's all in knowing how to look, you see." And she bent down to pluck a bit of heather to tuck under the straps of her own pack.

He realized that. In fact, it was precisely that point which was keeping him high on fear and low on optimism.

They began to walk into the hills, Annie sending out signals to Longjohn and Elliot listening. That is, listening in between tripping over rocks, slipping into marshy patches, snagging his trousers on gorse, and gradually getting more and more irritated. The thick heather would have been beautiful to lie on but walking over it, he decided, was rather like bouncing over an endless mattress. They tried to stick to sheep-tracks where they went in the right direction, but it wasn't always possible, and his calves soon began to ache. He glared balefully at Annie who was leaping lightly along ahead of him. Out of his dim memories of serving as a houseman in Obstetrics and Gynaecology, he recalled that pregnant women usually fitted into one of two categories—the weak and the buoyant. Feeling the pinch of too many cigarettes around his ribs, he saw he had impregnated one of the latter variety and it wearied him even more.

If they'd had one word, one flicker from Longjohn, he could have felt more enthusiastic, he supposed, toiling up another slope, but he was now beginning to doubt he'd heard him at all. The silence of the hills was absolutely incredible, and the only thing he could hear was the thudding of his own pulse in his ears, accompanied by an obbligato of gasps and wheezes. When they finally stopped to eat their sandwiches, however, he decided that God's grandeur was not too bad, if you were sitting down to view it. A thermos of tea, a ham sandwich, and thou beside me singing in the wilderness, Annie.

"This is bog cotton . . . here's stitchwort . . . and a violet, look." She held up a piece of grass with a purple lump at the end. "It's a shame we're too late for the primroses. I love primroses best of all."

"Never thought I'd come second to a bloody flower," he muttered.

She made a face and came over to tuck some heather under his nose. "You *are* getting crabby," she told him, and he sneezed. Sinking back onto her heels, she gazed at him for a while. "I don't think I'll like it when you go bald."

"I'm not going to go bald," he informed her through his

handkerchief. "My father and both my grandfathers went to their graves with fine heads of hair. What made you think of that?"

"Seeing you blond instead of brown, I suppose. Blond matches your eyes better, but not your face."

"What's wrong with my face?" What next indeed, he thought. Her with her twenty-four years and her lithe body full of rising sap and hormones.

"There's nothing *wrong* with it. I love the way it's sort of—rumpled."

"Rumpled."

"Yes. Lived-in and comfortable."

"I see. That's probably because I sleep in it."

"Mmmmm. And I love your ears, too." She took hold of them to prove how handy they were for pulling faces down to other faces. He got the handkerchief out of the way just in time.

A little while later he told her to put her clothes back on before she caught pneumonia.

"No," she said dreamily, rolling over on the blanket. "You're marvellous, you know that?"

"I know, I know. I'm also half frozen to death."

"Didn't you like making love under the sky?"

He stopped struggling into his cagoule and grinned at her. "Of course I did, you idiot."

So did I, said the cricket bat. *I didn't know you were so inventive, Phil.*

Elliot let Annie drop back down onto the heather and jumped up.

"Goddammit, where are you?" he shouted at the hills.

. . . ut . . . miles . . . come . . . ver . . . ttage . . . smoke . . .

Annie was shining triumphantly. *LONGJOHNLONG JOHNLONGJOHN*

. . . 'lo, shorty . . .

"Not far," she said, reaching for her clothes. Something about her complacent tone aroused Elliot's suspicions.

"You did all that on purpose, didn't you?"

"All what?"

"You know all what," he accused.

"Well, you did once mention that sexual activity raised the overall DC level of the brain and that—"

"You calculating little . . ." He didn't know whether to laugh or belt her one.

"It wasn't *just* for that."

"I'm so glad to hear it," he sulked, retrieving his back-pack.

"And you *are* wonderful."

He sighed. "Absolutely true, of course. Going bald as I am, and all."

I love you.

"Hmmmm." He fastened the straps of her pack, turned her around, and kicked her, hard, in the backside. "Next time *I* open the day's play, all right?"

"Chauvinist," she giggled, and ran ahead before he could get his knee up again. Shaking his head and smiling, he trudged after.

Their individual definitions of "not far" differed widely, he found. It was at least another three miles of ankle-aching heather, rocks, and hills, face into the cold wind that was being pushed toward them by the low bank of black clouds which now nearly filled the sky.

When at last he lifted his head and saw Longjohn's refuge a quarter of a mile ahead, there wasn't enough energy left in him to even groan. He didn't know why he had assumed the eyrie would be some God-forsaken shack somewhere, but he had. It was actually a lovely whitewashed cottage with a thatched roof, the smoke being whipped away from the chimney by the wind, with a nice old Land Rover parked next to it, just off the dirt track that led back over the hills. At *that,* he groaned.

Longjohn was there, leaning (as always) against the nearest vertical surface, in this instance his own open front door. There was no mistaking his long angular shape, even though it was now bearded. Annie gave a yelp of joy and ran up the last slope. Elliot followed, staggering slightly, the backpack pulling at his shoulders and his boots making one last attempt to saw his legs off just above the ankle. A few yards away he stopped and stared. Longjohn had his arms locked around Annie and looked at him over the top of her knitted cap.

"I hope you didn't forget the beer."

He hadn't—that was what was making the backpack so heavy. What made the rest of him so heavy, suddenly, was the sight of one of Annie's old headbands around Hawkins's temples. Suddenly the ragged quality of his sending made a terrible sense. Longjohn had used the bio-feedback to trigger his Omega, but he'd been in too much of a hurry to ask any of them how to build the Wall. For all these months, he had been wide open. As Elliot had been after his accident. As Annie had been on Mhourra. Wide open and defenceless, except for the untrustworthy bands.

"How many did you take with you?"

Longjohn smiled, briefly. "This is my last one."

Elliot drew a little closer. Longjohn's face was haggard behind the beard, his eyes haunted by shock and the memory of shock.

"You bloody fool," Elliot choked.

"And you," Longjohn reminded him. "And you."

The wind was hammering at the shutters and trying to put out the fire. Elliot had gone into Longjohn's head and taught him the mechanism of the Wall before he had even taken off the backpack. Longjohn seemed easier now, his head back against the rocking chair, the light from the flames playing tricks of age with his cheekbones and mouth. After they had eaten, Annie had gone to bed, leaving the two of them beside the fireplace.

"It was easy," Longjohn was explaining. "I flew over the

Inverpolly Nature Reserve until I had twenty minutes fuel left, set the auto-pilot, and chuted. I'd rigged a little cassette recorder to the radio on a timing device to send the Mayday call just before the fuel ran out."

"You chuted out of a plane in the *dark?*"

"Well, only dusk. Anyway, I couldn't risk anyone spotting me, could I?"

"My God, you could have been killed!"

"Not me—I'm built to bounce."

"But . . . *why?*"

Longjohn wouldn't meet his eyes. "It was the only way, Phil. You remember when you took Annie to the party at Curtiss's place?"

"Where you told her to 'read' Curtiss?" Elliot found he was still angry over that, although he'd never said anything to Hawkins. Perhaps because that evening was so private and special for him and Annie.

"It was her decision. Just as it was her decision to tell me what she'd found out, and not tell you. She didn't think you'd believe her—and you were still behind your Wall, remember?"

"I remember." Elliot's voice was bleak.

"What she got from Curtiss was very confusing for her, but she realized there was something very wrong in it. She gave me everything she could remember, and I told her I'd take care of it. It wasn't so confusing to me. I saw the direction Curtiss was taking, and it didn't take a clairvoyant to work out the worst that could happen if he wasn't stopped. I didn't know how to stop him—so I did the next best thing, and made provision for the worst. If a time came when you needed to run, and I was sure it would, then you had to have somewhere to go. A place to hide, a place to give you time to work out your next moves, if there were any to make. Just simple logic and working out the details."

"You were *that* positive I'd need to run?"

"Well, old friend—here we are, aren't we?"

And you set off your Omega mechanically, without any

buffering from a Group member, without any . . .

I only meant to set it off a little bit—to help you to locate me.

You can't set Omega off "a little bit."

So I've discovered as the months went by.

You'll be all right now—you have the Wall.

Can't you turn it off for me, Phil? I hate it.

Elliot got up and retrieved his cigarettes from the mantel-piece. *No. Since you left we've found it's a one-way street, Longjohn. Once your lungs start you can't stop them, and it's the same with Omega. Unlike lungs, you don't have to use it if you don't want to, but it never goes away.*

Longjohn sighed in resignation, as if he'd been told he had terminal cancer and would have to live—and die—with it. He turned his head towards the bedroom door. *She's prettier than ever.*

Pregnancy sometimes does that.

Hawkins lowered his head to stare at the stocky figure at the fireplace. *My God, is that why they're chasing you so hard?*

It's one of Curtiss's reasons, I suppose, 'Our' people don't know.

They won't find you here. They wouldn't even know how to look.

Elliot threw the empty cigarette packet into the fire. *No, but they could learn. They've got it all, the rest of the Group, our technicians, the Russian technology to build on . . . they could work it out. They probably will.*

Longjohn spoke aloud, suddenly and angrily. "You've built yourself a heap of crap, Phil, you and your big hopes."

"So it would seem," Elliot agreed. And he knew who was trapped underneath it, too.

20

Ari and Frances arrived two days later, guided in by Annie's strong signals. But Janet and Danny did not.

A week passed. Another.

It could have been a pleasant life there in the hills. Long-john had bought the cottage in a broken-down state, but had spent the lonely months improving it. He had worn the dirt track across the hills with his Land Rover carrying materials and supplies—which was why Elliot hadn't found it on any map. Locally he'd become familiar but not known, and he'd become friendly only in a two-pints way with some of the men from the Forestry Commission office in Clannach. They were loners, too, and accepted his story of being a geologist on sabbatical from McGill, writing a doctoral thesis on the Moine Thrust. A little burst of mountain-building that had taken place some four hundred million years earlier, he told Elliot. Very popular among geologists. He continued to shop in Clannach as before, buying the same amounts, but made some longer trips to Dornoch to stock up on supplies to feed the rest. Elliot and Annie returned to Clannach to collect the Honda and wave goodbye to their landlady. So endeth our trail,

Elliot thought, as they bounced over the trail to the cottage. So endeth the trail of Ari and Frances.

But where had Janet and Danny's ended?

During the time it had taken them to get to Longjohn, the papers had been full of the events at Talbot Hall, but there had been no hue and cry raised over their disappearance. In fact, according to the papers, they were all alive and well and working hard for His Majesty's Government somewhere—and there was a deal of editorial hand-wringing over *that*. The PM finally made his statement—all talk of "brain-washing" was nonsense, Dr. Elliot and his colleagues were engaged in vital research into brain structure, entirely medical, and the whole thing had been a storm in a teacup. As for the turmoil of the Little Summit, there had been an attempt at suicide by one of the lesser members of a delegation, purely personal, and Dr. Elliot had been called in merely because he was an expert on brain damage and there had been some worry concerning *that*. He deplored the concept of psychological manipulation, he deplored the excesses of hysteria which had brought about the destruction of Talbot Hall (at a great waste of taxpayer's money), and he deplored the role of the media in inciting such hysteria and everybody should be on their guard about *that*, dear me.

All very neat.

But Longjohn returned from Dornoch to report that the local police had been given secret orders to look for and detain, if found, the six who had escaped from Talbot Hall. This he gleaned from the mind of a constable whom he located and for whom he had bought a friendly beer at a pub in the High Street. The orders came from the Home Office, and had also been circulated through Interpol.

Longjohn said it was too far to swim to Brazil. At least at this time of year.

And still Danny and Janet did not appear.

Then, one Sunday, Elliot found some of the answers in

The Times, in an "aren't we clever" article about a new commission that had been set up to investigate "Human Potential."
An international body of Western scientists were going to explore the subject, and it would all be centered here in great
Great Britain. The Director of the new Commission spoke in
glowing terms of the "interdisciplinary" structure of the Commission, with economists, sociologists, psychologists, physicians, technologists, and many others who would take an
optimistic and positive approach to finding new ways for
utilizing mankind's strengths to improve the future of the
world. "While clearing up the problems we have at the moment is vitally important, it is also vital to be ready for the
time when those problems exist no more. We have to find new
horizons and opportunities for all. The future approaches
more quickly all the time," the Director said.

The author of the article thought that they had chosen
the Director well. Carter Hooks Curtiss was obviously the man
who could make things happen, as his previous record in Government showed.

Elliot read the piece aloud, put the paper down, and
looked around at them. Curtiss had convinced the Government
of his innocence, probably by convincing them of Elliot's guilt,
or duplicity, or insanity, or something similar. He had the rest
of the Group, he had the equipment, he was starting his new
kingdom in style. And he was absolutely right about one thing.

The future *was* approaching more quickly all the time.

A few days later, Ari happened to pick up one of the items
Elliot had grabbed from his desk before leaving Talbot, a gold
pen and pencil set Janet had given him the previous Christmas.
Elliot had been amused when he discovered it among all the
other things in his backpack, not knowing what had impelled
the selection except random hysteria. Now Ari's hand tightened
around the two golden pieces and he looked over at Annie
who was knitting in the rocking chair.

Elliot came in a few minutes later to find them locked

in mutual misery, Ari in front of the fire and Annie looking down at him. He put down the box of potatoes he'd dug from Longjohn's vegetable patch.

?

But he already knew.

"Janet's dead," Ari croaked. "Danny, too. Both dead." He began to lay the evening fire in the grate, his big body hunched over the task, slowly putting in the paper, the dried heather, and the first small pieces of coal. After a moment he mumbled something more.

"What?"

"Suicide," Annie said, softly. "That's it, isn't it, Ari?"

He nodded, dumbly, and his hands continued to put the fuel in place until the grate would hold no more. Some bits of coal rolled out onto the stones. He picked them up, put them back, and others fell out. He kept doing it, over and over again, with infinite and pointless patience.

When?

Weeks ago, now. Weeks ago.

Where?

Does it matter?

It might tell us whether Curtiss got hold of them or not. Elliot picked up the pen and pencil and carried them over to Ari, kneeling down next to him and holding them out. *Please.*

It hurts, Phil.

Please.

Eventually Ari took them, nearly enveloping them in his enormous fist. After a moment he let go and they clattered into the grate. Elliot retrieved them, accidentally dislodging more coal. Ari resumed his firebuilding silently.

?

Manchester. A lot of blood, no pain. Take the pen away, Phil. Please.

Elliot stood up and went out into the bright afternoon light. Longjohn was filling another box with potatoes, grubbing in the loose soil, whistling. When he'd pulled a couple out, Elliot dropped the pen and pencil into the hole.

Bury these, will you? Deep.

Hawkins rocked back on his heels and squinted up against the sun.

?

Elliot told him. After a minute or so, Longjohn went forward onto his knees and began scooping the earth out from under the two golden cylinders until they were a good three feet down, and then he started putting it back again, obliterating them.

Annie was standing by the window, looking out at the night.

Come back to bed. Come back to me.

She came slowly across the room and knelt on the edge of the bed, her knee pulling the nightgown away from her.

They died together. Will we die together?

Don't think about it.

Together?

He reached up and grabbed, pulling her over on top of him, forcing her mouth onto his, demanding she forget. She struggled for a moment, wanting to hold onto her despair as a kind of mourning gesture, but he would not let her. Gradually his hands drove the animal in her out of hiding and released it to run through both of them, wild and savage and hungry for prey, claw and muscle, teeth and tongue, the tearing hunting animal of limitless appetite. They mated, slept, and woke to hunt again until the night was chased away and the pale light of dawn redefined the window. The bed was a sea of twisted sheets and blankets, and they were two panting quarries, taking it turn on frantic turn to win, lost in the centre of the worlds they made together with their bodies and minds, an arch, a circle, an endless spiral with no beginning or end but just the turning and sliding and searching down and down and up into the morning to turn again and take.

Before he fled into the refuge of exhaustion, Elliot recognized with sorrow the need that had driven them through the hours of the night. A desperate defiance of death, a silent cry against those who were waiting to take them, a struggle against the hands at their throats.

That was all it had been.

That was all.

The weeks passed, and no one came for them. He wanted to believe they had truly escaped, wanted to believe that Danny's pessimistic prediction of the future had stopped with his own and Janet's death. That eventually Curtiss would settle for what he had and give up looking for them.

He wanted very badly to believe it. But he could not, because summer was over.

And it was getting cold again.

Everywhere.

21

His head ached, and the words swam in front of his eyes. He blinked and tried to concentrate on the book Longjohn had brought back from Dornoch. He didn't really see much point in learning how to build their own windmill and produce electricity, but Longjohn seemed to think it would be a good idea. He still kept thinking of good ideas. It would be an improvement on reading by gaslight, Elliot admitted, putting the book down and looking across at Ari who was also squinting at a book.

"Think we can do it?"

Ari raised his head but the frown didn't go away. "The theory is simple enough."

"Piece of cake," Longjohn said from the fireplace where he was poking and breaking up a lump of coal and heather. Fragrant smoke billowed up the chimney. "I can buy aluminium T-frame in Inverness, we can make the sails out of wood and canvas to start with, replace them with something more permanent later on, once we get the balance right." He rubbed his eyes with his knuckles, like a child.

Frances was asleep in the rocker. It was Annie's turn to wash the dishes in the bucket, but she was doing it slowly, sloshing the water apathetically onto the thick white plates and letting it run back.

"It would certainly be an improvement on these things," Elliot said, nodding towards the hissing gas lamp. "Between that and the smoke from the fire I feel as if somebody has been using my head for a gong."

"There you are, then," Longjohn said. "We have to make this place as self-sufficient as we can. The less we have to travel outside for stuff, the safer we'll be. Think you could learn to chop a chicken's head off?"

"I imagine so," Elliot said wryly.

"Good. Chickens to start with, then maybe a cow. Especially with the baby coming, a cow would be a good idea, wouldn't it?"

"I know how to milk a cow," Annie put in suddenly. "I used to steal milk from . . ." she trailed off. "I can milk a cow."

"Right," Longjohn said with a little too much enthusiasm. "Put a cow down on the list."

Frances woke with a start, looking around her crossly. "It certainly is stuffy in here," she complained.

Elliot pushed his chair back and stood up. "I'll open the door for a few minutes—any objections?" There were none, so he crossed to the door and opened it.

"Hello, Elliot," Curtiss said, smiling at him.

Instinctively he tried to slam the door closed, but another man came forward from behind Curtiss and knocked it back out of his hand. Elliot recognized one of the guards from Talbot.

"Hardly a welcome for an old friend who's come so far to see you," Curtiss said. His glance went past Elliot to the others who were sitting still and stricken, staring. "And everyone at home, too. How cosy."

Beyond Curtiss, Elliot could see others. Lots of others, all around the house and yard. They hadn't heard a thing. They'd developed a second-nature listening ability for human beings within five miles. And they certainly all recognized the hum of an implant, they'd heard them often enough. It wasn't a conscious alertness, but it was there, always there. And then a twinge reminded him—they'd all been complaining of headaches, hadn't they? They'd all felt claustrophobic. A new device. How simple. A new device, of course.

Of course, Curtiss echoed. *What else?*

Elliot swallowed, couldn't take his eyes from the smug face before him.

You didn't think yours was the only way, did you, Phil?

Curtiss's eyes left his and went round the room, passed over Annie, then returned to her. Her pregnancy was very apparent now, straining against her sweater and her safety-pinned jeans.

"Ah, Annie, how are you, my dear? Bursting with health, I see."

Elliot clenched his fists, stepped forward. There was a click from the yard outside. Not a loud click—just a rifle bolt. He stopped and the guard smiled.

"Now, why don't we all sit down and have a chat?" Curtiss suggested, his charm glinting from his nice even teeth as it had always done when he was at his most dangerous. Elliot remembered that smile very well. "It's *such* a long walk over those hills. Sit *down,* Phil." He glanced at Longjohn, bearded and shaggy. He'd only met him once and didn't recognize him. "And you too, whatever your name might be."

"Rumplestiltskin," Longjohn said evenly, and hunkered down in front of the fire, his hands clasped loosely between his knees.

Curtiss's smile tightened, but it didn't go away. Elliot wished it would. He went back to his chair and Annie came to sit near him, on the side farthest from Curtiss and the guards.

"That's *much* better," Curtiss enthused, drawing up another chair and placing it at the head of the table. "Well, now, I hope you've all had a pleasant holiday?" No one spoke.

"Yes, well, delightful as I'm sure it's all been, it's over I'm afraid. You're required back in London now. We have work for you. All of you, including Mr. Rumplestiltskin over there who George tells me is also an Omegan."

"George?" Frances whispered.

Curtiss's eyes focused on her for the first time. "Miss Murphy, isn't it? George speaks *very* highly of your abilities, Miss Murphy. I know he'll be glad to have you back. George? George?" He raised his voice and after a moment George Lomax appeared in the doorway carrying something in his hands.

"Yes, Mr. Curtiss?"

"Here's your Miss Murphy, George, safe and sound. Say hello."

"Hello, Frances," George said shyly. Frances closed her eyes and looked away.

"Never mind, George," Curtiss soothed. "She'll come around."

"Hello, Doc," George said, glancing at Elliot.

"George—how are you?"

"Okay, thanks. Okay."

"What's that you've got there? New toy?"

Lomax looked down at the box in his hands. "Oh, no, Doc. This is the real thing. This works."

"Everything George makes for *me* works," Curtiss said, taking out his cigarette case and offering it to Elliot. When he didn't accept, Curtiss shrugged and extracted one for himself. The guard came forward to light it, then stepped back against the door, his gun still level and his eyes fixed on Elliot. *"Unlike* those little gadgets you put on your famous show with, Philip. I was *very* disappointed to find out the things you showed my colleagues were worthless. I felt you let me down badly, there."

"I've been consumed by guilt ever since."

I'll just bet you have, you superior bastard. "Mind you," Curtiss continued aloud, "the ideas were good. They set

George to thinking, didn't they, George?"

"Oh, yeah, the ideas were *good,* Doc." George was feeling in his pocket, shifting the box in his hands to rest on one hip. Pulling his hand out, he displayed the silver egg. "I mean, *this* was useless, but once I began working on the theory . . . well . . ." he gazed down at the egg in a friendly fashion. "I brought this one along as a souvenir for you, Doc. Only one of its kind, now." Abruptly he tossed it towards Elliot. The guard moved to intercept it but it landed in Elliot's hands as if it was a homing pigeon still in the shell. He held it in his palm but it didn't rock, just sat there.

"Oh, pity," Curtiss observed. "All the magic's gone. Never mind."

"No magic about it," George persisted as if eager to justify himself. "All in the idea . . . just taking it and giving it a little twist until something new came out of it, see? I mean, Doc, when I started working on the DC levels and reversed the diodes so that the impulses ran on a cps of—"

"There will be plenty of time for that when we get back to the Centre, George," Curtiss interrupted, impatiently.

"Oh . . . sure . . . sorry." George backed up and stood against the wall.

"Ah, but don't think I don't appreciate you, George, I do," Curtiss said with diplomatic haste. "I do." He leaned forward slightly. "George has done some really marvellous things for us, really terrific developments."

"In the original semantic sense, of course," Longjohn observed.

"What?" Curtiss glanced down the table at him. "Oh, I see what you mean. Not at all, though, not at all. It's Hawkins under all that, isn't it? I *did* wonder about that plane crash, you know, but there wasn't time to . . . ah, well." He returned his glance to Elliot, drew on his cigarette, leaned back in his chair. *Your friends stick by you, don't they? What is it? Charisma? Money? Blackmail?*

Elliot stared at him wishing he could figure out how

Curtiss was doing it. Invariably, with Omega sending, there was a background of amplified and resonating images, word bounces, echoes, an enrichment of language that made mental conversation as much like music as anything. But when Curtiss sent his asides, they came across without anything extra, just the words, like a second person speaking aloud. And nobody else was getting them either, he realized, just himself. George *had* been busy.

Very busy, Doc.

Somehow Elliot managed to keep his eyes on Curtiss, stunned as he was to hear from George telepathically. He still clutched the egg George had tossed to him earlier, his fingers tight around its cool smoothness as it rested in his lap. When he shifted it, the egg did not have the same sensation of life it had possessed before, and it was heavier. Far heavier. His fingers moved slowly over the surface and he detected a fine line running round the ovoid, as if it had been cut in two and then put back together.

"You know, I don't know why you automatically assume I'm such a bad man," Curtiss was continuing. "My plans for Omega aren't so terrible."

"Oh?" Elliot's fingers continued to trace the fine line round the egg, turning it, turning it. It went all the way round.

"Certainly not. Mind you, the members of the Group you trained are very enthusiastic about all of it . . . goodness and kindness and exaltation and so on, they can really get rather *boring,* in fact, about the world of the mind. Like those two we caught in Manchester. So dedicated—so noble. Killed themselves in their cells, can you imagine? Bit through the veins in their wrists and quietly bled to death into their respective mattresses, during the night. Such a pointless waste—all because they wanted to keep the Omega power *inviolate* or some such nonsense. They couldn't see the possibilities, because they, like you, wanted to dissipate the thing. You think that if each man has a world in his head to share with humanity, then humanity will have a world worth sharing, isn't that it?"

"Something like that."

"Wasteful," Curtiss repeated, emphasizing it with a jab of his cigarette. "Time-consuming, high-flown, and inefficient. All it takes is a little objectivity and the whole thing falls into place. We can have a world worth living in far more quickly than that. Every man with a world of his own is *anarchy*, don't you see? But everyone with the *same* world in his head, that's peace, that's harmony, that's productive functioning."

"Whose world?"

"What?" He had been interrupted in full flow and it annoyed him.

"*Whose* world will there be in everyone's mind?" Elliot amplified.

"It doesn't really matter, does it, as long as they all match?" But he could not resist sending: *Mine, mine, mine.*

"And how will you accomplish this little miracle?" Elliot asked him. His fingers stroked the egg, the line around the egg. He had been trying to send to Annie, Ari, Longjohn, Frances, but had been unable to get through. His Omega was blocked, totally blocked, while Curtiss was zapping him every few minutes without any apparent effort.

"Oh, not easily, Phil, not overnight, I'll admit. But with George's help we've developed several new techniques . . . well, George and some others I've found who aren't quite as troubled by *ethics* as your lot were. We can develop Omega with bio-feedback, as you did, but now we can do it selectively, and within defined limits. We'll find the potential minds that are most useful to us and develop them just far enough, no more. And then we'll simply point them *out*, not in. You see? *Out*, to other minds less . . . enlightened, shall we say? And we can exert control and direction so easily they'll never even realize it. They'll even like it—that's the thing. Oh my, yes— we want everyone to be *happy* in our world. Contented."

"And if they aren't?" Ari wanted to know.

"Then we turn them off."

"Kill them?" Frances gasped.

"No no no, everyone is useful. Just turn them off."

"Moles in the mines, phantoms in the factories, drones in the hives," Elliot said quietly.

"Oh, Phil, you are so *emotional,*" Curtiss said in exasperation. "I can see I'm going to have a long hard job convincing you of my benign intent. How much longer before the helicopters get here?" he asked the guard behind him.

"Ten minutes. You said you wanted a clear half hour with them."

"I can see that was optimistic," Curtiss conceded. *And you'll be the biggest drone of all, you and your wife and that . . . thing . . . in her belly. What do you suppose it will be, a boy or a girl? Not that it will matter in the tank.*

Elliot's fingers tightened around the egg, wishing it were Curtiss's throat. He understood, now. Cart had begun to hate him for being the man he himself couldn't be in his own wife's bed. Then he had hated him more for possessing Omega—something else of which he was incapable. And, finally, he hated him for fathering a child when he himself could not. Once he had grasped the possibilities of Omega, he had used Elliot as a surrogate, an artificial inseminator for his own cockeyed concept of dynasty. Carter Hooks Curtiss, the "father" of a new order which would be people from Elliot's "seed." To have all this disaster grow from one man's frustrated sexual ambitions seemed impossible—and yet history was full of thwarted impotents who had misdirected their energies in similar ways. Elliot's dream of the mind of man raising him above his animal heritage to some finer destiny was just that—a dream. The animal was still winning. Perhaps the animal would always win.

"It all sounds lovely, Curtiss. Just lovely," he said.

"Still think man's greatness is within, do you?" Curtiss sneered.

"Yes, I do." Even in this moment of defeat, he knew it was. He'd touched a corner of it now and again, in the crowds they'd moved through, running away. Some man in a shop, another on a train, a boy playing football, a woman with a bag full of dirty clothes in a launderette. Every once in a while he had touched it—the light and the love. But he could imagine how well *that* would go down with Curtiss.

"Twaddle. Mystic twaddle. Just the kind of thing we have to eliminate if we want to get ahead," Curtiss snapped, as if he had heard.

"I can see you're convinced."

"As usual, Phil, you bore me." *You god-hunter, you easy-answer-fool, give up.* "No matter. We'll talk more at the Centre." He pulled back his immaculate sleeve to look at his immaculate gold watch. "Strylander, go and see if you can hear the helicopter, will you? And send a man in to help the ladies gather their things together. I know how ladies like to have their little bits and pieces about them." He smiled patronizingly at Annie and Frances. As they went into the other room, he glanced carefully at Elliot. "You won't cause any trouble, will you, Phil? I'd hate to see the ladies upset."

"No, I can't see there's much point in making trouble," Elliot agreed. Ari shifted in his chair, Longjohn settled himself more evenly on the balls of his feet.

"Well, of course not. Anyway, George has you all turned off with his little box, haven't you, George?"

"Yes. Sorry, Doc. Works on the same wavelength as the implants the guards wear." He gestured with the box, raising it slightly. "Sort of a damper effect, if you see what I mean."

"Is that what gave us the headaches a little while ago?" Elliot asked.

"Yes. We can detect Omega, even undeveloped Omega, at up to ten miles. Have to know the parameters, of course, that's why Mr. Curtiss had to bring me along. We did a high-fly over the country about a week ago, developed all the patterns we picked up, located the general area. You should have seen yourselves, Doc, shone out like stars in the sky up here. Simple, really. Then we just had to pinpoint you, that's all."

Elliot looked at him. George seemed really proud of it all. His face was proud, anyway. *Bartlett sends his regards, Doc. Says to tell you Joseph is fine, too, in case you were worried. Don't send. I can't hear you.*

Elliot wasn't sending. He was just sitting there trying to keep his face under control. It wasn't easy.

There are ten guards outside, Doc. And Curtiss and the fellow in with Annie make twelve.

Ari and Longjohn were looking at the floor, and Ari coughed. Elliot now realized George was sending to them, too, but Curtiss wasn't getting any of it. He was just puffing on his cigarette and smiling, waiting for the helicopters to come and waft them all away to his snake pit.

They're all implanted, even him, so you'll have to use your hands not your heads. He's got something more besides, a thing the other techs made him, on a harness. You'll have to get rid of that first before you can really get at him.

Elliot reached into his pocket and Curtiss's smile disappeared. "Just like a smoke, prefer my own," he said, meekly. Curtiss even lit it for him. What a gentleman, Elliot thought. What a true gentleman. George seemed to think it would all be very easy, and he couldn't ask him why. The odds were bad—plus the guns. And the helicopter was due any minute, carrying what? Reinforcements.

Been talking to you, hasn't he? It's all mechanics, Doc, his Omega rating is so low it's practically a vacuum. Just mechanics, don't worry about it. With me, it's . . . Bartlett did me, Doc. Like you did him. All in the head, Doc. There was a long pause. *I missed Frances, I couldn't . . .*

Elliot had dropped the egg into his pocket when he'd got out his cigarettes. He realized, now, that it was something George had meant him to have, but what?

It's bad back there, now. They don't use the Group,

*they've shut them up somewhere. The new ones . . . nobody
laughs, Doc. It's no fun.*

Elliot wondered if this was going to all of the others,
now, or whether George had developed the ability to handle
several simultaneous transmissions at once. Was Frances having a chance to hear him at last? He hoped so. Maybe George
was counting on the women, too—that helped the odds. He
started to draw his feet back slowly, ready to make a move.

No . . . wait for it.

Elliot stopped moving, and so did the others.

Didn't think I'd let you do it all alone, did you?

George's hand was moving across the face of the box
slowly, adjusting the dials and calibrated knobs delicately,
carefully. Oh, George, you sneaky bastard, Elliot thought,
you started it and you wanted to be in on this now, didn't
you? He wanted to say hello with all the trimmings, but his
head was still blocked and his mind was gagged. George's
fingers continued their butterfly work behind Curtiss's back.

*Don't worry about the helicopter, by the way. I set all
their watches ten minutes fast a while back. Frances ain't the
only one who can push things around.*

Elliot saw he was settling the box more firmly against
his stomach. Whatever George planned, it was obviously going to be awkward.

*I don't know how long I can give you, it might blow out
fast. Nod if you're ready, Doc.*

Elliot nodded, and George hit the button.

All hell broke loose. Literally.

"Jesus Christ!" Longjohn shouted, clutching his temples.
If they'd had headaches before, they were nothing by com-
parison. A rhythmic throbbing coruscated from the centre of
Elliot's brain, and everything in the room suddenly had a halo
around it—as if he had been swimming too long in chlorinated
water. All scents and sounds were intensified to such a degree
that the fried onions from the still unwashed pan by the bucket

practically tore out the lining of his nose, and the first step he took thundered through the room like a giant's. Fee fi fo fum, he thought, idiotically.

"Ma-ma," Curtiss said. "Ma-ma."

Elliot stared at him through the rainbows. Even as he watched, the beatific smile left Curtiss's face to be replaced by a rictus so extreme that the knobs of muscle round each joint of his jaw stood out like a baby's fists. Curtiss struggled to speak through his locked teeth but all that came out was a thin dribble of sound, rising and falling. His arms and legs began to jerk spastically, until he seemed to be dancing in the chair. Then the convulsion passed, and he was sneezing, sneezing, sneezing until his glasses flew off and smashed next to the chair.

"Wall! Wall!" Elliot shouted, his voice echoing through the room. Closing his eyes he concentrated on separating himself from his body, closing off the sensations that were bouncing around inside him one by one until he could handle them, opening his eyes to see Ari and Longjohn opening theirs. It wasn't good, but it was bearable.

Curtiss had stopped sneezing now, and had drawn his legs up to his chest, staring at something on the floor in pure horror. Elliot glanced down and saw an ant stepping quietly across the stone floor, a dart to the left, a scuttle to the right. "Wha . . . wha . . . wha . . ." Curtiss was gasping, and then his legs shot out in front of him and he wet himself, collapsing into the chair like an infant. He began slapping at the side of his head, desperately clawing at the skin and hitting his ear.

Elliot looked over at George to ask what—

George was crying. George was looking down at the box in his hands and sobbing as if someone had taken his last lollipop away. Then he sat down abruptly on the floor and began to bite his fingers until the blood came, growling like an animal, gnawing and . . . then he began to giggle.

"My . . . God . . . what . . . is . . . it?" Ari roared.

"The box," he managed to say. "He's turned it up to overload." He wished he could stop shouting. "Our perceptions are blasting us . . ."

"Egg," George giggled. "Egg . . . egg . . ."

Elliot hauled the silver egg out of his pocket and started to twist the two halves.

"*NO!*" George screamed. "Other . . . way . . ."

Elliot reversed his hands and twisted. Immediately things returned to normal. For them, that is. Not for George, not for Curtiss, or—to judge from the sounds they could hear outside and in the bedroom—not for any of the guards, either. Because *they* were implanted. And the implants were responding to the box, ricocheting their brain waves around like machine-gun bullets, reversing their perceptions, dumping their memories out like marbles to roll around the floors of their heads, cross-wiring their body functions, enhancing their emotions to unbearable pitch, and in general treating their minds like television sets carrying hundreds of separate and distinct programmes that changed from second to second as the maverick waves stimulated new areas of the brain in turn.

George had known it would happen. And George had known it would happen to him, too, because he was wearing an implant like the rest of them. His giggling rose to hysteria and beyond, and the box slid off his lap as he began to convulse, banging his head against the stone wall behind him. Elliot ran over and pulled him away from it, but that was about all he could do, except turn off the box—which would release the guards and Curtiss as well as George. He shoved the egg in his pocket."

"Tie them up," he shouted. "Get their guns and tie them up before the box blows itself out." He ran towards the bedroom. Annie and Frances were staring at the guard who had accompanied them. He was thrashing and moaning on the floor. "Get his gun from him and tie him up good and tight. Hurry," he directed. He grabbed a sheet and began to tear it into strips as fast as he could with his teeth and hands. After a second the women joined in, pulling another sheet from the bed and attacking it from both sides at once.

He ran back to Curtiss, and found him giggling and guffawing, roaring with laughter, slapping his thighs. Elliot reached for a hand to tie it, but even as he did so the implant in Curtiss did another shift and he grabbed Elliot by the front of his sweater.

"Not . . . not . . . not . . . funny," he snarled, his hands reaching for Elliot's face, nails out. Elliot ducked just in time to save his eyes, and then Curtiss was convulsing again, rolling off the chair onto the floor and kicking wildly. One foot caught Elliot's ankle and sent a jab of pain through it. Then Curtiss froze stiff. Elliot took the moment to try and tie him up, but Curtiss's joints wouldn't bend. To break the lock until he could get the hands together behind the back, he had to hit with the edge of his hand at Curtiss's shoulders and elbows. By the time he got the hands tied, Curtiss was off again into the wild blue yonder, screaming: "Fly, fly, flyyyyyyyyy." Elliot grabbed a leg, bracing himself for a fight, only to have it go limp on him like a piece of over-cooked spaghetti. He got the legs tied together just before Curtiss began convulsing again, his body slamming rhythmically against the floor.

Elliot ran over to George but there was nothing he could do for him. He lay on his side, curled into a foetal position, sucking his fingers. As he went towards the door, Elliot heard him start to giggle again. He had touched the box where it lay and found it was already very warm to the touch, the dials on the face fluctuating wildly. The field of the egg seemed to cover only natural Omega function, not the mechanical impulses of the implants.

The scene in the yard could have been painted by Hieronymous Bosch.

Between them, Ari and Longjohn had managed to tie up two of the guards with the spare clothesline, but there were still eight others on the loose. Their guns had been collected, and Elliot nearly tripped over the heap by the door. Two of the guards were crawling around the heather like rabid wolves foaming at the mouth and howling. Another was clawing himself as if searching for hot fleas, and one was hiccupping gently and staring at his fingers, counting "One . . . huc . . . two . . . hic . . . three . . . hac . . ."

Ari crept up on that one and started whipping some clothesline around the hands just before the implant shifted and the man began to flail like a thresher. Longjohn caught another in a flying tackle just as he started to attack a fellow guard, and the man who had nearly been strangled by his friend waltzed gravely away, turning and humming under the moon as if the girl in his arms was more than mere air.

Elliot took the bill-hook out of the ground where it was stuck point first and used it to chop down the main clothesline, stripping the shirts and underwear from it with one hand while coming up behind the waltzing wonder. Just as he reached him, the man stopped dead and began to scream, a high thin terrible sound of pain beyond bearing. Elliot could not think of any doctor alive who could have heard that noise and not felt his skin crawl, even a doctor who knew it wasn't real. He grabbed one of the guard's hands and pulled him down as he began to convulse, fought him flat and twisted his arms back. Finally, in desperation, he sat on the man's backside and rode him like a bronco, tying the hands with some of the strips of sheet while the legs kicked out behind, drew up, then kicked out again, whump, whump, whump.

Using his penknife he chopped off a piece of clothesline and secured the legs, then looked around to see who was next. He chose one of the wolves who had now become a tiger and was stalking Longjohn. He got to him just as the guard changed from tiger to opera star—his sudden basso profundo rendition of "Kill, kill, kill" sent an unsuspecting Longjohn two feet into the air. Even while Elliot finished tying him up, the guard regressed to infancy crying and rocking to and fro on the ground at a steady seventy-two beats per minute. Longjohn had recovered his nerve sufficiently to catch up with and immobilize the other wolf, who was also crying now, but with rage as he tried to claw his own eyes out and found he could not reach them.

Suddenly, over all the screaming and thudding and spewing and crying, Elliot heard another sound. The distant clacking roar of a helicopter coming closer and closer. The enthusiastic bastard was early.

"Let's get some of them out of sight," he shouted, catching hold of his latest captive under the arms and dragging him over to the rose bushes Longjohn had planted in front of the cottage, leaving him there to beat his head against the stone wall while he went back for another. The helicopter was nearly over the cottage now, and the pilot switched on his landing lights. The double glare threw everything below into spotlit clarity. They had managed to immobilize six of the guards, but four were still scrabbling in the dirt and grass, kicking, thrashing, insane with the torment they were enduring.

The note of the engine changed suddenly, and Elliot realized the pilot had taken in the situation below and without knowing precisely what it was, knew it for unreceptive at best. *He* obviously was not implanted or he would have crashed long ago. The chopper began to lift away rapidly, and Elliot knew he had to be radioing for help as he rose.

"Frances! Frances!" he screamed. She appeared in the doorway, holding onto the jamb on either side. "Bring it down! Bring it down! Stop the radio and bring it down—hurry!"

"No!" Longjohn shouted. "Stop the radio but don't crash it, for God's sake, I can fly the bugger . . ."

But Frances had let go of the jamb and was pressing her hands to her head, her eyes closed in intense concentration as she forced what power she could through the damping effect of the egg. The helicopter continued to rise for a few seconds more, and then the note of the engine changed again. A strange whine began to override the throbbing beat of the rotors, and the machine suddenly tilted and began to slide sideways out of the sky. For a minute Elliot thought it was going to right itself, then, with a blinding flare of light and noise it exploded fifty yards ahead of the cottage in an expanding fireball that set the thatch on fire in several places.

The burning wreck seemed to hang in the sky as the rotors flew apart, spinning away with centrifugal force to slice into the hill on one side and the jeep on the other, and then the blackened skeleton of the airframe splattered itself all over the heather. One of the bits of wreckage hit a guard who was still crawling over the grass and took half his chest away. Then there was only the silence of the night, the tick and lick of flames from the thatch, and the continuing screams of the three agents who were still under the assault from George's box. Longjohn was riding one as Elliot had ridden his, and Ari had nearly finished tying up another when George's box blew out.

Elliot had to chase the last one and hit him on the head with a rock before he could tie him up. Longjohn sat on the back of the one he had been fighting and stared across at the blackened twisted wreck of the helicopter that still burned fitfully, settling down inch by inch like a dying insect into the burn that gurgled and hissed beneath its superheated frame.

"Oh, drat," Longjohn said morosely.

"Never mind," came George's hoarse croak from the doorway where he had joined Frances. "There'll be another one along in a minute." He put a shaking hand on Frances's arm. "Maybe we can be a little neater with that one . . . litter is a terrible thing, you know, Frances."

She turned and buried her face in his shoulder.

Elliot stood up and looked around. The thatch had begun to burn in earnest. "We'd better put out that fire or . . ." he began, when Annie gave a sudden shriek inside the cottage.

George and Frances started to turn but were savagely pushed aside to stumble into the yard as Curtiss appeared in the doorway trailing strips of sheet and clutching Annie to his chest. In his other hand he held a gun—taken from the guard

in the bedroom, Elliot presumed. Curtiss's eyes went round
the yard in disbelief, then he located what he was most interested in—Elliot himself.

"I want you to watch this, I want you to see it all," he
snarled, raising the gun towards Annie's head, his eyes wild
with hate and worse. Elliot couldn't move, he was frozen. He
saw Annie's eyes widen as Curtiss's knuckles whitened around
the gun. And then . . . Curtiss's arm stiffened as the gun
began to fight him.

Frances, from where she lay half on her knees beside
George.

The gun slowly turned from Annie. Curtiss tried to hold
it steady, but it was turning inexorably away from Annie . . .
towards Elliot . . . past Elliot . . . towards Ari . . . past
Ari . . . towards Longjohn . . . and it went off even as it
flew from Curtiss's helpless grasp.

Longjohn went backwards off the guard he was straddling
as the bullet caught him in the chest and left him sprawled
across the soft cushion of the heather. Annie screamed and
Curtiss sent her towards Elliot with a vicious shove, turning to
run into the darkness. She stumbled and fell into Elliot's arms.

*So strong . . . tore the sheets . . . got up . . . I
couldn't . . .*

Trust Curtiss not to give up those squash games, Elliot
raged. Trust him to stay fit, trust me not to tie sheets as well
as I can tie sutures.

Are you all right? The baby?

Yes . . . yes . . .

He steadied her, then ran over to where Longjohn lay
terribly still, staring up at the sailing moon and the sky. Kneeling beside him, Elliot tried to see where all the blood was coming from.

Only . . . hurts . . . when I . . . laugh.

"Shut up." Tearing at Longjohn's shirt, Elliot exposed
the wound. High, it was high over the left breast, the blood
welling and flooding down. He heard the breath whistling in

and out of the hole—it had caught the upper lung but not the heart.

"You'll live."

Never thought otherwise. I have this ace doctor friend . . . Who didn't bring his bag with him.

So . . . improvise.

Elliot found all this faith in him touching, if wildly misplaced. Longjohn was losing consciousness, along with all the blood. Improvise with what—two spoons and a teabag?

"We've got to stop this bleeding," he shouted, getting up and running back to the cottage. The thatch was still burning but Ari had begun to do something about it, starting with the dishwater. He ran past Elliot towards the burn, swinging the empty bucket.

"We've got to stop that fire," he grunted. "Good as a beacon to that other helicopter."

"Have to stop the helicopter, too," Frances said, getting to her feet.

Elliot stood looking from Longjohn to the burning thatch to the sky in the south. "Great! Anything else we've got to stop?"

"Yes," said George, heavily. "Curtiss. He can Omega the chopper pilot to radio for help. That thing the other techs gave him has real power."

Suddenly Elliot knew how the boy at the dyke felt when another leak sprung out six feet away. "Get Longjohn flat and start some direct pressure to the wound . . . sheets, towels, anything," he instructed Annie. She was a better healer than he could ever be. She nodded and went into the cottage as George and Frances went towards Longjohn. Ari ran past him with another bucket of water from the burn. It seemed to Elliot a golden opportunity to say something spontaneous, inspiring, and original. He sighed. "Which way did he go?"

Being Curtiss, he had taken what to him seemed the logical and sensible direction—back down the track and towards the

main road. Not realizing there was nothing down the track
but six miles of track, winding the easiest way through the hills
for the jeep. Elliot knew that if Curtiss stayed with the track,
he would add a good two miles to his distance. Which meant
to head him off all he would have to do was go directly over
the hills. Through the thick heather. In the dark. With hardly
enough breath left to keep his lungs in business.

He set off down the track.

He did not hurry all that much because he knew that
eventually the distance would tell on both of them, and Curtiss
had been weakened by the attack from George's box. He, on
the other hand, had only had to deal with the guards, chasing
them around the yard, bringing them down, tying them . . .
he began to hurry a little more, cutting across some of the
stretches of hill he knew whenever the moon gave him the light.

How's Longjohn? he sent back to Annie.

Still unconscious—not bleeding so much.

Not bleeding outside so much, Elliot amended. God knew
what was happening internally. *Keep the pressure on.*

Yes . . . yes . . . Distance was beginning to tell, or
she was distracted. He knew he wouldn't be able to stay in
contact much longer. *Why* hadn't he spent more time on his
distance development? For the same reason he hadn't kept up
his correspondence with *The Times* Gardening Editor, he supposed, jogging along in the dark and nearly coming a cropper
in the burn where it crossed the track for the second time in
its meander through the hills. Too damn many hobbies, that
was his problem.

He sent his mind ahead, trying to pick up the hum of
Curtiss's implant, but heard nothing. Something extra, George
had said. The techs had given Curtiss something extra.

George . . . tell me about this thing on Curtiss. No
response. *George?* Then his ears picked up the distant sound
of the second helicopter and he realized George was too busy
to come to the phone just then.

Stopping for a minute to ease the pain in his chest, he

peered down the track. There was a long straight stretch ahead, but no sign of Curtiss. Had he turned off, was he waiting somewhere to try to signal the chopper pilot? Had he made a signal already? No, the sound of the helicopter was still growing, it was still coming. How close did Curtiss have to be? Maybe George's box had damaged the thing, whatever it was. Maybe . . . maybe . . .

Maybe he'd better get moving. Taking a last deep breath he started down the track again, listening for the sound, any sound, that might give him a clue as to where Curtiss had got to.

Curtiss ended the search by jumping onto his back and trying to knock his head off with a rock.

The shock of the attack provided Elliot with the best possible defence—he went down like a startled schoolmistress, pulling Curtiss with him. As they hit the track, the lump of granite fell from Curtiss's grasp and buried itself in the band of heather between the ruts. That freed his hand and he used it to catch hold of the other one and tighten his lock across Elliot's oesophagus. Elliot drove an elbow back and caught him just under the ribs. With a grunt Curtiss let go just enough for Elliot to turn within his grasp and go at him as best he could, biting, gouging. But Curtiss had let go as much as he was going to do. That was the trouble with attending the same schools, Elliot decided as he tried to thrust his knee into Curtiss's groin—you learn all the same tricks in the scrum. They rolled over and over in the heather, like two lovers in the moonlight eager for penetration, but the genders were wrong and they were both growling words and sounds no lovers ever turned to for effect.

Harness, George had said. Harness. Elliot tried to get a hand between them, scrabbling at the front of Curtiss's shirt, tearing at it, trying to locate whatever it was. Curtiss drew his elbows together to protect his chest while forcing his knee further and further up between Elliot's legs. Elliot brought his legs up and locked them around Curtiss's pelvis, using his opponent's body to protect his own. He decided to go for the throat, the hell with the harness. As his hands encircled Curtiss's neck he felt a thin ridge under the collar, leading to a heavier cord at the back.

Congratulations, Dr. Elliot, he told himself, you have just failed Basic Anatomy I.

The thing *had* to be on his back somewhere, over the spine. Dimwit. Curtiss had been defending his belly, hoping he would miss it. Cunning old Curtiss. He bit a piece out of cunning old Curtiss's ear and hitched himself further up his body, reaching down over the shoulders and searching for the thing that had to be there.

Suddenly Curtiss was in his head trying to blow his brains out through his ears. The technicians had given him power, all right, Elliot conceded. But he had been so intent on trying to kill his pursuer that he had forgotten it for a moment. Now, realizing that was Elliot's target, he had decided to use it.

LETGOLETGOLETGOLETGOLETGOLETGO

Despite all he could do, Elliot's body was obeying the stronger demand. He put the Wall up, trying to lessen the flow, but it was thin and getting thinner by the minute under the continuous close-in bombardment. He forced his hands further down Curtiss's back and felt a small square shape under the jacket. Flat, against the spine. His fingers dug at the edges, but the jacket was too taut over it for him to get any leverage.

HEARTSTOPHEARTSTOPHEARTSTOPHEART-STOP

Elliot's heart throbbed painfully in his chest, starting a disrhythmic hiccup that threatened to decay into fibrillation at any second, and his muscles began to weaken and slide within his skin.

NONONONONONONONONONONONONONO-NONO he sent back, trying to set up a counter-blast in Curtiss's head. He threw a blanket of sensory impressions over his perceptions, light, sound, colour, noise, whatever he could pull out of his own memory banks, smells, textures, movement. Still inching over the shoulders, reaching for the lower edges of Curtiss's jacket to rip it apart up the back seam from the vent.

Skyrockets and roses, sulphur and Stravinsky, blue, black, red, green, spinach in the mouth, dust in the nostrils, butter-scotch, pink, purple, vomit, Delius, jackhammers, hot coals, toothache, earache, falling down the stairs, Mummy, orange, brown, sliced onions, cat scratches, hay fever.

LETGOLETGOLETGOLETGOLETGO NOBREATH NOBREATHNOBREATH

As the air went out of Elliot's lungs in a whoosh, he got hold of the edges of the flat box through the cotton of Curtiss's fine handmade shirt and pried the thing away. He hoped it was wired directly into Curtiss's nervous system so he could pull out his spinal cord with it, like a long strand of grey spaghetti. But it only came away from the back with a rip of adhesive, and instantly Curtiss's commands to Elliot's body ceased. They were back to fangs again.

Curtiss had gone limp for an instant, only an instant, expecting Elliot to attack him with Omega at full strength. But there was still the old implant stopping Elliot from achieving anything more than a whispered version of the sensory bombardment, and Curtiss was getting used to that. With a manic burst of strength, Curtiss hauled himself away and brought his knee up hard.

Thirty million Elliots bit the dust and so did their progenitor, howling into the heather like a banshee. Curtiss jerked himself away as Elliot curled himself around the agony, gagging and heaving for breath. Generous to the last, Curtiss tried to distract Elliot from the pain in his groin by drawing his foot back and ramming his heel into Elliot's shin, producing a dull but unmistakeable crack of breaking bone.

Curtiss hung over the writhing figure, his torn jacket flapping round him like a shawl and his hair lifting and stirring in the night air, gilded by the moonlight into a gossamer crest.

"All *right,* Philip," he whispered. "Now we'll start *again.* Don't worry about your leg. Once I get you back to the Centre, you will part company with it for good. Along with everything else. When I say I want your head on a platter, I mean just that. I have the platter all wired up and waiting. And one for that freak of a wife of yours, although I think we'll see what she's got in her belly before we pry out what's in her skull, yes?"

Elliot vomited all over Curtiss's shoes—it was the best he could do at that moment.

Curtiss ignored it, he had better things to croon about. "Now, you just lie there like a good boy while I go and find someone to shovel you into a box. You and all your little friends."

He stepped away and then turned to start searching the heather for the box Elliot had ripped from him and heaved as far away as he could. Elliot watched the angular figure through his tears of pain. Curtiss bent over the thick heather, kicking with one foot, trying to part the growth and find the source of extra energy that would put him back in touch with his kingdom. The pain from Elliot's crotch was diminishing, replaced by waves of grinding pain from the splintered shin. He tried to summon the others, but he was alone, alone under the moon with a madman. Trying not to jar his leg, he turned and felt in his pocket for the egg. He knew what it could do in one direction, he remembered, but it was the only thing he had left that hadn't been stamped on, kicked at, gouged, torn, broken, or run out. If it didn't do anything, he could always throw it at Curtiss's head.

Curtiss was further away now, still kicking at the heather, sure that within minutes he would be able to control them all for good. Or rather, for evil.

Taking hold of the egg in both hands as he lay on his back and tried to focus over the pain, Elliot twisted the two halves. Is that what George had meant? Would that . . . ?

His head began to grow.

His mind began to expand, out, out, out, like the spreading bubble of radiation around the fiery core of Hiroshima . . . out, out, out . . . until he was filling the sky and filling the air and flowing out over the hills, everything small beneath him. He saw his own body lying in the track, the dark burn curling and chortling over the rocks, the cottage, the second helicopter hovering over the figures below it, the sheep in the hills, the rocks. He could see the rocks *under* the heather, he could see into the rock, he could see the molecules, the atoms, the electrons and protons whirling around the nucleii, and he was the rock and the sky and the night air and everything he saw was bright and burning with the fire of being, rainbows and scentbows and touchbows ran through him, circled him, lifting and rising and turning and flowing and growing . . .

And he could see Curtiss.

The shape of him, the flesh, the bones within the flesh, the black blot of his brain glowing with dark fire in his skull, there, far below in the bubble of Elliot's being he stood kicking the grass, searching, a small ant, a thing to be stepped on, a thing to be destroyed.

Elliot wasn't sure if he could be bothered, now.

His mind was still expanding, flowing, rushing, spreading, rising, rising, rising . . .

Curtiss bent, suddenly, and reached for something in the heather. Something that glinted and caught Elliot as he rose away. No. No. He couldn't do that. Couldn't be allowed to do that to Elliot's world, *his* rocks and *his* trees and *his* people and *his* spinning whirling planet, the very core of him, of *his* flesh . . . *his* flesh. *His* woman. *His* child. There in Curtiss's hand was the box in which all of them would be caught, dying and screaming to fall away . . . away . . .

Elliot focused all the loathing in him onto that reaching black ant in the heather . . . and it *stopped* reaching.

It fell down and began to twist and writhe in the heather,

in the dirt where it belonged. It began to beat out a circle in the heather as its arms and legs windmilled, as it gurgled and choked and screamed.

Elliot watched. For Valery, for Annie, for the baby.

Curtiss's body curved up into an arch of agony, the spine lifting a good eight inches clear of the ground beneath, his legs jerking and splaying out.

Elliot listened to him for Janet and Danny. Listened to the screech of agony as it ripped from Curtiss's throat. Curtiss's fists began to pound the heather, drumming, beating, his head was forced back until the throat was a white column of corded sinew. Suddenly, quite suddenly, blood began to stain Curtiss's clothes in a dozen places at once. It darkened the crotch of his trousers, it spread across the front of his torn shirt, it began to drip and slither like black snakes down his arms into the ground, to rivulet from his open mouth, his ears, his nose, his thrashing legs. It was everywhere. Where his shirt was torn it exposed the flesh, and Elliot could see it separating, the layers of epidermis, fat, and muscle opening into a hundred gaping wounds, each spreading wider and wider. Eventually he could even see the bared bones of the ribs, the glistening movement of dark viscera shifting within as Curtiss twisted and turned, trying to escape the flaying razors that slashed unchecked from Elliot's still-expanding brain.

Now Elliot could see the small grey houses of Clannach, the wide silver gleam of Loch Dour, the highways leading to the towns beyond the hills, the people in the towns, moving, laughing, talking, loving, singing, sleeping. And in the centre of it all—Curtiss.

His spine had lost its arch, now. He had dropped and lay motionless. Only the blood was still moving, coiling over what was left of his skin, pooling. Eventually he stopped making even the small guttural sounds and was silent. Eventually the blood snakes rattled in his throat and he was finished, literally torn apart by Elliot's hate.

Omega.

Omega as it was never meant to be.

Omega in revenge.

Elliot's mind soared higher, to the edge of the atmosphere, wider, to the sea on either side, free, endless . . . until it crossed another. New, waiting to be born, somewhere below.

No more. Come back. Come home. Need. Need. Need. Need.

Elliot returned to the body that was his, back to the pain and his smallness and the hard edges of reality, back to the sounds of his own sobbing in his own throat, back to the shame. Crawling, dragging his leg, he too searched the heather, reached for and grasped a rock, brought it down again and again on the silver egg, smashing it forever.

And then fell back to stare up at the stars.

He'd told them he was no saint.

He'd told them what he would do if someone hurt him, hurt the ones he loved and was responsible for.

He'd warned them.

Hadn't he? Hadn't he?

22

The two men sat on the dunes of Mhourra, looking out over the sea.

Elliot picked up a piece of rock and tossed it from hand to hand, his eyes following a gull that broke its level flight to dash itself head-first into the sea, a white dart thrown into the waves. He knew that if the gull went deep enough, it would see the shadowy shape of the helicopter on the bottom. Perhaps the current would be turning the big rotors lazily in the deep water as it surged in and out. He still felt sick when he remembered watching Longjohn lower the machine to the surface of the waves, cut the engine, and then calmly step out of the open door and swim away as the big silver shape sank silently behind him in the twilight. They had hidden since then here on Mhourra—as Annie had hidden so long ago.

"You'll have to leave Annie here, Phil." Longjohn's calm voice broke into the memory.

"Yes. I know." He forced the pain away, the sweet pain of seeing Annie's face bent over the shape of the baby at her breast, the red of her hair repeated in the fine gossamer of his son's baby fuzz, curling around the silver band that encircled the tiny head. "But I can come back sometimes. More, later on. And we can talk whenever we . . ." his voice faded. His mind could now touch Annie's at will from wherever he was— but his hands would be empty. "It has to be done, Longjohn. We have to *try*."

"Still the believer."

Elliot's smile was wry. "And still a pain in the ass?"

"As ever was." Longjohn stretched his arms out and wriggled his shoulder experimentally. "I think I need another session with Annie . . . this thing still hurts."

"I'll remind her." The gull reappeared, a flash of struggling silver caught in its beak. "Is Bartlett due for contact tonight?"

"Yeah. Around ten." Longjohn leaned forward to sift some of the white sand through his fingers. As the grains fell away, a small shell was left in the palm of his hand. "It's going to be like that, you know."

Elliot's eyes went to the small white circle. "Easier, I think. Easier for us than for them, anyway. They've only got the machines. They think they're a weapon—but they're a limitation, really. Have to be moved, have to be set up, have to be calibrated, focused, adjusted. All *we* have to do is listen."

Longjohn chuckled. "My God, when Frances worked out the numbers I just couldn't believe it." They both called up the image of the paper she had handed them. Without machines, without anything but their own awakened minds, they could find and open other minds to Omega. They had done it with Bartlett, and Bartlett had done it with George. It would be exhausting, it would be frightening, and it would be a race against the machines that the Commission technicians would soon be using. But the minds that they reached and released could reach other minds in turn. The circles would widen, and the family would grow. Because Annie had to stay on Mhourra with the baby for now, they would start with six. Longjohn, Elliot, Frances, George, Ari, and Bartlett. Each taking a country—Bartlett had organized the false passports already. At the end of the first week, they would have become twelve. At the end of the second week, twenty-four. At the end of the third, forty-eight. At the end of the fourth, ninety-six. Double, double, double, double. At the end of the second month the number would be one thousand, five hundred, and thirty-six Omega minds that could defend themselves and each other against the manipulation and destruction the machines threatened. At the end of only six months the number could be— Elliot smiled—over a hundred million. A week more, two hundred million. And so on. And so on. By the end of a year there would be quite a few of them around.

As George had once said, people have a right to their own heads.

"And you still think the good will outnumber the bad?"

Elliot shrugged. "They do now. I don't see why the ratios should change."

"They *seem* to, now. Once they've each got Omega, maybe the law of majority won't apply."

"Maybe the law of majority won't matter. Maybe we'll understand faster, act slower, judge a man by what's in his head, not the colour of his skin or the colour of his money or the colour of his religion."

"Yeah. *Maybe.*"

"The only alternative is to let Curtiss's people take over. Strangle the world instead of widen it? I don't like that prospect much."

"I noticed." Longjohn's hand dug into the sand again, and this time when the grains had sifted away, there were three small shells left behind. "Okay, Phil. Curtiss's successor will be going ahead, that's for certain. I guess we *don't* have any choice."

"No." Elliot's voice was soft, almost lost in the wind.

The sun was dropping into the sea, and the wash of reflected colour stretched above their heads, burning the flanks of the clouds with gold and a soft pink that hazed like smoke into the twilight. The gulls were swooping in and out of the sea faster and faster as the fish rose to feed. Catching up the silvery shapes, rising to swallow them whole, and turning to dive again.

The sea darkened slowly, until in the dusk they could only see the white froth on the waves that dashed themselves against the rocks, shattered into fragments, and fell away into darkness. Elliot's voice came again, even more softly, whispering as the wind whispered through the strands of grass that embroidered the dunes.

"We haven't any choice at all. Now."

PROLOGUE III

The sun had set in Ottawa, too, and the man behind the desk had been forced to switch on the small lamp next to his telephone in order to finish. The last page shone translucent in the light, the small dark writing slanting upward, slightly.

His grey eyes were clear and cold and very angry as they came to the end of the page. He looked up at the messenger who stood some steps away from the desk, lost in the gloom.

"Are you Bartlett?" he asked.

"Yes, sir." His voice was as shadowy as his outline.

"I had a feeling you must be."

"Yes, sir. I know you did."

"Perhaps . . . after I've . . ."

"Whenever you like, sir. Whenever you're ready to try."

"I have to approve this Bill before . . ."

"I'll just wait outside."

Light flashed from the outer office as Bartlett withdrew, closing the door quietly behind him. The man behind the desk looked down at the heavy official papers, and then at the last page of the letter he had dropped beside them. The flimsy airmail sheets stirred, moved, separated gently in the breeze from the window behind him.

Bartlett will ask you the questions we will be asking everywhere—of everyone—at first as they sleep, then again when they are awake and ready:

Do you dream in colour?

Have you ever felt something was going to happen that did happen?

Have you ever sensed someone watching you, and turned to find it was true?

Do you sometimes know what people are going to say before they say it?

Leave your mind open.

You'll be hearing from one of Us.

At least . . . we *hope* it will be one of Us.